Dorothy KOOMSON

The Friend

CENTURY

1 3 5 7 9 10 8 6 4 2

Century
20 Vauxhall Bridge Road
London SW1V 2SA

Century is part of the Penguin Random House group of companies whose
addresses can be found at global.penguinrandomhouse.com.

Copyright © Dorothy Koomson 2017

First published in Great Britain by Century in 2017

www.penguin.co.uk

A CIP catalogue record for this book is available from the British Library.

ISBN 9781780895987 (Hardback)
ISBN 9781780895994 (Trade paperback)

Typeset in 12/15.5 pt Baskerville MT Std Jouve (UK), Milton Keynes
Printed and bound in Great Britain by Clays Ltd, St Ives plc

Penguin Random House is committed to a sustainable future for our business,
our readers and our planet. This book is made from Forest Stewardship
Council® certified paper.

To my friends, near and far.

It's easy to say thank you when you've been supported by a great bunch of people. So, here we go:

Thank you

to my wonderful family and friends;

to my incredible agents Ant and James;

to my brilliant publishers Susan, Charlotte, Rebecca, Sarah, Aslan & Viola, as well as Jason, Wendy, Chris, Najma, Jasmine and everyone else. A special mention to the lovely Georgina, so very much missed;

to my amazing publicist Emma.

And an extra special thank you to E, G & M. I love you. Always.

As ever, I would also like to say thank you to you, the reader, for buying this book. I hope you enjoy it.

MOTHER-OF-TWO IN COMA
AFTER BRUTAL ATTACK AT SCHOOL

A popular mother-of-two is in a coma after being found on the premises of a local Brighton school after a vicious attack the police are investigating as attempted murder.

Yvonne Whidmore, 42, was found in the early hours of Saturday in the front playground of Plummer Preparatory School, New Hillingdon Road, having been brutally assaulted and, according to police sources, 'left for dead'. It is still not clear how Mrs Whidmore came to be at the school, which is still on summer holidays.

A close friend of the family revealed that Trevor Whidmore, 43, and their children, aged eight and 10, have not left her hospital bedside since Mrs Whidmore was admitted.

Friends of the blonde housewife, pictured here in a gold ball gown at a recent school event, which she organised for Plummer Prep's Parents' Council, took to the school's social media site to express their shock and upset.

'Can't believe this has happened. Yvonne is one of the nicest people on Earth. Big hugs to Trev and the girls.'

'Get well soon, Yvonne, Plummer Prep needs you.'

'Thought this area was safe! Urgh. This is just horrible.'

'Who would want to hurt Yvonne???!!!! She's the soul of this place. She's everyone's friend. Get better soon, honey.'

Mrs Carpenter, the head teacher of Plummer Prep, told us she and other members of the senior management team at the £15,000-per-year private school were cooperating with the police in every way they could but this incident would not prevent them from continuing to run the institution at its current, outstanding level.

Police are appealing for anyone who was near or passing the school between the hours of 10 p.m. on Friday, 18 August and 5 a.m. on Saturday, 19 August to contact them as soon as possible.

Daily News Chronicle, August 2017

Part 1

MONDAY

Cece

6:15 a.m. 'This is like the start of a TV drama,' Sol calls to me from the bedroom. 'Husband in suit, getting ready for work, kids downstairs having breakfast, and wife in her underwear rushing around trying to get everything organised.'

'Hmm,' I reply. 'I suppose it is.'

I rinse my toothbrush under running water before slotting it back into the plastic pot on the glass shelf. I take my time doing this because I like being in the bathroom. It's calm in here, it's *unpacked* in here. In fact, the only places in our three-storey new home that are 'fully useable' as averse to 'technically habitable' are the bathrooms.

I linger in the bathroom, enjoying the calm finishedness, and avoiding the oppressive chaos that is the bedroom. There's a bed, there are sheets and a duvet . . . and a huge pile of my clothes on the floor in front of the bay window, nicely flanked by boxes of 'stuff'. Not Sol's 'stuff' though. He has somehow managed to sort out his 'stuff' – it is hanging up in the walk-in cupboard/wardrobe (something that sold the house to both of us), his shoes are lined up, his ties are on a special tie hanger, his underwear is folded into the drawers. He's been living down here in Brighton in a hotel for the last three months and seems to have had no problems settling into our new place.

June, 2003
'Can I ask you something?'

The good-looking man came up to me as we were leaving the

3

library. The last few months we'd seen each other almost every day and had progressed from smiling to actually saying hello. Now he, who I'd named Library Man, was speaking to me properly.

'Yes, of course. I may or may not answer depending on how intrusive the question is,' I replied.

'Why do you come to the library every day? I mean, I'm here every day because I'm studying, but I don't see you get any books out or anything.'

A little shiver of excitement ran through me that someone had noticed me and hadn't dismissed me as another single mother to be ignored and vilified in equal measure. 'It's a two-mile walk here from where I live, and the only way I can get my child to sleep during the day is to walk with her in the pram. After mile one she nods off, wakes up when we get here, and then half a mile back she falls asleep again and then stays asleep for a good couple of hours so I can do some work.'

'Right.'

'What about you? Why are you always here? I mean, you've just said you're studying but surely that can't mean going to the library every day.'

'It's a good place to come to keep warm and be around people.'

'You do know of these things called pubs, don't you?' I said to him. 'They're warm and dry and they have people. There might even be people in there that you know from your course.'

'Ah, maybe. But I'm twenty-five, most of them on my course are eighteen, away from home for the first time and enjoying every second of it. I feel positively ancient compared to them.'

'What about going to a café every now and then?' I replied. 'You know, mix it up a bit.'

'I might be tempted to try out one of these so-called "cafés" if you – and your daughter, of course – will come with me.'

'I'll come with you if it's not a date.'

'What have you got against dating? Are you with someone?'

'Sort of.'

'What does that mean?'

I indicated to Harmony, my one-year-old with beautifully frizzy hair, almost-black eyes, pale brown skin and huge smile. She blew a raspberry and clapped her hands at the brilliantness of this. 'Everything is dictated by the demands, stability and well-being of this little one. I'm not planning on dating until she's eighteen and I don't have to worry about her any more.'

'All right, it's not a date,' he said with a grin. 'But I feel it only fair to warn you, from everything my friends and family have told me, you never stop worrying about your kids, no matter what their age.'

6:17 a.m. Sol comes up behind me in the bathroom, slips an arm around my waist and tugs me close to him. He's had a summer of going to the gym and running along the beach, so I can feel every exercise-devoted second of his muscles as my eyes slip shut and I almost melt against him. It's so long since we've been this close. I haven't missed the sex as much as I've missed having him next to me. Holding him, being held by him . . . He kisses my neck, holds me closer. I relax some more and the scent of him fills my senses. He's started wearing a different aftershave, but I can still detect his natural scent: slightly salty, musky, a touch of sweetness under there. I haven't seen him properly in a while, but he's still Sol. His grip on me tightens and his fingers creep down over my stomach and slide into the waistband of my black knickers.

'Yeah, I don't think so, TV drama boy,' I say, removing his hand. He certainly killed that moment. I step away from him and cross the corridor, heading for the bedroom and my 'wardrobe'. 'Didn't you say something about the children downstairs and the mother running around, trying to organise things?'

He follows me into the bedroom and stands beside me in front of the wardrobe pile. 'It was mostly the underwear bit I was focusing on . . . Tee. Bee. Haitch.'

I face my husband. 'Did you just sound out "to be honest"?' I ask him. '*Seriously*? How old are you to be using that? When did you even *hear* that to start using it?'

5

Sol stares very hard at my clothes mound. I know his heart will be racing right now, little beads of sweat will be prickling along his forehead, he'll be praying I'm too distracted by the move to still be the person who would pick up on such an obvious 'tell'. One of the reasons I was so good at my previous job was because I picked up on things that most people ignored as irrelevant. For example, Sol has just 'told' me that he's been spending a lot of time with someone much younger than him (and me) and certainly more female than him, who uses that expression enough for it to have rubbed off on him. Sol makes a big show of looking at his watch.

'Wow, I didn't realise the time. Shouldn't we all be getting a move on? Especially me,' Sol says.

I study my husband, observe him as he avoids looking at me while he mentally kicks himself. When he does risk a glance in my direction I cock an eyebrow at him. '*T. B.H.?*' that eyebrow says to him. '*Really?*'

He whips his gaze away. 'I really need to be heading off. See ya.' He disappears out of the door with that.

'Yeah, see ya,' I reply. 'And T. B.C.,' I whisper. 'T. B.C.'

July, 2004

'So, are you still waiting until Harmony is eighteen to go on a date? Just, you know, asking for a friend.' Sol asked this in a pub.

Our daytime coffees had segued to afternoons with the three of us going for walks and plays in the park, days out at play centres and safari parks. And, more recently, my mum babysitting so we could go out in the evenings. I was still fitting my home-based data entry job around Harmony's sleeping patterns, and he was still a student, so we were both skint and whenever we went to the pub, we didn't simply nurse our beers, we coddled them until the very last drop.

I gazed at Sol. I did a lot of gazing at Sol, because he was very easy to, well, gaze at. He had dark brown skin that was smooth and dewy-soft, he regularly shaved his head, which exposed its beautiful shape while emphasising his huge, black-brown eyes and amazing

6

lips. Sol was also extremely easy to be with and every time I gazed at him I was reminded that he had been single and celibate for nearly a year because he liked me. He made no secret of it, either, hugging me, stroking my hair, giving me lingering kisses on my cheeks, staring into my eyes when we spoke. Although this was the first time he had come out and said something.

'This friend, anyone I know?' I asked.

'Yes. It's me. Look, this is driving me crazy. I like you so much and I've never waited this long for a woman before. Can I kiss you? Will you turn me down if I do?'

I gazed at him some more. 'You can kiss me, but only if you listen to the story about how I came to be a lone parent.'

'Not a problem,' he replied, staring at my lips. He wasn't listening, not properly. He was thinking of the bit afterwards, when he'd get to kiss me. 'Although, I feel it only fair to point out to you that I know the biology bits so you can skip them.'

'I'm serious, Solomon. I'm going to tell you the story and you must only kiss me if you can handle what I've told you and what it means about me. And if you promise never to use it against me. If you can't, no hard feelings, but I need you to be honest with me and yourself.'

'I'm a bit scared now.'

'You should be.'

'All right. All right.' He inhaled and exhaled rapidly like a boxer about to enter the ring then visibly braced himself. 'Tell me.'

I told him: the unvarnished truth about my life before I became a mother, how my daughter was conceived, what happened next. I was honest, in a brutal way that I had never needed to be before. No one had needed to know this about me. My parents just accepted (and rejoiced at) having another grandchild to coo over and love, my siblings added another name to their Christmas lists and my friends drifted away once I became all about the baby instead of all about the partying. My story was a strictly need-to-know type of tale, and Solomon definitely needed to know. At the end of it, he had stopped gazing adoringly at me and instead he stared into the mid-distance, shell-shocked by what he'd heard. After a minute or two of silence, he could arrange his features enough to face me. I held my breath, tried to freeze time so it would be the moment before he told me he couldn't handle it for as long as possible.

He smiled at me, then very carefully, very slowly, kissed me.

6:25 a.m. I've parked Sol's 'tell' that he's been spending a lot of non-work time with someone else recently, and stare at the pile of clothes in the window bay. I had gone to sort and hang them up on Saturday morning, then I realised that sorting clothes was an indulgence when I had to unpack the kitchen so I could cook something, as well as organising the children's rooms as much as possible and getting the remaining uniform bits. After a weekend of organising everything else, I am left with this mound of clothes and no idea what to wear.

I want to run back to the calm of the bathroom and forget about this whole getting dressed to take my children to school business. Forget this need to find the perfect outfit that won't be too showy and won't be too anonymous and will say to every other parent at the gates: 'I'm nice, please be my friend.'

I hear Sol's footsteps on the stairs and I smile with relief and gratitude. I was being silly, he doesn't have anything to hide.

'Oh, Cee, I completely forgot,' he says when he dashes into the bedroom. 'My good suits will be ready to collect from the dry cleaner's today. The shop's not far from here. You just have to head in the opposite direction of the boys' school for a bit on the main road. The tickets are on the noticeboard and you can pick them up any time after eleven.'

With a deep frown grooving my forehead and narrowing my eyes, I rotate very slowly to look at my husband. I stare very, very hard at him.

'What?' he says after I have not spoken for two whole minutes. (I know because I counted them in my head.) 'Why are you looking at me like that?'

'Oh, Sol.' I sigh. 'Look, I know you're really busy with work and

8

all, but would it kill you to acknowledge the sacrifice we've all made for you? Even a little?

'I mean, our children have moved away from their friends and a life they loved because of *your* job and you haven't once acknowledged that over the weekend or this morning. Not only that – this is the first time we've all been together for three months but we've hardly seen you these past few days. You've not helped to unpack their stuff, you've not helped me with putting up their furniture, you didn't come to the uniform shop. Sometimes you've had meals with us.

'You know, they're starting at new schools this morning, and Harmony has changed schools at the start of her GCSEs. Would it have been the end of the world if you'd gone into work a bit later this morning so Harmony doesn't have to walk into school all on her own? I feel sick that I have to take the twins so I can't go with her. It never even occurred to you that she might need someone with her, did it? But you leave the house with barely a goodbye to any of us and then you come all the way back from your car, I presume, to order me to collect your dry cleaning like I'm your personal assistant. It's just . . .' I run out of words. Well, nice words. Instead, I flop my arms up and down in frustration and despair.

Sol, in response, physically draws back, as though someone has shown him his version of a Dorian Gray portrait and he is horrified by how unpleasant and downright inconsiderate he looks. 'I didn't think,' he says, shame and regret coating every letter. 'About any of it. I just didn't think.'

'No, I guess you didn't,' I reply.

'I've got a meeting, I can't cancel, it's really important.' He rubs his fingertips over his eyes, pinches the bridge of his nose. 'Not that you lot aren't important, but I can't cancel it last minute. I'm sorry. If I could cancel, I would.'

'It's fine, what's done is done,' I say. 'I just don't want you to start taking everything we've given up for you for granted, all right?'

'We've made this change for our family, not for me,' he protests.

Don't kid yourself, Sol, I almost say. *I did not want to move. I loved my life,*

9

my career, my friends I saw every now and then. I did not want to move. The
children did not want to move. But we had to, for you.

'We agreed: it'd be great for them to be in a city but right near the
sea, and that now we could afford it, we'd put them into private
education,' Sol is saying. 'We agreed that getting out of London
would be good for all of us, didn't we? *Didn't we?*'

'Yes, I suppose we did, but we should be seeing the kids off to
school together. That's how our family works, remember?'

His face falls even further. 'I'm sorry, Cee, I really am.' He takes
a few steps forwards until he is close enough to slip his arms around
me. 'I really am sorry,' he murmurs. 'I'll do better. I promise you I'll
do better.'

'I know you will,' I reply. I let him kiss me and even manage a
smile and wave as he leaves the bedroom. He'll do it properly with
the children this time – he'll hug them, reassure them, say a proper
goodbye.

My hands reach out for a pair of jeans, a white top. I'm always
trying to teach the kids to be themselves, to be who they are and
allow the worthwhile friends to gravitate towards them. I should take
my own advice. No, I didn't want to move, but I'm here and I have
to do this. So I have to do it on my terms – a special outfit won't do
that; what will do that is showing everyone I am comfortable in my
own skin.

I also need to get a bloody move on.

7:40 a.m. I have three children, all in uniforms, standing on the
pavement outside the house. I also have five minutes to spare. This
is a win. This is a win that was achieved with only a minimal amount
of shouting (me) and a tiny amount of scowling (them). Especially
since they then went on to be moderately cooperative with the obliga-
tory first-day-of-school photos in front of the fireplace. A miracle,
especially when they all explained to me, at various points, that school
started a week ago for everyone else, and so it's not really the first
day of school.

I look at my children while I run through my mental locking up

10

checklist. Then I look at them frozen on my mobile's new screen saver: Ore, the youngest twin, tips his head up and pushes his chin forward, showing off his missing lower teeth; Oscar, the oldest twin, smiling as always with his mouth closed and his head tipped slightly to one side. And Harmony, standing behind them, staring at the camera, radiant and beautiful, simply smiling. Simply Harmony.

I turn to my fifteen-year-old. I hate the idea of her rocking up there on the bus knowing no one as she walks through the gates. 'Are you sure you don't want to come with me to take the boys, and I'll drive you to school a bit later? Actually, it won't even be that much later since they start at eight fifteen,' I say to her. I've been there for every single one of her first days at school – even making the boys late the past three years, so I can be there – and I can't quite believe I am going to miss this one. 'Or you could—'

Harmony shakes her head. 'I'll be fine.'

When she says that, what she really means is: I've earned this trip to school alone.

If we *were* in a TV drama, right about now, there'd be a montage of all of Harmony's first days at school – every one with me sobbing, or holding back the sobs, or pretending not to sob as I clung to her and whispered over and over how much I loved her. Each new clip would show a bigger, taller Harmony wearing exactly the same expression: lips pursed, eyes raised to the heavens, patience itself sitting on her face as she waits for me to *get a grip*.

'I can't believe I won't be able to see you in on your first day,' I say to her. 'Especially since it's a new school.'

'Mum, thing is, I *can* go to school on my own.'

'But we're in Brighton. It's not like London. We're practically in the middle of nowhere here and you're having to get a bus all on your own, wearing a strange uniform and, you know, I should be doing that with you.' Tears fill my eyes at the thought of my poor unaccompanied daughter.

'Didn't you have two other children so I didn't get to be the sole focus of this craziness?' Harmony says with barely concealed contempt. 'I mean, isn't that what they're *for*?' She turns to her brothers. 'No offence,' she tells them.

'Lots taken,' Oscar, eight years of deep thinking, replies.

'Yeah,' chimes in Ore, 'lots taken.'

'Sorry boys, it's every child for themselves at times like this. I've had ten school years of this, you've had three, so don't "lots taken" me.'

'Right, well, when you've all *quite* finished being outraged at me, your mother, caring so deeply about you, shall we go?'

Before my daughter can even think to move, I fling my arms around her, kiss her cheeks, kiss her forehead, tell her over and over how much I love her and how proud I am of her. If I can't do it at her school, I'll do it here.

'Thanks, Mum,' she eventually mumbles, and untangles herself from me while in one smooth, practised move she swings her turquoise rucksack onto her shoulder. 'I'll see you later,' she says and then walks away. She doesn't get far before she runs back to us and bends to her brothers. 'See you two,' she says as she throws her arms around them. 'Have a great first day. Tell me all about it tonight, OK?'

'We will,' they say at the same time. She rises to her full height and I see it, a quiver of nervousness as it flits across her features. I'm not meant to know – none of us are meant to know – so I stop myself from grabbing her again and deciding to start home schooling. My daughter tucks her fears away behind her trademark cool nonchalance before she rehoists her bag. As she passes me, she presses a brief kiss on my cheek without looking at me, and then carries on, down the road, around the corner and to the bus stop. To the outside world she might be fifteen and taller than me, but to me, she'll always be five and not quite ready to do anything much on her own.

8:05 a.m. It's taken longer to arrive here at the gates of Plummer Prep than when we walked it yesterday. I'm not sure why. We practically strolled here yesterday, and today the boys have scooted while

I ran along behind, weighed down with book bags, rucksacks and hats, piling embarrassment upon embarrassment by shouting like a town crier to 'mind the road', 'watch out for pavement yuckiness', 'don't turn the corner until I'm there'.

Oscar and Ore slow down as we near the school. My heartbeat surges, becomes like rapid thunderclaps in my chest. Ore stops completely and I almost fall over him. Oscar stops next, and stands with his feet either side of his green scooter platform and stares. They saw the school yesterday, but didn't think – as I didn't, I suppose – what it would be like when there were so many people around.

Noise, disorder and chaos swirl through the warm, sun-blushed September air outside the school. Children are being herded in, most without lingering goodbyes; others cling to parents who are trying desperately to remove them. Clumps of parents stand like bundles of hay, left at various points on the pavement to untie themselves and go about their day; vehicles are double-parked, ignoring the yellow lines and the white zigzag lines as though those markings don't apply to them. Other cars pull up in the middle of the road, stopping traffic, while their drivers slap on hazard lights and jump out to open the back doors, virtually javelin-throwing their children out of their seats.

When I'd first come to look around Plummer Prep (Sol was working so he couldn't make it) I'd been impressed by the look of it: a red, double-fronted, rambling mansion-house, with white pillars that flank its large entrance, set on the corner of two main roads. Its roof is gunmetal grey, and its sash windows are painted white. It looks huge from the front, until you walk through the front and discover that it is, in fact, *mahoosive*, as Ore says. It has an extended glass walkway that is set like a large rectangle, with a large paved courtyard at its centre. The glass walkways lead to the art rooms, science labs and common rooms. Behind that are the three different playing fields, two that lie end to end, and the other is the cricket pitch, complete with its own weatherboard pavilion.

With the size of the place, I half expected there'd be a glut of people arriving at the same time in the mornings, but what I didn't expect was this frenzied, manic air. I didn't expect so many parents to hang around, acting like this is the last time they'll be together. They are acting like I do on my children's first days, but they've all been here at least a week, they should be over it by now. And most of them will have been doing this for years. My heart puckers in my chest. *What is going on?*

'Come on, boys,' I say, my voice jolly and excited, not terrified and wary about why they are behaving like this. 'Isn't this great?'

Ore turns to look at me like I've finally lost my mind and Oscar continues to stare – neither of them moves towards the gates.

'Come on, scooters.'

Without losing their different expressions of terror, the boys relinquish their scooters, and deftly, like I do it all the time, I scoop them up with one hand, still balancing their stuff, and negotiate the islands of talking, lurking parents.

As we approach, I see the headmistress, Mrs Carpenter, who isn't that much older than me, standing like a guard at Buckingham Palace, the epitome of poise and control. She is wearing a purple suit with a green shirt – the school's uniform colours – and her strawberry-brown hair is swept up and twisted into a perfectly constructed chignon. She smiles and greets every child entering the school by name. I keep my eyes on her, a beacon in the turmoil that surrounds us. She grins as we approach and I know it's going to be fine. She will welcome the boys, she will make sure other teachers welcome the boys; she will make the transition easy, smooth.

As we arrive in front of Mrs Carpenter, the noise suddenly stops, cut off like a switch has been flicked on the background hubbub. Silence, a deathly hush, is cast over us. *Have I gone deaf?* I look around. But I can still hear birdsong, the rush of traffic from the adjacent road, the click of flashing hazard lights, the sound of the boys breathing beside me. I look around again. Everyone is staring. Everyone is silent and they are all staring . . . at us.

The thunderclaps in my chest increase; my breath forgets to go in and out. Maybe I should have put more thought into my outfit? Maybe I should have driven, then I could have done a drop'n'run, without anyone noticing us. I look down at the boys. Ore has a determined-not-to-be-intimidated look on his face – ready, it seems, to slug it out if anyone says anything. Oscar is openly confused – his eyes dart here and there, trying to get a handle on the situation. Eventually he looks at me and mouths: *Mum?*

I shake my head and shrug: *I don't understand it either.*

I decide to ignore this, to not let the boys know that I'm scared, confused, worried about how the children will treat them if this is how the parents behave, and I'm about to move forwards when the space I was going to fill is suddenly occupied by a tall white man. His short wavy brown hair is scruffy but not intentionally so, I don't think. His navy suit is lightly creased, his white shirt could do with another iron, although his blue and gold paisley tie is in place. On either side of him he has two blonde-haired girls – their school uniforms look like they have been washed and an attempt has been made at ironing, but like their dad's shirt, it could all do with a re-iron. It's him – them – everyone is staring at.

The man has noticed the silence, of course he has, and he stops short of the school gates, ignores the now frozen smile of Mrs Carpenter, and looks left then right at the gawkers. Where his gaze lands, the heads turn away, embarrassed that they've been so obvious. When he has made everyone who stared feel uncomfortable, slightly ashamed, he carries on.

Mrs Carpenter seems to unfreeze then and her smile reignites itself. 'Good morning, Madison, good morning, Scarlett. It's lovely to see you both. Good morning, Mr Whidmore.'

In response, Mr Whidmore nods briefly to Mrs Carpenter before he lowers himself to his daughters' levels and hugs them.

'Have a good day,' he tells them quietly. The noise and talking has begun again but quietly, sombrely, like something bad has just happened and no one knows how to carry on. 'I'll pick you up from after-school club, OK?'

Both girls nod; neither speaks. They both stand very still, rucksacks on their backs and book bags in their hands as they wait for their dad to let them go, then both turn in a seemingly synchronised spin to walk through the school gates. Most children who have entered the school go straight to the playground, these children, Madison and Scarlett, don't even look in its direction – they head straight for the open front doors, step through and disappear.

Mr Whidmore straightens up, stares at Mrs Carpenter and her face says, *What can I possibly say to make this right?* while her mouth says, 'Try not to worry, we'll take good care of them, Mr Whidmore.'

He nods. 'Make sure you do,' he says.

As he turns away, he spots me and the boys, he stares at me, then stares through me, looking somewhere off over my right shoulder, then he swings left, glares in that area as though looking at someone specifically. Once he has stared, has made his point, he leaves. Like his daughters, he doesn't look back.

What the hell have I just brought my children into?

Hazel

8:05 a.m. *What have I forgotten?*

There'll be something. I made a list, and I checked it twice, just like Santa in the song, but I think I forgot something for the list in the first place. Let's face it, I've probably forgotten more than one thing. I stand very still outside the school gates ticking things off in my head while waiting for the bell so I can go off to work:

- Permission slips for trips/activities/various contentious subjects to be taught (tick)
- Said permission slips put into correct children's bags (tick)
- Correct uniform, clean and put onto correct children (tick)
- Correct bags with correct PE and Games kits (cos there's a difference) (tick)
- Navigated pre-teen's meltdown about phone/make-up/ sleeping over at her dad's place (tick, tick, tick)
- Arrived here on time (tick)
- Dressed in uniform ready to go to work (tick).

I have far too many ticks on that list for me not to have forgotten something. And it'll be something huge. So huge I'll probably be apologising to more than one person while reminding myself I'm meant to be getting better at being an adult. And even as I'm reminding myself of that, promising myself I will do that, I know I'll always be on the wrong side of being a mess.

I sigh. What I've missed will soon reveal itself, I'm sure.

For a mid-September morning it's quite hot; humid but not as sunny as it could be. I always think, though, that the heat in this area comes from the energy expended during the buzz of the morning drop-off. That moment when everyone rocks up, having put everything into arriving as close to start time as possible, in as much of the correct uniform as possible. That energy usually escapes into the atmosphere as soon as the children cross the gates and the parents can sigh with relief at getting them there. After that, most of us run – very few people used to wait until the bell sounds and the children have filed in to leave. But since term started again, very few people do the drop'n'run thing – most of us now do the drop'n'hang thing, or, the drop'n'fret thing, which is what I do.

Washing machine? I remember putting clothes in the drum, I remember pouring in powder, I even remember turning the dial to synthetics, but did I press 'go'? Is that it? The washing machine?

As well as the drop'n'fret, I drop'n'wonder . . . I wonder how I can stand to do this after everything? I wonder if I should have talked to Walter, as bad as that would be, and taken the kids out of school? I wonder where else it would be safe—

The frantic buzz is suddenly guillotined. In place of the chatter is now tension, hesitancy, *pity* and the unexpected quiet snatches my breath away.

That's what I've forgotten.

I've forgotten that today is the day that Trevor is bringing the girls back to school.

Everyone stands and stares, silent and wary, as the three of them approach the gates.

When Trevor has delivered the girls to the gates and hugged them, he virtually scowls at Mrs Carpenter, as though he holds her responsible for what happened to his wife. After that glare he turns away, and then stares at the black woman with two children who stands in front of him, before he stares on. He stares beyond the ghouls who are treating him like a horror show, before his gaze finally settles on who he was clearly looking for. Me. In this crowd, this group of spectators, his eyes are on me. Glaring at me, accusing me. *I know what you did, Hazel*, he's saying with that look. *How could you?*

I want to look away, to hide the tears that are stinging my eyes, but I can't. I can't look away until he lets me go. I try to breathe, but my chest is too tight; I try to think but my mind is frozen. I try to feel and I can't, not when all of their pain is so potent and apparent and exposed.

He sweeps his accusatory gaze away and I lower my head, take a few shaky breaths in and focus on the ground. *It's as if he knows. It's as if he can tell.* I breathe even deeper, and I know he's gone when the atmosphere around me releases a little and people quietly, cautiously start to talk again. Some people are staring at me, I can feel it. They know I was *her* friend. They remember how close we seemed. They're wondering what I could possibly have done to make Trevor glare at me like that.

The small tinny beep of my mobile goes off, making me jump. I remove it from my pocket and read the message.

We need to talk.

Maxie

8:05 a.m. I can't believe it's only been a week of this. It feels like I have been dragging myself from bed to do the school run for weeks and weeks. I feel that slow, creeping exhaustion that comes towards the end of term, when you've just got into the routine of it, remembering which bag, which uniform on which day, and then you're at home with them all day again. Except, of course, it's only week two of a new term.

Frankie has been ahead of me on his scooter the whole way up here. I'm carrying his full – and blinking heavy – rucksack, as well as his book bag and his sports bag because he convinced me last night that he has a football match today. They don't normally have matches on Mondays, but he's nothing if not convincing, my son. And often he's right. I almost went onto PPY3, the messaging group for Year Three, to ask about it. My fingers hovered over the keys, ready to type out the simple message, but I couldn't. In the days after *Yvonne* . . . in the days after what happened, the messaging stream had been overflowing with shock and very real fear about it; people talking and worrying and sympathising. After the shock faded and the constant updates stopped, it all switched: worry was replaced by speculation. Not about what happened, but about what Trevor would do.

'Will he pull the kids out, do you think?'
'I'd pull them out straight away. Why wouldn't you?'
*'Can't imagine how they'd feel going past that playground
    every day.'*

20

'I think they should pull them out. It's not fair on our kids to deal with that reminder every day.'

On and on and on and on it went. All wrapped up in concern, all 'just asking'. It was unsavoury, as though people were either asking to find out the latest piece of gossip, or asking because they wanted to know how his decision would impact them. Each time, when they asked a question, they would tag Anaya, Hazel and me. *Her friends.*

I'd been close, had been itching, to call them a bunch of mawkish, two-faced bastards and then leave the messaging group. But I'd held my tongue (finger) because I had to see them every day, I had to bring Frankie up alongside their offspring. I had to do whatever I could to not stand out any more than we already do.

Frankie moves like a green and purple needle, weaving himself in between the various mothers who stand on the pavement, zipping in and out of them, invisibly sewing their forms together. I have to keep moving left and right, rising sometimes to my tiptoes so that I can keep my eyes on him. 'Hi, Maxie,' someone says. I smile at her, pat her on the shoulder, and move on, without ever letting Frankie out of my sight. There's another 'hello' hand on my shoulder; a smile; a wave; a half-shouted mention of coffee soon, the usual greetings to arriving at the gate, and I respond to them all appropriately – a smile, a pat on the back, an indication to text about coffee, a 'call me' sign – all the while I watch my son make his way to the school gates. I am expert at communicating with others but never taking my eyes off Frankie.

He must feel like the most watched child on the planet because I rarely take my eyes off him. I know it's normal to worry about your child, to briefly have scenarios flit through your head about what could happen and to pause and then bat them away. And I know it's *not* normal to lie awake at 5 a.m. and stare into the brightening gloom, while scenario after terrifying scenario about how your child could be snatched away runs through your mind. For most people, though, the things I worry about amount to nothing more than urban legend, a good story to hear from friends, a great plot to watch on telly. For most people, what I worry about is fantasy, but I've lived it.

Frankie does one of his well-practised fancy sliding stops, then hops off his scooter, treats Mrs Carpenter to a happy, toothy grin before he whips off his black helmet. I come up behind him and take the helmet.

Among the faces I recognise there is a parent I've never seen before. She is casually dressed in jeans, T-shirt and teal-green leather jacket. Her skin is the same dark mocha of Mum's complexion, her shoulder-length black hair is in large, rope-like twists, and with her large, expressive eyes, she is actually quite beautiful. She so doesn't know it though. Not from the clothes she's combined, the way her features are set as she power-walks behind two young boys – who look about Frankie's age – carrying their rucksacks, book bags and school coats. One of the boys' green and purple caps is perched on top of her head. She's about to approach the gate, when an unearthly silence falls over everyone outside. Even the children in the playground stop for a moment when they notice that their adults are suddenly, brutally, mute.

My heart almost turns itself inside out when I see him. He's so much paler than normal, dark circles under his eyes, and a crumpled look about him. It's clear from how they look that Yvonne did everything. I never worked out how she managed it: how she looked so good, ran the Parents' Council – even before she was its official head – and managed to make sure her family were always in clean, ironed clothes. No, she didn't have a job, but a lot of people don't have jobs and still don't manage to excel at homemaking like Yvonne did.

My heart goes to my throat when I see Madison and Scarlett. They walk beside their father, straight-backed and apparently oblivious to the way those around them are behaving. *Those poor girls.* I should have been round. I should have offered to have them over. I should have done what Yvonne did if any of us had a crisis – stepped in to keep things as normal as possible for the children. If Yvonne were around, she would have drawn up a rota, she would have arranged food and laundry. She would make sure the person's other half was never alone. I should have done that.

I couldn't, though. I just couldn't.

Trevor walks through the school gates, nods cordially to Mrs Carpenter, then lowers himself so he can hug his children in succession. I imagine he's reassuring them that he'll be there later, that they'll be fine . . . that their mother will – eventually – be fine, too. She's still in a coma three weeks later, but she will be fine. I can tell, even from where I'm standing, that he's doing that thing that all parents have done at some point – making promises we can't possibly know if we're able to keep.

Trevor turns and looks again at Mrs Carpenter. Obviously they have spoken on the phone, have planned this return and how it will be 'managed', but they don't look like the conversation went well. Mrs Carpenter looks, in fact, like she wishes this wasn't happening. Despite the way she's greeted the girls so warmly, I wonder if she asked Trevor to consider keeping them at home a while longer, or if she suggested they leave? The whole thing has been the worst possible PR job for the school, and with the amount of parents who just pulled their children out – some simply saying 'sue me for the term's fees' – I wonder if they would prefer if the Whidmores quietly faded away.

But no one could be that cruel. No one could watch the tension that has made the girls' bodies ramrod straight and feel anything other than guilty. Guilty that your family is still intact, still safe, still fully awake.

After a brief exchange, Trevor turns and looks slowly at the crowd, stares at each and every person, probably silently cursing us. *J'accuse*, he says with his eyes. *J'accuse*. As his eyes trawl the people around him, his contempt for us clear, his gaze snags on the other side of the gates. He glares at a particular spot for just that little bit longer and then his eyes carry on until they reach me. We stare at each other, his anger at me, at what I've done, apparent.

I hold my breath, the air painful and burning in my chest. *Does he know? Has he found out? He can't have. There is no way he could have.*

But his eyes: they pause, they remain and they continue to accuse me. Harder than how he cursed the others. Much harder. He's upset, distressed about Yvonne, scared and hurt, too. *There's no way on Earth he can know.* His damning gaze moves on, finishing its angry sweep of the crowd, and then he stomps away without a backward glance. I want to watch him go, but I don't. I can't.

Frankie is wriggling against me; I've been holding him close, probably tighter than normal. He manages to break away from me. He holds out his arms for his bags, impatient enough to keep looking over his shoulder to where his mates are kicking a ball around in the playground. I suddenly can't look at that playground, at where she was found behind the usually locked gates. I suddenly want to snatch Frankie away, take him to another school and pretend I never met Yvonne, or Hazel or Anaya for that matter.

'*Mum*, see you later,' he says, indicating he wants his stuff and I'm holding him up. Reluctantly, I hand over his belongings, bend to kiss him before he dashes away, leaving most of my kiss hanging like a falling leaf in the autumn air.

Instead of turning away, I reach into my pocket, take out my phone. The atmosphere around the school hasn't gone back to normal, like the waters closing after a parting, instead everyone is still here, talking in hushed tones. This isn't what it used to be like. As well as the presence of a police car parked across the road, and the almost visible canopy of a heavy, crushing pall hanging over us, the daily reminder that something bad happened is the fact that the parents stay now for the whistle. All of us – even the drop'n'runners, the ones who work in London and other cities – hang around the gates, as though our presence alone will keep them safe. Into my mobile I type:

We need to talk.

and press send before I change my mind.

Anaya

8:15 a.m. 'I swear, you two, why are we always doing this?'

I turn into Plummer Place, and immediately know I'm not going to get a park. There are cars lined up on both sides of the street, and at the bottom of the road, near the school, I can see double-parked cars on the left and right hand sides. This wouldn't be an issue if these two wouldn't expend what feels like a lot of energy making sure we don't leave the house on time. I sometimes think they work against me because it's fun to see Mama, who at all other times is calm and sane, become a screaming monster. 'We need to get ourselves out of the house earlier, OK? This isn't good for any of us, this rushing.'

As I talk, my eyes are scanning, searching for a gap, any space that will let me pull up and drop them off.

'Do you hear me?' I say to them.

'Yes, Mama,' they chorus, probably not even listening to me. Priya plunges back into explaining to Arjun how she dunked a hoop in the boys' game of basketball last week and they were all jealous because they couldn't jump like she could.

There! A gap, a space between a Jeep and a BMW, the perfect size for this beast that Sanj bought for me. I push lightly on the brakes, start to slow the car and then realise it's a driveway. Seriously, I've been doing this for five years, when am I not going to get fooled by that? I drive on, past Plummer Prep, which has a swarm of parents standing on the pavement outside. I turn left at the end of the road because no matter how late we are, I can't do what other people are doing and double-park. It's just not in me. I'll have to find somewhere round here and we'll have to do that run-walk we're so good at first thing in the morning. I'm so tired of this. My day shouldn't start like this. 'I mean it, you two,' I interrupt them. Even around here, a smaller road, it's busy, because no one has left the school surrounds yet, no one has allowed me to get one of those latecomer spots. 'We can't keep doing this.'

'We know,' they say at the same time. Of course they know. This is the usual conversation when we get to this point in the school journey: I am craving caffeine at this point; they are wishing I would just accept that this is who we are, how we are, and stop going on about it. But I can't let it go, I can't allow us to become the perpetual late ones – I have to try to drum into them that we are in need of an extra five minutes. Just that extra bit of time so when we do park a little further away, we can walk to the gates. We can arrive calm and relaxed, instead of flustered and me feeling like I'm the one who the headmistress will take into her office to lecture on personal responsibility. Also, I want to get to that place where I can pretend that I am superwoman – able to wrangle two children with ease.

I glance in the rear-view mirror at them to see if I have in any small way got through to them. Eight-year-old Priya sits tall in her seat, her shiny black hair parted perfectly in the middle and swept back into a low, plaited ponytail; ten-year-old Arjun is slouched in his car seat, his uniform already looking like he's been at school all day, even though I made sure he was wearing ironed, clean clothes when we were getting ready. They aren't listening. Of course they're not.

My eyes return to the road and a large figure is suddenly there, in front of the car. I have to slam on my brakes in an emergency stop, throwing all of us forwards, the children already complaining before any of us have time to sit back in our seats. 'Are you OK?' I ask them.

'No,' Arjun complains.

'Why'd you do that, Mama?' asks Priya.

My eyes return to the person who caused me to brake, to see if they have any idea how they've put my children in danger, let alone themselves. 'I didn't mean—'

It's him. The figure standing in the road is him. I haven't seen him since it happened. I haven't seen him and, I suppose, I wasn't expecting to see him. I was hoping to manage to avoid seeing him for as long as possible. He stands in the middle of the road and scowls at me. His gaze is a piercing blue glare that burns through the windscreen and carves his anger into my skin. With a sneer and a shake of his head, he turns away and continues to stalk across the road to his car.

I'm shaking. Not just from the emergency stop, but also from what Trevor just did. He hates me. He absolutely hates me. I know why. I don't blame him. But it's horrible to see such a look on the face of someone with whom I have sat and eaten and drunk and danced and socialised. It's heartbreaking to see that look on the face of a friend.

My hands tremble as I move my foot from the brake onto the accelerator and move off again. I find somewhere to park and then immerse myself in getting the kids out of the car, grabbing bags and blazers, delivering them to the school gates, just in time for them to line up in their neat year-group lines to go inside.

I don't make eye contact with anyone, not even the mothers who usually just smile at me. I don't want to see anyone, to have them look at me like Trevor just did. On my way back, I am still on edge until I reach the end of the road and I can breathe again. The crowd is dispersing now that the children are going in, and the further away I get from the gates, from the playground where *she* was found, the better I feel. The freer I feel.

It was the same last week when we all went back to school. Every time I approached the place, my breathing would stall, my body would tense, I'd have to keep blinking to stop myself crying.

The other two are waiting by my car with their arms folded across their huddled, tensed bodies. They're not talking, they are standing there, looking how I feel: worried, scared, shivery. Hazel's brown hair was probably a neat bun when she left the house this morning, but it is a frazzled mess now; Maxie has obviously been spinning her curls around her finger so her hair is in clumps rather than ringlets. Both of them have unfocused gazes that are fixed on the mid-distance.

Since it happened, we haven't been near each other. We haven't messaged each other, we didn't meet for coffee last Wednesday, didn't stand together at pick-up and drop-off – it was like we barely knew each other. We didn't plan it, we just instinctively kept our distance. Even after the police questioned us because we were the last people to see her conscious that night, we didn't get on the phone to each other to compare notes, we didn't rush to meet up. Now we've seen Trevor, though, it's different. I'm deducing they have seen him. I'm thinking they must have had the same look from him. Why else would they look like I feel?

I come to a stop in front of them.

I'm guessing we really do need to talk about this now.

Cece

10 a.m. Sending the children to private schools goes against all my beliefs. Sol had tried to sell it to me as part of the moving down here package and I hadn't been interested. I believed in the state school system and that was pretty much that.

Then when I started researching schools in the area we could afford to buy in, I discovered that we were in the so-called 'dead zone' when it came to state schools. There were none within walking distance and the other nearest ones that were a short drive away were full – I didn't believe the woman I spoke to at the council so I rang them all and checked. My best bet would be going on the waiting list or driving half an hour every morning to get them to the one they would be originally allocated. Sol had helpfully piped up that maybe we should consider 'independent' education again (he'd changed the word 'private' to 'independent' to try to soften the impact of it) and were there any 'independent' schools within walking distance of our new home?

Plummer Prep came up. Plummer Prep, with its long history and its outstanding OFSTED report and shiny new website, and green and purple uniform, and mother who was almost bludgeoned to death in the front playground three weeks ago.

I'm hanging on the phone, waiting to speak to Sol. I left a million messages for him when I got back from school, managed a brief internet search, and he still hasn't called me back. When his personal assistant had said to me with an embarrassed tone, the last time I called, that he'd ring me back as soon as possible, I decided to hang on the line.

Plummer Prep. I'd liked the head teacher when I met her and when she'd shown me around I'd seen an array of happy girls and boys who reflected the multicultural world we lived in. I'd walked away, clutching my thick, shiny brochure and application forms, happy and, I'll admit it, excited about the boys starting at the school. In the last few weeks, with all the craziness of moving, I'd barely had time to eat, let alone check the news headlines. In all of it, though, I'd been comforted that the school thing was sorted, and I didn't have to worry about it.

'Mrs Solarin, do you still want to hold?' Sol's personal assistant asks. If possible, she is sounding even more embarrassed.

'Oh, yes, thank you.'

The first thing I had typed in about the school had brought up the news articles. The pictures. I'd looked at Yvonne Whidmore, standing with her husband and children, looking so happy, so contented with her life. And this was what had happened to her.

I had to take several deep breaths, had to walk around and around the kitchen several times to stop myself running down to the school and grabbing my children out of class and bringing them home. By home, I mean London. This place is not my – our – home. That sort of thing never happens in London. Well, of course it does, but not to people I could potentially know. Not on the premises of the place where I dropped off my kids.

The Whidmores looked like a nice family. He looked considerably different to the crumpled, highly stressed image I got of him walking into the school with his children, but they seemed so together. How could—

'Cee, yep, what's up?'

'Sol. Did you hear about what happened at the boys' school?' I ask.

'No, what? Are the boys all right?'

'The woman who was found on the school grounds in the summer?'

'Oh, that,' he says dismissively.

'So you heard about it? But didn't bother to tell me?' I ask.

Sol pauses now. He knows he's about to plunge himself into a whole world of trouble. 'I might have heard something. But it wasn't . . . I knew you'd just get yourself all worked up about it.'

'Get myself all worked up about it? Aren't you even worried, Sol? Because I am. What if it was part of a grudge someone has against the school? What if they come back and harm our boys? What if this is the start of something awful?'

'It'll be fine,' Sol says. That's it. To that devastating revelation, to my worries, to my assessment of the atmosphere at the school, all I get is 'It'll be fine.'

'You didn't just hear something, did you? You knew all about it,' I say to him.

'I told you, I heard something. But seriously, Cee, stop fussing, it'll be fine.'

Over the last three months Sol has been doing this: dismissing me and anything I try to bring up with him in a condescending manner. 'I really hope you're right,' I say to him.

'I am. Look, Cee, I have to go. Stop worrying. See ya.'

He hangs up before I can even say a proper bye and the anger I've been suppressing flares up like an inferno in me.

I really didn't want to move. But I had to. The longer Sol and I were apart, the more distant he became. When he first got the promotion, six months ago, he was commuting down to Brighton three or four times a week because none of us wanted to move. And he'd get back late, grumpy and irritable, unpleasant and hostile. When we decided to try him living down in Brighton for a month he began to disappear. His texts during the day stopped completely, his replies to my texts dwindled, and on the phone he was short and distracted. Then we'd go three days sometimes without any communication. I didn't want to move, but I didn't want to lose him either, so I said yes to us moving, I convinced the children it was going to be a big adventure. And I ignored the fact that I was the one who lost the most in this. I didn't want to be a stay-at-home parent – I didn't have the strength for it. I liked working, I liked being independent and not reliant on anyone for anything. I truly thought once we were here that Sol would go back to who he was. But no, he is still being dismissive and condescending. He is still treating me like an after-thought. *Is that because someone is 'see ya'-ing and 'TBH'-ing with my husband?*

April, 2005

'So, I have two questions to ask you,' Sol said to me. We were cooking in my little kitchen, and Harmony was sitting in front of the television, counting her toes in time to something on *In the Night Garden*.

'Go ahead, but just remember, I may not answer depending on how invasive the question is.'

Sol smiled and put down the carrots he was washing. He came to me, took the knife out of my hands, and stood behind me. He wrapped his arms around my waist and nestled his cheek on my shoulder. 'They are kind of interlinked.'

'Go ahead.'

'Right, well, the thing is, I was wondering if I could adopt Harmony?'

I froze. That I was not expecting. I was expecting him to ask if we could move in together, not this. 'What's the other question?' I managed to squeeze out.

'Well, will you marry me?'

I froze again. I was not expecting that, either.

'Do you see how the two are interlinked now?'

'Yes,' I squeaked.

'Have I scared you?'

'Yes,' I squeaked again.

'Cece, I love you. You love me. Let's get married. Make more babies.'

'Is it really that simple?'

'Of course it is. Come on, Cee, when you think about it, if we weren't together, how would you feel? I mean, I know you'd cope and you wouldn't fall apart, but how would you truly feel?'

How would I feel? Devastated. Hopeless. Broken. 'Not good,' I said to him. 'But adoption and marriage, they are huge things.'

32

'What sort of an answer is that? I'd be broken if we weren't together. Devastated. Hopeless. Broken. That's why I want you to marry me and to let me adopt Harmony. You're my family.'

'OK,' I replied as he wrapped his arms around me. 'OK, I will marry you and I will let you adopt Harmony. OK.'

Sol spun me in his arms and picked me up, holding me above him, his grin so wide I could barely see his face. His grin, of course, matched mine, because I couldn't remember a time when someone had made me so happy.

10:20 a.m. I toss my phone onto the table and pick up my tablet again. I need to stop reading about Yvonne Whidmore. I need to focus on something else, anything else, because if I start down that road and discover stuff about her that makes her life in any way similar to mine, I will be leaving before Sol gets back tonight. I look around at the boxes that need unpacking. I need to focus on something else. Just not that, either.

Anaya

11:15 a.m. I was dubious about this car when Sanjay first suggested it. It's too flashy, I'd told him. And not that brilliant for the environment. But he'd gone on about the safety record, about how the children would be better protected in a crash, and I'd asked him if we'd just have to ignore what sort of planet they'd grow up to inherit then? And he'd replied that he would make the equivalent donation in the car price to any environmental charity I chose. Fair play to him, he did as well.

Since leaving the others, I couldn't go home. Sanj is working up in London most days for the next few weeks, so the house will be empty, echoey and empty, and I can't be alone in there right now. I can't be with the others, but I can't be alone at home.

My foot presses down on the accelerator and the car surges forward, eating up the black line of road that leads upwards through the green hillside to the top of Devil's Dyke. Sometimes the way to Devil's Dyke feels like an almost vertical incline. When I used to come running up here, I had to dig deep, concentrate on every step, push through the shuddering of my leg muscles to reach the top, to stand at the very summit and throw my arms in the air, victorious like Rocky Balboa after his famous run. I was humming the *Rocky* theme tune in my head, of course.

Now I'm driving up here, climbing all this way to be closer to the sky, to be as far away from the beach as I can while still being able to see it. I want to think about that night with Yvonne and forget about it at the same time.

When Trevor wasn't bringing the girls to school, last week, when it was simply everyone hanging around until the kids went in, and no one really talked about it, it was easier to act as if it hadn't really happened. To pretend that I hadn't seen her *that* night, that . . . I'd told the police all about it, of course. Apart from the bits I couldn't tell them. Wouldn't tell them. What does it matter, the semantics of it – I didn't tell them everything. Most, but not all. It's always that detail that catches you out.

I almost knock the car door off its hinges freeing myself, pushing myself into the windy top of the hill. I can see for miles and miles, but you have to know exactly where to stand to see the beach, to see the sea, to see where one of my former best friends began the night that would end with her in a coma. Without thinking, I stand in that spot and cover my eyes. Hide myself. It's too much. Too much. I have to tell. I have to tell Sanjay everything. Even if it ruins my life.

I have to tell.

But I can't.

I won't.

I mustn't.

April, 2003

I stood behind the metal mesh railings of the balcony of this hot new London club, looking down at the party I had put together. I'd organised it to celebrate the merger of two huge companies, and it had gone off without a hitch. Obviously we'd had the usual tantrums – the clients not liking the decor, food, location, about three minutes before the event was meant to start. *Obviously* I'd discovered that the people I'd put next to each other on certain tables had once been married/caught having affairs/threatened to kill each other and so I'd had to rearrange EVERYONE to make sure they were properly far apart. But those were mere glitches to be expected and I wasn't in danger of losing my job over them.

I was aware of the tall, handsome man moving up the metal staircase as though he glided, and I pretended not to see him. He was Sanjay Kohli and he'd arrived with the bigwigs who'd spent the best part of a year negotiating this deal. He didn't work for either company, he was the man who'd made it happen. He was a matchmaker for companies who often didn't know they were looking for someone to hook up with, and he'd been all over the business pages as the hot new thing. He was certainly the best-looking thing. I'd read all about him when my company, Logan & Lachlan & Lockhart, had won the pitch for this account. When I'd seen a picture of Sanjay Kohli, I'd actually gasped. They were all polished, these people involved with big business and mergers, but he was that handsome reserved for movie stars who had access to filters, make-up artists and time to take care of themselves. His saffron-brown skin was smooth and unmarked, his large eyes were edged by thick midnight-black eyelashes, his features were framed by thick black eyebrows. The way he was smiling at the camera gave the impression that he knew something about you but he wasn't going to tell you what – in fact, he wasn't ever going to tell anyone. I knew I'd see him at the launch and decide he would be my event crush.

When he'd walked in, told me his name, and smiled that smile as I ticked it off, I'd felt my cheeks grow warm. I'd stared very hard at the sheet in front of me and pretended I was immune to his looks.

I'd watched Sanjay Kohli from my balcony, moving from group to group, talking, engaging, making everyone feel at ease, while most people were slowly descending. I was fascinated by this process: the sloughing off of sensibility and decorum; the formal layers peeling away with every sip of the drinks in their hands and becoming a different breed to the ones who'd walked in the doors. It would end in tears. Tantrums, tears and taxis. Always. No matter who, no matter how refined, these parties, these events that kept me employed, always ended the same way. And I always came away a little deflated that the person I'd decided was my event crush had descended with the rest of them.

'I hear you're the one to thank for this splendid event,' Sanjay Kohli said to me. Most of the time, my event crush did not speak to me beyond telling me his name on the door, or to complain about something that wasn't in my power to change. Beyond being the gateway to the end of the night and a body full of alcohol and good food, I didn't exist to most people.

I took a fake sip of the champagne glass in my hand and smiled at him. 'I am part of the team that put this event together,' I replied.

'I see,' he said. Amusement danced around his mouth and eyes, as though he was mocking me for being self-effacing. 'Part of the team.' He nodded. 'You wouldn't happen to be Anaya Harshani, would you?'

I gulped, discreetly, so he wouldn't see how flattered I was, positively brimming with excitement that he might know who I was. 'Yes, yes, I am.'

'I seem to remember that most of the emails about this event came from you. Sometimes late into the night.'

'I didn't know you were on the email list.'

'My assistant is, and she forwards everything on to me. I always like to know what is going on with my projects.'

'Good plan,' I replied. 'I'm the same.'

He took a fake sip of the drink in his hand and I smiled because he probably wasn't going to descend. '*Tuhānū rāta dē khāṇē la'ī jāṇā cāhudē hō?*' he said quietly, while staring straight into my eyes.

I had to rewet my lips, take a deep breath and remind myself to smile before I could speak. Those eyes. They were like whirlpools that drew you in and then swirled you around. 'I'm sorry, my parents are from Sri Lanka,' I said. 'I don't speak or understand Punjabi.'

'Ah, shame,' he replied. 'That will teach me to make assumptions based on a name and a picture. OK, in English: would you like to go to dinner?'

'I would like to go to dinner. But I am not going to go to dinner with you.'

'Ah . . . And why not, may I ask?'

I glanced at the event below and spotted my boss, with his sun-induced wrinkles and expensive glasses, staring up at us. He'd been hired after me so had 'inherited' me. I'd overheard him, on a night when he had descended with the rest of them, say that I was too pretty to try hard enough, too ethnic to be promoted, and too fuckable to not be a sexual harassment suit waiting to happen. He'd been mortified when he'd realised I'd overheard, and had been trying to get rid of me ever since. I knew he was going to watch how this interaction with someone important would play out and add it to the list of things he would use to get me out.

'Because I can't get involved with clients, no matter how tenuously a client they may be.'

'So you know who I am?' he asked.

'Doesn't everyone?' I replied.

He laughed, his face cracking from the fixed, knowing smile he'd worn all evening. 'Well, isn't part of your job giving the client what they want?' he asked.

'No.' I shook my head, and I watched his eyes follow the movement of my hair, transfixed like it was black water flowing from my head. 'My job is to give the client what they need, because rarely is what a client wants what is good or right for them. And anyway, I'm not part of this or any deal.'

He reached into his inner pocket and pulled out his business card. 'When you leave your job, give me a call,' he said.

I didn't take his card – I couldn't with my boss watching. 'And if you ever leave your job, give *me* a call,' I said. 'I really must go,' I added. I did not want to stop being around him, but I had to. It was the only way to stop myself descending with the rest of them except my overindulgence would be with Sanjay Kohli.

11:35 a.m. The wind whips at me up on this hill and I close my eyes, put out my arms. I want to jump off. Jump off and float away from all of what happened and all of what's to come.

Cece

4:35 p.m. Ore comes out of the building first, and he looks like he has all his belongings with him. He always does. It's almost always Oscar who has to go back for his book bag, his hat, his jumper, his homework folder, his . . . his . . . his . . . Ore walks beside a girl with saffron-brown skin and shiny black hair swept back into a plait under her green and purple hat, talking avidly about something. Oscar brings up the rear, carrying some of his stuff in his arms, but I can see his cap is on his head, and he has both his rucksack and book bag, as well as his blazer, so that's a good start. He walks beside a boy with pale skin and brown hair, they are also immersed in intense conversation.

'How was your day, boys?' I ask them as they trail up to me and I relieve them of their belongings while handing over their scooters.

'Great!' Ore says.

'It was so cool,' Oscar says.

'Really?' I ask. I was hoping they'd have a good day and a tiny little part of me was kind of hoping they wouldn't like it so I'd have an excuse to move back to London.

'Yeah,' Oscar says. 'It's like, the best school.'

'Ever,' Ore ends. '*Ever.*'

I look from one face to the other: both of them are so excited and happy. I guess that means we're staying.

Hazel

5 p.m. 'Coats off, shoes off, then straight upstairs with your bags to wash hands and start homework. I'll bring you up drinks and snacks.'

I sound convincing. My voice is clear, my words are easy to understand and yet, and yet . . . I watch Russell chuck his green rucksack and mud-splattered purple sports bag down in the middle of the hall, just in time for Camille to half trip over it before she goes on to do the same. Russell rips off his blazer, and drop it behind him without missing a beat, then he sideswipes Camille so he can run into the living room and throw himself onto the sofa. Calvin brings up the rear, stepping over the detritus of his older siblings and shedding his book bag, then heads for the kitchen. Camille has gone for the playroom. I stand at the bottom of the stairs, watching the intention behind my words evaporate like wisps of steam in the ether. They just do not listen to me. But, fair play to them, do I listen to me?

I inhale deeply, turn away from the mess that my children have left and turn towards the kitchen. Calvin has disappeared into the pantry and is probably knocking things onto the floor to find where I hid the chocolate biscuits. I ignore him, and go over to the far side of the cooker. I need to heat the oven, get this lasagne in, but I can't move from here. I keep seeing Trevor's face. Scarlett's face. Madison's face. I keep seeing their faces. All day they've been hounding me, coming to me when I've been trying to concentrate at work. I keep seeing what being without her is like. I grab the side to steady myself, bend forwards and take a long breath in. The out breath chokes in my throat, causes a loud sob. *Oh God, what did I do? What did I do?*

Another sob, and I almost double over, the thought of it ripping its way through me, almost tearing me in two. 'Oh God,' I sob. 'Oh God.'

'Mum? Mum, are you OK?' Calvin says suddenly.

I jerk myself upright, try to pull myself together. I shouldn't do that in front of him. Or any of the kids. Or anyone. No one can know about this.

'Yes, yes, I am.'

His face is creased with concern, wrinkled by worry. I go to touch his cheek but I'm trembling so I have to return my hand to my side without touching him. 'I'm fine, sweetheart, really, I'm fine.' I force myself to stand like everything is normal.

'I'm sorry we didn't listen to you,' he says. His voice is panicky. Scrabbling around to find a reason why I'm acting the way I am. 'I'm sorry, Mum. I will listen to you from now on. Promise.' He holds out his little finger. He wants me to hook my pinkie through it, to accept his promise by linking with him. 'Promise.'

'When do you lot ever listen to me?' I say to him. 'I'm not upset about that.' I shake my head. 'I mean, yes, it's not great that you lot never listen to me, but you know, that's not what has upset me right now.' I start moving the pans off the stove, onto the saucepan stand at the end of the kitchen. *Oven! I'm meant to be turning on the oven.*

'Did Daddy tell you off again?' Calvin asks. He's not going to be fobbed off as easily as he used to be. He has been growing into that stage when children are more worried for those around them than for themselves. I like this phase he's in, but it also means that the baby years are over. I'll have that void in my life which a very young child has filled for years.

'No, sweetheart, Walter – I mean, Daddy – didn't tell me off again.' Walter hasn't been in touch since the night . . . Since he made that call that led to what happened to Yvonne. I can't think about that, though. I can't.

I bend down and hug Calvin, then I let him go, and with my hands on his shoulders, I march him out into the hall.

'OK,' I say loudly from my place at the bottom of the stairs. 'I am about to put dinner in the oven. In that time, you need to pick up your stuff, and get upstairs, wash your hands and start your homework.' I know they can hear me, but they're all ignoring me. Even the one I am holding in front of me. 'If that does not happen, I will be putting it all in the bin. And you'll be the ones explaining to Mrs Carpenter why you've got no sports kit, no homework books, or library books. And don't think I'll be buying you new stuff until next year, either. It'll take me five minutes to get dinner on. After that, it's *aaallllll* up to you.'

Calvin gasps; he believes me and breaks free to quickly gather his belongings. First he attempts to hang up his blazer, but when he can't quite reach the hook, he throws it down and snatches up his bag and then runs up the stairs, heading straight for the bedroom he shares with Russell.

The other two stay in place, messing with the instruments in the playroom and flicking through channels on the television. 'Cool, guys,' I say. 'You do what you think is best. And when your stuff is in the bin, you can think up the right excuse to tell Mrs Carpenter. Of course, "my mum threw it in the bin because I wouldn't move it and wouldn't do my homework" might not get the sort of sympathy you hope it will, but I guess we'll find out tomorrow, heh?'

Calmly, I walk back into the kitchen and shut the door behind me. I head for the clingfilm-wrapped lasagne, which has been defrosting on the side all day. Once I've freed it from its covering, I press at the top, checking that it is properly defrosted. I prod a little more, before I pull a large metal baking tray from the small second oven and line that with greaseproof paper. Carefully, I place the large ceramic dish on it and slide them into the oven. From the fridge I take out broccoli and green beans, then take my time to remove the florets from the stems, to top and tail the beans, to wash them, place them in the steamer, ready for them to go on when the lasagne is nearly done.

I do all this slowly and precisely, giving the other two time to think about whether I was serious, whether they should maybe not test me. By the time I open the kitchen door, all their belongings have been removed from the hall, their blazers hung up, and they have also disappeared upstairs.

I stand at the bottom of the stairs and smile to myself. A momentary sense of smugness washes over me. I don't get to experience that very often when it comes to being a parent. Usually I feel like I am running at a hundred miles an hour just to stand still; often I feel like I am working very hard to not permanently damage one of the children. I've never been one of those serene parents who breezes through life, managing to do it all and do it well. I'm not like Yvonne, who made it look easy to run her family and life with precision; who was perfect in every way.

I'm thinking about her in the past tense. And she's still here, she's still with us, hanging on. Waiting, I think, to tell everyone all about me and what I did.

Cece

5:45 p.m. Oscar and Ore are both standing in the kitchen, looking at me like I have wronged them. I do not have snacks beyond apples and oranges and slices of pineapple. I am going to serve them cottage pie for dinner. And the television still hasn't been hooked up, so they have to make do with reading their books and doing their homework. The end of the world, *apparently*.

'You see, the thing is, Mum—' Oscar begins, ready to talk his way out of having to consume the mash-topped pie. He's cut short by the key in the lock.

Harmony! lights up in both their eyes – she'll save them from this disaster that is the first night after school with Mum.

'We're back!' Harmony calls. I look at the cooker clock. She's back early, since she finishes at five-thirty and it's at least half an hour on the bus. And who's this 'we'? I hope she hasn't been getting lifts from strange people. We've only just moved here; I'm about to run into the corridor when Harmony comes into the kitchen followed by Sol.

'Dad came to get me from school,' she says, dumping her rucksack by the kitchen door.

'How was your day?' I ask her, staring at Sol.

'Oh, fine. Fine,' Harmony says dismissively. 'Lessons were cool and lots of cool people.'

'I didn't know you'd be picking her up from school,' I say to Sol.

'Ah, I had a reminder this morning that I need to do more,' he replies with a smile. 'Anyways . . .' He comes further into the kitchen. 'I can see from those two faces that there's a potato-topped pie for dinner,' he says to the boys.

Harmony stops bending down to hug her brothers and fires her gaze in my direction. 'Oh, *what*?' she says.

'What is wrong with my pies?' I screech.

The children all move to explain the problem and 'Nothing,' Sol says over them. He looks reproachfully at the children, telling them not to say a word. 'They are delicious. I think the thing is, we seem to have them quite regularly? We don't get a chance to appreciate them because they're often on the menu, but anyway, I'm sure this one will freeze rather nicely for another day, because I'm going to take you all out to dinner to celebrate first day of school, first Monday in our new house and first weekday of us all being together.'

'No potato pie?' Ore says excitedly.

'We're going out for dinner,' Sol confirms.

'Not unless you all get changed and wash hands and all that stuff,' I say, feeling bad for my poor maligned cottage pie.

The room empties in seconds.

'So . . .' Sol says once we're alone.

'So . . . ?' I reply.

He slips his arms around my waist and gazes down at me. 'So . . . Are you going to stop with the potato-topped pies?'

'Git,' I say, and dig my fingers into his sides while he tries to wiggle away from me.

'Beautiful,' he replies and tries to tickle me back.

It doesn't seem so bad right now, being here. With him. And them. It doesn't feel so bad at all.

Hazel

6 p.m. The children are joking and talking with their mouths full as we sit around the dinner table, eating lasagne and vegetables. I'm here with them but I can't help my thoughts drifting over to another side of Brighton, to what it must be like in the Whidmore household. They will have gone from after-school club to the hospital to visit their wife and mother. They will have sat by her bedside, praying for even the smallest sign that she knew they were there. Then home, to homework, to dinner, to another night climbing into bed and hoping she'll wake up. Hoping she will tell all about the moments leading up to her attempted murder.

January, 2012
I stood in the middle of the supermarket and convinced myself not to scream 'CAMILLE!' at the top of my voice. Calvin was in a sling on my front and Russell had been, uncharacteristically, glued to my side all shopping trip. To balance the cosmic scales, of course, Camille, who was usually unfailingly good, had decided to disappear. I'd been scouring the shelves for a particular brand of whisky that Walter had screamed at me about not finding last time, and I'd turned back to put the bottle in the trolley to find her gone. Actually disappeared. I hadn't heard her unclipping herself or climbing out of the trolley seat; I hadn't heard her footsteps as she'd made good on her escape plan.

I'd wanted to start screaming but stopped myself. Because if I didn't panic outwardly, the bad things that happen to children you take your eyes off for two seconds wouldn't start. If I stayed calm, controlled, collected, things would work out all right.

'Which way did your sister go, Russell?' I asked calmly. I gently placed the bottle in the trolley – if I dropped it and smashed it dramatically, that would start *that* scenario where something bad was going to happen. Russell, in turn, looked surprised that I was speaking to him; in fact shocked that I knew his name. 'Russell, sweetie, can you tell me which way Camille went?' I said, crouching down as far as I could with a sleeping, dribbling Calvin strapped to my front. 'Just point – was it that way or this way?'

Come on, you stupid woman, I was telling myself while I tried to stay calm. *Someone could be leading your daughter through the car park to an unmarked van as you stand here trying to stay calm and trying not to make bad things happen.*

'Russell, sweetie,' I said in a shrill voice, 'tell Mummy which way Camille went.'

He took a step away from me, terrified by my rictus face and scary, falsetto voice. If I wasn't careful, he was going to run for it too.

'Excuse me,' a voice said to my right.

I swung towards her, ready to bawl her out for interrupting me while my daughter was missing and my son was preparing to run away, too.

'I think this little one belongs to you?' she said. This woman, this stranger, had her hands on Camille's bony little shoulders. 'I saw you with her earlier. She was trying to climb into one of the freezers.' She smiled at me, and the first thing I noticed about her was the twist of the left-hand side of her top lip, the way it could so very easily be a bitchy sneer but this smile was rueful and understanding. Still, she was a stranger and she had her hands on my daughter.

I snatched Camille away, held her protectively against me and took another look at this 'rescuer'. She was slightly taller than me. She wore an expensive-looking black skirt suit, high heels, and had a sky-blue handbag hooked over her left arm. I was suddenly, glaringly, aware of how casual I was, especially compared to this stranger. 'Casual', of course, meant dishevelled, messy, unkempt. I had on red and blue shoes that didn't match – Russell or Camille had hidden one of each last week and I still hadn't got around to finding them. I had on jeans that were baggy and unflattering, though you couldn't really see the breast milk and mashed banana stains on the front of my black top because Calvin was rather kindly hiding his work under the sling I carried him in. And my hair . . . my hair was so far at the other end of the spectrum from this goddess in front of me.

'She reminds me of my youngest child,' the woman said, conversationally. 'I look away, she makes a break for freedom as though life with me is so awful she has to re-enact scenes from *The Great Escape* every chance she gets.'

'You have children?' I said. I looked at her *again*. She had hips that did not carry extra weight; her breasts, impressively emphasised in the V of her suit jacket, were generous but perky. She didn't look like her body knew what a stretch mark was.

'Yes, of course. Like you.'

'You are nothing like me,' I said. I sounded awful, bitchy and jealous, but I didn't mean it like that.

Her lips twisted again as she smiled. She reminded me of those Hollywood actresses who made their fortune from the shape of their lips. 'I really am like you,' she said, completely unfazed by my snippiness.

'Sorry, shouldn't have said that. It was nasty and uncalled for. Especially when you found my daughter. I'm just so . . . and you're so . . . I can't see how you would say we're anything alike.'

'Oh, but we are alike. I just happen to know the secret to not going insane in the face of being a mother, that's all.'

'Oh, and what's that?'

'Childcare,' she said simply. 'I promise you, it will change your whole life.'

'I can't use childcare – I don't work. I can't justify that sort of expense when I don't work.'

'Sweetheart,' she said, 'you do work. Of course you work. And the secret to being successful at any job is the simple art of delegation.'

'Delegation?'

'Delegation. Learn that word, love that word. Because, believe me, two half-day sessions a week with your children in nursery and you will feel like a new woman.'

'Delegation.' The possibilities of having some time to myself or some time for me and the baby opened up in front of my eyes. The children out somewhere being educationally stimulated while I got to sit still for a few seconds *before* rushing around doing all the jobs I never seemed to get around to. 'Delegation.' I almost sighed the word. That was the sort of word that Walter respected. It didn't sound 'emotional' or 'female', it was a good, decent business word. One that he would understand, far more than: *I'm going insane. I only agreed to a third because you said you'd help out more, or at least be home relatively on time so I can go to the loo by myself. Never mind have a cup of tea, I'll forgo the tea, just let me do the toilet thing and we'll call it quits.* Admitting that sort of thing would be seen as emotional and weak by Walter. 'Delegation' as in *We need to delegate our responsibilities so we can become more effective, efficient parents* would not.

The happy grin spread right across my face.

'I'm Yvonne,' the stranger said. 'And I am going to change your life.'

June, 2012

We sat at my kitchen table with coffees.

Despite my new-found ability to delegate, I still didn't look like Yvonne. I don't think anyone did, if I was honest, but my whole life had been opened up by being able to drop the older children at nursery. I could take the baby to playgroups. And I could meet people for coffee. In this case, Yvonne. Who was as perfect as always: blonde hair all bundled up into a casual bun, a beautiful red shorts suit and bejewelled sandals. I'd graduated from mismatched shoes and baby-food-stained tops to clean clothes and washed hair. Delegation was liberating.

Right now, Yvonne was overjoyed that our children were going to be starting at Plummer Prep that September. 'I can't wait for us to be school gate mums together,' she said. 'We've got a head start on everyone else. Do you think you'll get a job, then? You've talked about it ever since I met you, which, it has to be said, feels like years ago, not months ago. So, any idea where you'd like to work?'

'Oh, no, there's no point thinking about that – Walter's been talking about another baby.'

Slowly Yvonne set down her coffee cup and blinked at me a few times as though I'd started screaming at her. She seemed truly horrified by what I had just said.

'Do *you* even *want* another child?' she asked, horror in her voice.

I glanced over at Calvin, asleep in his cot on the other side of the kitchen. My happy 'surprise'. My third that I would not have if I'd had any real choice in the matter. And that was a terrible thing to think, an awful admission. I was satisfied with two. As Camille and Russell got older, closer to some semblance of independence, Walter had started talking about having a third child. I'd told him no. I was just getting my body back, I was just getting to sleep through the night, I was just remembering what it was like to go somewhere without having a small person hanging off me. We'd talked and talked and talked about it, then he'd got me to agree to at least just using condoms instead of the Pill. Foregone conclusion after that. I'd used condoms all my sexual life, but after only two weeks of them this time around with Walter, I was pregnant again. I didn't want to be suspicious of him, and I loved Calvin when he was eventually here . . . but being pregnant with two older children who had only eleven months between them had been a hell I'd never wanted to revisit. A fourth would mean getting a job would be a pipe dream. A fourth would mean I would never get my life back; it would mean being known as nothing more than 'Mum'.

'Do you want another child?' Yvonne asked again.

I shook my head. 'I don't think I do, no.'

'So why are you entertaining it? It's your body.'

'It's hard to explain,' I replied simply.

'Tell him if he wants another one he can get a womb and do the necessary hard yards,' Yvonne said firmly.

I laughed at what she had said, as though when I had said that to him, he hadn't smirked at me and said, *Why bark when you've got a dog to do it for you?* before scratching behind my ears and saying, *Good girl, Lassie. Good dog.*

'Tell me you're at least still on the Pill,' Yvonne said.

I glanced down. How could I tell her that we were back where we'd been twenty-two months ago, with him having convinced me to stop taking the Pill while we talked about having another?

Yvonne's face softened, she softened. Slowly she reached out and covered my hand with hers. Her touch was steadying, calming. She'd not touched me like that before and I realised how I missed touches like this. I had no friends to touch me, soothe me; Walter only touched me as a precursor to sex. 'Hazel . . .' She stopped speaking, shook her head. Her eyes misted up. 'Does he force you, you know, to do it?'

'Of course not,' I replied. Because it wasn't how she made it sound.

'OK . . . is your "yes" actually an "all right" so you don't have to accept it's the R-word when he does it anyway?'

That was more like it. But I couldn't admit that to her. Or to anyone. 'I love him,' I said instead. 'We've been together since uni and he's all I know. And I love him.'

Yvonne curled her hand around mine and nodded understandingly. 'You mustn't have another baby with him if it's not what you want.'

'It's fine, we're still using condoms.'

Yvonne pointedly looked over at Calvin, even though I'd *never* said anything to her about how he came to be here. 'OK, look, I'm going to help you,' she stated.

'How?'

She smiled at me in the same way she'd smiled at me the first time I met her. 'Oh, Hazel, in many, many ways.'

6:10 p.m. I can't eat. I haven't eaten properly in weeks. Even before that night with Yvonne. I was so wound up, stressed, anxious. I was on a knife-edge, I knew that. That's why I should have walked away that night. I should have walked away.

Forcefully, I rip my mind away from thinking about that. I look at the faces of my children, laughing and relaxed. I'm here to see that. I need to focus on that. I need to focus on that as much as I possibly can. Because you never know when it's all going to be taken away.

Maxie

11:25 p.m. I wanted to tell Ed about to seeing Trevor, today. About how he looked at me, how he looked at Hazel, about how Anaya said he'd looked at her. I wanted him to understand, to sympathise.

I'm in bed waiting for him now. When he came in earlier, he had dinner with me and Frankie, we all chatted and laughed and ate together. We watched the end of Frankie's DVD on this very bed and when Frankie eventually went to sleep, Ed smiled at me, that friendly, affable smile you shoot to vague acquaintances, carried Frankie to bed, then went downstairs.

Not tonight, I thought. *Tonight I need to talk. We need to be open, honest and united with this.* So I followed him downstairs to find he'd opened his one bottle of beer and was flicking through the channels. There were many channels to go through, and methodical, logical man that he has been for as long as I have known him, he was clicking on them all one by one. That sort of thing drove me insane because it was such a waste of time, but I couldn't bring that up with him. There's lots of stuff I can and do bring up with him, but for some reason, things like that, which mention something that drives me to distraction, are off-limits.

'Hi,' I said and flopped down onto the sofa next to him.

He grinned at me again, genuine affection in his eyes, and then patted the hand that was nearest him, like an owner quieting his pet. That was it. The sheer soul-mangling humiliation of being petted by the man you've been married to for seven years was too much for me. I choked back a sob, and I knew he heard it because he stiffened in the seconds after it left my mouth, braced himself for what I might say, but he didn't even move in my direction.

Here I am, instead, waiting for him to come up here. So I can try again. So I can find my voice and tell him what happened today. He's waiting, I know, for me to go to sleep so he can avoid me. So we can avoid all those unspoken conversations that are piled up between us like invisible bricks.

March, 2005
'Knock, knock,' a voice said softly as someone opened the door to the nursery.

I sat in the rocking chair with the brakes applied, reading by a tiny nightlight. My eyes were heavy and tired; the temperature of the room was perfect for a sleeping baby, and perfect for me to want to curl up and nap, too. I couldn't, of course, not when I was working. I'd got this job as an au pair because it was the perfect way to make money, have somewhere to live and have time to study. The family I was working for treated me as though I was a servant, and expected me to do much more than was in the contract, but it was fine. The older child was fun, and the baby was calm as well as cute. Tonight was a dinner party at their grand London house and I had decided to settle myself in the baby's room so if she woke I would be right there to resettle her, and not disturb the people downstairs.

I lay down my book and stood up, ready to redirect the person who'd entered to the toilet or downstairs.

'I'm sorry,' the woman whispered. 'I couldn't resist coming to look at the baby. You don't mind, do you?'

I gawped at her. My eyes were properly out on stalks as I stared at her masses of corkscrew curls and perfectly made-up eyes, and small, pink rosebud lips. My gaze then skittered over to the cover of the book I'd just put down. It was *her*. Bronwyn Sloane. The woman whose book I was reading. She was standing in the doorway, letting all the heat out, and the light in. The baby was sensitive to even the smallest of changes in her environment –

she liked a continuous equilibrium to sleep so was likely to wake up any second.

Not completely believing what I was doing, I indicated for her to come in, to shut the light out, to let the warmth take over again. She grinned at me. Bronwyn Sloane smiled at *me* as she came in. 'Love babies,' she whispered. She theatrically crept across the room to stand beside the cot. She smiled down at Marilyn, who was flat on her back, her arms thrown up on either side of her head.

'Oh, but she's beautiful,' Bronwyn said. 'And, obviously, that is not the only way she'll be judged in later life as I'm sure she'll be clever, ambitious and talented, too.' She was gently laughing at herself because the books she wrote often focused on how people usually judged her on how she looked. I couldn't help myself staring. This woman was brilliant. Funny, insightful, cutting, and she let any unfair criticism wash over her in a dignified manner. And she was talking to me like I was someone she knew.

'Is she a good baby?' she asked and looked at me. I jumped a little, because I'd been staring so intently at her.

'Yes,' I whispered back.

'Awww,' she cooed in reply. 'I'm Bronwyn,' she said to me.

'Erm, erm, Maxie,' I replied, having forgotten for a sec who I was. 'I'm Maxie.'

'Pleased to meet you, Maxie.' Her eyes scanned the room, as though she'd never seen a nursery before, and then they alighted on her book on the floor by my seat. 'Oh, I see you're a reader.' She looked amused. 'What do you think? Too pretentious? Full of obvious crap that anyone could have thought of? A load of old narcissistic nonsense?' Clearly she had read the same reviews I had.

'No, not at all,' I gushed. 'I think it's brilliant. Your best yet, actually.'

'Is the correct answer.' She bobbed down, her bag falling off her shoulder, and picked up the book. When she stood up again, she hooked the bag back into place. She looked at where I had splayed the book open. 'I know really I shouldn't ask, but what's your favourite bit so far?'

'Erm . . . Probably the bit where all those people kept touching your hair. And you told them to stop and that your hair isn't a toy and if people kept touching you, you'd do them for assault since assault is actually touching someone against their will. I love it because the amount of times, being mixed race, people have put their hands on my hair as though it's their right to touch me because they're curious . . .'

'Urgh! Don't get me started on the people who think you should be somehow grateful that they're interested in you,' she whispered back. 'I like you, Maxie.' She grinned, seemed to look me over again and then looked at the baby. 'I could talk to you all night, but I should be getting back to the dinner party.'

I nodded, smiled. I'd be texting all my friends the second she left and letting them know I'd bonded with a genuine celebrity over the hair thing even though she was white.

From her bag, Bronwyn Sloane got out her flashy mobile phone. 'What's your number?' she asked.

'My number?' I replied.

'I'd like your number. I'd like to see you again. Not like that – I know how that sounded and I know what people say about me despite all the stuff I write about my sex life with men, and my husband, but I didn't mean it like that. I think you're interesting. I'd like to go for a coffee sometime.'

'Me?' I pointed to myself.

She giggled. 'Yes. You. I know if I give you my number you won't call me because you'll think I wasn't serious. So I'd like your number, and I'll call you and we can meet up. If you'd be interested, at all?'

Of course I'd be interested. I slowly read out my number and watched her type it into her phone. I was going to wake up in a minute. I'd obviously dozed off while reading Bronwyn Sloane's book and had imagined the whole thing. She grinned at me one last time, then waved at me, blew a kiss to the baby and then off she went, creeping over the soft-pile carpet, slowly shutting the door behind her.

I sat back in the chair, closed my eyes and then waited for myself to wake up. A few minutes later there was another knock on the door before it was pushed open. This time it was a man. He had unruly brown hair and was dressed in a tight-fitting royal-blue suit with a pencil tie. He crept in, shut the door behind him. 'Hi,' he whispered as he crept over to the cot.

'Hi,' I replied.

'Bronwyn sent me up. She said I had to come and meet her new friend Maxie and to see the most gorgeous baby. Not in that order, I don't think.'

He was talking to me but staring at the baby. He turned to me, did the smallest of double-takes and then stuck out his hand. 'You must be Maxie,' he said, holding out his hand.

'Yes.'

'Hello, Maxie, I'm Bronwyn's other half, Ed.'

11:55 p.m. Moonlight is dancing into our bedroom from the open curtains, but it's not quite the full moon. I remember Frankie once asking me if there was only a proper full moon once a year because that was the time it took for the Earth to go around the sun and we could only see the moon at certain points. I'd stared at him for a second, not understanding the question because I wasn't sure four-year-olds were meant to know that much about astronomy. And then I'd been taken aback because what he said reminded me of what my relationship with his father was like – I only got to see the proper full him about once a year, when he seemed to relax and remember how to be with me.

I feel Ed's presence in the room before I see him. He's walked quietly – probably crept – upstairs so as not to wake me and when I haven't moved, he's obviously felt it safe to walk into the room. I listen to the rustle of him unbuttoning his shirt, the soft thud of it hitting the laundry basket, then him undoing his belt, holding on to it to stop it jangling, the quiet tug of undoing his trouser buttons. I roll over then, look at him.

He stands at the foot of the bed, and pauses in pulling down his trousers when he sees I'm awake. We stare at each other across the divide. I know what will happen next: he will do up his trousers, grab his shirt and leave. He'll go and sit downstairs until the small hours, or he'll sleep on the sofa. He rarely sleeps in the spare room because he doesn't want Frankie to know, doesn't want me to know, either, I suppose, that he doesn't want to be around me for too long.

Slowly I move back the covers, show him that I'm naked, that there is a space on my side of the bed that he can slip into. In the dancing moonlight, which I know he likes, I watch his chest lift and then fall as he inhales deeply and then exhales just as deeply. He's torn. Usually he's able to walk away, but it's been a while. More than a few weeks have passed since we've . . . And I know he wants to. Wants me, probably. Only probably, because I can never be certain it's me and not simply sex that he wants. He inhales and exhales again, then finishes taking his clothes off. His desire, his want, has overridden his need to not be around me.

He takes my nipple in his mouth first of all and my body responds by pushing itself towards him, begging for more. He moves to the other breast and his fingers slip between my legs. We revel in the closeness, the familiarity, the openness of foreplay with each other. He becomes more forceful, his fingers moving fast and hard, his lips covering my body in hot, passionate kisses. Suddenly he pulls his fingers away, holds himself over me, staring down at me, asking if I'm ready for him to enter me. I stare back, begging him to bring us together. He registers my need, my desperation for him, and sits back to open the bedside table and pull out a condom. Always. *Always.*

I try not to mind, to tell myself it's for the best that he always uses one, but I always have to sneak into the bathroom later, to bite into the soft, fleshy part of my forearm and stop myself crying at the fact that my husband always needs protection to have sex with me.

Ed pushes inside me, keeping me engaged with eye contact. I want him to lower his head, to kiss me. If he has to wear a condom, fine, but for once I want him to kiss me, to act like we're a real couple. But he doesn't, he never has – he probably never will.

We move together, we groan together and we orgasm together, and when he rolls off me, and we stare at the ceiling, our breathing slowing down together. Our bodies can do that: make love, be in harmony, find mutual pleasure together – it's everything else about us that doesn't completely work.

Does it bother you that the only time our lips have met in a kiss is the minute after we were pronounced husband and wife and we needed our marriage to look real, at least in the photos? Do you wish it was different? After seven years of marriage, do you wish you could allow yourself to forget why you had to marry me, and just kiss me?

He gets up and heads for the bathroom to sort himself out. *I wish you'd kiss me. I wish, just for once, you'd kiss me.*

TUESDAY

Anaya

1:15 p.m. When I return from yoga, the deadlock is thrown and the alarm is silent as I push open the front door. Any other person, who knows their children are at school and their husband is at least sixty miles away, would be panicking right now. They'd be backing out carefully, they'd be reaching into their pockets for their mobiles and hoping their keyboard doesn't give them away as they carefully dial 999. Me? I feel a gut-wrench, not of terror but of irritation. I have an intruder in my house, but my husband gave her the key and she feels entitled to come and go in my home as she pleases.

September, 2004
'You're a mystery, Ans. Such a beautiful mystery.'

I sat astride Sanjay, looking down at him, listening to the words he said to me every time we got together. If we went for a coffee, to a bar, to a restaurant, or if we spent the afternoon at his house making love, he'd say it. He ran his hands down over my bare shoulders, over my chest, onto my breasts, where they stayed.

At first I'd liked the idea of being mysterious and beautiful – the heroine heroes go insane for in books and movies. The compliment had started to wear a little thin now, six months later. Now, it felt like part of the big act that was Sanjay Kohli. I'd begun to suspect that he spent all his time acting, holding himself back, hiding his true nature because he didn't think the real him was good enough to be seen.

'There is no mystery or depth to me,' I said to him. I was tired of it now. He'd called me a year after we met because he'd been poached by another firm and I – miracles of miracles – had managed to hang on to my job. We'd started as a mutual crush so I'd expected a bit of reservation with each other, but after six months I thought we'd both have been able to relax. But no, I couldn't relax because he seemed to be constantly doing the emotional equivalent of sucking in his stomach whenever he was with me.

He ran his fingers over my body and the tingles raced through me, igniting the fire deep inside, between my legs. I rocked against him in response, felt him go hard and waited for him to start again. 'Oh, there is so much depth there,' he said. 'So much mysterious depth.'

I rolled my eyes, climbed off him, and lay back on the bed. I tugged the white sheet up over my breasts, then stared at the ceiling. It was a very nice ceiling as ceilings went, I'd been seeing it for many months and I would have liked to keep on seeing it – since it was obviously more real than the man I was actually seeing. 'I don't think we should see each other any more,' I said to him. I was testing it out for size, and, yup, it felt right. It was the right thing to do.

'What?' he said. He'd been confused when I had climbed off him; now he was shocked. 'What do you mean?'

He had a beautiful house in Brixton, the sort of place you walked past and knew you would never afford to live in. I'd expected someone with his reputation and wealth to go for a Thames-side apartment or a loft in east London, but no, he'd apparently grown up around Brixton and wanted to stay close to his roots. Obviously modern Brixton wasn't the Brixton he'd grown up in; he often spoke about how the soul was being systematically ripped out of the place he loved. He adored its imperfections, its crazy shops under and around the arches, the characters who hung out by the Tube station, the mini dramas played out on the streets every day. He'd talk about Brixton, the things he got up to – the feuds, the loves, the schemes – growing up there with such warmth and passion that I knew he had it in him. I knew there was more to him than the man who was always emotionally holding in his stomach. But I never got it. Six months and I never got the real him unless he was talking about 'his' south London home.

'I mean, I can't be doing with this any more. You never relax with me. You act like I'm some precious, delicate goddess that you have to be careful how you touch and speak to and I can't be doing with it any more.'

'I'm really confused? I respect you and I want to treat you well,' was the best he could manage.

'There's a difference between treating someone with respect and treating them like they're a deity.' I sat up so we were level, but I kept the sheet covering my chest. 'You seem to be holding back with me. Now, I don't want to know everything all at once, I don't want to be your therapist or anything like that, but I'd like you to be real for once. It's like . . . It's like you're always on your best behaviour. Like I'm some auntie who's going to berate your parents if you don't behave well in front of me. And when you're not acting like that, you treat me like I'm a business acquaintance that you have to schmooze.

'Do you realise you've never once sworn in front of me? You rarely go to the toilet, you certainly don't let one off. And that's fine, it's not normal, but it's fine and respectful like you say, but when it's combined with the rest of it, it's exhausting. That's it: it's exhausting. I always feel like I have to be on my best behaviour because you are.'

Sanjay's face creased up a little more with every word, until he didn't have a face any more, it was one giant wrinkle. 'But how else am I supposed to be?' he asked.

'Be yourself,' I replied.

'This is myself,' he said.

'Then yourself is fake, and I need to be going.'

'Anaya, come on,' he said.

I held on to the sheet as I leant over the side of the bed to pick up my bra. From downstairs, the front door banged shut. I hadn't heard a key in the lock, so I assumed he was being burgled. We both froze, eyes wide and alarmed. 'I'll call the police,' I said.

'Sanjay? Where are you?' a woman's voice called from downstairs. 'I know you are here because the alarm did not sound.'

A shockwave of fear about being on the scene of a crime in progress (I watched *The Bill* like anyone else) was swept away by the giant shockwave of him being married. That made everything clear: why he was holding back all the time, why he was never relaxed. He was married. *The bastard.*

'Oh, fucking shit,' Sanjay said, picking that moment to break his six-month run of not swearing in front of me.

Wife? I mouthed at him. It was not going to end well. Women in these situations rarely blamed their lying, cheating spouses, they always blamed the other woman until the shock had eased off. I was about to get into a fight with his wife and I was naked.

He shook his head. 'Mother.' He whipped aside the sheet and leapt out of bed and was round my side of the bed in less than a second.

His mother's footsteps went towards the back of the house, although she continued to call for him. 'Sanjay! Are you asleep?'

'You have to hide,' he hissed at me, and grabbed my jeans, top, bra, knickers and bag into a bundle in his arms, then pulled the sheet off me.

'Don't be ridiculous,' I said. I reached for the sheet to pull it back. 'Sanjay!'

He pulled it off me again. 'Trust me, you do not want to meet my mother like this. She will never accept you, if you do. And you will wish I had a wife if you meet her like this, I promise you.'

I could hear his mother's footsteps pause at the bottom of the stairs. 'What is it that you are doing up there?' she called. 'I brought you food and your ironing.'

'Please, Anaya,' he begged in a whisper. 'I love you. I want to marry you, but that will not happen if this happens.'

'You love me?' I asked.

His face relaxed into a goofy smile, and he started to nod, then remembered what was happening, what those footsteps meant. 'Not the time,' he said.

'All right, all right,' I mumbled, then got out of bed. He thrust my stuff into my arms and then pointed to the large oak wardrobe that sat on the other side of his room. 'You're having a *giraffe*,' I said.

He pursed his lips at me and then pointed to the stairs. 'You so owe me,' I said and ran naked across the room to the wardrobe. Thankfully it was nothing like my wardrobe and everything was neatly hung up, the shoes carefully lined up at the bottom. You wouldn't be able to find Narnia let alone space to hide in the mess at the bottom of my wardrobe. He slammed shut the door with me crouched in the corner, my belongings in my arms, just as his mother arrived at his bedroom door.

'Sanjay, did you not hear me calling you?' she asked.

'Yes, no. I mean, I was trying to sleep – it's been a heavy few days. But when I heard you, I thought I'd check to see if there was space in the wardrobe for the ironing.' His voice was quite loud and clear, so obviously he was standing in front of the wardrobe.

'What is that smell?' his mother asked. 'Perfume? Have you had a girl in here?'

'Depends what you mean by a girl,' he said. 'I did have a woman in here earlier checking out the . . . erm . . . ceiling? Yeah, she was checking out the ceiling. I wasn't sure if there was a fault with it or not and she was looking at it.'

'A woman was a structural engineer?' his mother asked.

'Something like that,' he replied. 'Anyway, there is no room in here. Can you hang those up in the spare room? Come, I'll show you.'

'You haven't greeted me properly, Sanjay. I come all this way to see you and you don't even bother to greet me properly.'

'Mum, you live three streets away.'

'Do not measure your journey by the miles travelled, but by the distance you know that you have crossed to arrive there.' That sounded almost Buddhist, I thought, slightly awed that such wisdom had simply tripped off her tongue.

'Yes, Mum,' Sanjay replied. He sounded far less impressed by his mother's wisdom than me. 'Sorry.' He began to speak to her in Punjabi and she replied, their voices growing quieter and quieter as they moved away from the wardrobe and out of the bedroom.

Once I was sure I was alone in the room, I carefully stuck my hand into my bag and rummaged around until I found my BlackBerry. I checked the time while I was turning off the ringer. The last thing I needed was my boss to ring me – which he did on every single one of my days off, just to remind me that I was lucky I had a job – and for all of this to have been a pointless exercise. I shifted carefully and quietly so I could stop crouching and instead sit down – and immediately regretted it as the cold of the wardrobe's floor flashed across my bare bottom. I pulled my clothes towards my chest to try to warm up a little. I didn't want to move too much in case they came back or they could hear me below.

Sanjay loved me. It didn't sound like he was saying that for effect, it seemed like he meant it. The second after he'd said it had been the most real I'd seen him if he wasn't talking about his beloved Brixton. He loved me. I liked that. I liked that a lot.

I wasn't feeling quite so lovey-dovey when he opened the wardrobe door thirty minutes later. *Thirty minutes.*

'I am so sorry,' he whispered, throwing the door wide open.

I was almost frozen solid; I'd had my head on my knees and had been drifting in and out of naps as I'd waited for him to get rid of his mother.

He held out his hand, and if I hadn't been so stiff and unable to move on my own, I would have told him to F-off. He reached into the wardrobe and slipped his arms around me before helping me to climb out.

'I've been in there for half an hour.' He walked me over to the bed and I tried to unkink myself. I was stooped like a woman whose eighty or so years of a hard life had rested on her back and kept her constantly bent and burdened. I could barely shuffle as my thighs were almost locked into their legs-up pose. I was taking up yoga again, I decided. I'd stopped a while back, had decided I didn't need it, but I did. I clearly did. 'I thought you'd get rid of her quickly. *Half an hour.*'

'Anaya, that *was* getting rid of her quickly. Usually, if she comes by and I'm home, she stays for the rest of the day. She cooks, cleans, and then basically browbeats me about not being married and not

65

giving her grandchildren like my sisters who have all got married in good time. I had to tell her I had a business meeting overnight before she'd go. If I'd said I just had a meeting she would have waited for me to go and come back.'

I fell gratefully onto the bed and began trying to unlock myself. Definitely back to yoga. 'So, what this whole day has taught us is that you're a giant mummy's boy,' I said with a laugh.

'No,' he said. He started to massage my thigh, loosening the muscle with his expert touch. 'What this day has taught us is that I have to be honest with you about how I feel so I can introduce you to my mother as soon as possible.'

'You don't have to be honest about how you feel,' I replied. 'You just have to chill the hell out and stop being on your best behaviour all the time. That's if you want this thing between us to work out.'

'I do, I really do.'

'Well then, you need to be more like Sanj and less like Sanjay Kohli, businessman.'

He said something in Punjabi and then kissed my forehead, my nose, my mouth.

'What did you say?' I asked.

'I said: "For you, my love, anything."'

1:16 p.m. 'I thought I heard you!' she says. Her hair is perfectly blow-dried to frame her slender face and she is dressed in a burgundy, pink and pale blue silk sari with an embroidered burgundy blouse. I used to feel inferior around her, like she is the template of what women are meant to look like no matter their age, no matter their state of mind or health. 'Anaya, hello.'

'Oh, hi,' I reply. I'm expected to walk to her, to greet her warmly with an embrace, carry on this farce that's been going on between us for thirteen years.

'I was wondering where you were. Sanjay is not here.' She says this like a woman whose house I have wandered into looking for a man that she knows and I don't. 'I knocked but there was no answer.'

She didn't knock; she never knocks. She uses the key she has to my house to come and go as she pleases. When I once mentioned that we should probably have a key for their house and their alarm code like they have for ours, she was horrified. 'She's joking,' Sanj told her to get that look of horror off her face. 'You're joking, aren't you?' he said to me, his eyes wide, his lips set, and his face telling me to take it back.

I'd laughed that fake laugh that always comes out whenever I am around his parents and said, 'Of course I'm joking.'

'I so wasn't joking,' I told him later.

'I know you weren't,' he said. 'But of all the things there are to fall out with my mother about, that was the one you were going to pick?' He'd been right, of course, but it still niggles even now. Our house is clearly an extension of their home to them, and their home is something private and secure, a sanctuary they won't have invaded by anyone at any given second of the day.

'He's working in London this week, didn't he tell you?'

'My son never tells me anything these days. I am often the last to find out anything about his life.' She shakes her head. 'But no matter, it was fortuitous that he was not here.'

'Oh? Why?' I ask. *Idiot. Anaya, you are an idiot.* I want to bite back those words, but they're out there, they've opened a conversation, they've made me engage with her.

'It gave me a chance to tidy up. You are so busy with your life, I know this, but it didn't take me long to clean the kitchen and strip the beds and put the bedclothes in to wash. Nor to run the Hoover around.' She smiles even wider; each one of her teeth is perfectly white and unnaturally straight. I suspect my husband paid for those teeth. Like I suspect he paid for their house, but I try not to think about that. 'After all, that is what we women were raised to do, is it not? To create the home, make sure everyone is comfortable? A family cannot function without the heart of a woman to beat at its centre.'

When I was young and still fresh from crouching in wardrobes, those sort of words impressed me – now they irritate me. They're profound, thought-provoking and sometimes rather poignant – but it's who is saying them that negates everything about them.

'Thank you for the help, as always.' Every syllable is forced through gritted teeth having been flambéed by my rage. 'I always appreciate it.'

'I know you do. You modern girls are so busy, busy, busy with your lives, it's no wonder you have no time to run your homes. And obviously you, my dear daughter-in-law, you are especially disadvantaged because your mother was forced to work and did not have as much time to spend on your development as a woman. There are so many women nowadays who have suffered the same neglect, so do not trouble your heart.'

I stare at my husband's mother and have the urge to shout at her. *It's your fault!* I want to scream. *If you didn't go around trying to find out stuff about my past, Yvonne wouldn't be in a coma right now. This is your fault! And it's my fault, too.*

WEDNESDAY

Hazel

5:05 a.m. I can't stay in bed any more. I've had to get up, shrug on my silk dressing gown and then bring myself down here. It seems worse in the bedroom, trying to sleep. I feel more cloistered. Smothered. I hate the bed being empty, too. I wish I wasn't alone right now. I wish I wasn't walking around the kitchen touching things – the stainless-steel kettle, the white taps, the large cooker hood, the wooden kitchen table, the three different timetables on the noticeboard. I wish one of those things would give me what I need.

I need to feel all right with all of this.

I need to be OK with it.

My mobile, sitting on the counter beside the cooker, lights up.

> Coffee? M x

I read the message, then immediately delete it. We agreed on Monday that we have to delete all texts to each other. Not just some, that would look suspicious. *All* texts.

Once her message has gone, I know I can't reply because I'd love to go for a coffee, I'd love to sit with Anaya and Maxie like everything is normal, but I don't think I can.

October, 2012
'Hazel, you're going to join the Parents' Council, aren't you?' Yvonne was, as always, surrounded by people. They flocked to her like the bright, pretty, shining light she was. Right then, she stood outside the large, black iron gates of Plummer Prep, while we waited

for our children to emerge, trying to sign up people to the Parents' Council.

The former head of the PC had left suddenly under shady circumstances – we'd *all* heard the whispers about drugs and money laundering. She'd seemed so nice, too. Always had a friendly word to say to people, smiley, happy; nothing was ever too much. But once she'd stepped down – well, moved out in the middle of the night, never to be heard from again – all the other board members had stepped down too. I'd heard those *other* whispers that they had been, if not involved or complicit, certainly talented when it came to overlooking where the extra funds came from to throw the lavish parties with low ticket prices and still make a profit afterwards. A couple of the more senior, more financially responsible board members had left the area as well, but most had just stepped down and taken to wearing huge sunglasses at the gates no matter the weather.

We had only been at the school six weeks and Yvonne was already a popular bod. She'd gone for the position at the top of the Parents' Council but hadn't been around long enough to get it. But she was on the board and here she was, trying to recruit people. I was standing beside two other mothers whose children had started in Plummer Prep's Preppy classes for pre-schoolers at the same time as Camille and Russell, and Yvonne's Madison. I recoiled in horror at Yvonne's suggestion – I did not need to invite more stuff to do into my life. I jiggled Calvin from one hip to another. He'd managed to escape his pram and if I didn't keep hold of him, he would be re-enacting the Great Baby Escape his older sister was so famous for.

'No, Vonny, I'm not going to join the PC. It's not for me.'

'Maxie?' Yvonne asked, turning her smile on the woman to my right who had a son Camille's age. 'You're creative with all your copywriting work, you'll join, won't you? We need someone to write flyers and compile the newsletter.'

The woman shook her head. She'd pushed her black ringlets back with a silver hair band, and had her hands deep in the pockets of her denim jacket. 'I'm not a joiner, Yvonne.'

'Anaya?' Yvonne asked the woman standing on the other side of me. She had two children, one who was in Preppy and one in Reception. If there was anyone at the gates who could make Yvonne feel inferior it was Anaya. She was so serene with her innate beauty and style. Although she was always expensively dressed, she didn't seem stuck up, more content to just *be*. I'd found myself gravitating towards Maxie and Anaya, standing near them hoping Anaya's calmness and Maxie's ability to say no without apologising would radiate outwards and infect me.

Anaya smiled at Yvonne then shook her head.

'Oh, come on, if there's anyone I would expect to get involved it'd be someone like you,' Yvonne said.

Anaya blinked. 'Someone like me? What do you mean?' she asked.

'Yes, *Vonny*, what *do* you mean?' Maxie asked.

'I mean someone who works in marketing, who runs her own business and who is always attending lavish events with her husband. I'd have thought this would be right up your street.'

The first time Yvonne had done that to me, I'd been taken aback. I had said that Walter was complaining about spending money on sending the children to Preppy and Yvonne had replied, 'Really? Are we or are we not drinking coffee from Wedgwood cups? Are these or are these not original Chippendale chairs we're sitting on? Are we or are we not sitting in a house worth nearly two million pounds?'

'Why do you know so much about my financial situation?' I'd asked her.

'Because I'm a nosey bitch!' she'd said with a laugh. That was one of the best things about Yvonne: she was honest about her failings. She didn't lie about the fact she could be shallow and vacuous and would rather be late for something than turn up make-up-less. 'I did research on you and your husband. So? More fool you if you didn't at least check up on me before you let me into your house and your life.'

I'd laughed. 'I trust people,' I'd told her. 'I take them at face value until they prove otherwise.'

'Yes, I do that too. But only for people I don't want to be friends with. I liked you so much the first time I met you that I had to find out if you had the potential to be a psycho killer or stalker before I saw you again.'

'You,' I'd said with a laugh. 'You're so lucky you're otherwise nice, because you could seriously piss someone off.'

Yvonne clearly wanted to be Anaya's friend with the amount of research she had done on her.

'Although you have clearly looked me up on the internet, Yvonne, you actually don't know me at all if you think that. No, I'm sorry, I'm not going to join the Parents' Council.'

Yvonne was nothing if not perceptive, and with the look Anaya was giving her, she knew being somewhere else was a good idea. She moved away to try to engage other people in conversation.

'You should take that as a compliment, you know,' I told Anaya quietly. I felt bad for Yvonne, who didn't understand that researching someone was one thing, but repeating what she found out was another. I also felt bad for Anaya, who probably thought Yvonne had been gossiping about her. 'I know it might not seem like it, but it's only cos she likes you.'

Anaya raised a sceptical, unconvinced eyebrow at me.

'Honestly, Yvonne only ever researches people she wants to be friends with.' I swung my gaze around the other people who were arriving to pick up their children. 'I bet very few of these plebs even got so much as her logging on to the web on her phone, let alone spending time doing extra reading about them.'

'Hmmm,' was Anaya's reply.

'Well, cheers for that,' Maxie said. 'It's always nice to be reminded that I'm so incredibly dull that someone won't even bother to type my name into a search engine.'

I couldn't tell if she was genuinely offended or not. 'No, no, come on now, Maxie. Did you tell her you were a copywriter?' I said quickly.

'I did not,' she replied.

'Well, there you are then. Research. Proper, *proper* research.'

'Yeah, well, good luck with that, Yvonne and anyone who wants to do searches on me – my surname is Smith, there are billions of us,' Maxie replied with an amused giggle. 'I'm surprised she even found out I was a copywriter.'

'And I've changed my name a million times,' Anaya added, giggling too.

'And you might as well call me an international woman of misery,' I said.

'I think you mean "mystery",' Anaya corrected.

'Oh no, I've seen her first thing in the morning, she definitely means "misery",' Maxie helpfully supplied.

'Rudeness!' I exclaimed.

'Truthness!' they both replied. And all three of us cracked up laughing. Calvin sat on my hip, unimpressed – or rather, uninterested in what we were doing. This was the first time I'd laughed with adults in a long time. At the events I went to with Walter, they always seemed to be laughing at an in-joke someone had told five minutes before we arrived, even if we'd been there for hours. I would laugh and pretend I understood why they were laughing, feeling like a fraud all the while. I laughed with the children at their TV shows, at their back-to-front jokes. And Yvonne, my only real friend from recent times, wasn't the type of person who I laughed and joked with. She was serious, and she was fun, but we didn't do silly laughing. I enjoyed it so much, standing at the school gates with Maxie and Anaya laughing and laughing just for the sake of it. We didn't know each other, we were all doing this for the first time, and we found the same things funny.

'Coffee, tomorrow?' Maxie said. 'Down at that Milk 'n' Cookees?'

'Yes, sure,' Anaya replied.

'Count me in as long as you don't mind me bringing this one with me,' I said.

'No problem at all,' Maxie replied.

'Shall I invite Yvonne?' I asked. 'She really is a sweetheart and she has a heart of gold.'

They both looked in her direction. 'Not tomorrow,' Anaya said. 'I think I need a little distance right now. Next time, for sure.'

'All right, next time.'

5:10 a.m. My mobile buzzed.

> **Maybe. Let me think about it. A xxx**

November, 2012

'Isn't this exciting? The first meeting of the official Wednesday Morning Coffee Club,' Yvonne said to us. She was very close to clapping her hands in excitement.

'Don't be trying to Parents' Council this, Vonny,' Maxie said. 'This is just four friends having a coffee and a chat. And besides, this is like the third time, so I don't know what you're on about.' The second she said it, I could see Maxie knew the mistake she'd made.

Yvonne looked at me first, trying to find out if this was right – we'd met up twice before I'd officially asked her along. When she'd taken in my look of horror, she looked at Anaya, then finally at Maxie the Mouth (as I had decided to rename her). 'You've met before?' Yvonne asked in a quiet, hurt voice.

'It wasn't like that, Yvonne,' Maxie said. 'We just kind of ended up here at the same time.'

Yvonne, in response, glanced at me again.

'And that's why we asked you this time,' Anaya said quickly. She knew my guilt-soaked face would give the game away. 'We knew it wasn't as much fun because you weren't with us.'

'Yeah,' Maxie said. 'And we were talking about meeting when we all had a bit more time, like in the evenings, and inviting you.'

Maxie was lying, but she – all of us – could see Yvonne was hurt and Maxie wanted to make up for running her mouth off.

'Yeah,' Anaya said. 'I was trying to convince these two that they should come over one evening and I'll get a yoga tutor over and we can all throw a few yoga moves.'

'You can imagine how well that went down,' Maxie said. 'But Hazel here then said out of all of us you were the one who would look best in yoga gear. Even better than gym bunny here.' She nodded towards Anaya. 'You can imagine how well *that* went down.'

Anaya eyed Maxie distastefully. 'Then the idea of making cocktails was floated,' Anaya said. She bobbed her head towards Maxie. 'Guess who suggested that?'

'And then we were discussing . . .' Maxie ran out of steam. We weren't good enough friends or even long enough acquaintances to keep up the pretence.

'Knitting,' I said. 'That was what I was going to suggest last time before we all had to dash off because we weren't here for very long.'

'Knitting?' Anaya and Maxie repeated at the same time. They both looked as though I was suggesting wrestling with crocodiles.

'Yes,' I said firmly, decisively. 'Knitting.'

'I don't knit,' Anaya stated.

'Neither do I,' Maxie added.

'You do, don't you, Yvonne?' I said to her.

She smiled at me, and her body, which had visibly clenched when she'd found out we'd met without her, finally loosened up. 'I do. I'm a champion knitter.'

'As am I,' I said. 'So, it's settled then, two against two. Knitting it is. We meet up once a week to knit.'

'Bollocks do we,' Maxie said.

'I think that's a brilliant idea,' Yvonne said.

'I'm not spending whatever free time I have learning to knit,' Maxie protested.

'Oh, shut up,' Yvonne said. 'Of course you are. It will be fun. We get knitting needles, we get wool and we meet up at Hazel's for knitting fun.'

'Erm, probably not the best idea,' I said. 'If I'm doing something, I need to be far, far away from where the kids are because even if Walter is there, I'll spend the night going up and down to them.'

'Same,' Anaya said. 'If I'm there, they only want Mama.'

'Same,' Maxie said.

'Same,' Yvonne admitted.

Eventually, Maxie sighed and eyed us up as though she was about to induct us into a secret society, one that we could only leave on pain of death. She licked her lips and sighed again, this time resigned to her fate. 'All right, the weather's not too bad at the moment so maybe we can go knitting at my beach hut.'

'You have a beach hut?' Yvonne said. 'I've *always* wanted a beach hut. Trevor will not hear of it because we technically live within walking distance of the beach. I am so jealous you have one.'

'Yeah, well. If we must knit, at least we can do it on the seafront.'

'This is going to be perfect,' Yvonne said. 'I've always wanted to spend time in a beach hut.'

'Me too,' Anaya admitted.

'Right, so next Friday?' Yvonne suggested. 'I'll bring nibbles, a couple of bottles of champagne?'

She looked at each of us in turn, happy and excited. Her excitement was infectious, something that enveloped us all.

'Ah, knitting-smitting,' Anaya said. 'At this stage, I'm just in it to see what amazing nibbles Yvonne's going to conjure up.'

'Me too,' Maxie said. 'They'd better be good, Vonny. None of that shop-bought muck – I want your hard work to be a vital ingredient.'

Yvonne grinned her twisty-lipped smile. 'Trust me, ladies,' she said. 'Just trust me.'

8:30 a.m. When I enter Milk 'n' Cookees, they're both already sitting there, in our favourite table that's nearest the booths by the window. There are four spaces, and I take up mine, the one with my back to the window. The fourth one sits empty but heavily occupied. We stare at each other, all of us a little surprised that we have turned up like it is any other Wednesday.

'Coffee?' Maxie eventually says.

'Yes,' I say. 'Flat white.'

'Espresso, please,' Anaya says.

'Cool.' Maxie gets up, her purse in her hand. 'I'm going to resist the cake today. I honestly am.'

'Yeah, right,' Anaya replies. 'While you're resisting it, please get me a piece.'

'Yeah,' I add, 'I'll have a slice of all that resistance, too.'

'I am,' Maxie says indignantly. And with that, we all know that we're going to try to get back to who we were, how we were with each other, even with that spare seat at our table.

Part 2

THURSDAY

Cece

8:55 a.m. The nearest café to the school is called Milk 'n' Cookees. It's a large space with orange padded booths lining the area underneath the large picture window; the main space has silver, mottle-topped tables and silver bucket chairs. The walls are the colour of buttermilk, the rubber-tiled floor is the colour of freshly baked vanilla biscuits. The glass display counter is a crowded cornucopia of sweet delights. I never say 'cornucopia', it's not the sort of word I've ever had occasion to use, but today, seeing what is being paraded in front of my taste buds, there is no other word that would be suitable.

I can almost taste the breakfast cookies in my mouth, melting and teasing and soothing away every single second of those moments this morning that saw me very nearly resorting to shouting at the boys to get them out of the house. After the first raised words, I gritted my teeth as I reminded Oscar for the third time he really would need to be wearing underpants to classify himself as 'finished' and 'the winner even though Ore brushed his teeth first'; and I almost cracked those very same teeth clenching them to stop myself screaming at Ore for forgetting he was meant to be getting dressed – while he was getting dressed.

The stress of it, of almost going back to being the shouty, frantic Cece I used to be every weekday morning, is spiralling in my stomach. *Calm, I need to be calm.* Everything is meant to be different now. I need to remember that being late won't kill me or the boys. I need to keep in mind that this is all a work in progress, that I'm no longer the woman who needs to get everyone out of the house, drop them at school and then get myself to work by a certain time. This life is not only physically new, but also mentally. I need to change my mindset and that will take time.

'What can I get you, Cookee?' the Australian woman behind the counter asks. She has a smile that goes nowhere beyond the surface. Not that I blame her – I'm sure my smile would be merely functional if I had to call people 'cookee' all day.

I order a milky coffee in a takeaway cup and wait for it to be made and handed over with an 'enjoy your day, Cookee'. To the right of the counter a set of stairs leads down. The woman behind the counter shows no interest in me at all, so I go down the stairs, wondering how different it is underground. The stairs take a turn and I find myself in another comfy space, the walls lined with booths, the same type of chairs and tables as there are upstairs. The difference between upstairs and downstairs is the party atmosphere because it is almost full with people, or should that be . . . parents. I look at them, and I recognise more than a few from standing at the gates over the last few days. In the past four days, I've even nodded to a few as we wait on the pavement for our children to go into the building and come pouring out at the end of the day.

Although the layout of the café isn't conducive to sitting in a group, they manage it, the fifteen or so of them. They sit with coffees and toast and wraps and the opened wrappers of complimentary coffee biscuits in front of them, and chat like the old friends they are. One of the parents, who I've stood next to and whose child has left the building with Oscar, glances up and spots me. She smiles and lifts her hand in a brief wave. I smile back, lift my hand too. I should go and talk to her. Try to make friends. Things will be so much easier if I make friends. I gather every molecule of courage I have, and move to go over and say hello. Maybe she'll tell me to pull up a chair, ask my name, introduce me to a few other mothers . . . Maybe I'll be a part of them, even if it is for a few sips of coffee, but I can sit with the group I sort of belong to now, and I can try to fit in, continue to convince myself that Brighton is actually our home. I brighten up my smile, go to take a step towards the table – and her face clenches in horror at the thought of me speaking to her. She then quickly cuts eye contact and lowers her head. A couple of other people see the look on her face and turn to look at me, and do the same thing, offer a weak, vague smile, nod or raise a hand, then lower their heads in horror in case I want to join them. This causes a ripple effect amongst the group when others spot what those sitting next to or opposite them are doing.

Is it me? Well, obviously it's me, but what part of me? Is it 'the new person' that is me? A stranger they don't want to take the time to get to know?

Is it the way I look? Am I dressed too differently? Is my skin the wrong shade for them?

Is it the timing of my arrival? Do they think I've followed them here, expecting to be allowed access to their group because I have stood next to them in the playground? Or are they having a super-serious discussion that they don't want anyone – let alone a stranger – to hear?

Whatever it is, it's clearly something that means I can't go over and say hello, ask their names, vaguely introduce myself. I plaster what I hope is a pleasant, unbothered smile on my face, and go back up the stairs.

Of course, this was never a problem in London. In London I was always a drop'n'runner. I was also, on my picking-up days, an 'arrive at the last minute/pushing the limits of the teachers' patience'-er, who rarely saw other parents except at school events and performances. I could small-talk with those people because we'd all been new at the same time, we'd all watched our children change and grow, while we changed and grew into the different roles that being parents demanded of us.

Everyone else in my family seems to have friends: after four days Ore and Oscar are always leaving the school talking intently to a different person; Harmony's phone never stops pinging with messages from her new friends; and Sol clearly has friends after being here for three months. It's only me who hasn't had much luck. Yes, it's only been four days, but I'd like someone to notice me and want to be my friend.

The bell of the café tings as I allow it to close behind me. My skin is burning with humiliation and rejection. Would it have killed even one of those people to smile and say hello? Obviously. *Obviously.*

To spite them, I smile and say hello to every single person I pass on the road from the café to home. *That'll show them*, I think as I push the key into my front door and the alarm starts to bleep. *It takes nothing to be a friendly, decent human being. It takes nothing at all to welcome someone when they're new, and vulnerable and unsure of their place in the world now they don't have a job and they have hours to fill until they are with their children again.*

SATURDAY

Hazel

5:05 a.m. Another night of not brilliant sleep and I'm here in the kitchen again. My mobile, sitting on the counter beside the cooker, lights up.

> Have to go back to the beach hut today. Frankie has been asking all week. Feel sick thinking about being there. Mx

I read the message, then immediately delete it. Once her message has gone, I know I can't reply because there's no way I'd go back there. And there's nothing I can say that will make it any better for her.

5:10 a.m.

> *Hope it's not too awful. Will be thinking of you. A xxx*

Anaya is so good at that. I couldn't think of a single thing to say, but she was straight in there. Poor Maxie. Poor Maxie.

Cece

12:35 p.m. It's September but the sun is high and fierce, a shimmering, bright disc in the pure, undulating blue of the sky. I inhale and the briny breeze of the seafront fills me up.

I thought the kids would want to chill out, having moved last weekend and gone straight to school, that they would have wanted to sleep in, at least stay in their pyjamas and maybe start unpacking their stuff, but no, they wanted to go out. They've been itching to get out there and walk along the beach, because that's why we moved, after all. I sold it to them that they were going to get to go to the beach every day if that's what they wanted. And that's what they wanted on this glorious Saturday.

Four of us left the house together, Harmony 'yeah, yeah'ing me when I repeatedly told her to keep in touch with me all day as she was going off to Brighton to meet some new friends. Sol is working. After his grand gesture on Monday, I thought we were getting back on track and we'd be spending Saturdays together, but no. Nothing any of us said could persuade him to come for a walk, even for a few minutes. He barely even looked up from his laptop while we were having an early lunch, while we rifled through boxes, gathering things together to take out with us, even while we were putting on shoes.

Work is Sol's new best friend – his wife, too, it seems. Work has slipped into the spaces where I belonged, where I *belong*. I park those thoughts; they're not helpful, and they'll only make me miss this gift of a day.

We are heading down towards the pier, which shimmers in the

distance, passing the beach huts Brighton is famous for as we walk. I've seen them in pictures, on television, even in the flesh when we came house-hunting, but this is the first time I have seen so many of them opened up and full of people.

The seafront is transformed by them and it is like wandering through a colourful market bazaar. Some people recline on stripy deckchairs, the doors propped open, showing the stuff they have crammed inside; others have placed tables out on the promenade; others still have large, brightly coloured parasols anchored with concrete blocks. A group of good-looking men sit on green fold-up chairs around a small fold-up table playing cards with a pile of money in the middle, and cans of beers beside their hands. They are playing so intensely, I think they've forgotten they are on the beach. A woman has spread a tartan blanket on the hot ground outside her hut, and is playing with a huge camera, regularly lifting it to her face and taking shots of the vista. We walk on, past two women hunched over slowly sizzling sausages on a tinfoil disposable barbecue that they have perched on top of a fire they've created in the centre of a ring of stones. We all look in wonder at the couple who have a dog up on its hind legs, performing tricks in return for doggy treats. Another beach hut is home to people stripping off shorts and T-shirts and struggling into shorty wetsuits, ready to head down to the beach. A man sits in another hut, holding a six-month-old baby on his knee, while his other half reclines on a spread of cushions, playing with an older toddler.

'There's Frankie,' Oscar says as we pass one of the beach huts.

'Who's Frankie?' I ask.

Oscar stops and turns around, points to the hut we've just moved on from. Its green doors are propped open, and two blue-and-white deckchairs are placed facing each other. On the ground is a picnic blanket and to the side is a large cream parasol, anchored, like most of the others we've seen, by a large marble-coloured concrete block. In one of the deckchairs there is a woman with black and brown ringlety hair wearing sunglasses, with her legs pulled up reading a book. It's a good one, that book, I read it a while back. On the purple picnic blanket sits a boy about Oscar and Ore's age, who is playing with a small yellow bucket, a stick and a pile of stones. He's wearing a blue fisherman's hat, and his arms have been slathered in sunblock. He's playing intensely and I can barely see his face, so how Oscar saw enough of him to know, I have no idea.

'He's in my class,' Oscar says.

'Are you sure?'

'Yeah, that's his mum and that's him.'

'Oh, right. Do you want to go and say hello?' I ask my son.

'Hi, Frankie,' Oscar calls from quite a distance. The mother looks up, takes her sunglasses off, and I realise I have seen her this week. I saw her on the first day, and I've seen her since. Most of the time she looks harried, stressed, particularly unhappy. This is the first time I've seen her look relaxed, and when she smiles, she looks like the first person I would go and talk to if I walked into a roomful of strangers.

'Hi?' she says getting to her feet. She comes towards us, as Frankie stands up. She extends her hand and the bracelets on her wrist tinkle as she does so. 'I'm Maxie. I think I've seen you at the school gates.'

'Hi, Oscar,' Frankie says before I can reply to his mother. 'Hi, Ore. Do you want to play with me? I'm making a scientific formula that's going to power cars in the future.'

'Cool,' the boys say at the same time and dart across to the front of the beach hut. The three of them huddle down onto the blanket and begin playing, as if they've been together all morning. Frankie shows them what he was making, and the boys listen while picking up and examining his collection of pebbles.

'I'm Cece,' I say to Maxie. 'We were kind of heading to the pier. But apparently not. Sorry to invade your Saturday afternoon.'

'Not at all,' she says and brushes away my concerns with a light wave of her hand. 'Frankie talks about Oscar all the time. He says he's got a cool twin brother – Ore – I'm guessing that's him.'

'My son has not mentioned anyone from his class. To hear him tell it, you'd think there was no one else in his class except him and the teacher. Oh well, at least they've made friends. That's the biggest worry when you go somewhere new, isn't it? That they'll make friends and won't feel like the new kids for too long.'

Maxie moves back to her seat and beckons me to come and sit down with her. I do as she asks, although I almost collapse back into the seat as I'm not used to sitting on something so low and unsupported. Maxie unclips the cool box beside her seat, which I didn't notice before, and hands me a cold, sweating bottle of water.

'Frankie said you moved from London?' she asks.

'Yeah, north-west London. My husband landed a big promotion down here so we eventually all packed up and came too.'

'And you didn't mind leaving it all behind?' she asks.

Of course not, is the answer I should be able to hand out. *Of course I didn't mind.* 'Honestly?' I say, lowering my voice. 'I wasn't sure. The kids weren't sure. But him commuting a few days a week, and then living here on his own and coming back some weekends, was no way to have a family life. So, no, I don't suppose I did mind in the bigger picture.'

'That's a very good way of looking at it.'

'Have you lived in Brighton all your life?' I ask. I sit back in the deckchair. If I aim for a certain angle, it's not too odd to sit like this. I can't move, of course, but it's all right. And if I unclench a bit, it's almost comfortable. And the hazy sun, the salty air, the beach sounds, all make it impossible to keep myself tight and tense. Maxie sits back, scoops her legs under herself and unscrews her water bottle.

'No, I'm from up North. Can't you hear the accent?'

'Honestly, no,' I reply. 'You sound like you're from . . . Oh, I don't know. I'm rubbish with anything but the most obvious accents.'

'Well, blooming hell, what if I talked like that? Would you be able to tell I'm a Yorkshire lass born and bred, then?' She giggles at the end of her sentence. And her face creases. She's pretty *and* beautiful. I'm guessing one of her parents is white as she has light brown skin, darker brown freckles are dotted across her nose and over her cheeks, her eyes are a deep chocolate brown and her lips are glossed with a red-brown colour.

'Well, yes, when you speak like that, of course,' I laugh. 'How did you end up down here, then?'

'Do you know, I'm not entirely sure. I've lived in various places and we moved here just before Frankie turned one. Can't imagine living anywhere else, now. Ed, that's my husband, he travels a lot for work, but if his work took him elsewhere permanently, I'd have to seriously think about letting him go on his own.'

She looks wistful for a moment, as if she's thought it through and seriously doesn't intend to leave this place. I don't blame her. If I had a seafront property, even in the form of a beach hut, I wouldn't leave, either.

'Thankfully Ed's never really been interested in leaving here. If that moment—' She stops talking, and looks at her son, suddenly aware that he can probably hear every word she's saying. 'Anyway, how are you finding it?'

'Fine.' I wonder if I should ask about what happened on our first day, about the atmosphere that hangs over the school, the way parents drop their children off, even the ones who are clearly in a rush to get to work, and don't leave until all the children are inside. I wonder if I should ask her if the reason why she has looked so harrowed and stressed all week is because she knows Yvonne Whidmore, the woman who was attacked and left for dead on the playground?

Maxie must know her because Madison, Yvonne Whidmore's daughter, is in Oscar's class with Frankie. 'Has anyone been in touch to welcome you to the school yet?' she asks.

I place our out-for-the-day rucksack on the hot tarmac of the seafront and glance at the boys, playing on the blanket still, even though their collection of stones, rocks and other pieces scavenged from the beach is modest. I'm not sure how the game has held their attention for so long but I'm grateful for the rest. I've been running on high these past few months; my life has been an adrenalin-fuelled race to wind up life in London and relocate down here. Sitting down has not been allowed. The longer I sit here, the more my body dissolves into the seat and I realise it's going to be difficult to get up again.

'No, no one's been in touch yet. The headmistress did say, just before the boys started, that the Year Three class coordinator would make contact but I haven't heard anything yet.'

Maxie inhales deeply, almost dramatically, through her nose, then slips her sunglasses into place. She's masking those striking, expressive eyes. 'I thought Mrs Carpenter would have chosen someone else by now,' she says thoughtfully.

'Howddya mean?' I ask.

Even with her mask I see that she rolls her eyes before she turns her head slightly and stares off at another point on the horizon. 'The head teacher chooses the person who works as the class coordinator. I thought she would have found someone to fill that role by now. Even temporarily . . .' She shakes her head slightly, obviously trying to clear a particular thought. 'Look, I was an admin for the Year Three instant messaging group called PPY3. That's Plummer Prep Year Three. The other years have their own PP system. I'm not the admin any more, but I think I can still add you. I'll do that, if you want? You just have to give me your number. When Mrs Carpenter has found someone to replace our last class coordinator, I'm sure they'll be in touch. Most of the stuff that's organised, the stuff about what to take in when, and people trying to track down lost uniform, etc., is done by PPY3 anyway. And someone generally knows the answer to most of your burning questions so we're not in desperate, *desperate* need of a new class coordinator.'

I have a burning question: *Who tried to kill Yvonne Whidmore, and why?* For me, the why is always as important as the who.

'Did your last class coordinator suddenly move to another school or something?' I ask.

Maxie stares at me long and cool, wondering if I am taking the piss, which makes me realise how dumb I have been. I'm generally not that stupid but in this instance, I am.

'No,' she eventually replies. 'She . . . A few weeks ago she . . .'

'Oh, I see,' I reply.

'Yeah,' she breathes. 'Yeah.'

After a long, awkward silence that not even the market-bazaar atmosphere can alleviate, 'Do you know her well?' I ask. I'm careful to use the present tense, to not assign her to the past.

'I suppose so . . . I mean yes, I knew her, she was my friend.'

'Oh, well, I was sorry to hear about what happened to her.'

Maxie nods slowly, accepting my partial condolences. She slips off her sunglasses and suddenly she's back to being open and friendly. 'So anyway, tell me about you. Where are you living? And do you need a list of the best cocktail bars around here? Because I can get you that. No charge.'

And with that, Maxie makes it clear she doesn't want to talk about Yvonne Whidmore.

Maxie

8:35 p.m. Why did I do that with Cece? I didn't have to bring up anything about her being contacted by the class coordinator. I would know if there was a new class coordinator, wouldn't I? Why the hell did I have to bring her attention to it? Maybe I was just desperate to get it in there first, to bring up Yvonne and see how gossipy she was. I liked Cece, in that way I liked Hazel and Anaya when I first met them, but I suppose I was testing her to see if she had the potential to be ghoulish, to show that fake-gilded concern that so many others have shown on PPY3 and in real life. They don't say anything to my face, but they will stop talking when I approach, they will ask me how I am, if I've heard from Trevor at all, if there's anything they can do. They all have his number, they all have his email, if they are that concerned they can contact him. They never do, though. Cece seemed to know when to stop asking questions and let me talk about something else. I like that in a person.

'Mum?' Frankie says.

My gaze goes up to my boy. He filled the bath himself, added copious amounts of bubbles and Octonaut toys and then climbed in. The Octonauts are cool and he loves toys that are designed for in-water play. I have to smile when I look at him. He's a big boy now. He's shot up so much. I didn't even really notice. You don't, when that person is right beside you all the time and you spend day after summer day with them. I was with him for almost every waking minute and even though I looked at him in wonder, as I always do because of what I went through to get him, I didn't notice how tall he's become. When we went for his new uniform I knew he'd got bigger because that's what children do, but it wasn't until the afternoon pick-up on the first day that I saw him without the daily filter. He came out of the school gates with Oscar, I now realise, and I did a mini double-take. He was taller, he was broader – a proper boy. Not my little boy any more, not my baby-boo; he was a proper boy. That winded me for a moment because he was going to be my only, and that stage had gone by so quickly, I'd been so embroiled in getting it right, I had forgotten to enjoy it.

But he hasn't fundamentally changed, not yet. He still likes his Octonaut toys, he still does things like make polar bear ears from bubbles and puts them on his head.

'Yes, my lovely?' I reply to my boy.

'Can Oscar and Ore come to our house to play?'

He doesn't usually ask. He knows what the answer will be, what it almost always has to be. He's obviously taken with Oscar and Ore.

'We'll see,' I say, because much as I want to, I have to remember how dangerous it is right now. I have to think of Yvonne and how that turned out.

'Oh please,' Frankie says. 'Please?'

'I said we'll see,' I reply.

'But Mum, please. They're really cool. And they both know so much about sea creatures. Please, Mum. Please don't say "we'll see" again because that just means no and it's not really fair. I hardly ever have friends over. So please, Mum, please. I'll be your best friend.'

Usually Frankie accepts a 'we'll see' and moves on. He knows that he can go to the park with his friends, he can play with them at the beach, he can even go to parties as long as I can be there. My anxieties, my husband's worries, allow me to leave him very, very rarely and only with trusted people. And for the same reasons, rarely do people come here. I won't let him go to theirs as is the done thing, and I won't let him out of my sight unless I have to. So he knows not to ask. The only friends who are allowed over are Hazel's three, Anaya's two and, of course, Yvonne's two. Other than that, no one comes over, and certainly no one is begged over.

'I'll make you a deal,' I tell Frankie. 'If their mother sends me her number before bedtime, I will invite them over for a play. How does that sound?'

Frankie's face lights up. I haven't seen him so happy in such a long time that I stare harder at my phone, willing her to text. Not for me, but for Frankie. Like him suddenly growing up, it is only when I see that smile, that joy shining from every feature, that I realise how long it's been since I saw it. He smiles, he laughs, he plays around. But he's not been *this* type of happy in so long. And that's what parents are supposed to do, isn't it? Make your children happy whenever you can. And when you can't, you're supposed to step in and do the best you can to change a bad situation for the better. Trevor comes to mind. How he obviously can't change his current situation, but he is doing his best. He is braving the school gates every morning, head held high, ignoring the lowered voices, the looks, the atmosphere that descends every time he appears.

Part of that, part of what he is going through, is because of me. But only because I was trying to do what any other parent would do: change a bad situation for the better.

'I won't tell Dad about them coming over,' Frankie suddenly says. His voice is very decisive, as though they are definitely coming over and he's made up his mind that this is the correct course of action.

'Why ever not?' I ask. 'Keeping secrets from your mummy and daddy isn't good, you know? You should tell him. I mean, I'm going to anyway. I'm sure he'll be really pleased that you've got new friends you want to come over to play if I get their mum's number.'

'Please don't tell him,' he says. He is serious, solemn. I watch his features set into a face that wouldn't look out of place on Ed's visage. 'Please. I know he will get sad. He always gets sad when I talk about having friends over.'

What? 'He doesn't,' I reply. I'm not forceful or probably even convincing in my reply. Ed does do that: he dons a cloak of despair and worry whenever we try to make connections with people outside of the three of us, especially if they involve Frankie. I simply never realised that Frankie noticed his father's moods. I thought I shielded him from that, thought that the fun we had together was enough to make up for his dad's unhappiness.

'Yes he does, Mum. All the time.' Now his voice is cajoling, asking me to acknowledge this fundamental truth about his father. He really isn't a little boy any more. Or maybe he is, and he's always known what his dad is like – it's only now that these boys are so important to him that he has to say something.

My cheeks are set alight by shame, by the absolute bloody shame of having my eight-year-old point out the faultline that runs through our life – the emperor's new clothes nakedness of our perfect family persona. To the outside world, we are Maxie: loving mother, attentive wife, perfect friend; Ed: loving, attentive, hard-working father; and Frankie: small boy who likes sea animals and the planets, who doesn't notice that we have no substance beneath what we show to the outside world.

What was I thinking just now about taking a bad situation and making it better for your children? If only I could.

'All right,' I say, 'I won't tell him and you don't have to either. Not until afterwards, anyway.'

'But—'

'That's the deal, take it or leave it,' I tell him.

'Ooooo-*Kay*, deal,' he concedes.

I stick out my pinkie finger, ready to hook his and for us to pinkie-shake on it. When he sees what I'm doing, he draws back in disgust and one of his bubble polar bear ears almost topples off his head. 'No one does that any more, Mum. I'm not a baby.'

'Right-o,' I reply. My face is still a smouldering, guilt- and shame-fuelled wreck. How have I managed to convince myself that Frankie doesn't know what our marriage is like?

My phone beeps and the sound is magnified by it echoing along the tiles. There's a number I don't recognise and my heart leaps in my chest.

> Hi Maxie Here's my number. Boys had a great time with Frankie.
> Let me know if you fancy meeting up again. Cece x :)

'Is that her?' Frankie asks.

I nod. And despite myself, despite everything, I can't help but grin.

> Nice to hear from you, Cece. Do the boys and you fancy coming over
> for tea next week? Maybe Thursday? Maxie x

Almost straight away my phone beeps again.

> The boys would love that. See you next week. C x

11 p.m. In my kitchen, there is a photo that I took of Frankie with Madison (from his class) and Scarlett. I'd driven Frankie and I to the nearest out-of-town shopping centre. I'd wanted to get some extra bits and pieces and thought going away from Brighton would mean we wouldn't bump into anyone we knew. Obviously not the case because we were there less than twenty minutes when we stepped off the glass lift and there was Yvonne with her daughters. They looked like mini models of her, with their colour-coordinated versions of the same jeans and off-the-shoulder top Yvonne also wore, and their perfectly waved blonde hair falling to their shoulders.

I stare at the photo. Frankie asked me to take it on my phone, then went on at me until I printed it out and let him stick it on the fridge with the dinosaur magnet. For some reason, he often talks about that day. Always different parts of the day, but it is a day he likes to recall over and over again.

October, 2014
We stood on the sidelines and watched the children climb through the play area in the shopping centre. It was a huge plastic monstrosity, with different-coloured netting, cut-outs, tunnels, covered slides that rose upwards almost at a vertical, and connected to netting-covered walkways. Saturday, of course, meant this place was rammed with people. The heat, the noise, the smell of sweat and feet, undercut by gentle notes of wee-soaked nappies, all conspired to drive me insane. I had never liked these places, had been to far too many of them in my life, mainly because Frankie loved them.

His idea of heaven when he was younger had been for us to go to a play centre early in the morning, run around the place as it was empty, climbing on everything available, bouncing on the bouncy structure, then stay for a lunch of dark brown sausages, yellow chips and coagulated bright orange beans, then spend another couple of hours running around.

Those were the days when I was most paranoid, when I couldn't stand to be away from him even if it was a few metres, so I'd crawl through the holes, the plastic tubes and netting to make sure he wasn't out of my sight.

'It's funny,' Yvonne said as we watched our children, 'Frankie doesn't look like you at all.' She made her voice conversational, as though she hadn't been working up to saying this since the very first day she saw Frankie run out of the school gates and into my arms.

'What's funny about that?' I asked her.

She was right, but it wasn't funny. Frankie had brown hair, hazel eyes and pale skin.

'I don't mean funny ha-ha, I mean a bit strange.'

'In what way?' I took my eyes off Frankie for a moment and focused on Yvonne, the woman who spent her entire life, it seemed, either trying to corral people into joining the Parents' Council or scouring the internet for information on the people she wanted to be her friends. It never occurred to her that being friends with someone should include allowing them the luxury of telling you what they wanted you to know. She wanted to know everything, all of it. Even the bits you would not share with a friend. I knew she would have searched and searched and searched for stuff on me and Frankie and Ed and would have found very little because our surname was Smith (and both had been before marriage) and there would have been so many of them around.

Added to that, we weren't part of the social media stuff, we didn't put everything online, which must have driven her insane. I wondered, often, how far she would go to find out stuff about me. If she would go and try to get a look at Frankie's birth certificate. If she did that, it would all be over. Everything Ed and I had done would come undone.

'I don't know. He's just . . . He's pale and you're not. And it's not like you've got different skin colours and he still looks like you – he looks nothing like you.'

'What are saying, Yvonne? Speak your speak. I can't stand people who hide behind "it's funny" or "it's a bit strange" – say what you want to say.'

'All right . . .' She shimmied her shoulders a little, as though trying to shake off the shackles of propriety. When she didn't manage it, when she couldn't quite step into being outright rude, she instead said, 'I just think it's odd that he's pale and you're not.'

'My dad's white, Yvonne,' I said. I hated having to explain myself, but there was something about her line of questioning that meant I had to control this. She'd probably already made comments to other people and if she carried on, it could get out of hand. 'My mum's black. And I'm sure you've seen how pale Ed is. There is no accounting for genetics. And anyway, why am I having this conversation with you, Vonny? Do I ask if you actually had sex to have your children or if you cloned them because they are exact replicas of you? I do not.'

'Oh, don't take offence – I was only wondering if he might be adopted or something? Or if you were maybe Ed's second wife?'

'Are you Trevor's second wife?' I asked her.

'I am, actually,' she replied.

'Really?'

'No, not really.'

Her face dropped its usual mask for a moment, and she looked smaller, plainer, more ordinary. 'Do you ever worry about being boring?' she asked. I turned back to watch the children. Scarlett was hanging upside down from the highest point of the climbing structure; Madison and Frankie were climbing into the gaping yellow hole of the twisty slide that would bring them all down to the ground. 'I mean, there is nothing remarkable about me. I can't really get a job because of having to be here to make sure the kids are OK.

And I have no backstory. I'd never tell anyone else this, but that's why I look up people's backstories on the internet. I want to find out if other people are as uninteresting as me. Beyond the children, beyond the Parents' Council, I have nothing. I'm simply not interesting.'

'You are interesting, Yvonne,' I said to her. 'You don't need to be married a trillion times or to have some high-flying job – you're interesting because you're a human being. That's what human beings are about. We're interesting. I mean, it's remarkable to me that there are so many of us, with all the same basic template for looks – you know, eyes, nose, mouth, ears – and we're all different. It's the same with our stories. We're all different and we have these interesting tales to tell, even if we aren't off fighting dragons or coming up with amazing scientific discoveries. You are interesting.'

'And you are so "peace, love, hope" about everything,' she sneered.

I turned to her and stared. 'Was there any need for that?' I eventually said.

She shrugged with one shoulder, as petulant as a teenager caught out after curfew. 'I opened up to you and you just dismissed it with some New Age bullshit,' she said.

'All right: Yvonne, you are dull and unremarkable. Is that what you want to hear?'

'Well, no.'

'Well then stop it. I wasn't dismissing you. You may or may not have valid concerns about being boring. Or whatever. But I don't see it. I genuinely don't see it and I'm not going to coddle you about it when I can't actually see it. I think people are interesting. Actually, I find them fascinating. But I also find you fascinating for so many, many different reasons. The main ones being you're my friend and I know you would drop everything to be there for me if something happened.'

'Sorry,' she mumbled.

'It's fine.'

'Am I really your friend?' she asked quietly.

'Yes, Yvonne. You think I knit with just anyone? Or do yoga or mix cocktails or cook at your house for that matter? You're my friend and I haven't had many of them over the years.'

'So you like me as much as you like Anaya and Hazel?'

I wasn't sure where Yvonne's neediness was coming from. We'd been meeting up for nearly two years. Had she really been doubting our friendship all that time? 'Yes, Yvonne, I like you as much as my other two good friends.'

She grinned at me.

'Right, that's about as much as I can stand in here. We need to head back anyway. Ed's coming back tonight and I need to do some serious tidying up.'

'Where's he been?'

'New York? Washington? Possibly Tokyo? Somewhere with a time difference, I know that.'

'You don't know where your husband is?'

'No. I can honestly say, I don't know where he is. He travels so much, I only really find out where he's been when I check the flight number on the noticeboard to see where he flew in from.' Yvonne looked horrified. 'Trust me, it's easier that way. If Trevor was away as much as Ed is, you'd lose track too. It's not like he ever actually tells me anything about these places or brings us back souvenirs. He spends most of his time in horrible hotel rooms and horrible meeting rooms and lecture halls; he doesn't get to see whichever city he's in. Most of the time, he could actually be in a room in Worthing for all the culture he manages to soak up.' It wasn't always like that, of course. When we were first married, I would hang on Ed's every word. I would check up where he was, the weather forecast, the time difference, the places he could visit while he was there. Over time, like a lot of things with Ed and me, it got easier to stop engaging. To have my interest not acknowledged or noticed with a vague smile and a few sentences dulled my emotions. I trained my heart not to care, to accept the reality of our situation and make the best I could of it. We had sex, we talked, we lived together quite contentedly. I mostly accepted that.

'I could never let Trevor out of my sight if I didn't know exactly where he was . . . Doesn't he even call you?'

'Yes, every day.'

'And he doesn't tell you where he is?'

'We don't really talk about his work on the phone. We talk about Frankie, how my day's been, what's going on at home, the news. Remember, this is what our relationship's always been like.'

'No video calls?'

'Not often.'

I could see the cogs whirling in her head. She'd watched too many movies, had read too many mystery books, had done far too much internet researching. She thought he wasn't where he said he was, that he possibly had another family. Or was a two-timing so-and-so. Nothing could be further from the truth. Ed was always where he said he was. Always. I knew other women said that sort of thing all the time and had been caught off guard when their husband's secret life was revealed. But Ed wouldn't dream of going 'off plan'. Doing anything out of the ordinary could ruin everything for him and he would never risk it. He had as much to lose as I did. Except, as time went on, I found that I was the one who had more to lose. And that thing to lose was about to go back up to the top of the soft play area and throw himself down the large yellow slide tube again.

'I could not live like that,' Yvonne stated.

'I know. Most people couldn't. It works for us though.'

Yvonne was eyeing me up – I could feel the intensity of her blue gaze, burning into the side of my face like twin blowtorches. *Let her look*, I thought to myself. *She can't even begin to understand what my marriage – what my life – is all about.*

11:05 p.m. My phone bleeps and makes me jump. I was lost then, back with Yvonne and how, I suppose, that was the start of it. That's where it really began.

How did it go today? Was it awful? Sending hugs. Axx

11:10 p.m.

> Not too bad. The two new boys in Year 3 walked past and played with
> Frankie. Was fun, actually. She's called Cece, the mother. Frankie loves
> her twins. Sleep tight. M xxx

11:11 p.m.

Xxxxxxx A x

11:12 p.m. My phone bleeps again and the little (1) appears at the
top of Anaya's text, meaning there is a message in the list waiting
for me.

I scroll back to the message list, to see if it's Hazel, who hasn't
replied to the text I sent first thing this morning. Instead:

> *Maxie, I need to talk to you about what happened that night with*
> *Yvonne. Why didn't you answer my calls that night? I know she was*
> *with you. What's going on? I thought we were friends? Please, just talk*
> *to me. Trevor*

I drop my phone, it's a miracle it doesn't smash on the tiled floor. I
stare at it, shaking. Shaking, shaking, shaking. Just like that night
when I got in after being with Yvonne and the others. Shaking,
shaking, shaking.

Anaya

11:05 p.m. I've not been able to get Maxie out of my head all day. I don't know how I'd cope if I was forced to go back there. Sanj and the kids think I've gone mad because I've been so jumpy, but I can't help it. It must be awful for her.

How did it go today? Was it awful? Sending hugs. Axx

Sending hugs. That's all I can do. Send hugs. Keep quiet about what happened.

March, 2015
Until I'd started meeting up with this lot at the beach hut, I'd never really been down to the beach beyond sunset. I'd obviously walked home that way sometimes, but I'd never come down here in the evening, for the specific reason of being here. I didn't know what I was missing. The darkening sky had inky, blue-black clouds stained upon it like the potato prints the kids made in Reception; the moon carefully but gloriously sprinkled its light on the ripples the sea made; while the slick pebbles seemed to gently glow like a Hansel and Gretel path down to the water's edge.

When we came down here to knit and sometimes to mix cocktails if Maxie could be bothered to bring it all down here, we generally sat in the same places: Yvonne at the 'head' of the table with her back to the beach hut, facing the sea; Maxie didn't seem to mind craning her neck to see the sea so she sat with her back to it; Hazel sat to Yvonne's right and I sat to Yvonne's left. We each of us had our rocks in front of us to keep the tablecloth flat on the metal fold-up table. I'd found those large palm-sized rocks, made sure they were all a similar size and shade, then used a scrubbing brush and soap to clean them up. Once clean, I'd used gold paint to inscribe them with our initials. It was ten years now since I'd changed my name for the first time and I'd even changed it when I got married, but I still hesitated over writing my surname initial. It was fake. I always felt that. It wasn't my true name, but what was done was done and I'd pushed aside my thoughts to make the stone mine. After the gold had dried, I'd varnished them to keep the lettering, to preserve our names as part of the friendship. I'd done it because, for once, I had friends.

I'd had friends at school. I'd had Candy, who was what people would nowadays call a frenemy in that she was a friend who had so many issues with me that she often behaved like an enemy to me. But these three were lovely and they were my friends. I could talk to them, I could trust them to look after my children at a moment's notice, and I could be who I was without them expecting anything in return.

'Do you ever have that heart-stopping, terrifying moment that you're turning into your mother?'

Yvonne asked this. It was spring, but it was also chilly. We had on thick jumpers and blankets over our shoulders. Maxie and I wore fingerless gloves; Yvonne and Hazel wore full gloves because they were experienced enough knitters to do that. We'd all brought flasks of hot drinks, and Yvonne kept topping up her and the others' plastic drinking cups with shots of whisky.

Yvonne often asked questions like that. It was the way she got to know people, I'd come to decide. We all knew that she was an obsessive when it came to spending hours on the internet searching for information about people, hunting out their secrets, especially with those she called her friends. (We all knew she still did it because sometimes she'd forget herself and let things slip. But since my two name changes, I was reasonably certain she would find out nothing significant about me.) But her questions worked both ways: the answers to these odd, sometimes intrusive, questions also allowed me an insight into her.

'Nope, no such worries here,' Maxie said. She was much more comfortable with her knitting needles now. She held them like a pro, and she could even do it with the fluorescent pink gloves, from which I'd watched her brutally cut off the fingers. 'I love the very bones of my mother. She's proper strict, a real no-nonsense Yorkshirewoman. If I turn out like her, no problem.'

'I *have* turned into my mother,' Hazel said. 'It's spooky. I mean, Mum's husband, my dad, ran off with another woman, too. And although he kept going on about how the other woman was better and prettier and amazing at blow jobs – yes, he said that more than once in front of me – he still spent a lot of time trying to make Mum's life hell, trying to screw her financially, and using us children to get back at her. I swear, I am my mother. And you know, I'm all right. So no, I don't worry about it. And if I did, it's too late, cos tah-dah!' Hazel didn't even have to think while she was knitting, she moved her needles together as if it was an automatic function to her, like breathing.

'You're so lucky,' Yvonne said. 'I live in fear of becoming my mother.' She was another accomplished knitter. I was always a bit curious about how she managed to be so perfect at everything – she looked amazing, she could knit, she could sew, she could make cocktails, she knew how to get herself into perfect yoga asanas. 'She's nuts, by the way. And not in an endearing-middle-class-English-lady-who's-a-bit-batty-but-harmless way; she's pretty much a psycho. Everyone loves her and she loves everyone until she doesn't, which is when she sets out to destroy that person. She drinks all the time, she's always slagging my dad off for his multiple affairs, but has had just as many. I mean, she's toxic. I spend my life trying to make sure I don't turn into her. Thankfully, seeing as I have friends whereas she's always had acquaintances, I think I'm safe. For now.'

They all looked at me, wanting to know what my mother was like, but after Yvonne's confession, I felt bad talking about my amma. 'I'd love to turn into my mother,' I confessed. 'She's one of the coolest, most amazing people I've ever met – present company included. No offence. She was always so laid-back when I was growing up but in a way where she tried to let you make your own decisions while guiding you to do the right thing. If you chose to do the wrong thing, she'd try to get you to change your mind, but ultimately, she knew she couldn't stop you. It was so hard for her. I mean, when Arjun or Priya make mistakes, it takes all my strength not to lose the plot; imagine watching all four of your children do some pretty terrible things and letting them get it wrong but being there for them.' I shook my head. 'I don't know how she didn't go completely insane, to be honest.'

'What terrible things did you do?' Yvonne asked.

Her question niggled me. The frequency with which she was doing things like that – jumping on a small portion of something someone said and then trying to find out more so she could play detective – was alarming. And annoying. And worrying. 'Thankfully, Yvonne, ya'll never know.' I grinned at her to take the edge off my rebuke. 'But I suppose the thing I love most about my mother is that she taught me to pray.'

'She *taught you to pray*?' Yvonne was pissed off that I hadn't spilled my secrets, I could tell by the clipped off edges of her words. 'Don't you just like slap your hands together, at a push get on your knees, open your mouth and words come out?'

Maxie and Hazel bristled at the same time. They also didn't like this side of Yvonne that seemed to come out the second things didn't go her way.

'No need for the snarkiness, Yvonne,' I replied. The others left it; I always challenged her because, well, being friends with someone requires you sometimes to tell them when they are out of line. 'By praying, I mean the type of praying that uses your body, mind *and* soul. When you do it right, or even when you don't do it right, it's a way of using the whole of who you are in worship.'

They all looked at me blankly.

'For pity's sake. Yoga. My mum taught me how to do yoga. Because, of course, you all knew that yoga started off as a system of worship, didn't you?'

More blank expressions. 'Oh, please, you lot. Why do you think I get that woman who has an emphasis on meditation as well as the asanas to come out to teach us yoga?'

'Because you're so rich even King Midas feels poor next to you?' Maxie said.

'Cheeky mare,' I said to Maxie as we all laughed. 'No, it's because when we do the yoga with her, she's trying to get us to connect with our inner selves, to find our calm centre. She's as close to using yoga to pray as I can find around these parts. But obviously I don't know which religion you lot are so I wouldn't push that on you, but yoga is all about connecting with your centre. If you use that time to meditate on your version of God, all the better.'

'You're actually quite a deep person, aren't you?' Hazel said. 'I mean, I knew that, but wow, you really take it to another level.'

'She certainly does,' Yvonne mumbled. She lifted her white plastic flask cup to her lips and sipped as she said that.

'Look, I have to confess,' Maxie said suddenly. 'When we're meant to be meditating and all that, usually, I'm trying as hard as I can to not fall asleep. I mean, come on, lying there, all chilled out, no worries about suddenly hearing "MMUMMM!", it's like a non-stop train to Snoresville.'

'Yeah, me too,' Hazel said. 'It's the best time because I get to stop and not think, so obviously I want to fall asleep. And I can't. So I start writing shopping lists and to-do lists and going through the kids' timetables to stop myself falling asleep.'

'Me three,' Yvonne said.

I stared at each and every one of them with my mouth wide open in shock. All that time, *all that time*, and they'd not— 'Ya'll a pack of bitches,' I said and laughed because it was hilarious. I'd thought I was enriching their souls and, really, I was giving them a chance to have a lie-down.

They all started to laugh too.

'You should have told me. We could do something else, you know.'

'I don't want to do something else,' Hazel and Maxie said at the same time. They looked at each other and went, 'Jinx!' like they were their children.

'I love doing the yoga,' Maxie said. 'I'm not kidding, I love it, and I like the meditation part, but I didn't want you to think I was getting some big spiritual kick out of it when I wasn't.'

'And me,' Hazel added. 'But I do love it. It's the only chance I get to lie down without the worry of someone coming to disturb me. And hey, I need that time. But you know, now you've told us all this stuff, I'm going to tune into it better.'

'Exactly,' Maxie said, using her free knitting needle to point at Hazel. 'And hey, it might get me to relax some more if I try to tune in. And if it'll help me relax properly, I'm there. I am so there next time.'

We all looked at Yvonne. She took her time moving the cup away from her mouth and then slowly licking her pink lips. 'I don't *love it* love it, but, you know, it's fun. And if the others want to still do it, then I'll keep doing it too.' She smiled at us, a bright, happy grin.

I couldn't challenge her on *that* because she hadn't technically said anything to take issue with, but we all knew she was being a bitch. And we all knew that Yvonne could do that really quickly when she was pissed off about something. The rest of us were just a bit short; Yvonne seemed to go in for the hurt if she perceived you had in any way slighted her.

'Why do you look so sad when you're talking about your mum?' Maxie asked me, to cover over Yvonne's bitch moment – or 'B-mo' as I called her flashes of bitchiness. 'Is she still alive?'

'Yes,' I replied. 'I guess it makes me sad that I let her down and I guess I don't see her as much as I'd like because I always get this sense of quiet disappointment from her. She's never said anything or been anything but supportive, but I suppose because I feel it for myself, I kind of expect her to feel it too, which makes me retreat from her.'

'But would you feel the same way if Priya or Arjun did what you did?' Yvonne asked. I looked at her, shocked that she had asked something insightful when she'd been having a 'B-mo' seconds ago.

'No,' I replied. 'I suppose I wouldn't.'

'Then aren't you doing her a huge disservice by keeping yourself from her for something you imagine she feels? I mean, you talk about her being really cool, so why are you punishing her?'

'I never really thought about it like that,' I confessed. I was punishing my *amma* for what I did.

'Well, maybe you should,' she said gently. 'I'd really hate to think of how your mum feels.' This was the real Yvonne. I was never sure why the other one came out sometimes, but I liked someone who thought about other people, who gave them something to think about. That was why we didn't just cut her off or cut her out when she had her 'B-mos'.

'You know, you're right, Yvonne. Thank you.'

'No problem,' she replied with a genuine smile. 'No problem at all.'

11:10 p.m.

Not too bad. The two new boys in Year 3 walked past and played with Frankie. Was fun, actually. She's called Cece, the mother. Frankie loves her twins. Sleep tight. M xxx

It feels odd, deleting this message. It's so innocuous. But that's what we agreed. So I text her back a line of xxxxs and then hit delete.

MONDAY

Hazel

9:30 p.m.

Hazel, I'm really confused. Why are you ignoring me? Ignoring the girls? You and Yvonne have been friends for years and it's been four weeks but you haven't even been to see her. What's going on? Why haven't I heard a thing from you? Did something bad happen between you and Yvonne that night? Tell me what's going on, please? Trevor

I don't need to read his message more than once to have it seared into my brain. I delete it like I've been deleting Anaya's and Maxie's messages. I start to hyperventilate like I do whenever I think about that night with Yvonne.

TUESDAY

Cece

9.15 a.m. *And breathe, and relax and breathe and move.*

The yoga teacher's voice glides smoothly through my mind. I don't think I've ever had a yoga lesson where I've actually relaxed and breathed and moved and relaxed and moved. Those yoga lessons I have been to in the past, there's always been a bit of me that is frantically trying to organise things, trying to find the best way to make the jigsaw puzzle that is family life – every piece needing to be in its right place or the whole thing doesn't function – work that bit smoother. Today, I have no such thoughts. I stand, lie, balance and allow myself to simply 'be' in a room with six other women.

I finally get it, too. What all the fuss is about. I finally understand the urge to yoge, what it can do for you if you do it properly. If you dare to concentrate. Or if, like me, you have the chance to tune out everything else and tune into what your body is being asked to do and finding a way to do it.

10:15 a.m. I am standing patiently, because that's what I do now I am not in any great rush, in a queue at Milk 'n' Cookees, waiting for a hot drink. I was going to go for a coffee, as usual, but I won't undo all that good, breathe-and-relax work by sprinkling mole-cules of caffeine into my bloodstream. I will take my herbal tea, and walk along the seafront, continue the theme of connecting with myself and allowing myself to just 'be'. Yes, yes, there are a thousand other things I could just 'be' doing at home, but they don't seem important right now.

Out in the fresh air, I take a sip of my lemon and ginger tea and I don't gag. Well, I do, but I tell myself I don't. I am at one with myself and with nature. I *will* drink this tea and I *will* enjoy it. All right, I *will* drink it. Coming towards me from the direction of the yoga class I recently left is a woman who was in the class with me. She could have been teaching it though, the way her muscles seemed to bend without much effort. She has reams of thick, black hair that she has secured up in a neat bun, beautifully smooth skin and a perfectly shaped body. She is dressed in über-expensive gym gear. I noticed that when I kept sneaking looks at her, trying to work out where I'd seen her before. It could only have been from the school, I decided in the end. Or from our road. But then, the labels of her clothes, the very neat manicure, suggested she lived somewhere with a lot more commas in the price of the house than ours. I smile at her and she smiles back, the same 'where do I know you from?' expression in her eyes.

'Plummer Prep,' she says, suddenly. 'I've seen you at Plummer Prep. Haven't I?'

'You have,' I say. 'My two boys have just started there.'

'Oscar and Ore?' she says as though she knows them. I know what that usually means: they've made an impression, and probably not a good one. Although they both know to incur the wrath of Mum and Dad, which you are risking if you misbehave at school, you must do something pretty spectacular to make it worthwhile.

'Erm, yes.'

'Oh, they're lovely boys. I go in to read with the children once a week and I've read with both of them. Beautiful manners, the pair of them, and amazing reading.'

'I'm very pleased – and relieved – to hear that.'

'I'm Anaya,' she says and holds out the hand not curled around her yoga mat.

'Cece,' I reply.

'Cece? You've just appeared on our instant messaging group, haven't you?' she says. 'All the pieces are coming together now. Maxie mentioned she'd run into you on the beach the other day.'

'You know Maxie?' I ask. Which means she must have known *her* – Yvonne Whidmore.

'Yes, quite well. Her, me and another mother, Hazel, we used to go down to Maxie's beach hut for our nights out, which sounds more debauched than it actually was, especially since I don't drink.'

'Some of my most debauched nights have happened without the excuse of drink,' I say.

Anaya grins at me. I like her. There is something open and relaxed about her. 'Sorry, am I holding you up getting a coffee?' I say to her. Her eyes widen in alarm, and then dart around, checking who might have heard.

'Shhhh,' she hushes. 'Don't be shouting that around. As far as the world knows, I go to the gym three times a week, I do yoga four times a week, I juice a farmyard full of vegetables every day, and I don't drink alcohol, I don't have a sneaky cigarette or five and I certainly don't drink coffee. All right?'

'All right,' I say carefully.

'Oh, lighten up,' she says, bursting into a huge laugh. 'People see me in my gym gear and they make up all these ridiculous stories about me. Yes, I do go to the gym a lot, but that's because I like to exercise. That's having spent most of my twenties doing anything but going to the gym. When I hit thirty a switch flicked in my head and I couldn't get enough of the gym and exercising in general. I am a total gym bunny now and to most people that must mean I spend my life spreading all that Earth mother stuff.'

'Right,' I say.

'I sound completely crazy to you, don't I?' she says with a wrinkle of her pretty nose.

'Not completely crazy,' I reply. 'Only a little.' I raise my hand, move my forefinger and thumb close together. 'A tiny little.'

Another huge grin. 'I really like you,' she says with a laugh. 'And just for that, I'm going to do you the huge favour of making you ditch whatever it is you've got in your hand and buy you a real coffee.'

'No, no, this tea is the best thing to drink right now. I'm sure that's what the yoga teacher said.'

'I won't hear of it,' she says and snatches the cup out of my hand. 'I really won't. Life is too short to drink tea if you want coffee.' With that she suddenly becomes still, her whole being transported to somewhere else in her head, it seems. Yvonne Whidmore, probably. Maybe she said those words to her and now that her life hangs in the balance, Anaya is remembering and wishing she'd done more to make sure Yvonne did enjoy those times that led up to that moment.

'Who says I don't want this tea?' I interrupt. She looks like she is spiralling down into something dreadful, she is remembering something that will be her undoing. My words bring her out of the stupor and she refocuses on me.

'Hmmm?' she asks, confused.

'Who said I don't want that tea?' I repeat.

'You did,' she responds with her upbeat voice back in place, her smile fixed on her mouth, her endearing wrinkling back on her nose. 'I saw your face when you took a sip – it was not what you wanted at all.'

'True, but I could learn to like it.'

'I doubt it. I come from a land where we know how to make proper tea and this herbal "tea" that's made with a bag crap should be banned.'

'You could have a point,' I say.

She dumps my cup on one of the small black metal tables outside Milk 'n' Cookees and then moves forward to push open the glass rectangle of the door. 'Come on, have a real coffee on me. It's my way of saying welcome to the neighbourhood.'

FRIDAY

Hazel

8:55 p.m. I'm slamming things around my kitchen. It's not subtle, and I know all of them sitting in the living room can hear me, but I don't care. I DON'T CARE!

I opened the door five minutes ago and there was Maxie. There was Anaya. And there was this woman I had seen all week at the gates but had never spoken to AT MY HOUSE! When Maxie had suggested that we try to get back to normal, that Ed was back for a stretch of time so she could come over for knitting, and then Anaya had said she was free, I'd thought, finally, *finally* we're going to move forward. We're going to put *Yvonne* behind us. I'd even bought a bunch of pre-mixed frozen margaritas and had downloaded some of that yoga music Anaya likes as a nod to the things we all did together. I knew Maxie would be horrified by the idea of pre-mixed cocktails and it'd be the wrong type of music, but they wouldn't say anything because they're my friends and they'd know I'd tried. But no, it wasn't a getting-back-to-normal experience – they brought someone else with them. I open the cupboard with the tinned goods and slam it shut again.

Oh, that felt good. I fling the door open again and slam it even louder. I'm so glad I couldn't afford the soft closures when the kitchen was fitted.

That last slam does it: Maxie appears in the kitchen and shuts the door behind her.

'We can all hear you, you know,' she says.

'Good!' I say loudly.

'Shhhh, keep your voice down.'

116

'NO!' I shout.

'OK, what is your problem?'

'Are you insane, bringing someone else here? After everything that's happened, you've decided to bring someone else into this mess?'

'Look, she's new, she needs friends and I thought, you know, we are nice people. We don't sit around in Milk 'n' Cookees only deigning to speak to people if they've got the right clothes and look desperate enough to settle for scraps of attention. No one else has really bothered with her and I can see how difficult and awkward she feels at the school gates. And Frankie loves her boys. When they came over for tea, I got to talk to her properly and she's really nice.'

My stomach flips. 'They came over for tea?' I ask. Maxie rarely lets anyone come over for tea. My children have been less than twenty times over the years I've known her, but she met this woman seconds ago and she has had them in her home.

'Yes, I thought I told you.'

'No, you didn't. We've barely been talking let alone anything else. But you seem to have time to do stuff like make new friends.'

'Anaya has met her as well.'

'So Anaya thought it was a good idea that she comes tonight too?'

'Well, yeah,' Maxie says.

'Have you three had coffee without me?' I ask. 'When I couldn't make it the other day, did you have this woman with you instead?'

'We asked her to come so she could meet you. Obviously when you couldn't come because you were starting work early, you didn't get to meet her.'

This is how Yvonne felt. I can see it now. How easy it is to become The Friend. The one who is the outsider and people start to unintentionally plot against. Which is even worse when you think about everything else that is happening. About the secrets we now have to keep for each other and ourselves.

'You could have asked before you brought her here,' I tell Maxie. I am not going to become Yvonne. Or the person who goes down for this, as they say on the television.

117

'I know. I'm sorry. I just want you to get to know her. She really is nice. And she was so excited to meet you. She was saying that Camille and her son Ore are really good friends. She's wanted to text you a few times to arrange a play date but wasn't sure how you'd take it.'

I look over Maxie, seeing her how Yvonne must have seen her. She's intimidating in that she's so open and effusive, when she likes you. But she isn't actually that open. She keeps her home and her husband off-limits to all but the most select. She very rarely joins in our talks about our relationships. I don't, for example, know how she met her husband. I don't know why she and Ed moved to Brighton. I don't know if she and Ed are planning on having any more children. We've been close friends for years, she's held my hand through some of the biggest disasters I've faced to date, and yet I hardly know her. Same with Anaya. I share a huge secret with her, but I hardly know her. I know as much about them as I do about this new woman sitting in my living room right now.

I lick my lips. I need to think about this. I need to think about who I am trusting with one of my biggest secrets. Not right now, though. I have to put all of this out of my head and concentrate on being friendly to this stranger my friends have brought to my house.

I walk to the cupboard I was just abusing, and open up its neighbour to take out an extra cocktail glass. 'Well, all I can say is, she'd better be able to knit because I sure as hell ain't teaching her.'

Maxie smiles at me. Relieved. That I'm going to give this Cece a chance? Or that I haven't worked out what she's up to yet?

March, 2014
Yvonne called them.

I was grateful and resentful at the same time. I was still numb around the edges, the fingers of my mind grasping for anything familiar to hold on to. I didn't really want anyone else here to see it. It was like that monster you can pretend doesn't live in your wardrobe – the moment, the absolute second someone else sees it too, it becomes real. The minute Anaya and Maxie walked in, gathered me into their arms and told me how sorry they were, was the minute it became real.

I had to accept Walter had left. I used to dream of it, of not having to fend off his aggressively lewd advances, not having to pick up after him, or listen to his rants about how much I cost and how little I contributed. I dreamt of it, but when it had become reality, I'd begged him not to do it. I'd got down on my knees, literally, and begged him to stay. Pleaded with him for another chance. Promised I would change every little thing about me if he wouldn't leave.

The more I'd begged, the more contempt he had developed for me. I hadn't been able to stop, though. Russell, Camille and Calvin deserved to grow up in a home with two parents and if that meant doing anything, promising everything, then that was what I'd do. 'We can try for another baby,' I'd said in desperation and the sneer had become set on his handsome features. He'd looked me up and down then spat: 'What makes you think I'd even be able to get it up with you? You repulse me.'

It was almost as if Yvonne knew – she had come over to drop off a knitting pattern and had leant on the doorbell until I opened it. 'What's he done now?' she'd said when she saw the state of me. My eyes had hurt when I blinked they were so swollen from crying, my lips were raw and sore because I had chewed on them so constantly and I'd practically pulled off my fingernails clinging to him. He'd waited until I'd got the children to bed before telling me his plans for the future and how they didn't involve me.

'He's gone, he's left me,' I'd said. 'I don't want him to be gone. I don't want him to be gone.' I'd said that so she wouldn't say anything bad. So that she would understand this was the worst thing in the world to happen to me and she wasn't allowed to trash him.

Her arms had been warm around me, then the others were there, and their arms were around me too. Then it was real, then it had happened and he was gone and he wasn't coming back. None of them said I was better off without him. They held me, they comforted me. Yvonne organised a rota with the three of them to each collect the children from school, take them home for tea and a sleepover, while another sat with me and stopped me calling him for as long as possible before they gave in, gave me the phone, then let me cry in their arms after I'd subjected myself to his absolute, unrelenting cruelty. He was all business, all talk about how long he would let me live in 'his' house until it had to be sold and I would have to find somewhere to rent, how we wouldn't need solicitors if I didn't get greedy, how he had to think about his future and his money. After every phone call that Yvonne was there for, she would say afterwards: 'When you're ready, let me know, and we can turn this whole thing around.'

On the tenth day, Yvonne's turn to sit with me, after he had screamed at me to leave him alone, I realised that he hadn't once asked about the children. How they were coping, how I was managing to make sure they were fed and clothed and taken to school on time. These were the children he'd been so desperate to have, so keen to see me stay at home and look after. Once that realisation hit, I saw all of it like standing in front of a door. The door had finally been opened and I could see not daylight but the night, the stars that lit the way to my new future. There was nothing to be afraid of in this dark – it was another part of the way I was existing in the world. The only thing to be scared of, absolutely terrified of, would be standing in front of the door, seeing the night, the darkness rich with possibilities, burgeoning with the many, many paths of my life, and staying where I was because I thought that I could somehow will my life back to the way it had been.

I dried my eyes on the too-long sleeves of the cardigan I'd been wearing for four days, and I looked across my kitchen table at Yvonne. I remembered the conversation we'd had here about whether I wanted a fourth child; how Yvonne had tried to tell me that I didn't have to do what Walter wanted just because Walter wanted it. She had been trying to tell me, in a roundabout way that I might listen to, that I was in charge of my own life, my own destiny. And I was in charge of the lives, the destinies of my children, too. If I kept on as I was, I would be homeless, penniless, and so would they.

'I'm ready,' I said to her.

Her lips twisted into a smile I hadn't seen before, and a determination took over her face. She carefully unhooked her little sky-blue bag that hung on the left-hand corner of the chair she sat on, and slowly she unzipped it. She pulled out a rectangle of white card and slid it across the table.

'He's not going to know what's hit him,' she said. With her words, I took that step. Pushed myself through the doorway into the dark unknown, looking up to the stars and knowing the only way out of this place was to go forwards, to follow the line of stars until I reached the next phase of my life.

June, 2015

'Thanks and everything, you lot, but no thanks. I'm going to use this time when they're not here to really centre myself. You know, I haven't been without the kids since . . . well, since they were born, except for those nights out with you all at the beach hut and stuff. I'll be fine, honestly, you don't have to worry about me. It's so lovely of you to care. I'll be fine.'

Clearly, they had spent time training like Olympic athletes in a synchronised sport because they all looked at me, glanced at each other and then rolled their eyes. In unison. Walter had left over a year ago, we'd been divorced six months and in that time he'd barely asked about the children let alone seen them. But when the divorce didn't go the way he envisaged – and I wasn't living in rented accommodation far away from family and friends, begging him for scraps of money, and he'd had to pay for his children and share 'his' money so I could house and feed his children – he'd decided that he wanted to hurt me by having the children overnight after all.

Which is why my friends were all dressed up and standing in my house demanding I come out with them. They, like Walter, thought that me being without the children for two nights, being in my house all alone, would traumatise me. He was wrong, of course – I wasn't going to suffer without them. I would be fine. And my friends were wrong, too. I was fine. Absolutely fine.

'Just go and get changed,' Maxie said after they listened to me explain how fine I was.

'No—'

'I swear, you do not want all three of us dragging you upstairs and dressing you,' Yvonne stated.

'Yeah, Haze,' Anaya agreed. 'We are mothers: we got wrestling clothes onto wriggling beings down to a fine art a long, long time ago. Do you seriously think we'll have any trouble getting you dressed and made-up?'

'Guys, thank you. I honestly couldn't have got through this divorce without you all, but this is a time I need to stop and pause and really take it all in.'

'You can do that in the new wine bar down near George Street,' Yvonne said.

'Do you know what it's cost me in babysitting for tonight?' Maxie asked, although it was clearly rhetorical. 'I've had to bribe my husband with all sorts of promises so he won't let Frankie stay up watching horror films while eating sweets and drinking pop . . . It's costing me a lot to be standing here tonight so I am going to make sure we all enjoy every single second of it, even if it kills you.'

Anaya spoke next: 'And you know what? If my teetotal witch of a mother-in-law finds out I've been on the same street as a bar, let alone inside one, she'll have those divorce papers she's had drawn up since the day we got married under Sanjay's nose before I can even explain to him that I didn't touch a drop. This is costing me big too. So go and get dressed, OK? Get dressed and things don't need to get unpleasant.'

I focused on Yvonne, waited for her to tell me the price of coming here to take me out. She stared at me blankly. 'Well?' I coaxed. 'What's it cost you to come here tonight?'

She screwed up her beautiful face, deeply offended at the idea. 'Nothing,' she exclaimed. 'This is part of our deal, isn't it? I tell you what to do when I know it's for the best, and you do it.' She nodded towards the hall and stairs. 'Go get dressed. That's the last time any of us is going to ask nicely. Next time, we'll be treating you like an unruly toddler. I don't know about these two, but my children only ever wriggled once. After that first time, even at their young ages, they knew not to mess with me.'

Later, I threw my arms around Yvonne. 'Thank you for bringing me out,' I whispered into her ear. I was grateful to her, and the others, but especially to her, for all she'd done for me.

'No problem, baby girl, absolutely no problem.'

Cece

9 p.m. 'It'll be fine,' they said. 'She won't mind,' they said. 'She'll love to meet you. Especially if Ore and Camille are friends,' they said.

It is not fine. Hazel took one look at me and had some sort of internal explosion.

'Sorry about that,' Hazel says when she and Maxie return to the living room.

'No problem,' I say. I'm starting to wonder if I should fake some sort of problem and then go home. I do not want to be where I am not wanted.

'You look like you're thinking of ways to escape a bad date,' Hazel says.

I smile nervously. 'Do I?'

'Yes, and I'm sorry about that. I was just surprised about you being here seeing as my friends didn't even tell me you existed.' She adds another glass to the table in the middle of the room. 'But you're here now, so I'm sure we'll have lots of fun.'

I nod.

'So, can you knit?'

Can I knit? Well, the internet was very helpful in giving me the general idea. But, can I knit? 'Thing is, Hazel, I'd like to be honest and say no, but I suspect if I do, your kitchen will be the one to suffer.'

When she bursts out laughing, the atmosphere in the room breaks and we all relax.

Part 3

MONDAY

Cece

4:30 p.m. 'Oh, hello, are you Cece?'

The woman who stops me is the one who I saw in the café that first week, the one who smiled and then looked horrified when it seemed like I was going to go and speak to her. She is a perfect mother: well turned out, well made-up, sweet-smelling with long blonde hair. She actually reminds me of Yvonne Whidmore in the pictures I've seen of her.

'Yes,' I reply. Now I have three friends who actually seem to like me (Hazel's initial kitchen abuse notwithstanding), I know I don't actually need to speak to this woman.

Over her shoulder, I keep an eye on the school's front door, waiting for the boys to appear.

'Oh, hello, I've noticed you around and wanted to say hello. There never seemed to be the time,' she gushes. 'I'm Teri. My child is Nettie, she's in the same class as one of your twins? Such lovely boys. I've been meaning to talk to you.'

Inside, I roll my eyes. She is rewriting history. What is the point? We both know that she wasn't interested in me before. Outside, I offer a vague smile so I'm partially but not fully engaging with her nonsense.

Surprise flashes in her eyes, probably a little disconcerted that I'm not gushing in response. I've never been that good at faking it in these situations. 'Well, anyway, I'm sure no one has properly welcomed you to the school. It must be so hard for you. Moving here and everything. Well, Mrs Carpenter has asked me to be the class coordinator, in place of . . .' she places a hand over her chest, 'well, in place of Mrs Whidmore. Yvonne. I'm sure you heard what happened to her.' Her concern, I notice, doesn't go beyond her words, and her body movements. The real seat of concern – her eyes, the set of her mouth, the way she holds herself – are untouched. 'She was my dear, *dear* friend, so obviously I feel terrible about it, but Mrs Carpenter thought she wouldn't mind. I've taken over the role of head of the Parents' Council as well. Like I say, I feel awful about it, but Mrs Carpenter *insisted*. I was so close to Yvonne so I know she wouldn't mind me taking over from her.'

'Until she wakes up, you mean?'

'Pardon?'

'She won't mind you looking after the roles until she wakes up,' I say. I wish the boys would hurry up so I can have a legitimate reason to stop talking to this woman in front of me.

'Well, yes, of course,' she says with a smile that tells me that isn't what she meant at all. 'Of course, that's what I meant. Yvonne wouldn't want it any other way.'

'What can I do for you?' I ask.

'It's what I can do for you,' she says. 'And that is, to officially invite you to the class, we'd like to take you to coffee. We often meet on Thursday mornings at Milk 'n' Cookees. Thought you might like to join us? I'm sure everyone would love to meet you.'

That would be the Thursday-morning coffee where you could have asked me over when I was new and scared? That would be the Thursday-morning coffee when you completely blanked me and left me feeling small? 'Oh, thank you, that's so sweet of you, Teri,' I can gush now. 'I'm really busy the next few Thursdays, but I'll let you know.' *Where are my children?*

Teri's face contracts a fraction. I was not meant to say that. I was meant to gush at her before, and I'm meant to fall over myself now I'm asked to join her gang. 'Oh, lovely. *Fine.*' She manages to gather up a smile. 'Just let me know. I'm on PPY3.'

'Yes, of course,' I say.

'And if there's ever anything I can tell you about how things work around here . . .'

'I'll ask.' *Someone else.* 'Thank you so much, Teri,' I say and I walk up to the gates to ask the teacher releasing the pupils what is taking my children so long.

FRIDAY

Cece

8:30 p.m. Sol wasn't happy when I'd asked if he could be in tonight so I could go out again with my newly found friends. He'd thought about saying no, then he'd huffed about leaving work on time in the middle of a big project, then he'd sulked at me – there is no other word for the scrunched-up lips and glower as he'd walked through the door at seven o'clock. He'd sulked some more as I put out dinner, as I washed and tidied up. Then he'd 'hmmm'-ed me as I got ready. And had finally 'right'-ed me as I left.

I, for the most part, ignored it. Things haven't been brilliant between us the last two weeks; we've both been ignoring the fact that we haven't had a proper conversation in the last fortnight beyond 'what time will you be home?' and 'I won't be back for dinner'. We haven't even touched each other, let alone anything else amorous in months. I am feeling better because I have friends and the children have friends, but I am also unsettled and more than a little scared because I am clearly losing my best friend and lover. I am clearly headed down . . .

I do what I have been doing for weeks, months now, and decide not to think about it as I arrive at Maxie's house with a bottle of Kahlúa, ready to mix cocktails.

'OK, mixtras,' Maxie says as we stand in her kitchen. 'We are going to be mixing a new cocktail tonight. One that we are going to call "the Cece".'

'Oh, just get on with it,' Hazel says. She is sitting beside me in front of Maxie's table/mixing area, and has been glued to me since I arrived. I think she feels a little guilty about how she behaved last week and is trying to make up for it by never leaving my side.

Anaya stands on the other side of the table, with her array of 'virgin' ingredients. 'Yes, Maxie, get on with it,' she says.

'You lot, you have no respect for the process,' Maxie said.

'Oh, please. "The process." I've heard it all now,' Hazel says.

'Oh, oh, I'd forgotten about "the process",' Anaya giggles. 'The process, the process, let's all respect the process,' she sings.

'You mock, but has anyone ever mixed cocktails as beautifully as me? I don't think so.' Maxie looks at the array of spirits and mixers on the table in front of us. 'For The Cece, since she has brought Kahlúa, I am going to need this, this, this and this.' She pulls towards her a bottle of Green Bols, a bottle of Blue Bols, my bottle of Kahlúa and a bottle of Irish Cream. From the side, she collects four small clear glasses that are shaped like tulips with short stems. Behind those glasses she has small, jewel-coloured cordial glasses similar to the ones I gave Sol for Christmas one year.

'We need these glasses and we need a very steady hand.' She opens the Green Bols and pours it carefully until there is a layer of green at the bottom of the glass. She then pours in a dash of Blue Bols. Carefully, carefully she pours a layer of Kahlúa so it sits on the green-blue layer. She then pours a layer of Baileys so it sits on top. 'And, ta-dah! Here we have the Cece.' She grins at us, her face so much like that of a child who has finally cracked a problem move they've been practising for weeks and weeks. 'What do you think, Cece? How do you like your namesake cocktail?'

'It's fantastic,' I reply. Truly. It's a thing of beauty. 'I especially like the nod to my teal-green jacket.'

'That does look lovely,' Anaya says and tips her head to one side to look at it a bit better.

Hazel is silent for a moment longer than necessary. We all look at her and she visibly gulps, as though swallowing back some emotion. 'It's beautiful,' she whispers. 'Truly. It's one of the most beautiful things I've ever seen.'

'Steady on,' Maxie says. 'It ain't the Mona Lisa—'

'*You* steady on,' I cut in. 'If Hazel thinks The Cece is beautiful, then The Cece is beautiful.'

Maxie opens her mouth and Anaya's mobile ringing replaces her words. 'Oops, sorry. That's not Sanjay's ringtone so I'll need to take this,' she says. 'It might be work.'

While she talks, she is reaching into her bag and pulling out the silver phone. She looks at the screen and is visibly shaken by the name that pops up. I can't see who it is, but she stares at it like it is a ghost, then she looks up at Hazel and Maxie. Her hand starts to tremble violently enough for us all to see. The other two frown at her reaction. 'Erm . . . I don't need to take this now,' she says and virtually throws her phone back into her bag.

Hazel's phone lights up next, ringing on the side where she left it earlier. Puzzled, she goes to it, then blanches when she sees the screen and takes a step back. She then looks at Maxie and Anaya, with the exact same expression that Anaya had seconds before. Anaya returns her look, but Maxie is still openly mystified. Hazel backs further away from her phone and then returns to her place beside me, still pale and trembling slightly. Maxie's mobile starts after that. The others avoid looking at her, and she frowns as she moves towards her phone like a woman approaching the gallows.

I wonder if my phone's going to ring next and I'll discover that by coming here tonight I've accidentally walked into the plot of a horror movie. When Maxie reaches her phone, she looks at it and doesn't react. She stares at the screen, which is probably flashing the name and identity of the person who is calling her. I watch her, the others watch her: she stares at the screen and breathes deeply a few times, then pushes the phone back against the cream-coloured blender. It rings desolately a few times before cutting out. I'm sure she takes a second to fix her face before she turns to us again.

Seconds later, her house phone starts to ring. All three of them stare at the white-and-red landline phone that sits on the counter. Maxie marches to the other end of the kitchen and snatches the white phone cord out of the wall socket. Instead of coming straight back towards the table, she grabs her mobile from the side and switches it off.

Hazel and Anaya in robotic fashion do the same with their mobiles.

'Right, where were we?' Maxie says.

'Erm . . .' Hazel says, as though fuzzy-headed.

They're clearly being harassed by someone. I know that look – I had it more than once in my last job when people used to find out what I really did and would take to calling and calling me, trying to intimidate me by rarely leaving messages.

'Are you all right?' I ask them all.

Anaya smiles, Maxie nods, Hazel stares at a point in the middle of the table. 'It's not been a brilliant time,' Maxie says.

'Yeah.' Anaya rubs her eyes with her fingers, pinches her nose like she is about to develop a migraine. 'It's not been a brilliant time. But I'm having fun tonight. Like I had fun last time with the knitting.'

'Me too,' Maxie says. 'Shall we go back to the cocktail and try to move on?'

'Yeah, good idea,' Anaya says.

Hazel doesn't say anything. She sits very still and stares at the middle of the table.

'So, Hazel,' I say to her loudly, to bring her out of whichever trance she's in. 'Tell me how beautiful you think The Cece is.'

She looks at me then. 'Hmmm?' she says.

'You were telling us how beautiful The Cece is? You got rather breathless about it, if I recall?' I say to her, still speaking with a raised voice to keep her attention.

'I did not say that!' she says, back in the room with us at last.

'Er, yes you did. "The Cece is the most beautiful thing I've ever seen", to quote you.'

'That's hilarious!' Anaya laughs. 'She sounded exactly like you.'

'She didn't!'

'Oh, but she did,' Maxie laughs.

'I don't sound that nasally with a hint of Brum.'

'You do, actually,' Maxie and Anaya say together. They turn to each other and shout, 'Jinx!'

We slide back to where we were then, laughing and joking and making cocktails. And now we're back here, in this room having fun, I'm going to pretend that interlude with the phone calls didn't happen because it is nothing to do with me.

Part 4

MONDAY

Cece

9:15 a.m. I haven't gone to Milk 'n' Cookees today to grab a coffee before I walk home. Instead, I've strolled down onto the seafront, along the beach, quite far from the school, then cut up towards the centre of Brighton.

Once I've bought a coffee in this café, I plan on wandering all the way into the centre of Brighton to have a proper look at the shops. I haven't had a real chance to do that yet without having the boys with me, so today is the day for it.

A small queue has formed behind me and I step out of the way to wait for my coffee and, once I have it, I begin to leave.

'Cece,' a voice says from the line. 'Cece, hi. Hi.'

I stop short, causing the person who was coming up behind me to tut and then sidestep me to get out. *It can't be*, I think. I take my time turning to the man in the line. It can be and it is.

He is taller than me, the same height and build as Sol or thereabouts. He's white, though, with blond hair that he wears short, green eyes that focus intently on whatever you're saying. He also dresses like an off-duty policeman with black trousers that sit snuggly around his rugby-player hips, white shirt with the top button open and a brown leather jacket.

'Hello, Gareth,' I say. I want my voice to be flat and unemotional. I do not want him to know that my heart actually stopped beating when I heard his voice and that my insides melted when I saw his face.

He smiles, overtly relieved that I remember him. *How* could I forget him? Every time I look at Harmony, I'm reminded of him. 'It's good to see you,' he says. His smile deepens, moves away from relief into something that could be genuine pleasure.

'Bye then.'

Gareth steps into my path. 'Do you fancy a coffee?' he asks.

'I've got mine to go,' I say. 'Maybe another time.' *As in, never.*

'You don't mind if my friend has her coffee here, do you, Norman?' Gareth calls over my shoulder to the barista. When he has his answer, he says to me: 'See? He doesn't mind.' His high-wattage smile dims a little – he's nervous, worried that I'm not going to give him a chance. It's not as if he's sought me out over the years, made a nuisance of himself through the myriad ways available to not let the past stay in the past. But now he's here (there's no *way* this meeting is a coincidence – no one would be dim enough to believe that) and he wants something. What that is, I have no idea. But in the grand scheme of things, I'm probably better off finding out what Gareth wants now, instead of him turning up again when I'm with Sol, or, even worse, Harmony.

March, 2001

Heat. Gareth and I were all about sizzling, fizzing, burning heat. Whenever we got together we were like a fire that got way out of control way too quickly. 'Ah, ah, ahhhhh,' he gasped between huge great gulps of air as he flopped back onto the bed. 'Ah, ah. I never . . . I never . . . *never* . . . knew *that* could be like *that.*'

My fingers slowly let go of his shoulders and I moved my legs over and away from him as I rolled off and flopped down beside him on his narrow single bed. How he could talk right then, I didn't know. I was sure my mouth would spill out incomprehensible burbles if I tried to speak. I was tingling all over, every part of me alive with the afterglow of being with him.

'I thought I was going to have a heart attack at the end there,' he gasped, through deep, laboured breaths, 'so I did.' In moments like this, after we'd done stuff like that and his guard was down and he seemed free to be who he was, his Irish accent crept out from behind the bland blanket he threw over his voice most of the time. 'You could quite possibly be the death of me if we carry on like that,' he said, still breathing hard.

I wasn't risking a burble so I said nothing, continued to melt into the uncomfortable bed and waited for my body and mind to reconnect.

Gareth lazily stroked his fingers across my stomach, probably to remind himself that we were still naked and together. 'How . . . ?' He broke off from the question he frequently asked. He couldn't fathom it. We'd spotted each other on the first day, both of us sharing that seconds-too-long glance, both of us acknowledging the heat even across a crowded mess hall, and we'd both known it would be good when we finally got together. 'Good' was underestimating ourselves though, as we'd found out three days later. That was why he always asked this question: *How the hell did we get to have such great sex when we barely know each other?* I never had an answer.

Casually, I looked around his room, small and functional, just like mine. Neat and orderly, too, like mine. The room felt like him, and smelt like him. As I scanned the room, my eyes happened to glance at his desk clock. Immediately I sat up. 'No!' I said. 'We are going to be late back.'

'Nooo!' he said. He checked his wrist, got confirmation from his watch that we had too few minutes to get dressed and get back out there before anyone knew we were missing. 'Nooooo!'

I was out of bed first. Over the last ten years or so I had managed to perfect the art of getting dressed and getting to where I needed to be – school, sixth form, outside the Peel statue downstairs every morning for inspection – with seconds to spare. Knickers, bra, tights were on before he'd even managed to roll off the bed and start to locate his trousers. Blouse. Skirt. Tie. Feet shoved into shoes. I grabbed my tiepin and slipped it into place in the middle of my black and white chequered tie. I quickly ran my fingers through the strands of my cheek-length black bob, to make sure it looked respectable and not like I'd grabbed a quickie during refs. He was still trying to straighten out his trousers.

'I'm sorry, I'm going to have to go,' I said. I grabbed my books and pen from the floor by his bed.

'Yes, yes, you go,' he fussed, his accent rinsed clean of his heritage and now as unremarkable as someone who grew up in Generic Town, UK. 'I'll screw you later,' he added as I headed towards the door.

I laughed. He probably didn't even realise what he'd said. 'Not if I screw you first,' I replied as I opened the door, checked no one was in the corridor and then made a dash for it. I was not meant to be in the male accommodation and I would be in big trouble if I was caught. If I hurried, I would make it to 'Searching Premises and Suspects in a Policing Context' without anyone knowing I'd skipped lunch to go screw another cadet. I turned the corner and as I neared the end of the corridor, ready to take the stairs two at a time, someone barged into me from behind, bouncing me into the wall.

'Oh, Cee-*Dee*, didn't see you there.' Duke. If Gareth was heat, Duke was cold. Frigid, bleak, cold. Despite some stiff competition, he was probably the most alpha male on the course, and he constantly looked like he had something spiky and unpleasant shoved up his backside. 'You've shoved yourself into a wall.'

I said nothing and was about to move towards the stairs when he barged me against the wall again. 'You've done it again,' he said. 'You really should be careful.' Obviously he wanted to say something. He did this – cornered me when no one was around, said something vile to make me believe I wasn't wanted in the police force. I didn't move; it was easier, quicker to hear him out and let him walk away. 'I saw you,' he said, a nasty hitch of his lip to go with it. 'You and Gareth think you're so clever, don't you? I saw yer. I know what you're doing.' He looked me up and down. 'I don't know how he can bring himself to dip his nib into your type of ink.' He leant in close. 'Or maybe I should have a go and see what it's all about.'

In reply, I raised my hand and examined my nails. They needed clipping and filing and buffing. An essential part of being an officer was making sure you were neat, groomed and well presented. I was in every other way, but I'd let my nails run to ruin. My nail-examining, of course, enraged Duke, but he didn't have time to do anything about it. We were both now late for a class, and anyone could come along at any minute. He used his shoulder to shove me forwards. 'I'm going to make sure you don't finish this course, Cee-*Dee*. You watch and see.'

Yeah, good luck with that, I replied silently as I ran for the stairs.

9:20 a.m. We sit by the window, Gareth with his cappuccino in a proper coffee cup, me with mine in my beige takeaway cup.

'So, how've you been?' he says. His voice still has the shadow of a hint of Cork, where he was born, running through it.

'Fine. And you?'

'Fine,' he says.

'Great. We're both fine. Isn't that lovely.'

Gareth grins at me, lowers his gaze. I used to love it when he'd do that. (I never told him that, *obviously*.) I used to imagine all the things going through his mind when he smiled and didn't meet my eye. 'You've not changed,' he says.

'No, I haven't. People generally don't change. We are who we are, especially when we hit adulthood.' So much is loaded into those three, innocuous sentences. Will he notice?

From the way his green eyes are suddenly on me and wounded but defensive – he took those words *exactly* the way I meant them. 'People can and do change. I did, anyway.'

'Of course you did.'

'I have,' he insists, both words stern and clipped.

I give him a one-shouldered shrug, but it is my turn to deliberately lower my gaze.

'I'm sorry,' he says, gently. 'I never got the chance to say that. To apologise. You just disappeared – I had no way of getting in touch with you. I knew virtually nothing about you to even know where to start looking. I was young and stupid and scared. And I'm sorry. I really am.'

*

I had earned the Baton of Honour. Rather than leaving the course as Duke had been determined to make me do and had tried very hard to make happen, I had actually finished the police training course with the highest honour a cadet could receive. I'd had to force my face to set in a serious, worthy expression at the passing out parade because I'd been so desperate to smile. *Grin.* I could barely believe *I'd* achieved such an accolade. The excitement and, I'll admit it, pride at having been adorned shone through me as I walked to the pub after waving my parents off at the train station.

As soon as I opened the door to the Sunny Arms, the heat from the other officers – excitement, relief, pure joy from having done it – rolled over me like stepping off a plane in a tropical country. We had made it; we were on the way to becoming proper police officers.

As I made my way through the crowd, searching for the people I'd become closest to on the course, I was aware of the sour grapes, the 'she got it because she's black, she's female, wouldn't be surprised if she was a lesbian too' looks and whispers being aimed my way, and I ignored them. I knew how hard I'd worked, what I'd put up with; I knew I had more than earned the right to be on the course *and that* I had done enough to be awarded the Baton. I continued to gently push my way through the throng, stopping to smile and say thank you to those who were normal enough to congratulate me with a smile and a pat on the back. Between the gaps in the bodies collected in the bar, I saw Gareth and my stomach flipped.

We had both circled the sticky topic of what would happen when we left. Yes, we'd lain together, naked and post-coital, talking about how we were going to help the good people, lock up the bad, weed out corruption wherever we saw it, but that was post-sex talk. It was talking while we were dressed and unbefuddled that caused us to grow shy and mute and to dance around each other. He'd broken first, though. Had asked if we could keep in touch, meet up and see where it took us. I'd said yes, of course, and now we were here, the end of the road, ready to go forth. I wanted to clink a glass with him to mark the end, start the future.

My group of friends were standing in a slightly out-of-shape circle formation by the hollow of the unlit fireplace, pint glasses in hands, relaxed and relieved, euphoric and ecstatic. As I arrived at the edge of the group, I saw faces fall. It took less than a second to find out why: Duke. He was holding court, the alpha male at the centre of things, imparting his wit and wisdom in the form of a joke. It was this particular joke that made people's faces fall.

Everyone else's faces fell, but his lit up. He held my eye and raised his voice as he continued to tell his 'funny' story that was designed to remind everyone how much he hated me and my 'kind'.

Heat. The heat was back. Not the sweaty, tropical heat that surrounded me. Not the heat that ignited whenever I was with Gareth. The heat of humiliation, the burning pain of listening to what Duke was saying and having no one step in. They all stared into their pints, stared at their feet, stared at anything other than me.

When he was done, had paraded his 'punchline' and laughed at his own joke, loudly, heartily for an extended period, Duke raised his pint glass to his face and then spoke to me: 'Didn't you think that was funny, *Cee-Dee*?' he asked. 'Don't be so sensitive, sweetheart. It was only a joke. You can take a joke, can't you?' Right beside him was Gareth. His eyes were on his feet, his head so low I could see the blond whorl of the crown of his head, his mouth so firmly shut it was hard to believe that I'd ever heard him speak. I glanced around the group of friends, all of them with their heads lowered and their mouths shut.

I looked again at Gareth while Duke grinned and sipped his pint. I breathed in, as far as I could. Smiled at Duke with the same victorious smile he was aiming at me, and then walked away. I could feel the crowd closing up behind me, almost as though I had never been there. They'd forget about me soon enough, I realised. Even Gareth.

9:25 a.m. 'Cece, I really am sorry,' says Gareth. 'I have felt sick about it ever since. When I heard you'd left the force, I was devastated. Believe me, I haven't done anything like that since. Not once.

Any hint of that sort of racist crap, no matter who it's by, and I speak up, speak out. I've got myself into a lot of bother over the years with it, I've been more or less told I haven't been promoted as much because of it, that I'm not going to go any further than this, but I don't ever back down.'

'Good for you,' I tell him. 'But just so you know, you don't get hero points for not ignoring racists because it's not you who's been targeted. Speaking up and not backing down is what all decent human beings do as standard.'

He closes his eyes and screws up his mouth. He used to do that when he was trying not to say something. I used to suspect that he did that when he was trying to not confess that he'd fallen in love with me. But that could have been my utter naïvety and arrogance. I mean, no one stands there and lets someone they love be abused. 'I know,' he eventually says. 'I thought you were made of stronger stuff though. I didn't think you'd give it all up because of him.'

'That's just it, Gareth, I didn't give it all up because of him. I could handle him and people like him. I left because of you. And all my other "friends" who listened to what he was saying and did nothing.'

July, 2001

I resigned the next day. It was a little more complicated than I thought it would be, but they didn't really try to stop me. My commanding officer asked me why and I could have said: *Yes, yes, me walking away from all that I've worked for the last four months could be seen as letting people like Duke 'win' but it's not about that. Duke is Duke is Duke. People like him are a pound a dozen. There are vocal racists all around me. But those other people, the ones who looked at their feet and closed up their mouths? They were meant to be my friends. I had thought all this time that if he did in public what he'd been doing to me in private, everyone would berate him, defend me. But no, it wasn't quite like that with my 'friends'. If even one of them, just one of them, had said something – even a 'shut up, mate' would have done – I wouldn't be resigning. I would stick around because I would believe that my* friends *would be there when I needed them. As it is, they all listened and said nothing. They didn't laugh, no, but they didn't say anything or walk away from him; they stood there and waited for me to leave.*

I could have also said to him: *And I'm good at learning, sir. I was given the Baton because I excelled in academic achievement, so I know what could happen next. Those people, my friends, the ones who I would be relying on for backup, have shown me they're not capable of it. So I don't have to walk into an actual life-threatening situation and learn that lesson the hard way. So, I'm going to leave, not only because Duke is a vile little specimen, but because I saw very clearly how my 'friends' didn't and probably never would back me up.*

I could have said all that to him. Instead I smiled sweetly (that's kind of what he expected female officers to do when in his presence but not 'out there' amongst the public) and said, 'I've realised that this isn't the job for me after all, sir.'

He stared at me with inquisitive grey-blue eyes. 'Has something happened, Baswale? Something you're too frightened to tell me about?'

'No, sir. I'm not frightened of anything.' The absolute truth.

'I genuinely wish you'd change your mind, but you have to make the right decision for yourself.'

'Thank you, sir,' I replied.

9:35 a.m. 'You live in Brighton?' I say to Gareth. I still have no idea what he wants.

'Yes.'

'Wife? Kids?'

He shakes his head. 'Married to the job, me. Think I always was.' He takes his time to meet my eye. Heat. It radiates between us again. We stare at each other, almost like we're back in that canteen all those years ago, staring and knowing we could be so good together. Staring and fantasising about what could happen.

'It's the job I wanted to talk to you about, actually,' he eventually says. 'I need your help.'

'*My help?* I'm a data entry supervisor,' I say to him. 'How can I possibly help you?'

'We both know you're not a data entry supervisor,' Gareth replies. 'We both know that's what you tell people as a cover for what you really do.'

'You make me sound like a spy,' I say. I talk plainly, simply, disguising my heart fluttering, trying not to let on that I'm panicked – if he knows what I really did in London, then he must know all about my daughter.

He smiles. 'Some people might say you are.'

'Why have you been checking up on me?' I ask. There is an edge to my voice now. He must know about Harmony – that Sol isn't her biological father, that in the space on her original birth certificate under 'Father' it says: 'Unknown'. I know who her father is, of course I do. But Gareth doesn't.

He sighs. 'I haven't been checking up on you as such. I saw you talking to someone the other day, and I had a bit of a shock, then I got a bit nostalgic, wanted to see what you were up to.'

Who on Earth was I talking to that would make him reignite this acquaintance? If he just saw me in passing, then he'd maybe send an email, but to come here and start talking about help with his work . . . I barely know anyone down here. The only people he could have seen me talking to were . . . 'Is this about Yvonne Whidmore?'

He sits back and nods almost triumphantly. 'You always were two steps ahead of the rest of us,' he says.

'So it *is* about her? Well, I don't know why you're asking me – I moved here after she was attacked. Never met her before.'

'Yes, but you know her friends.'

Maxie, Hazel and Anaya. 'So?'

'It's a bit like you've taken her place in the group, actually.'

'How can you know that unless you've . . . ? You've been watching them? *Why?*'

'Come on, Cece, you're the smart one. Why do you think?'

'You think one of them did it?'

He says nothing, simply stares at me.

'Really?' I repeat: '*Really?*' when he doesn't reply. 'Oh, please. I don't believe that for one second. Have you actually properly met them? None of them would harm a fly. And I mean that literally – I've seen Anaya practically break her neck to free a fly rather than kill it.'

'Cece, it's true. One of those three women tried to kill Yvonne Whidmore. And I want you to help us find out which one.'

October, 2001

I sat on the bed of my little bedsit and stared at the white stick, sitting like a ticking bomb on the other side of the room. I couldn't see its results window from here – my room wasn't *that* small – but I didn't really need to. I bunched my fingers together and pressed them firmly over my lips.

I had a passenger on board.

This little passenger was unexpected. I'd been sitting in the same position for over an hour and I still hadn't worked out if said passenger was unwelcome as well as unexpected.

I thought about my life: I had no proper job, having walked away from the one thing I'd wanted to do most of my life. In the stark light of day, the aftermath of a positive pregnancy test, it was clear I could be breathtakingly immature, selfish and reckless. All things that would need to change if I was going to become a mother. But, wow, I had a passenger on board. The idea of it was pretty darn amazing.

9:45 a.m. 'That would be no,' I say to Gareth.

'No? You are seriously saying no to helping us investigate this?'

'Us? Oh, right. I get it, you spot a picture of me talking to three suspects in an investigation and you say in your best accent: "Don't worry, lads and lasses, I'll get her to help us. I'll rock up, remind her of what we shared, apologise for letting her down, flash my accent at her, and then she'll be putty in our hands. Putty, I tell you. Just leave it to me." Is that the sort of thing you said to them?' I'm being a little unfair – he hasn't exactly flashed me his accent and he didn't realise that his accent was one of the things I liked most about him.

'No, but that's what you're going to think no matter what I say, isn't it?' Gareth replies.

'Yeah, pretty much.'

Gareth rubs at the centre of his forehead with his forefinger and studies me for a few moments. Slowly he runs his hand through his hair. 'Cece, you should help us. It's nothing to do with me; I'm just the person making contact, a familiar face, if you will. I can get you to talk to someone else if you'd prefer. But I think you should help us.'

'Why would I?'

'Because it's the right thing to do.'

'It's the right thing to do to spy on my friends then sneak back and tell on them? To be disloyal and backstabbing? Not generally how I conduct friendships.'

'I remember how important justice and doing the right thing were to you when we were training. And you say you haven't changed so why wouldn't you do this? I mean, someone tried to kill Yvonne Whidmore and they didn't succeed. If she wakes up, they may try it again. What's to say they won't try and kill someone else? I can't see how you'd live with yourself if you don't help.'

'I think you're wrong. I've spent time with these women, I know them. None of them are capable of it.'

'Wouldn't you have said the same thing about me all those years ago? That I wasn't capable of doing and saying nothing while someone was horrible to you?'

I draw back, stunned. 'Wow. I can't believe you've used one of the worst experiences of my life against me like that. That takes a special kind of arseholery.'

'I'm sorry, I'm sorry. But doesn't your upset at that kind of prove my point? You never really know how dangerous a person is, not even your friends.'

'True enough,' I concede. 'But I'm not helping you.'

'At least think about it.'

'No.' I push my coffee cup away, across the table, not quite imping-ing on his part of the table but close to it. A boundary I am erecting around my life. Of course I'm going to think about it. Not the help-ing him and his police buddies bit, but how can I not think about the accusation? The fact that they are so convinced about this they are following them, trying to recruit spies to help their cause, says a lot. I mean, these are the women who have welcomed me into their fold and made me one of their own, but the police think one of them could do something as extreme as nearly killing someone. Not even accidentally. With intent. That could, technically – well, not technically, that could *actually* put my family at risk.

If I am honest, too, the way they have been behaving is really weird. They are all of them on edge. After the phone call business the other night, they kept exchanging looks, unspoken worries they thought I didn't notice. If I look at the pattern of behaviour of my new friends, things only add up properly, make a full and complete pattern, if you place what Gareth has said at its centre. That then becomes the piece that every part of the pattern grows from.

I could be friends with someone dangerous. But aren't we all? Aren't we all capable of being dangerous under a particular set of circumstances? If you are threatened, for instance. If someone is planning on hurting you or someone you love, wouldn't that make you deadly? There's a difference between reactive dangerous behaviour, when you're trying to protect yourself or someone else, and planning it. Planning it and *then doing it*. Gareth hasn't actually said which type of dangerous he thinks my new friends are.

I slip my hands into the armholes of my leather jacket, appalled that this is now in my head. For the first time in what feels like years, I have friends who I haven't met through work and who I talk to about things not related to children and school. For the first time in what feels like years, I have proper friends. Now I have to worry that one of them may be a killer. Thanks, Gareth.

9:55 a.m. 'So I hear you have a teenage daughter,' Gareth says.

I continue to shrug on my jacket and take care not to sit back, not to slump, not to tense. This is a man who is trained in interrogation techniques, who is trained to spot any change in demeanour that will give someone away. The whole time we have been talking, he has probably been studying my responses to the different types of questions: *Does she hold her breath when she's angry? Does she twirl her hair when she's thinking? Does she sit back when she wants to distance herself from the truth? Does she look directly into my face when she wants to hurt me?*

I've been spectacularly stupid. Yes, he probably is trying to get me to help him with the Yvonne Whidmore case. But the chat beforehand, that was so he could relearn my 'tells'. No one liked to play card games with Gareth at Hendon – he almost always won because he was so naturally good at reading people and using it against them.

'What of it?' I say, looking him directly in the eye.

'How old is she again?'

'I'm sure you wouldn't be asking if you didn't already know the answer to that question.'

'All right. So this question I don't know the answer to: is she?'

I keep eye contact, necessary so he doesn't make any assumptions about me, doesn't get anything from any of my 'tells'. 'Is she my daughter who I'm not going to talk to you about? Yes.'

Heat is creeping through my body, spreading out from the painful throbbing at the centre of my stomach; it pumps through my veins, causes sweat to break out over my top lip, my forehead. It speeds up my breathing, makes my heart skip beats in its race to keep me calm.

'Is she my daughter?' he asks.

'No.'

He takes a moment to allow my answer to settle, like shaken flour over a bread-kneading surface before he throws down the dough and starts to work at it. 'I don't believe you.'

'I can't do anything about that.'

'The timings are too close.'

'If you say so.'

'No, I don't say so – your daughter's date of birth and the last time we were together say so. Unless you were sleeping with someone else at the same time.'

'Is that a question?'

How would I hold up under a real police interrogation? Obviously we learnt all about it in training, we did role play, we were fake criminals who were being interrogated, and we learnt how to get the

150

answers, the truthful answers, but in the real thing, how would I stand up? Especially if I wasn't telling the whole truth.

'No, that wasn't a question. This is: were you sleeping with someone else at the same time as you were sleeping with me?'

I keep eye contact, keep my body in the exact same position as earlier. I mustn't give anything away. He only needs to know what I tell him, nothing more. 'No,' I say.

'So, I'll ask you again: is she my daughter?'

'*My* daughter is not your daughter.'

'All right . . .' Two spots of colour appear in his cheeks, betraying him, showing how frustrated he really is under his cool, rational exterior. I wonder if he ever loses it like this in real interrogation situations, or if it's only reserved for the people he's slept with. 'Did I father your daughter? Was it my sperm that helped to create her?'

'No.'

'I don't believe you. Tell me who her father is and I'll let this drop.'

'If I haven't told her, what makes you think I'm going to tell you, who has absolutely nothing to do with it? And,' I twist my body out of the seat and stand up, 'you'll let this drop anyway. I've told you all you need to know. It's not my problem if you don't believe me.'

'Cece,' he says, his voice back to normal, out of interrogation mode. 'I'm sorry, I shouldn't have come on all heavy. Please, at least say you'll think about what I asked you about helping us? Please?'

I shake my head. I wonder if his gall, his blatant, in-your-face guts, is what has got him as far up the food chain as he has got. Despite what he says, he is a detective sergeant in CID. I've more than thought about Gareth over the years – I've kept an eye on him. Every so often I do a search, seeing where he has got to in life. I knew he was here in Brighton. And that was one of the reasons why I didn't want to move here. I wasn't sure it would be big enough for me not to run into him and start all the mess that would bring. 'No, Gareth, I won't think about it because I'm not going to do it. Have a nice life.'

'See you later,' he says. For a moment, I'm sure it sounds like *Screw you later,* like he used to say all those years ago.

Part 5

TUESDAY

Anaya

4:10 a.m.

Can't sleep. Feel so awful about everything. I thought it'd get easier but it's not. Mx

I feel dreadful, too. H x

Did it even happen? I keep thinking it didn't. A x

Me too. It's like it happened and I was just there watching it. M x

I started it, do you think they'll come down hardest on me? H xxx

I shoved her too. A x

And I ended it. M x Oh God, what did we do? Xxx

Let's just go to the police. H x

I can't. For other reasons, I just can't. Believe me, I would if I could. M x

Me too. If I could, I would . . . I hate this. I hate this so much.
Look, I have to go. I can't cope with this. I'm going to try
to go back to sleep. Suggest you both do the same. A xx

I know, you're right. Night. H x

I press the off button on my phone, wait for it to go dark in my office. I'm not going to sleep. How can I sleep? I just can't talk about it any more. Especially if Hazel is going to start on again about going to the police. Slowly, I lift the lid of my laptop and log on. I'll do some work. Take my mind off things. Sanj will be up soon to go to London and I can focus on getting him on the road. Then I'll focus on getting the kids ready and on the road. Then I'll go to yoga. That will take me up till ten o'clock? After that, I will come back and do some work. Focus on that, make some calls, drum up some new business. By then it will be pick-up time. If I do that, if I divide up my day, I'll have less time to dwell, to worry, to fret, to make myself ill contemplating things that will most likely never happen.

Maxie

11 p.m. I stand in front of Ed, obscuring his view of the television. I want him to talk to me. Properly talk to me. I want a way to reach out to him and have him respond. I need to speak to someone and I can't talk to Anaya or Hazel because things are already too fraught with them. I keep wanting to talk to Cece to hear what my secret sounds like out loud and to see what the reaction is from a normal person. I can't do that, so Ed is the only person left. I need to speak to someone and that person is Ed. That's what being married is meant to be about.

'Max, I can't see the TV,' he says.

'That's the point,' I reply.

He stops trying to look through and around me and focuses on my face instead.

'Hi,' I say and smile.

He looks suspicious, on edge. 'Hi?' he says cautiously. I'm glad the only light in the room comes from the flickering of the television so I can't see all the expressions on his gorgeous face.

I drop down to my knees so we're closer in height. I rest my forearms on his thighs and I ignore the way he tenses, as if he's repulsed by my touch. 'How was your day?' I ask him.

Ed's features are guarded. He doesn't know what to do, how to react. 'Fine, I suppose. How was your day?'

'I missed you,' I tell him. I did. I do. I miss the him that I met all those years ago. The him who I thought might one day kiss me. The him who might one day fall in love with me. My husband takes a deep breath in, releases it very slowly, measuredly. He's trying to work out how to deal with me. I haven't been like this with him before. I'm desperate, though. I'm desperate to connect with him and I'll do it in any way I can.

Nothing. He says nothing.

I'm panicking now. I don't know what to do but panic. There has to be a way to make this better. I know he still blames me after all this time, but I want him to forgive me. To love me. I reach for his belt, then his button, then his zip. He doesn't move, doesn't react, just continues to watch my face.

'You don't have to do this,' he eventually says when he's free and I'm about to lower my head. 'I don't expect any of this.'

He gasps loudly, loses his fingers in my hair, sits back and lets me pleasure him. Of course I have to do this. I have to do this and everything else so that one day, he'll forgive me.

March, 2006
'It pains me, really pains me to know that my affection for you is, at its heart, completely narcissistic,' Bronwyn said to me.

'I don't understand.' I was helping her to clear up after another of her fabulous dinner parties. We had all sat around the table, talking and drinking and eating excellent food, and I had felt like one of them. The other guests had all gone to top universities, they worked in amazing jobs and had breathtaking houses, but they hadn't patronised me. I was a girl who worked as an au pair and babysitter to save up enough money to do a master's degree, but they had talked to me like I was one of them, they'd discussed big theories and assumed I understood, they'd asked my opinion, they'd laughed at some of my jokes. They had acted like I was one of them and the effect it had had was a little like drinking too much – I'd spent a lot of time grinning to myself, feeling swirly headed and hoping that I didn't say anything stupid.

'I mean, I like you so much because you remind me of myself when I was your age, which makes me a borderline narcissist, I think.'

'I think you need other traits for that to be true.'

'I'm sure they're there, you simply haven't seen them yet,' she said. 'Which leads rather into something I wanted to talk to you about.'

She set down the pile of plates she was stacking and then pulled out a seat, and indicated I should do the same. Ed stood in the doorway, watching us. I sat, feeling a sense of dread creeping up inside me.

'I'm not sure if you know this, but we actually live in a cottage up in Cumbria most of the time. We borrow this London place from our friends if we need to be down here. We're heading back to Cumbria soon – I have a new book to work on for the next few months. Plus, there's a lecture series I have to compile and I've been talking to a television production company about a few new ideas.'

Gutted. Gutted. Dot. Com. 'Oh, right,' I said.

The past few months had been fantastic. Almost surreal in how amazing they were. I'd learnt so much, felt so mature, and I didn't want to think it would all be over when she left. I adored her. She was like the sun. I came alive around her; she brought out feelings and ideas in me that I didn't know were possible. Every so often she would say something, lightly touch me, or glance at me in a particular way that would make me want to kiss her. And now she was leaving me, in dull, grey London, which had only become so bright and vibrant because of her.

'Don't sound so pleased for me, eh?' she teased.

'I *am* pleased for you,' I said. 'I'm also a bit sad – I'll miss you.'

'Not if you come with us you won't.'

'Pardon me?'

'I need a research assistant for the lecture series and Ed would need lots of admin support, won't you, Ed?'

I turned to look at him and he pulled a smile that seemed tinged with sadness across his face. 'Yes,' he said.

'So,' Bronwyn continued, 'you could be that. It'd be up to a year initially, possibly longer. We'd pay a decent wage and you could live with us – we've got a big old farmhouse that's a bit in the middle of nowhere – or we could find you somewhere to stay in the nearest village and you could come over every day, if you think it'd be too weird living with and working for us. What do you say? Would you be possibly interested?'

I wondered again if I was still asleep in the nursery, if I was about to wake up very suddenly with a bad taste in my mouth and Mrs Ledbetter telling me off for not waking up when the baby started crying. I waited a few minutes, allowed myself the time to slowly and carefully wake up, but nothing. I even closed my eyes and opened them, waiting for the moment when all of this would fall away and I would be an au pair, asleep on the job.

As time ticked on and Bronwyn kept her gaze and smile on me, I accepted I was awake. This was happening. I had the chance of the most amazing adventure. I could save my money, go and do a master's degree.

'Can I think about it?' I asked her.

'Of course!' she said with a grin. 'But I think we'd have a lot of fun, the three of us. A lot of fun.'

11:15 p.m. 'I'm going to bed. Are you coming?' I ask Ed.

He won't look at me. He can't look at me. Whichever it is, he's keeping his gaze on the television, the redness in his cheeks bright and alarming. He's embarrassed at what I've just done to him, how much he enjoyed it when he wants to avoid me.

'Soon,' he says. 'I'll, erm, be up soon.'

Tears are clouding up my eyes, tightening my throat. 'OK. OK. Don't be too long.'

'I won't.'

He's going to sleep on the sofa. I know that. He'll sleep on the sofa, he'll get up at five o'clock and he'll go to work. He'll leave me here alone with Frankie, when he knows all I want is to be with him, too.

WEDNESDAY

Hazel

12:55 p.m. I stand in the kitchen because it's easier to think about what to make for dinner. They were at Walter's last night, which means when I collect them from school tonight I probably won't get all their uniform back (even though he won't contribute to the – astronomical – cost of it); they may have brushed their hair and washed their faces, if Camille stopped being eight and a half and became an adult to do it; and they'll have had lunch at school because he won't have made them packed lunches even though he refuses to pay for lunch. *Breathe, Hazel, breathe. It's all right. They enjoy their midweek time with him.* Actually, they don't always, but I tell myself that to make myself feel better for sometimes forcing them to go. Walter doesn't realise that the contempt he has for me often spills over into contempt for them and they hate him for it. But I have to make them go because they do mostly enjoy their time with him. Also, Walter is very good at playing the victim. My real friends knew the truth, but while I was still reeling and crying and begging him to give me another chance, he was able to get out there with his story first.

And people usually believe the first story they hear. In Walter's case: nagging shrew of a wife who spent money like it was going out of fashion, who made him cheat, and who is now raking it in with maintenance while simultaneously blocking his access to the children. If only the people who believed him knew. If only they could read some of the texts he still sends; if only they could be a fly on the wall to hear some of the things he tells the kids. If only they could see how his nastiness still has them crying and tantrumming for hours after they come home to me because they have no other way to let out the negative emotions they've had when with him. If only. If only. If only. If only. If only.

I sometimes think I live with 'if only' embroidered into every element of my life.

'Hello, gorgeous,' Ciaran says as he comes up behind me. His warm arms slip around my waist and his face nestles against my neck, in that space that's made for someone you love.

October, 2016

I read a book once that said women who sat alone at the bars in hotels were looking for 'business'. Prostitutes, basically. At the time, I thought the book was over the top, that the person who wrote it had no clue. That women who sat alone in hotel bars weren't *all* sex workers. But, it seemed that a lot of the men in this hotel had read the same book – they kept eyeing me up, raising an eye, tilting their heads suggestively. I stared through them, repulsed. I mean seriously, I was wearing my building society work uniform suit, I had a space where my name badge clipped on, I had on sensible shoes. What more did I have to do to tell all these losers that I wasn't interested? Or working. Or whatever.

I decided to finish the glass of wine sitting in front of me, and then go sit in my hotel room for the rest of the night. The room was so tiny, it felt like it was closing in on me and I couldn't really breathe, which was why I'd decided to come and sit here. To (apparently) be ogled by men who should have known better.

'Can I buy you a drink?' a voice said beside me.

I inhaled crossly, and sat up straight before I turned to the man who had spoken to me. *Wow, he's handsome* – neatly cut brown hair, buttermilk-pale skin, eyes a sparkling blue. I was thrown for a minute, surprised that someone that good-looking was talking to me. Then I remembered why he was talking to me, why he was offering me a drink. 'No!' I replied sharply. 'Thank you!' I added because I had to. Even if he was a sleaze, it shouldn't make me forget my manners. I tipped my nose in the air and turned back to the bar, and stared at the row of bottles lined up in front of the smoky mirror.

'OK, sorry I asked. Didn't meant to offend you,' he said.

I tipped my nose even higher, picked up my drink and sipped it. I wasn't going to speak to him again. Men like him didn't deserve to have decent people speak to them. He probably thought it was all right to do that sort of thing while away from home. And to other people it probably was. But not to me. Especially since it'd come out that all those cash withdrawals on the bank statements over the years hadn't been signs that Walter was a spendthrift, but were actually evidence of Walter using the services of sex workers while away on business. Although, towards the end of our marriage, it hadn't even been while he was away.

'I don't think you're a hooker, by the way,' the man said to me. He said this at a normal level so the barman heard and turned to look at him, then at me. The barman seemed surprised that it might have even occurred to him I was one, although I didn't know whether to be offended by that or not. 'I was just offering to buy you a drink. From one lonely business traveller to another.'

'I'm not lonely,' I said to him without turning in his direction. 'I'm just trying to have a drink. I have a lot of reading to do for my course, and I just needed a drink and some fresher air before I headed back up. I don't actually have time to be lonely.' I was loving my new job in the building society down in George Street near our house. It was more than just the ten-minute commute from the school gates to work; it was the being among adults, being spoken to like a human being, having the freedom to spend money as I wanted to. When they'd suggested me going on a training course so I could maybe move up the ladder I'd jumped at the chance. I'd arranged it so the course fell on the night Walter usually had the children, and Yvonne was to collect them on the following night for a sleepover.

'Why would you think I was a hooker?' I said to the man beside me. 'I don't look like one. And it is 2016 – women are allowed to sit on their own in bars without a man, you know.'

'I know that,' he said. I could see in the reflection of the smoky bar mirror that he was smiling at me. 'I also know that the high-class "business ladies", as a Japanese friend of mine calls them, are always very good-looking, very confident and very well dressed.' He looked around the room. 'That's probably why all the men keep staring at you. It's not because they think you're a "business" lady, but because they know you're *not*. You have all those things – the looks, the confidence and the sense of style – but you're so obviously not. And they haven't got the guts to come talk to you.'

My goodness, he was spinning me a line, but it was a good one. A 24-carat-gold one that made me feel warm and fluttery inside. I hadn't felt like that in such a long time. It was such a good line, I gave my head a wobble (as Maxie often said), reminded myself that talk was cheap. One night away from my kids, wine, a compliment or two . . . it could lead anywhere. 'Good line,' I said without looking at him.

'Good? Not great?'

I shook my head. Stupid though it was, now he'd said it, I did feel more confident. I felt like more than the frumpy, chaotic mess who lurched from one day to another, grateful that she got it right 90 per cent of the time. I felt like a proper human being. An adult. I felt like that person I had been chasing all those years in my marriage when I'd wanted a job, when I'd wanted to remember what it was like to go for a few hours without having a small person hanging off me, or worrying about if they were being looked after properly if they weren't hanging off me. Suddenly I realised that it didn't matter if all these men were looking at me thinking I was a prostitute, I should be savouring every second of being me, existing for the simple reason of existing. Not waiting for washing to finish, not waiting for meals to cook, not waiting for work to finish, not waiting for pick-up time, not waiting for the alarm to go off and start another day. Not even waiting for the end of a glass of wine to go back to my room and read over my course notes. Right then, in a hotel in Essex, I was a human. Being. Simply, being.

'Not a great line,' I said to him. 'But I'm sure you can work on that.' I drained my glass and then placed it in front of him. 'And you can buy me that drink while you work on it.' Confident is as confident does. Yvonne had been trying to drum that into me all these years. I finally understood what she meant.

'My name's Ciaran,' he said as he gave the nod to the barman.

'Hazel,' I said.

'Hazel,' he repeated. 'I've never met a Hazel before.'

'I've never met a Ciaran before,' I replied. 'Tell me, Ciaran, are you married?'

'No, ma'am,' he said with a smile and a shake of his head. 'I most certainly am not married. Nor otherwise engaged.'

I grinned at him. He clearly knew what I had in mind.

'Will I see you again?' Ciaran asked the next morning. Every part of my body had been brought to life with having sex with him. Every part of me throbbed with the pleasurable ache of having been explored, caressed, stroked, licked, sucked and fucked. I'd forgotten what it was like to have sex outside of the covers, to feel confident enough to have those silvery stretch-mark lines, reminders of the years of carrying children, on display. I'd forgotten what it was like to not wonder if the man I was naked with was revolted by the shapes and sags that made up my body as my ex-husband had constantly told me he was. Whereas Ciaran, he seemed to delight in every part of my physical form.

We were in his hotel suite – 'opulent', I think the appropriate word was to describe it. From its separate rooms to its huge bed to its antique-looking furniture, it was awash with luxury, wealth. It was a world away from my room on the lower floors, a galaxy away from rolling over in the night to find my bed had been invaded by younger children while confident head lice strolled across the pillow looking for the next head to infest. Even on those very rare occasions that I'd travelled with Walter, we hadn't stayed in places like this. He would never have spent that cash. But Ciaran didn't seem to be flash, or to want me to be impressed – he'd asked me after I leant across and kissed him in the bar a few hours earlier if I wanted to see his hotel room and we'd come up here.

'You said you live up in Durham, I live in Brighton, it's not like we're only a few towns over,' I replied, a little cruelly, I realised. But seeing him again, although a nice idea, was a fantasy.

'I can afford to visit you, you know. But only if it's what you want. I don't want you to feel at all pressured, so if you'd rather it stayed like this, I'd be sad, but I'd accept it. Things like distance, though, they don't need to come into this. Just decide if you want to see me again, and we'll work it out if you do.'

'The thing is, Ciaran, I'm not sure. My life is so complicated; I'm not sure.'

'I understand,' he replied sadly. 'OK, I said I would accept it. So this is me accepting it – apart from giving you my number. I won't ask for yours, but I will give you mine so if you ever change your mind, call me and I'll come to see you.'

'OK,' I said to him. Knowing that I wouldn't. I just couldn't call him. My life was too complicated. Would Ciaran want me if he knew the real me? Ciaran, who was sophisticated, educated, gorgeous, was not looking for a woman in my position. 'If I ever change my mind, I'll call you.' Of course I wouldn't.

1 p.m. 'Hello, you. I didn't hear you get back,' I say.

'I got the early train because I missed you so much. I have missed you all so much.'

Ciaran's body is firm, solid, but also welcoming and comforting. So different from Walter's body, which was doughy but unyielding – as though, in those moments when he couldn't do anything but let me be close to him, his body was as keen as his mind was to keep me away, apart, separate. It's only looking back now that I can see all those little instances where he told me by his actions, by his physical coldness towards me, that he felt nothing but contempt for me. I shudder a little as I remember how I used to twist myself into all sorts of knots to try to make him want me, appreciate me, to even act like he didn't hate my very existence in this world.

'You OK, babe?' Ciaran asks in response to my shudder.

'Yes, I'm fine, I'm fine,' I reply. 'Just a little flashback to the past.'

Ciaran kisses my neck and tugs me closer to him, reminding me of how physical he is, how physical we are. With Walter, I started to think I had no sex drive at all. Since he left, since Ciaran, I've discovered that my sex drive issues have virtually evaporated. I can feel Ciaran against me, growing hard.

Without meaning to, I sort of sigh and moan. I love this. *This.* That moment of suspension between the bubbling up of desire and the sliding into being physical. I love to be held here, the physical feelings matching the swirling in my veins, in my head. It's like a suspension in time when I feel alive. It's like I am fully aware of every part of my body, every cell, every synapse firing. I feel like I am connected to everything, tethered to nothing; I am an elemental part of the universe.

Ciaran's hands slide up my green work pencil skirt and his thumbs hook into my knickers on either side of my hips. He tugs them down until they naturally fall away. He pulls my skirt down into place again and pauses. I know what he's thinking. He's told me often enough – he wishes that I would go to work knickerless so he can imagine me, sitting there, talking to customers about their accounts, giving them money, listening to their tales of woe and know that he could come in at any time . . .

I gasp as his fingers bring me back to where we were. I can feel him unbuttoning and unzipping his trousers, pulling them down.

'Condom,' I whisper as he gently pushes me forwards.

'We don't need one, remember?' He punctuates those five words with kisses on the nape of my neck.

'Ciaran—'

'I've been living here three months now and we said we'd try, didn't we?' he cuts in. While he talks he gently, but definitely, opens my legs. 'You want us to have a baby, don't you?' he adds. I gasp as he slips his fingers back into me. 'Don't you?' he repeats.

'Yes,' I breathe.

His mouth moves up into a smile against my neck and he barely hesitates before he pushes in, groaning as he does so. I sigh, almost in relief that he still wants me, that the desire that has been winding itself up through my veins is being satisfied. Before I let go, slide into being with Ciaran, the absolute love of my life, my eyes flick guiltily to the wall cupboard to the right. On the top shelf, pushed quite far back, behind the tins of peaches and black-eyed beans, there is my bottle of one-a-day 'vitamins'. When Ciaran started talking about having a child and convinced me to go off the Pill so we could use condoms and then maybe try for a baby, I was all for it. For about five seconds. I couldn't do it. I just couldn't. For so many reasons, I couldn't. I told him. I explained all the reasons why. Almost all. There was one that I didn't want to think about, but the reasons he heard, the worries he listened patiently to, he understood. But at the end of the day, he loved me. He saw his future with me. And he wanted us to have a child together. A baby he could watch growing inside me, then growing more outside of me. A child that was half me, half him. A child we wouldn't have to live without one night in the week, every other weekend, and almost half the holidays. Once I was pregnant, we could talk about marriage if that was what I wanted. He made it sound so possible, so easy, uncomplicated, *perfect*. I saw my future with him, of course I did. And when he watched as I chucked my supply of the Pill into the bins on the day the bin men came to collect them, I knew I was doing the right thing. That this was what we wanted and what my family needed – a stable, kind, generous, loving man who was connected to us by blood.

And I feel horrible about it. Yes, I really do. But I'm not going to think about what Yvonne suggested I do back when Walter wanted a fourth and I didn't – empty out a bottle of vitamins and replace them with my new prescription of the Pill. It really isn't like it was with Walter, though. Ciaran only wants a baby because he loves me, so I'm not going to think about that bottle of vitamins. Instead, I'm going to concentrate on this quick, before school run fun with the love of my life. And I will tell him one day soon.

3:25 p.m. 'Any news on your friend Yvonne?' Ciaran asks.

We walk along the road towards the school. When he's here and

I'm here, we often do the afternoon school run. If I don't do half-days on Wednesday, he often comes to work. He takes a complete interest in me and my work and lots of the people there know him by name, to chat to. I know I have to stop comparing the two, but Walter would never have done that. He only ever came to events at the school – even the concerts – because he might see Yvonne. He liked her. He saw the alpha in her and wanted a bit of it for himself. Ciaran isn't like that.

February, 2017

'Are you hiding this new man of yours from me, Hazel Lannon?' Yvonne had cornered me at the gates on a Wednesday afternoon.

'Hello, Yvonne, nice to see you. Seeing as I just saw you for coffee a few hours ago.'

'Oh, please, don't "hello, Yvonne" me. I practically invented shaming your friends into social niceties so you can distract them from what you're hiding, OK? Why haven't we met your new fella yet?'

I'd never heard Yvonne use words like 'fella' before. It sounded almost ordinary coming from her.

'What's with all the sneaking around? I thought we were friends? I thought we told each other everything? Well, not everything, because that would be weird and totally stupid, but you know what I mean. Why are you keeping him a secret?'

Because he is mine, I wanted to say. I loved him so very much and he was mine and I didn't want to share all the fizzy, giddy excitement of being with him with anyone else. Not even Yvonne and the others. This was the first time in a long time that I had something – *someone* – who was all about me, all for me. With Ciaran, I didn't feel like poor Hazel. I wasn't single mum Hazel with the three kids whose ex-husband's favourite pastime was abusing her. When Ciaran was travelling hundreds of miles – sometimes just for an afternoon – to see me, and we spent that time in bed, having sex and talking, I was the woman he'd met in the hotel. It hadn't bothered him at all when I'd had to tell him that I had three children. He'd said no problem and we'd planned for him to visit when I had the house to myself and I wasn't at work. I liked not being pathetic single Hazel any more. Actually, I *loved* not being single any more. That he was good-looking and great in bed didn't hurt at all.

'There's no secrecy, Vonny, I just . . . you remember what it's like when you're first falling in love? How excited you are about every-thing and you just want to keep it close to your chest and not share any of it with anyone in case you jinx it?'

'No!' Yvonne said. 'I've never been like that. I tell people every-thing all the time. Hello! It's what friends do. You share.'

'But not this, you must see that. I don't know where it's going, so I don't want to talk too much about it. Especially when he might – *might* – be moving in this year sometime.'

'Wow! That is huge!' Yvonne said.

'I know, which is why I'm not talking about it. I don't want to jinx it.'

'Do Anaya and Maxie know about this?' she asked. Even now, years later, she was still convinced that we didn't like her as much as we did each other, that we didn't include her in *everything*. We did all we could to make sure she knew she was an integral part of our group, right down to helping out at Parents' Council events for her sake. None of us would normally get that involved, but we did. And still, when she had seen us dress up as bunnies and elves and, in Maxie's case, get dunked on one of the stalls at the summer fair, she still felt like an outsider.

'No!' I almost screeched, then remembered we were surrounded by other parents. 'No one knows about that because of what I just explained.'

'I want to meet him,' she said.

'Not going to happen.'

Yvonne screwed up her perfectly made-up lips and stared at me. 'All right, fine. But only for now. You have to let me meet him sometime.'

'And yes, you will. But not yet. Not yet, OK?'

'OK,' she replied. She wasn't happy about it, though. She wasn't happy at all.

*

3:30 p.m. I link my arm through Ciaran's, and snuggle close to him as we walk. I don't want to talk about Yvonne. Even obliquely. It's all too painful, this. From all of it, I didn't expect this pain. It's painful because I know the other two must blame me. They must. They were both shocked at what came out of my mouth that night. And if I hadn't started it then Anaya and Maxie wouldn't—

'Babe?' he asks when I don't speak.

'Hmmm?' I reply.

'Is there any news about your friend Yvonne?'

'No, I haven't heard anything,' I mumble.

We're about to turn into Plummer Place, where the school is, and he stops. He tugs me to a standstill and spins me so I am right in front of him. 'I hate that you fell out with her because of me,' he says.

'It wasn't about you.'

'Maybe, but if I hadn't told you about—' He stops talking and looks around, checking that no other person, no other *parent*, will hear what he is about to say. I slap my hand over his mouth. It's bad enough he had to tell me once; I don't need to hear it again.

'It's nothing to do with that,' I lie. 'It was a long time coming.'

'Maybe, and I don't know the ins and outs of it, and maybe it really is nothing to do with *what I told you*, but I still think you should go and see her.'

I shake my head. I don't think I can. I'd have to face Trevor, and the girls. After his texts and his calls, the way he keeps asking what was going on, I can't do that. I really can't.

'Just think about it, Haze. She was your friend for so long, you and her went through a lot together. Think about how bad you'll feel if she dies. Just think about it.'

What does he think I've been doing since 19th August? All I keep thinking is: *What if she dies?*

'OK,' I say to stop him talking about this. 'I'll think about it.'

'Good,' he says and smiles at me. 'Good.'

You wouldn't think that if you knew what she did, I decide as we carry on towards the school. *You wouldn't think that at all.*

FRIDAY

Cece

7:45 p.m. My dress – a tight, satin, jewel-blue creation that is ruched around the middle and stops just below my thighs – elicits a low wolf whistle from my husband when I enter our bedroom. He is in his dinner suit and stretched out on the bed, one arm behind his head, the other holding his mobile as he avidly reads something. He's reading the sports pages, of course. Or the news. Or something, anything other than whatever has set off the suspicious thrumming at the back of my mind. Since the 'T. B.H.' 'tell', since his grumpiness, since he seems to have forgotten how physically affectionate we usually are with each other everything Sol does sets off my suspicions. There is a new pattern of behaviour developing around Sol, and I do not like that idea.

In my old job, I was paid to be suspicious, but I always left it at my desk. It never infiltrated my life. Until now. Until Sol and I have not been getting on. When he is here, he's moody, snappy and disengaged. When he does speak to me, it's to make barbed comments about stuff not being picked up, there still being boxes that need unpacking, how I've managed to fill an entire day without actually having a pristine house. In response, I've bitten my tongue.

Sol presses the 'lock screen' button on his phone and, rather than toss it onto the bed like he normally would, he slips it into his inside jacket pocket.

'You look amazing,' he says after another wolf whistle. 'Give us a twirl then.'

I pause, wait for him to get his phone out to take a picture – and nothing. He puts his other arm behind his head and waits for me to perform for him. 'Go on, twirl. Nice and slow, though, so I can get a proper look at you.'

Downstairs, from the living room, I can hear the children, all three of them, talking loudly and excitedly to my mum. She's come down to babysit while we go to Sol's work's autumn ball. Apparently, with the amount of overseas employees they have, they find it virtually impossible to have a proper Christmas party in December, so they hold an event in early October to have a chance at the biggest number of people attending. The children are so happy to see Mum. They used to see her and Dad all the time in London, as my parents did a huge chunk of the childcare. Their voices carry all the way up here, each of them – Harmony included – wanting her attention and approval. I know they're especially excited because the other significant adult in their lives spends a lot of time either at work or growling at them.

'Go on,' Sol prompts again. 'Give us a twirl.' And there's something . . . He does this all the time when we get dressed up to go out. He lies on the bed waiting for me to finish getting ready and then asks me to twirl, to show him what I'm wearing so he can take a photo. It's nothing out of the ordinary, but this time it feels as though I am being asked to perform, somehow. Maybe it's the hitch of the eyebrow, the unfamiliar leer that is shading his lip, but this almost feels like I am on the receiving end of a voyeur's attentions. It's a ridiculous thought, of course. He's my husband, I'm not working in a strip club and having to display my body for an entitled man who has handed over cash to see me, but there's something . . . It's hard to put my finger on it; it's an imbalance, a shift that has occurred between us. I am being silly, I know that. Sol is still the same man I fell in love with, have been raising three children with, who I have trusted with almost all of my secrets. But I'm not going to twirl for him, not this time. Maybe not any other time. Not until I know what this shift is; and that hitch of the eyebrow, the hint of a leer on his lips, disappears.

I reach out and grab my white wrap from where it hangs like

a frozen waterfall over the end of our wooden-framed bed. 'We're going to be late,' I say. I avoid looking at him. I don't want to see the disappointment on his face, the result of rejecting something that was very much a part of who we were as a couple when we lived in London. We're not in London any more, and every day it's becoming more apparent that we're not that couple any more.

'What's the matter now?' he asks.

'Nothing. Why?'

'You just seem . . .'

'Seem what?' I ask. I'm still avoiding looking at him as I go to stand by the door. Or rather, I am still avoiding looking at the black, silk-lined pocket of his jacket where he slipped his mobile phone, his little box of secrets, out of sight.

'I don't know, distant?'

'No, probably more like nervous. I'm going to be meeting your very important new colleagues for the first time.'

'You have nothing to worry about,' he says. 'They really won't mind that you're a housewife. I'm pretty sure some of the other men have wives who don't work either.'

Excuse me? I do look at him then. 'Why would they mind that I'm a stay-at-home parent? Is looking after children, making sure there's always someone there when they get home, making sure they get fed and homeworked and put to bed, something to be ashamed of where you work?'

'I didn't mean it like that, Cee,' he replies.

'Shall we go before we're late?' I say to him, not acknowledging the non-apology.

In one move, Sol springs off the bed and comes to me, gently takes me by the elbow and turns me towards him. Carefully, as though he thinks I might break – or make a run for it if he makes any sudden moves – he loops his arms around me and stares at me until I am forced to look at him.

'You're not upset about what I said, are you?' he asks.

'Why would I be upset?' I reply.

He shrugs. 'You just seem a bit over-sensitive these days.' He says this gently, as though simply saying those words will light the touch-paper of my temper.

Sensitive. Right. You're rude but me minding is me being over-sensitive. 'We're going to be late,' I tell him. I break away from him and begin down the stairs. That now-familiar feeling of holding my tongue, trying to keep the peace at all costs, stomps repeatedly on my chest with every step I take.

SATURDAY

Cece

1:45 a.m. 'Keep your dress on while I fuck you,' Sol slurs once we've crept up through the house to our bedroom.

I haven't seen him this drunk in a very long time. His whole body is consumed by swathes of prosecco, wine, beer and whisky, and he has to lean against the bedroom door to stop himself swaying – actually, probably to stop himself falling over. I haven't drunk more than a glass and a half of prosecco, because I have to drive the boys to martial arts later. I'm aware that it's the drink making him irritating, but what about before he got drunk? What about that?

He didn't exactly cover himself in glory tonight. Apart from renaming me 'My Wife' to everyone he introduced me to so I had to follow up with 'Hi, I'm Cece', he revealed quite clearly what he currently thinks of me. At one point during dinner the CEO's wife, Brenda, asked, 'Do you work, Cece?'

'If you can call shopping and having coffee working, then Cece works very hard,' Sol replied and laughed. A couple of other men laughed but none of the women at the table did. Even when I worked full-time I wouldn't have laughed.

'No,' I said to Brenda, when the laughter stopped. 'I don't work outside of the home. That's to say I don't currently earn money for taking care of my kids and running the house and covering for the other parent.'

'Ah, yes, I remember those days well,' she replied wistfully. 'I remember that moment of *utter* frustration and *absolute* blinding fury when Rex would call me up and announce he was going away without a single thought as to what my plans might be. It was almost as if, because he earned the money, he had no respect for me and my time and thought I should be there waiting to define myself by whatever it was he was doing. Rex doesn't know this, but I often thought at moments like that that I had three choices: walk out and see how he'd cope with sorting out childcare and running the home; or smother him to death in his sleep. Obviously I went for option three – which was to put up with it. But it was touch and go a few times.'

Rex, her husband, froze in putting a sauce-covered prawn in his mouth and I felt Sol stiffen in shock beside me. After that Sol, for the most part, kept the barbed comments to a minimum and I scanned the room, looking for who could potentially be his 'T. B.H.' friend.

'I love that dress, keep it on while I fuck you,' he repeats in the dark of our bedroom. Funnily enough, now that I'm fully aware that Sol has minimal respect for me because I'm no longer earning money, I'm less inclined to have sex with him. I roll my eyes at him and start to cross the room to take off my clothes, when he grabs my wrist and pulls me back towards him. He moves his other hand to my waist and holds my body tightly against his. 'I said—'

'I heard what you said and no thank you.'

'Oh, why not?' he says. 'It's been months, Cee. *Months*. I think my balls are going to explode.'

'Yeah, well, good luck with that.'

'What is wrong with you now?' he snarls. 'I just want us to make love. We haven't done it in months. What is wrong with that?'

'Sol, I'm really very tired. I'm actually tired enough to climb into bed fully clothed right now, so no, I don't want sex.'

'You don't have to do anything, just lie there and I'll pull your dress down when I'm done.'

I rip my arm away and step back, absolutely revolted.

Even in his drunken state, he realises that what he said is out of order. He closes his eyes and then opens them again, squinting like he is expecting me to scream at him. 'I'm sorry. Shouldn't have said that. I was well out of order.'

'I'm going to pretend this whole conversation didn't happen,' I tell him. 'Now, please step aside so I can go to the bathroom. I really hope you're in bed pretending to be asleep by the time I get back.'

'I'm sorry, Cee,' he says while he stumbles away from the door. 'I'm sorry for being an arsehole tonight. I'll do better. I promise.'

You keep saying that. You keep saying that, but your pattern of behaviour is showing me that all you're going to do is keep getting worse.

9 a.m. This feels like middle-of-the-night o'clock. I feel hungover, my head is banging, my mouth is achy and dry, and my eyes are barely open. I didn't drink enough – a glass and a half of prosecco – to be in this state. I know the real reason why I'm tired and emotional: Sol. He wisely pretended to be asleep until I had left the house with the boys while Harmony was making cakes with Mum. *Oh Sol*, I can't help thinking. For him to say that when we both know he wasn't joking . . .

I take a sip of the coffee in front of me; it's not as nice as the stuff from Milk 'n' Cookees, but I haven't any other option. This café attached to the dojo is populated by people who look as shell-shocked as me while they wait for their children to finish learning how to defend themselves. Each of us sits at individual tables, or on one of the low sofas, with a drink in front of them, either staring into space or scrolling through their phones. One woman is using her time wisely and sits marking a pile of books. Most of us are simply stranded here, washed up like large pebbles on the beach of waiting.

'Do you mind if I sit here?' a male voice says to me.

I glance up and begin to say, 'Of course n—' and my voice falters. 'Not. Of course not.' I move over, slide the boys' coats and bags towards my body to make room for Trevor Whidmore to sit down. He piles his daughter's belongings beside Oscar and Ore's stuff, then carefully drops his lengthy frame onto the other end of the small sofa. The café has a large wall of glass, and we are sitting in the seats next to it.

'This is going to sound like a chat-up line, but don't I know you from somewhere?' he asks. He has a deep, melodic voice.

'I, erm, my children, well, two of them, have just started going to Plummer Prep.'

He sighs, nods his head, purses his lips for a moment. 'Right. I see.' He looks wiped out. I was complaining in my head mere minutes ago about being tired, and here I am, confronted by someone who is properly tired, justifiably exhausted. I remember what it was like when I first had the twins. I thought I'd be all right, having done it all before on my own, but the tiredness, the bone-crushing, eye-watering, mind-altering fatigue, didn't leave me for a good two years. He looks how I used to feel.

'How are you getting on?' I say to him.

He stops staring out of the window and spins on his bottom to look at me but he doesn't say anything. 'I'm not rubbernecking,' I explain. 'If you don't want to talk about it, that's fine. And I'll shut up and not say another word to you. I only asked so it doesn't seem to you that I'm one of those people who'll cross the road to avoid you rather than have an awkward conversation.'

The woman from behind the counter brings his coffee in a take-away cup to the table and places it in front of him. This gives him a few more seconds to decide how he's going to respond to me. Once she's gone, he glances at the parent sitting on the sofa opposite who has her headphones plugged into her tablet and has it on very loud.

'We're all right,' he says. 'As all right as we can be. I've brought the girls back to their classes so we can try to get back to normal. Except I got it wrong and Madison is in the later class here and Scarlett's ballet class is now down the road. So I've had to beg both people to let them stay in the wrong classes for today. So this is as normal as we can be with all this going on.'

'That's all you can do, I suppose.' There isn't a lot to say, really. I don't know him well enough to offer him comfort.

'Do you have any idea how frustrating that is?'

'What is?'

'Not being able to do anything but carry on as normal? I like to fix things but I can't fix this.' He speaks in a low tone, doesn't want anyone to hear him. 'This sort of thing makes you feel so powerless. And I can't stand to see her like that. She was always so "alive" and vibrant. And now she's there, not moving, hooked up to machines.

They keep saying she should wake up soon. They don't understand why she hasn't. She hasn't responded either way, not even when they've tried to bring her out of it.' He sips from his coffee cup without uncapping it, and rubs his hand quickly and anxiously over his brow. Wiping away worry, soothing his sorrows. 'How many children do you have?'

I was reaching for some words that might be appropriate, trying to think of what to say and coming up short. What do you say when someone's wife has been almost murdered and no one is sure when she'll wake up to tell them what happened and who did it? Not a lot. So I'm grateful to him for asking another question.

'Erm, three. One is older, she goes to school on the other side of Brighton. Middelson High? She loves it. Has fitted right in and doesn't really need me, much as it pains me to admit.'

'Sort of thing Yvonne would have said. I know she became so involved with the Parents' Council because the children needed her less as they were getting older.'

'Maybe that's what I should do,' I say. 'I mean, apart from needing me to run them around and take them to school and cook their meals, do their washing and stand over them while they do homework, they don't need me much at all.'

'Yeah, maybe the Parents' Council would be good for you,' he says.

'Sorry, that was insensitive,' I say.

'Not really. Yvonne was always trying to get people interested in it. I'll tell her tonight that I may have got her a new recruit. It may bring her round if only so she can shout at me for not running it past her first.' A ghost of a smile hovers over his lips.

'It must be so hard,' I say. 'How are the girls doing?'

'Mostly fine. They seem to have taken it in their stride, really. They don't talk much about it. The school have been very good about making sure there's no gossip or such.'

'That's good. With the school I mean.'

He nods and stares into the distance. 'Yeah, shame about the others really.'

'How do you mean?'

'Yvonne had a lot of friends and acquaintances. Some of them she was really close to and she spent a lot of time helping people out. The first couple of weeks after it happened, it was fine, people were falling over themselves to help out, bringing round food and offering to have the girls. They were posting all this stuff about how she was the heart of the school, how the place wasn't the same without her. Now they've all pretty much scrolled on like they do on the internet – because it doesn't appear on the newsfeed any more, they've kind of forgotten about us. On the good side, they've stopped all the ridiculous over-the-top stuff on social media; on the other side, they've forgotten we exist in real life, too. Except when they see me at the gates. Then they just stare and probably start gossiping the second my back's turned.'

'I haven't heard any gossip, if that's any consolation?'

His face relaxes into a tired smile. 'It's not, but thanks for trying.'

'Look, I know you don't know me, but take my number – if you need a hand then give me a call. The boys have talked about Madison because she's in their class, and they really like Scarlett, too. I'm sure we could have them over for a playdate sometime. You don't want me to be cooking for you all, trust me, but if I can help in any other way, just let me know.'

Trevor Whidmore's eyes roam over me, wondering what sort of person would make such an offer to someone they barely know. He's probably also wondering what I'm hoping to get out of it. 'I don't even know your name.'

'Well, my parents named me Cece, but everyone at Plummer Prep probably knows me as Oscar and Ore's mum. I'll answer to either.'

His face drops its dour, defeated expression for a moment and he grins at me. I grin back, glad to have helped him in a small way. 'I'm serious, you know. Take my number and call me if you need a hand. Hopefully you won't need it for much longer, but if you do, it's good to have a backup.'

'OK,' he says. We exchange numbers and the door to the dojo slides back. The boys are in the middle of the queue to exit, bowing deeply at the same time to their black-robed sensei before skipping over to our table.

'Mum-Mum-Mum-Mum,' Oscar says with his excited stutter, 'you'll never guess who's in our class?'

The noise level in the room has shot up now the children are out and ready to properly start their weekend.

'Madison,' Ore says over him. 'Madison Whidmore is in our class.'

'Yes, I know, I was just talking to her dad,' I reply.

Oscar's fingers are straight in his mouth, feeling his back teeth as he often does, to check whether any more are coming through. Ore raises his hands and runs them over the back of his hair while they both look to the pale white man sitting next to me.

'Hi, Madison,' Oscar says when she arrives at the table. He whips his hands out of his mouth and straightens up.

'Hi, Madison,' Ore says. 'My mum's been talking to your dad.' He says this as though I have done something wrong. 'I don't know what about.'

Madison looks at her dad and he smiles at her. 'They were probably talking about school. That's all adults talk about,' she says without smiling at her dad. 'School and results and how much they're paying so what they should be getting for it.'

'Paying to go to school?' Oscar says, affronted.

'Yeah,' Madison replies. 'Weird, I know.'

'Really weird,' Ore says. As a child they all turn to me and start to eye me up as though I am the source of this weirdness.

'Anyway.' I stand up, still under the scrutiny of three pairs of eight-year-old eyes. 'Let's get going, boys.'

'See you later, Maddie,' Ore says, his eyes still fixed on me.

'Bye, Madison,' Oscar adds, watching me too.

'Bye, Oscar, bye, Ore,' Madison says, also still fixed on me.

I look over their heads at Trevor Whidmore, who is finding the whole thing highly amusing. He grins at me, and hides a smirk.

Well, even if he doesn't call me, at least I've given him two things to smile about today, I decide as I bundle the boys up the short flight of stairs and out into the street.

Part 6

MONDAY

Hazel

2 a.m. I don't know my friends. They know everything about me. My life is an open book to them and I know nothing about them. I tested this out the other night: I asked Cece loads of questions and she answered them. She opened up to me with no effort. But I don't know half of that stuff about Anaya and Maxie. These are the people my freedom rests upon. I pick up my mobile and stare at it. I bet they're asleep. I bet they're fast asleep and not even thinking about it. I can't sleep. If I'm honest, I haven't been able to sleep since way before what happened to Yvonne. Obviously it was because of Yvonne, but I haven't been able to sleep properly for months now.

2:20 a.m. 'Babe, you really need your sleep,' Ciaran says.

I love him so much. But I resent him sometimes, too. When he's been away and he comes back, I know that I can't live without him. He's my rock. He has transformed me. But because of him, I am under this yoke. I know he didn't do anything wrong, he explained it all to me, but if I'd just been able to tell Yvonne to back off when she started her usual digging into his background, I wouldn't have had to . . .

'I can't sleep,' I say to him.

'Is this about Yvonne?'

'A little bit,' I say. *A little bit and a lot of bit because of what you told me. Because of your secret that I have to keep buried deep inside.* Am I turning on my friends because I can't be honest with them? If I tell them, they'll never let me near their children again. My children will be shunned. It's a big thing, living with his secret.

'I'm sorry, babe. This whole thing is rotten.' He takes my hands and tugs me to my feet. 'But come on, you're going to make yourself ill if you carry on like this. Come to bed. I'll cuddle you until you go to sleep. OK?'

'OK,' I reply. I can't sleep, but I'm too tired to argue. 'OK.'

Anaya

8:15 a.m. 'Hazel! Hazel!' I am calling and running after my friend, who has just blanked me at the school gates. We arrived on time for once and I spotted her, standing a little way away, waiting for the bell that signalled that we could all leave.

I went to speak to her, because we all agreed after Cece joined us for the knitting and then for cocktails that we'll try to act normal in the outside world, despite Trevor ringing and texting. We'll speak at the gates, we'll text each other but still delete them, just in case. But when I went to speak to Hazel, she'd stared right through me. As soon as the bell sounded, she turned and walked the other way, back towards home instead of towards work. I carried on trying to get to her in the dispersing crowd and she sped up. I called to her and she sped up some more. And she's practically running now and I'm jogging to catch her while calling her name. I break into a full-on run, slipping on the blanket of leaves that has fallen and has not been dealt with by the council yet. Eventually, I catch up with her as she turns the corner not towards her home but the other way.

'STOP!' I cry and put my hand on her shoulder.

She does stop but doesn't turn around. I step around her so that I can see her face. She's deathly pale; her bloodshot eyes are scored underneath with grey and her lips are dry and look like they have been chewed and chewed. This is what she looked like when Walter first left her. 'What was that about?' I ask her. 'Why did you blank me and run like that?'

'I didn't want to talk to you,' she says. She's so plaintive about it I have to take a step back.

'What? What have I done?'

'I don't know, what have you done, Anaya?'

'What the hell is going on? I thought we agreed we had to stick together, especially right now?'

She scoffs, a small, dismissive sound, and cuts her eyes at me. 'Yeah, right. How's your new friend Cece? Is she part of the sticking-together thing? And how's Maxie? You and her having tea together soon?'

I step back again. It's like Hazel has been possessed by the mean spirit of Yvonne. 'What's wrong with you?'

'Nothing, nothing a little attempted murder shouldn't put right, anyway.'

'I didn't try to murder Yvonne, if that's what you're saying.'

'How do I know that? Hmm?'

'Because I'm telling you so. And you know me, you know I'm not capable of such a thing.'

'Do I know you, Anaya? Do I really know you? Because I've been thinking a lot over the past couple of weeks and I've realised I don't know you, or Maxie for that matter, very well at all. I know more about Cece than I do you.'

'That's not true.'

'I know where she met her husband. I know that her oldest child is someone else's. I know she saved up all her money from her first job in a department store to buy that leather jacket she wears. I know she grew up in south-east London but moved to north London. I know her husband waited nearly a year to kiss her because she was so determined to not date until her daughter turned eighteen. I know all that about her and I've known her two minutes. I know none of that stuff about you.'

'But those are just facts. You know the real me. The stuff you don't get from answering questions. I'm your friend.'

'My freedom could hinge on you and I don't even know how you met your husband. I'm actually scared that you and Maxie could conspire against me to make me take the blame for what happened to Yvonne. I thought I knew you, but the more I think about it, the more I realise I need to find out more about you both to keep myself safe.'

What?! WHAT?! 'Who died and made you Yvonne?' I say. I should feel bad, I should be desperate to bite back those words, but I'm not.

'You know, it's funny, because I'm starting to see what she was so paranoid about. I lied to the police for you and I'm not sure if that was such a wise thing to do.'

I take a step closer to her and lower my voice. Generally people come down here in cars, but you never know who is listening. You never know if one of those parked cars has got plain-clothes police officers in it. 'We all lied to the police, for all of us and for ourselves. You're the one who suggested it. You're the one who came up with what we should say. I wanted to tell the truth, but you reminded us what it would look like. So we all lied and we all agreed to it.' I lay my hand on her forearm and I'm sure I can feel her racing pulse through the rough material of her coat. 'I know you're stressed, Hazel, believe me, we all are. But turning on Maxie and me isn't the way to go.'

'Is that a threat?' She snatches her arm away. 'Are you threatening me? Who's being like Yvonne now?'

'I'm not threatening you, Hazel. But I am scared of you right now. I don't know how to reassure you, but I am your friend. I love you. I can't tell you any more than that.'

I have to walk away from her before I break down. I've never seen her so close to the edge. So brittle and vulnerable and terrifying at the same time. I'm scared for her but more than anything I'm scared *of* her. She is slowly unravelling; the strain is obviously too much. And I feel the same. We didn't tell the police everything that happened from when Yvonne arrived at the beach hut that night to when she was found at the school later. We didn't all leave together after Yvonne walked away. We didn't all go straight home. I know I didn't. When they asked Sanjay, of course he said whatever time he saw me, and that I'd been sitting downstairs for a while before I came to bed. Because that's what I told him. That's what we all told the men at home. And it wasn't true.

Maxie

9 a.m. I'm sure I saw Anaya chasing Hazel up the road earlier. Actually running they were. I'd almost gone after them, wondering what on Earth was happening. Then I realised: I didn't want to know. Really, I didn't. I wanted a break from it all. When we're together and Cece is there, the Yvonne effect is mitigated. We're able to relax and enjoy being around each other. When Cece is not there, all of it is blown up, writ large all over our faces. If Anaya was chasing Hazel, even though we'd agreed to act normal, then something I didn't want to know about was happening.

I sit down at my desk with a cup of coffee and look at the pile of paper. Large A3 sheets, designed with cut marks, marked up in different-coloured pens with multicoloured Post-it arrows stuck to the margins. I've been working as much as possible since June. Preparing, I guess, for what's about to come. Right now, I know I should dive in, get on with it. But I can't face it. The sight of Hazel and Anaya running up the road comes to mind. So much for acting normal. So much for not drawing attention to ourselves.

May, 2017
'Have you seen the way those jeans look on her?'

'She actually looks like a sack of potatoes in them. An actual sack of potatoes. All those lumps on her hips. I mean, does she not have mirrors in her house?'

Yvonne smirked at that. A nasty, derisory smirk, like she was so much better than the person she and another mother, Teri, were talking about. 'I ask myself that every morning. I swear, you'd put a bag over your head if all you had to wear were those clothes.'

'I bet that's what her husband does every time he wants to get some action.'

I looked across the playground at who they were bitching about. Her name was Alysa or something like that. She wasn't as polished as Yvonne and the bitch she was talking to. But she looked like most of us did most mornings – just grateful to have got out of bed and made it to the gates before the bell went and Mrs Carpenter magically produced a clipboard to start marking down the names of those who were late. She was talking to another mother, and laughing, gesticulating, existing like any of us in this world.

This was a side to Yvonne that I really didn't like. In fact, I hated it. When she was in the playground at drop-off and pick-up, when she was surrounded by a particular type of person, she had to play Alpha Mama. She had to become a mega-bitch, to prove to everyone that she was superior.

Lately, Yvonne would arrive, Scarlett and Madison in tow, almost always wearing sunglasses, always perfectly made-up, with lipsticks to match her suits, a hairstyle to match her jewellery (hair down to suit dangly earrings and long necklace, hair up for small studs and choker), and the sky-blue bag she always carried no matter what colour her shoes or outfit. Yvonne *never* came out without looking perfect. And she had a habit of judging those who did.

'That's a horrible thing to say!' Yvonne exclaimed. 'Like her husband would actually want to have sex with her.'

The two cackled quietly and the laughter tore through my bones like hot pokers. I looked again at the woman. She'd obviously thrown on a pair of red jeans that didn't flatter her, she'd pulled on a crumpled T-shirt and a crumpled knee-length cardigan. Her hair was pulled up into a messy ponytail and she had not a scrap of make-up on. But those were just outward looks. Outward looks weren't everything.

I remember a time in my life when I could barely get dressed. When I did get dressed I didn't look in the mirror for fear of seeing who I truly was. I remember not caring if my clothes were creased, if they had the faint smell of the laundry pile, if they made me look like I had gained six stone just on my bottom and thighs. I just didn't care. I would brush my teeth, most of the time, I would remember to tie up my hair sometimes to stop it tangling. I'd get around to washing my hair some weeks. I was a mess. And even when I stopped being a mess, when I stopped feeling like everything was pointless, I still struggled not to look like I had. Maybe Alysa (if that was her name) was coming out of a time like I had been through. Maybe she wasn't. Maybe that was how she looked and she didn't need to be made-up or designer-clad or crease-free to feel like a human being. Maybe how she looked was how she looked.

'She's one of those women who would complain if he went off with someone else.'

'Instead of thinking, "who could blame him", she'd actually call him a bastard.'

'When it'd just be a case of him wanting someone who looked like a woman for a change.'

I rotated on the spot and glared at them. They both stopped talking but in that naughty-schoolgirl way – like they were going to carry on once my back was turned, like they hadn't really been doing anything wrong. 'You two are a pair of bitches,' I said to them. I didn't intend to, but my voice was raised, enough to draw the attention of a couple of other mothers. They all looked over at Yvonne and Teri. The pair of them flamed up, even under their perfect make-up. More people had joined the queue to see the school's summer choir recital, and they were all staring. This was my moment to bring down the mean girls, put them in their place. Make a name for myself as the bully slayer.

But I couldn't. Not really. Not at all. I just couldn't stand by and listen any more. Every time I'd heard this type of bitching and had not challenged it, I'd walked away feeling dirty, low, like I had done something wrong. I should ignore it – it was nothing to do with me, it was never aimed at me – but that didn't make it acceptable to not put a stop to it. To not even speak up, especially when I was pally-pally with one of the main perpetrators. Teri I could easily continue to ignore. But I had to deal with the other one.

I pointed at Yvonne. 'I can't be friends with you any more, Yvonne. Not if you're going to behave like this.'

Yvonne's eyes widened in horror. 'What's with the holier-than-thou routine, Maxie? We were only joking. And anyway, it was a private conversation. You can't eavesdrop on a private conversation and then take issue with it. You shouldn't have been listening.' Teri, her clone friend, nodded her little blonde head so vigorously it looked like it was going to fall off.

'That's what you're going to say to me?' I replied. 'Seriously, Yvonne, I've called you out, as the Yanks say, about being a bitch and you're going with the "you shouldn't have been listening" defence? Well, yes, you're right, I shouldn't have been listening to the bitchy conversation that you were having in my earshot. And, if we're going down that route, you should, technically, have been having that "chat" telepathically if you had issues with people hearing it.' I stopped talking and looked again from one of them to the other. Shook my head slowly, disappointedly, at Yvonne. 'Just delete my number, Yvonne. It's just better all round if we stop being friends, all right?'

Before she could protest, the gates were opened and the line of parents began to move towards the door and the hall. I folded my arms across my chest with the air of finality of a judge who has delivered her verdict. I didn't look at Yvonne again the whole way through the concert, even though Madison and Frankie stood next to each other in the back row, the two tallest in the choir, and I could feel her eyes on me whenever our children weren't performing.

She called out to me across the playground on the way out, obviously wanting to talk, needing to make things right, but I ignored her. Some things you just couldn't make right, not even with the sincerest of apologies.

Anaya

9:30 a.m. Sanjay's mother is in my house. Again. I can hear her clattering around in the kitchen. Probably cooking something and tutting, quietly cursing because I don't have the right spices, the correct equipment, the right breeding to be the daughter-in-law she really wanted. She'd been desperate for her son to get married, simply not to me.

I can't deal with her right now. I should tell her to leave, remind her that she has a perfectly good house not far from here and she can do all the cooking she wants there, but I decide to shelve that discussion. I've already dealt with one crazy woman today, I can't face another before lunch. I sneak up the stairs and then go to the top floor before she knows I'm there, and I go to the en suite in the spare room and lock myself in. I probably should have brought a magazine or a book, because I plan to be here a while. Until she goes, basically.

I sit on top of the lowered toilet seat lid and allow my face to fall into my hands. This is all such a mess. How was I to know that something I did twenty-odd years ago would come back to haunt me in such a huge way?

My mobile bleeps in my handbag and I rush to grab it before it echoes throughout the house and lets my mother-in-law know I'm here.

What was going on with you and Hazel earlier? M x

Craziness. You actually don't want to know. And I can't tell you anyway because she thinks we're plotting behind her back. A xx

???!!!! M x

Don't. Just don't. Enjoy your day. A xx

I delete the messages, turn off the phone's ringer and drop it back into my black handbag. This is what Yvonne did. How she controlled us, by making us feel guilty if we dared interact without her. I remember one time in Year One, Madison wasn't invited to a party. Priya hadn't been, neither had Camille or Frankie. I suspected that it was down to Hazel being a single parent, Frankie and Priya not being white and Madison because Yvonne wasn't über-rich along with her good looks. If she had been both, Madison would have been on the invite list. Hazel, Maxie and I didn't bat an eyelid. We told our children that they couldn't be invited to everything and it didn't matter if they were left out of stuff because their lives were full and interesting anyway.

Yvonne, though, took it personally. Nothing any of us said could stop her mounting a vendetta against the mother. I don't know what she eventually did, but she told us that the mother had decided to move her three kids to another school on the other side of Brighton – before the woman had even handed her notice in to the school. We joked at the time that Yvonne must have uncovered some serious dirt on her for that to happen. Everyone in that year group learnt a valuable lesson from that – leave Yvonne out at your peril. (Yes, it was the children who were meant to be invited, but it was actually all about Yvonne.) After that, Madison was invited to *every* party – even the boys-only ones. I was sure it was because they knew what might happen if they didn't.

With us, it wasn't about uncovering dirt, not then, anyway. With us, she guilt-tripped us into including her in everything. That's what Hazel is doing now, whether she realises it or not.

April, 2017

The alarm didn't sound when I opened the front door and since Sanjay's car wasn't there but his mother's was . . .

I tried very hard not to roll my eyes. I tried to channel my mother and her yoga calm. I tried to think of all the ways I was a successful person and I did not need Sanj's mother's approval to feel like a complete human being. I tried very hard to remember the tradition of respecting your elders and making all visitors welcome in your home.

Suhani, though. She had a way of getting to me. She had a way of making me feel like I wasn't good enough for her son, no matter what I did.

I walked into the living room with my coat on, just to show her that I wasn't staying as long as she was staying and to tell her that Sanjay wouldn't be back that night so there was nothing for her to hang around for. Even her interactions with the children had to involve her son so he would see what a wonderful grandmother she was. She couldn't be her without an audience, I'd realised.

My feet tripped over themselves when I entered our living room and found not only Suhani but Yvonne, too. The pair of them were sitting in my house with a full tea service on the coffee table in front of them. It was our special, fine bone-china crockery Amma and Tatta bought us as a wedding present. Amma and Tatta had their own wedding tea set and I had been fascinated by it for as long as I could remember. I would repeatedly beg Amma to get it out of its packaging and ask her about it: its images, its curves, why it was so important to them. She and Tatta had been so pleased at my expression when I unwrapped our very own tea set when they came to visit the day after we got back from honeymoon.

The only people who used that crockery were Sanjay and I, to enjoy our tea, to remind ourselves of our wedding day. We had other, perfectly nice, hugely more expensive tea sets, but Suhani, knowing its significance, had got it out to use it with a woman she had never met before. Why didn't Suhani and Yvonne go upstairs and root through my wardrobe, get my wedding sari out of its layers of tissue paper and put it on while they were at it?

'Ahhh, Anaya, my daughter-in-law,' Suhani said. 'It is so nice that you've finally decided to come home. We have been waiting for you. Your friend here, Mrs . . . ?'

'Whidmore,' Yvonne supplied.

'Yes, Mrs Whidmore has been such delightful company,' she said.

'I completely forgot you were working today,' Yvonne said. She got to her feet and smoothed down the wrinkle-free lap of her tight black skirt suit. She was wearing a pearl necklace and pearl earrings, her hair secured back in a low bun. 'I popped round to see if you fancied going for a coffee, but you weren't here. Your delightful mother-in-law persuaded me to stay for tea. She is so fascinating. I was so grateful that she had that time to spend with me.'

Suhani, who was actually blushing at the compliments gushing out of Yvonne's mouth, replied: 'The pleasure was absolutely all mine.'

Maybe it was true, maybe Yvonne had forgotten I was at work – why would she, who didn't work outside the home, remember my schedule? But there was something sinister about her being here, about her car not being parked outside on the drive, which can hold up to four cars. That meant . . . *No, Yvonne is nosey, she's a bit of a cow sometimes, she can be bitchy, but she's not completely sly and evil*, I thought.

'Well, I must be off,' she said.

I frowned. Why was she leaving if she'd been waiting for me?

'Thank you ever so much for the tea, Mrs Kohli. And I hope we can catch up again soon.' She focused on me. 'I'll see you in about an hour, Anaya, at the school gates.'

I nodded. And I tried to pretend I didn't notice how much that sounded like a threat.

Once she was gone, I returned to the living room, where Suhani was clearing up the tea set.

'How long was Yvonne here?' I asked.

'Oh, not long at all. Maybe an hour.'

'And you didn't think to maybe ring me to ask how long I was going to be?'

'Oh, Anaya, my daughter-in-law, I did not want to disturb you. What is two hours between two women, two strangers, essentially?'

'You said it was an hour a second ago.'

'An hour . . . two hours? What is the difference?'

With Yvonne, a lot. A hell of a lot. In the first hour, she would be getting warmed up; in the second hour she would have done enough buttering-up to find out every single scrap of information she needed.

'What did you talk about?'

'Why, all sorts of things.' My mother-in-law clanked my delicate, special china as she moved. 'The weather, politics, you of course.'

'What about me?'

'All positive things, Anaya. Do not be so paranoid. She was asking about your family. What your family name had been before you were married. She wondered if you had been married before because you had a different surname to your mother.'

'Pardon? She was asking about my mother?'

'Yes. She was curious – as I was – why your mother and father are Ranatunga and you were Harshani before you married my son.'

'You told her all that? You told her my parents' name?'

'Of course, we were discussing whether you had been married before my Sanjay found you and made you into the respectable woman you are today.'

That was it, then. Game over. She would find out my real name, she would find . . .

Bloody, bloody Yvonne.

'You look worried, Anaya my dear. Not too tired, I hope?'

I shook my head and moved across the room. I tossed my bag onto the sofa and relieved her of my tray of my stuff. 'No, I'm not too tired. But I do have a lot to do and Sanjay is away all night, so you're most welcome to leave whenever you feel like it.'

'I will, thank you. I will simply go and finish stripping and remaking all the beds. They were in a terrible state.'

I was tempted, sorely tempted, to shout at her. To let her know she'd ruined everything. *Bloody, bloody, bloody Yvonne.*

TUESDAY

Cece

9:45 p.m. 'I didn't know who else to call,' he says. He is frantic. He sounds it, any way. And, let's face it, he'd have to be to call me. I am a virtual stranger. Someone to nod to at martial arts and in the mornings at the school gate. If the roles were reversed, I doubt I'd be calling him. Not unless I was a special kind of desperate.

He moves into the house and I look around the place as we walk through to the kitchen. It's as large as our house, maybe bigger because they have three rooms downstairs and a large kitchen where he leads me to, picking up dropped items along the way. This is what our house looked like when both Sol and I worked full-time. It still looks like that sometimes now, and I have to put out of my head the snarky comments I get from Sol about it. His guilt at what he said to me the night of his work's autumn ball has subsided now. Superseded by his disdain for my lack of having morphed into a 1950s housewife, complete with pinny and dinner on the table when he gets home at whatever time he chooses to stroll in nowadays.

'I didn't really appreciate how much Yvonne did.' Trevor Whidmore seems to be talking to himself more than to me. 'She was just always there. I could work late, could dash back to the office at the drop of a hat without worrying about leaving two children on their own. I never had to clock-watch coming home like I do now. Most days now I have to work really late into the night because there's no way I can get it all done and pick up the girls. God, I don't know what I'm going to do if she doesn't . . .' His voice ebbs away, like a wisp of his breath. He shakes his head slightly, then firmly. He needs

to dislodge the very thought that follows 'if she doesn't'. It's unthinkable and he doesn't need to do that to himself right now. 'I literally
need you to sit here and make sure they don't come down and set
the place on fire, or try to leave. I'll be an hour, an hour and half,
tops. Is that OK?'

'Fine,' I say. I pull out the chair he pointed to at the kitchen table.
'I sit here, right?' I say. 'Just here?' I lower myself into the seat and
he stops moving around, looking for keys and who knows what else.
I raise a mocking eyebrow at him. And he smiles; his face relaxes
into a small grin that says he's realised how he sounds. This is how
I sound when I am in über-parent mode. I don't mean to sound like
like a drill sergeant and tyrant, but that's how it comes out. It's hard
to not slip into that mode when you're trying to deal with a myriad
of things all at once.

'Sorry,' Trevor Whidmore says. He holds the keys to the sporty
BMW parked outside in one hand and a table tennis bat in the other
one. He looks at the bat, shakes his head and tosses it onto the kitchen table. 'I'm trying to be two parents at the same time. And trying
to visit Yvonne. Trying to keep the kids going. It's hard not to start
barking out orders while everything is going at a million miles an
hour in your head.'

'I know,' I reassure him.

He shakes his head again. 'I can't believe I'm ringing up strangers
to come sit with my kids so I can leave the house on my own for a
little while.'

I wonder where his family is, her family is. If something happened to me, Sol would have a bun fight on his hands to look
after the children. My parents would pretty much move in and my
siblings would be setting up round the corner. How come Yvonne
Whidmore has no family stepping into the breach? Have they all
passed away? Is there another twist in the story of Yvonne Whidmore
that I don't know about? Popular, not *that* popular; hated enough
to be attacked and almost killed. That is the story I have now. But
is there more?

'Don't worry, I can get like that and I have no excuses. It's good to have someone speak to me like that every now and again so I can remember not to speak to Sol and the children like army trainees.' I grin at him and sit back in the chair.

'Thank you so much, Cece. I'll be back soon. Very soon. I won't be long. I won't be long.'

Then he is gone. And I am alone. Not completely alone, of course – Madison and Scarlett are upstairs. They know me from the school and that time at martial arts, so they won't be too distressed if they come down and find me here. But hopefully Trevor won't be gone too long. Sol's mouth actually hung open when I told him that I was going out to take care of Trevor Whidmore's kids while he dashed out to run a few errands.

'You're going out to look after someone else's kids when I don't have a clean shirt for tomorrow?' he said.

'How are the two connected?' I asked as I grabbed my mobile from the side of the bed. I'd actually been in bed reading when I'd got Trevor's call.

'I don't have any clean shirts for tomorrow, Cece, and instead of sorting that out, you're going to someone else's house to play babysitter.'

'Why would I be sorting out your clean shirt problem?' I asked.

'What the hell else do you do all day?' he snapped. 'I have dirty shirts, I go to work and I come back to find them not washed. Why?'

'I do the washing every other day – if something's not in the hamper, they don't get washed,' I replied calmly.

'But they're right there!' He pointed to the other side of the room. Where he drops his clothes when he undresses at night.

'And the hamper's right there,' I said and pointed to where it sat, by the entrance to the walk-in wardrobe. 'I repeat, if something's not in the hamper, it doesn't get washed. Even the children know that. Anything doesn't make it to the hamper in their rooms, it doesn't get washed. It's quite simple really.'

'What do you *do* all day, Cece?'

'Not wash stuff that's not in the hamper, obviously,' I replied. 'But you've still got time. You can wash and tumble and iron them before the morning. I've got to go.'

'Unbelievable!' he muttered.

I look around the Whidmore kitchen. It is in disarray, a state that's been building over the last few weeks, by the look of it. I'm not the tidiest of people, but this would break my heart if I came back to find my house in this state. I stand up, even though I was sort of ordered not to, and gather together the dinner plates on the table. They clink together and I try to stop them making noise. I do not want to wake anyone up. I do not want to have conversations with her children and have them potentially ask me when their mother is going to wake up and why I am in their house and what it means for the rest of their lives. The rest of their lives is a very big place, another country I do not want to give them peeks of or insights into without some sort of knowledge and guidance from their dad.

On the very large, shiny, red and designer-labelled fridge, I am aware of the picture that I have seen in Hazel's and Maxie's houses: the friends. The perfect friends. Yvonne at the centre, Hazel on the left, Anaya on the right, Maxie standing slightly behind between Anaya and Yvonne. Their heads are leaning towards each other, their faces are showing their best smiles to the camera. They are the close friends. With their perfect friend at the centre.

I stop, my hands full of dishes, and stare at the picture. Could one of them really have done it? It doesn't seem possible, not really. I've spent time with all of them and that seems so beyond the realm of possibility.

Would one of my new friends have really done that? Knowing that she had a husband and children who would be forced to remake their lives without her? Would one of those women I've sat and knit-ted with and concocted cocktails with and laughed and laughed with do something like that? No one I know would do that, would they? No, they wouldn't. That's all there is to it. No one would do that. With that knowledge lodged carefully in my mind, I turn towards the sink and place the dishes on top of the other dishes and pots and pans. No one I know would do that. No one.

Hazel

10 p.m. I'm shaking. Shaking. The children are asleep and Ciaran is watching television and I am sitting here in the dark kitchen, shaking. I'm scared. Really scared. I actually don't know what I'm scared of. Being found out? Fine, they'll arrest me. Not being found out? Fine, I won't be arrested. Yvonne dying? I don't know. Maybe. Whatever it is, though, I am scared. I am really, really scared.

Are we meeting for coffee tomorrow?

I press send and immediately regret it. I wasn't fair on Anaya yesterday. That is fear. That is me being scared.

No, sorry, can't. A x

Me either. I have a huge deadline. Maybe next week. M x

One kiss from each of them and no real excuse. They're going to meet without me. I'm sure of it. I'm sure of it. I'm sure of it.

Cece

11:30 p.m. I stopped myself going through Yvonne Whidmore's kitchen drawers, reading the franking marks on the letters littering the kitchen table and the sides. I have not looked at the notes hooked onto the fridge with various magnets, or pinned onto the noticeboard by the kitchen door. I have not violated the privacy of the woman in a coma and her family. It was torturous not to, of course. I wanted to work out who she is. What sort of person she is and what kind of life she lives. I wanted to complete more of the pattern that is Yvonne Whidmore, but I have stopped myself using this unfortunate opportunity to do so. Because the second I did that, it would mean I believe what Gareth said. I'd believe that one of my new friends is truly that dangerous. That someone I have become friends with is capable of murder.

Trevor Whidmore is full of gratitude when I leave over an hour later. He can't thank me enough for tidying up, for sitting with his kids, for actually meaning it when I said I would do anything I could to help. Of course, I don't mention as I walk away from their front door that the scent of jasmine and calla lilies from another woman's perfume dances around him, that he has a very pronounced glow in his previously pale cheeks, and that, in his obvious haste to get dressed, he's buttoned up his shirt wrong.

I was thinking before that whoever attacked Yvonne had to know that she had a husband and children who would have to remake their lives without her. What if that was the point? What if whoever did it, did it to create a vacancy in Trevor, Scarlett and Madison Whidmore's lives?

*

204

11:55 p.m. Harmony is in the kitchen when I get home. She has the downlights of the wall cabinets on and she's sitting at the table playing with her phone.

'Harmony? What are you doing awake?'

She shrugs and sags a little. I shut the door and go to her. I gather her in my arms and when she doesn't immediately shrug me off, my heart flutters. I've been so focused on the boys and that school – have I missed something vital going on with Harmony? 'Has something happened at school?' I ask.

'No,' she says, eventually shrugging me off. I crouch down beside her, unwilling to leave her now that I know there's something wrong. 'School's cool. Home is not so much.'

'What do you mean?' I say.

'I mean . . . Things are not good with you and Dad, are they, Mum?'

I sit back on my haunches, study my daughter and say nothing.

'You two really don't seem to like each other at the moment, do you? Before, you were a bit too kissy-kissy for my liking, and me and the boys thought it was weird that you were all over each other, but we'd all prefer that to what it's like now.'

'It's not that bad, is it?'

'The little one said you two were probably going to get divorced like Camille's parents. And the big one said that it'd be fine cos you'd then have another baby like Camille's mum.'

All right, it is that bad. I didn't realise they'd noticed. Well, not only noticed, but noticed enough for Harmony to say something. For *that* to have happened, they must have talked about it several times.

'I know it seems dire at the moment, but you know, it's only right now,' I say. 'Everything is so new and different, and for adults, it's harder for them to get used to something new and find our way in all that. But it's only temporary.' *I hope.*

'Can't you just, you know, be, like, friends again?' she says. 'It's not hard when you love someone.'

It's not hard when you love someone – she's right about that. It's not easy though, either. Especially when we're both so incredibly pissed off with each other all the time. 'It won't be like this for ever,' I say to her. 'I promise you.'

'You really promise?' she asks, like she is four years old.

'Yeah, I really promise.' Things are not going to stay the same; they're actually likely to get a lot worse before they get better.

Part 7

SATURDAY

Cece

11:45 a.m. 'My name is Gareth Prentice, I'm a police officer.'

I pause in folding up one of Sol's red T-shirts from the huge dryer pile on our bed when I hear his voice. *He wouldn't. He bloody wouldn't.*

'I'm here to see your mother,' he says to Harmony. I throw down the T-shirt and almost vault over the bed. *He bloody has.*

Sol has 'taken the day (Saturday) off' and has taken the boys into Brighton for lunch and to get their hair shaved. Harmony decided to stay home and do her homework. Which of course means watching television in the living room because she rarely gets to do that without one or both of the boys.

'Has she done something?' Harmony asks. Her voice tremors with worry and I bet she's about to start chewing the inside of her cheek. There are also a few threads of fascination, too – she's a little thrilled by the possibility that I might be a criminal.

'No, no,' his voice reassures. 'No, not at all. I've been trying to get her to help me with something and I thought if I turned up to talk to her again, she might change her mind.'

'She won't do that,' Harmony says with certainty. 'She's not like that. When she's made a decision about something there's pretty much nothing that will change her mind.'

This is the problem with having a big house. It takes an age to clear the bedroom, race down a flight of stairs while trying not to sound like a woman who is desperate to stop her daughter from talking to someone she did not want her daughter to ever even meet.

'I remember her being like that.' A pause. 'I suppose I was hoping she might have mellowed over the last few years.'

The accent. He is turning on the accent, I think as I round the bottom of the upper flight of stairs, dash down the corridor and turn at the top of the next flight, which curls and kinks down to the ground floor. *Or is he so unguarded, starry-eyed by the thought of who he is talking to, that he is forgetting himself and how he 'normally' speaks?*

'Are you basically trying to tell me you knew my mother before I was born?' my very clever daughter says.

As I hit the last curve to the ground floor, I slow right down, walking quickly but measuredly. 'Harmony?' I call from halfway down the stairs. 'Did I hear the d— Oh, hello.' My voice is, I think, normal and then surprised. Especially when I ask: 'What are you doing here?'

'Hi, hi,' he says with a smile. 'As I was just explaining to . . . Sorry, I didn't get your name?'

'Harmony,' my daughter supplies.

'Harmony. What a lovely name . . . As I was explaining to Harmony here, I've come back in the hope you will change your mind about helping me.'

My daughter is reading carefully from the small white business card he has managed to slip her. Sly git. Even if I take it off her now, it'll be too late – if she hasn't already memorised his number, she will know his name, and will be checking out all online sources of information about him. And I'm sure that he will suddenly be an open book on the internet. Providing many, many ways to be contactable by the girl he thinks is his daughter.

SHE'S NOT YOUR DAUGHTER! I want to scream at him.

'I told him you don't do that sort of thing, but he seemed to think that age might have mellowed you or something. Anyway, laters.' She turns on her heel without even acknowledging him again. On her way past, she hands me the white card. 'Think this was meant for you,' she tells me. She stops and leans towards me. 'I think he wants to renew your acquaintance.' She squeezes her nose up towards her eyebrows and nods. Then she heads upstairs, instead of into the living room, from where I expected her to try to eavesdrop.

I step outside, closing the door almost fully behind me, which forces him to take a step backwards. 'What the hell do you think you're doing here?' The anger bubbles in my words like ingredients in a witch's cauldron.

'You left me no choice,' he says, not at all fearful of my anger, not at all regretful of what he's done.

'Keep your voice down,' I hiss at him.

He's about to tell me no, that he won't keep his voice down, but I slap my hand over his mouth. Of course Harmony went upstairs. When we first moved in, she walked through the house several times, standing at different points in every room, listening. Listening and absorbing the acoustics of each area so she could work out the optimum place to practise her violin. She knows that the best place to capture every last syllable of our conversation is in the front bedroom.

'I will report you for police harassment if you say one more word,' I snarl under my breath. I remove my hand from his mouth and hold a warning forefinger up at him while I reach inside and grab the first pair of shoes to hand. I only have on a short-sleeved T-shirt and jeans, but I'm not sticking around to get my jacket, my keys, my purse. I do not want Harmony to hear any of this conversation.

I point to the end of the path, and push him slightly to indicate we need to go. While he walks down the path, I slip Sol's best running shoes onto my feet. He will go radio rental if anything happens to these shoes. He spent so much money on them and they have become perfectly moulded to his feet, like running gloves.

I jerk the 'move!' finger left, indicating Gareth should go in that direction. When he moves too slowly, I fold my arms across my chest to show how proper angry I am, and then overtake him. I lead the way across then down onto one of the streets that bridges our road and the main road and which has a red post box that stands like an exclamation mark on the pavement. I stop there and wait for him to catch me up.

'What the hell do you think you're doing?' I say to him.

'I had to see if she could in any way possibly be my daughter, and she is.' He indicates over his shoulder. 'She's the living image of me. She is my daughter.'

'She is not!' I only just manage to stop my voice from screeching at him. 'What is wrong with you? If she was your daughter, I would have told you. I wouldn't have wanted to, but I would have . . . And don't you dare flatter yourself with the whole "living image of me" bollocks. She looks like herself. Her gorgeous, beautiful self. All right?'

'What it comes down to, Cece, is that I don't believe you. I just don't. You can't dispute the timings. Until you tell me who her father is . . . Actually, I want a DNA test.'

'You can go whistle,' I say. *Find your calm, find your calm.* I close my eyes and run my fingers over my face, trying not to get any more annoyed than I am right now. 'OK, her father is . . .' I cringe every time I think about it. Every time. And when I think about it, I think about Gareth and I cringe even harder. 'OK, her father is . . .'

OK, her father is a man who I should never have gone near. You have to understand that after I left the Met, I slid very fast into a very bad place. Being a police officer was all I'd ever wanted to do. And when I realised that I couldn't, and why I couldn't, my mind kind of collapsed in on itself for a little bit. I had made what I thought of as friends, I had met someone, you, who I knew spent a lot of time trying not to tell me he was in love with me when he so obviously was. All of that had been wiped away because I'd gone to a pub one night to celebrate an achievement.

I moved into a tiny little studio, well, bedsit, but everyone calls them studios now, and sort of checked out for a while. And by check out, I mean going out and getting as drunk as possible whenever I could. I was properly messed up by leaving that job. I mean, it was the right decision, there's no doubting it, and, over the years, I've looked back and thought, What the hell were you thinking going down that career path? *but right then . . . I still remember it, in a very real, visceral way. Sometimes, I get that drop from the very top of a rollercoaster feeling in my stomach when I think about it. The years have rolled on over me, I've grown up (emotionally), I've grown out and in (physically) but I still can't completely erase that falling-away feeling, that sensation of feeling completely destroyed. Dismantled, broken. It was the making of me, sure. But at the time, I was in a terrible place, wrecked almost.*

This guy, Elion, was in a pub one night. He bought me drinks, we went to a club, he came back to my place and we spent most of the night having drunken sex. And then in the morning we had hungover sex. He stayed most of the day, and we both sobered up, we hung out, messed around a bit more, and he ended up staying the night. Next morning, he had to go, and I lay in bed thinking about what I'd done with a complete stranger.

I didn't even realise for a month. And then, one night, I lay in bed, having been out till the small hours almost every night, thinking over the past few weeks, and then sat bolt upright when I realised what I hadn't been doing for the past month or so. I had been on the Pill since I was eighteen, never missed a day, always took it at the same time every day, followed the instructions to the letter because that's what I'm like, and then I had stopped when I left the Met. But, of course, I'd had (a lot of) unprotected sex with that guy. And then I did a test, blah, blah, positive. Have a passenger on board, blah, blah. Oh my God, what a disaster. Oh my God, maybe it's not such a disaster. Oh my God, am I really going to do this? Oh yes, I am, which means I should probably tell the father.

Do you get what I'm saying? I remembered enough about him to find him again, to go to his flat – more than once, actually – to go tell him. And I did my very best to tell him. Because that's the sort of person I am. I did what I had to do despite it being uncomfortable and he being one of the worst people to have gone near, let alone have all that unprotected sex with. But anyway, there you are. Do you understand now?

'I did what I had to do despite it being uncomfortable and he being one of the worst people to have gone near, let alone have all that unprotected sex with. But anyway, there you are. Do you understand now? You are not my daughter's father. Not biologically, not emotionally. She has one of each and you are neither, OK?'

Gareth stands and listens to my confession, my explanation of one of the most humiliating, uncontrolled parts of my life, with an impassive face. He reads my body language, he reads my facial expressions, listens to the words I use and the way I deliver them. He knows I'm telling the truth. No one would admit to that sort of messed-up behaviour unless it was the truth. Or as close to the truth as you could possibly get.

'Why was he one of the worst people you could have got involved with?' he eventually asks.

I roll my eyes at myself. At what else is going to have to come out of my mouth. 'Because he was a druggie. It was so obvious when I met him. That was the reason why I had to keep going back to tell him. He was so out of his head every time I came near him that he never remembered what I said. I thought he'd remembered the last time, by the way he nodded and asked a couple of questions, but when I bumped into him in the street when Harmony was about two months old, he remembered me but was totally blown away by the idea that I had a child. Even asked if me and the father were coping with having a new small person around. He wasn't messing around or trying to deflect any sort of claim I might make – he was genuinely surprised I had a baby.'

Gareth frowns, narrows his eyes. He's been watching me; he knows this is the truth. Or does he? He might be good at reading people, but he knows he's not infallible, he knows that I may be the one person who could lie to him and get away with it.

'If he was so obviously a mess, why did you go near him?'

Another eye-roll. I have to do this, don't I? I have to tell him everything. And get judged accordingly.

'Well,' I say in the soft folds of a deep sigh. 'Well, I did that because . . . I can't even believe I have to tell you this . . . I went with him anyway because, urgh, because he reminded me of you. I was really hurt and stressed and heartbroken and he looked so much like you and he had an Irish accent like you, and I wanted to pretend for a little while. OK? Not proud of myself for any of it, but there you go, no one's perfect.'

There it is: the smug little smile from a man who has had his ego boosted in the most unexpected way.

'It was only that one time, though. After that, I remembered why I wasn't a police officer, why I didn't see you, how you'd hurt me and why I was in the mess I was in and all positive thoughts of you went out of the window.' Even that doesn't stop the self-satisfied little twinkle that sits in his eye. 'Do you believe me now, Gareth?'

Thankfully, that acts like a hose of water turned on him, and splashes him out of his fantasy world where he is a sex god, and he focuses back on me.

'Not completely, no,' he says. 'I was really stupid not asking about contraception, simply assuming you were on the Pill.'

'I *was* on the Pill. I've been on it since . . . Oh my . . . I can't *believe* I'm starting to justify myself to you. I was on the Pill. I was completely stupid not using condoms with you – you could have had anything.'

Offence at the idea of it flashes across his face.

'It's true, I was totally irresponsible – twice. Which isn't generally like me. Actually, it's not like me at all. I don't know what I was thinking, really. Obviously I wasn't thinking. But you know what? None of that means anything except the fact that you are not the biological or anything else of my daughter.'

Gareth has that look that tells me he still doesn't believe me. He wants to say more but hasn't got any foundation. 'I don't have any choice but to believe you, do I?' he says.

'You can believe whatever you want, Gareth.'

He nods. Suddenly his face softens, the lines smoothed out by a deep affection, transporting him back to how he used to look at me in 2001 when we'd moved beyond simply fucking at every opportunity we got, to long, languid love-making followed by talking, sharing, planning.

'You were right, you know, I did love you,' he says, staring right into my eyes as though I am sixteen years younger. The look and what he's just said repulse me so much, I have to look around to check I'm not going to step into anything unsavoury on the pavement behind me – people don't often scoop in this area – before I take myself a step away from him.

'What the hell has that got to do with anything?' I reply.

'Nothing. Everything. I don't know. I want you to know that. In case . . . in case it changes anything. In case you realise that if we did make a child, it was conceived with love.'

'What are you talking about?' I ask.

'I wanted you to know in case it changes anything.'

'What could it possibly change?'

'It could . . . Look, Cece, when you love someone, like I loved you, you do remember the important things about them. Like I remember, not long before we finished our training and we broke up, that you got a kidney infection. You were so insistent that I didn't look after you, even though you clearly knew how much I felt for you.'

Like he really remembers that. I barely remember it and I lived it.

'And I remember you had to go to the doctor's in the end because you were in so much pain and couldn't carry on ignoring it any more.'

'And?' I reply. 'What's that got to do with anything?' I am panicking inside, of course. I know where this is leading. It is hurtling down the road of thought my mind has meandered down several times over the years. Of course I've had the luxury of having my mind simply wander and knowing it is a dead end because, well, it wasn't really possible with the timings, but Gareth has spent these past few days hurtling up and down this road, trying to find a theory that fits with the one that has clearly taken over all his sensibilities. He was always like that, though: he will have a theory and will find everything he can to make that theory true. Even if it isn't possible. That's why that line of thought is always a dead end in my mind: it wasn't physically possible. I am the one with access to the timings, I know my body, I know all those other things that Gareth doesn't and I know the truth.

'You started taking antibiotics, didn't you?' Gareth tells me. 'I remember because you were so meticulous, would make sure you took them at the same time every day. Just like you said you did with the Pill. I remember that really clearly – other people kept saying it didn't matter if the timing was a bit out, but you were insistent that it was at exactly the same time.'

'So?'

'So, don't antibiotics often interfere with how the Pill works? Can't antibiotics often render the Pill ineffective?'

'Until thirty seconds ago you wouldn't believe I was even on the Pill,' I say, 'and now it's all "rendered ineffective"? Go to hell, Gareth. Go right to hell.'

I begin to walk away, but then return to him. Get so close I can feel the heat from his body. The heat that used to ignite heat in me but now makes me want to rage at him. I do not want this – *him* – in my life. 'Stay away from me, and especially stay away from my daughter, Gareth, I mean it. She is nothing to do with you.'

I don't wait for a response, don't need to listen to anything else he has to say. I know what he's thinking, though. In response to my warning to stay away from my child, he is thinking: *Not until I get a DNA test.*

12:05 p.m. Harmony is sitting on the third step of our staircase and glares at me with her dark-chocolate eyes, angry and betrayed by the fact I have robbed her of the knowledge she could have gleaned from eavesdropping. That was one conversation, probably of all the conversations I've had since she was born, that she feels she had a right to hear. Instead, I have snatched away the chance to find out if the tall, handsome policeman who came to our door and gave her his number is in fact the father she has never asked about. I wonder sometimes if she never asks about him because she's not curious, because she's worried it will upset Sol or because she doesn't trust me to tell her the truth. I've never been brave enough to find out which it is.

'Harmon—' I begin, but before I even get to the 'y' of her name, she has jumped up and stomped her way upstairs. Once at the top, she stomps to her bedroom and slams the door so loudly that part of the house shakes.

'Thank you, Gareth,' I mutter. 'Thank you very, very much.'

SUNDAY

Anaya

11:45 a.m.

Do you fancy coming to the gym with me later? Give yourself a proper workout? A xx

11:50 a.m.

Depends . . . is this really a trip to the gym or a euphemism for doing something other than working out? Cece x

11:51 a.m.

No, it's a euphemism for going to the gym. Are you coming? A xx

11:52 a.m.

Yeah, sure, why not? Cece x

Cece

10:30 p.m. With an arm that feels like it has tripled in weight, I tug back the covers and go to climb in. I am a fit woman. But a tiny bit of time at the gym earlier today has turned me into a wreck. It was fifty minutes. Fifty whole minutes with Anaya. I collapse onto the bed and starfish. Except I'm not starfishing. Not at all. But I can feel the mattress underneath me, moving and shifting so it can comfort and hold me, caress away those aches that Anaya's idea put there. She texted and asked if I fancied going to the gym. After yesterday's Gareth debacle, I thought pumping iron was just what I needed to get my head straight. Harmony was barely talking to me, Sol was talking less to me than that, so it was only really Ore and Oscar who noticed when I said I was going to the gym.

While I was there with Anaya, I got the impression that she hadn't told the others she was meeting up with me and she wanted to tell me something important. She didn't, but she wanted to.

I have to get up, I have to go and brush my teeth. I have to get up, I have to go and brush my teeth. If I say it many, many times it will, of course, happen. My body will magically move itself to the bathroom and I will find my toothbrush in my hand, moving up and down, foaming away the bacteria in my mouth. But, you know, right now, that bacteria doesn't seem so important. Staying flat and still is the best option for me right now.

Sol comes into the bedroom, wearing nothing but his dark blue jogging bottoms, his body like a smooth, dark sculpture. Under his arm he has his little black laptop; his glasses are perched on the top of his head.

'Please get into the bed carefully, OK?' I tell him. 'No unnecessary jiggling about – my body cannot handle it.'

'Oh, poor you,' he coos. Gently he pulls back the covers and then jumps in, causing me to bounce up and down, enough to jangle every aching muscle.

I stare at the ceiling, trying not to glower. Three months ago, that would have been funny; six months ago that would have been expected and he would have been quick to kiss away every little ache. In this timeline, the way we are right now, I know he's done it to annoy me.

'Was that a very nice thing to do?' I say to him.

'No, it wasn't. Sorry.' His apology is so throwaway, so dismissive, I don't know why he bothered. I turn my head to look at him and he is pulling a pillow onto his lap before he settles his laptop on top of it. Carefully, he takes his gold-framed glasses from on top of his head and pushes them onto his face. He flips his laptop lid open and edges it back and forth until he finds the right angle. A familiar feeling of irritation undulates in my chest. I hate it when he does that and I hate it even more when he does it to my computer. Usually that irritation flits across my mind and doesn't even really register. Nowadays, like everything we do, it causes deep, long-lasting ripples. The edges of those ripples wash up on the beach of resentment that has been building up inside my chest, and leaves behind another deposit of something that is damaging to our relationship. I have many, many resentment deposits sitting in my chest. They seem to be added to almost daily at the moment. The other day, it was hourly.

He turns his head to me, and suddenly we're staring at each other. I can see it there in his eyes, clear and present on his face: the same type of resentment that I feel towards him.

Can we just be friends? I want to say. *Can't we just get over ourselves and be friends? That's what was always so different about us – we were friends first, so let's go back to that and hope our relationship gets better.*

220

But he speaks first: 'So, Harmony tells me that her biological father turned up yesterday, gave her his number, got all googly-eyed at her, and you went for a cosy chat down the road with him out of sight of the house so she couldn't hear what you were talking about but she was pretty sure he was trying to rekindle things with you.' He is rather nonchalant in his delivery, although that's probably not what he is feeling inside. 'Anything you want to tell me?'

I return my gaze to the ceiling. 'That our daughter is really, *really* pissed off with me?' I say.

Not the only one, I can almost hear Sol reply.

Ignoring the aches, I slide myself upright until we are almost level in the bed, then I turn to look at him. 'That is not what happened,' I say to him.

'Is that why you agreed to move here?' Sol asks. 'Because you knew he was here and you wanted him to meet Harmony?'

'No. Look, Sol, he isn't Harmony's father, all right? I told you, her father was . . .' I glance at our bedroom door, see that it is slightly open. She'll be somewhere, listening. That's why she dressed it up as something more than what it was when she told Sol, why she hasn't said a word to me about it but has been frosty. She wants us to argue, for us to shout at each other so she can find out what she didn't yesterday. My daughter is devious . . . and possibly a bit too much like me for my liking.

I throw back the covers, go to the door and shut it properly. Back in the bed, I use the remote to flick on the TV and wait patiently for the screen to burst into life. Then I quickly flick through the on-screen guide until I spot a shoot 'em up movie that will be loud enough to mask our voices, especially if we start to raise them. Once the room is sound-obscured I put the remote down between us and pull my legs up to my chest. The backs of my legs, the muscles I used the most when I was doing squats earlier, protest, but I feel a bit better sitting like this, a bit more protected from the onslaught of the row we're about to have.

Sol hasn't moved the whole time; he has sat in the same position waiting for me to explain myself.

'I told you,' I start again, my voice low enough for him to hear, difficult for anyone else to hear especially when things are getting blown up on screen, 'Harmony's father was a very brief fling with a very unsuitable person. It wasn't exactly a mistake, but it wasn't my finest hour.'

The first time I told Sol this, said he could only kiss me if he listened to the story and decided if he could handle it, I added in more unflattering details than I did with Gareth yesterday, because I wanted him to know everything all at once so he could decide whether to walk away. I suppose I was testing him, too. Trying to see if he could handle living with a black woman who was once almost a police officer. Trying to see if he could handle the fact I'd gone home with a stranger and had unprotected sex with him because he reminded me of someone else. Trying to see if he understood that I wasn't perfect and I'd made some pretty heinous mistakes. Sol asked several weeks later if I was going to tell Harmony the truth about her father and I told him that if she asked, I'd tell her in age-appropriate language. But she never asked. Never even hinted once that she was curious about not having a father before Sol.

'I told you all this. I told you about what he was like. I doubt he could ever get himself together enough to turn up here. That's if he hasn't overdosed years ago. It wasn't him that turned up.'

'Who was it then?' Sol asks after a long, silent look.

'The ex before Harmony's father.'

'The one who Harmony's father reminded you of?'

'Yes, him.'

'So he tracked you down for kicks?' Sol says. He doesn't believe me. He thinks that Gareth is Harmony's father. Actually, he thinks I'm a liar.

'No!' I reply. 'He wants my help with something to do with his work and yes, he's still a police officer. I told him no, but he'd decided, after hearing – not from me, I hasten to add – that I had a fifteen-year-old daughter that she must be his. So, he turned up, pretending to try and coax me to help him but really to see if Harmony looks like him. Which she doesn't, because she's not his daughter, as I said to him – biologically and emotionally, she is nothing to do with him. All right? Or do I have to start talking in Portuguese to get you to understand?'

'I don't speak Portuguese.'

'Neither do I, but I'll try if it'll get you to believe me.'

'I do believe you,' he says quickly. He knows the damage that him practically calling me a liar will do.

'No you didn't,' I reply.

He virtually called me a liar, when he is the one with the honesty problem at the moment. I have caught my husband out in many, many 'little' lies over the past few weeks – about where he is, how late he's working, when he actually makes it into the office at the weekend and not some 'team bonding' trip away day. But I have not wanted to accept that our luscious, comfortable peninsula of honesty has been eroded quite severely by the waters of mistrust and lies. I have not wanted to admit that our marriage has gone way beyond us simply resenting each other over silly, solvable things, that we have drifted way past being snappy and unreasonable, and we're now rapidly heading towards those places of no return, where no matter what we do, we will never completely erase the bad behaviour we have visited upon each other. My husband has become a liar and I have turned a blind eye to it because I do not want my life to change.

'You didn't believe me at all. You thought I was lying.'

Sol swallows. His face has lost its superior air; he is now scared, in reality, that I am going to mention where our relationship is currently drifting. Once that has been named, exposed by being talked about, there is no going back.

One of the reasons why I was so good at my job was that I didn't take things at face value. My job, which I rarely talked about, *was* – in a convoluted way – supervising data entry like I originally told Gareth. Like I told anyone who asked. I used to supervise the people who entered data about staff in the company – which has many, many branches all over the world – but I also used to supervise the data that staff entered themselves be it emails or text messages or expenses claims. In other words, I was an internal corporate watchdog, who had the freedom to check everything people did on work computers and in work time. Yes, it's not the sort of job you win friends from having, but there it is, I did it and I was good at it. Mainly because I knew when to keep my mouth shut and I didn't let the power go to my head. (They went through a lot of people in my position before I joined the company because that amount of power goes to people's heads really, *really* quickly.)

Most people don't realise that my former position even exists and are often – very vocally – outraged when they discover such work does exist. But they don't realise that it's all there in the fine print of the contract they sign. Of course, when you have a job, especially one you really, really want, you're not going to turn it down because your company says it has the power to read anything and everything you do on their computers, or logged into their Wi-Fi or on the time in the office they pay you for. You're going to sign on the dotted line safe in the knowledge that no company has the time to read your emails and no one will care if you're arranging to meet your buddy who works for a rival company for drinks a few times, because, seriously, who is going to sit there and read the hundreds of thousands of emails sent every day? Who's going to bother trawling through all the hundreds of lines that lead to you having an affair with someone in accounting? Who's going to bother reading all those words to find out where you've bragged that the extra-expensive meal you claimed on your last trip wasn't really for you but to get someone into bed? Me. I read them. I deciphered them. I created a pattern. I worked out what it is you shouldn't be doing. And, as I said, I was good at what I did. At finding the corporate spies, the people who were intentionally and often unintentionally leaking vital secrets. I was excellent at seeing who was about to jump and take valuable information with them. I excelled at finding out those who were taking the piss when it came to expenses and corporate kickbacks. Like I said, I was never going to win any popularity competitions doing what I did. But I was good at it because I never took anything at face value. And I was good at spotting patterns.

Whether we realise it or not, we live in patterns. And our most deliberate actions – lying or hiding things or trying to deceive – follow even more pronounced patterns. The way you get dressed, make breakfast, the order you shower your body in, drive down a particular street, get on a certain train and aim for the same seat . . . Patterns, patterns, patterns. Loose, changeable, malleable patterns that are thrown off and altered, negatively and positively, by the chaos theory that is life. When people lie and hide things, their patterns become far more set because they can't afford for chaos to ruin things. Lies and deception need an even keel, because the smallest changes will reveal all.

I can see when certain patterns become more pronounced, when people start to send emails to the same person more or less at the same time every day or every week. When they change one little thing about their morning routine. When they suddenly start to wear more expensive clothes or visit the gym more or see certain people less. Legitimate, ordinary, chaos-influenced change always goes back to a familiar pattern. Less innocent patterns intensify.

Sol's lies are intensifying. This is what I used to see all the time – the intensification of lies, the concentration of deception. The inevitable.

'Why didn't you just tell me all this? Why did I have to hear it from Harmony, with her spin?' Sol says to my silence. 'All of this could have been avoided.'

I finally look at my husband with the eyes I once used to look at the emails and travel expenses and phone bills of people under scrutiny. I never thought I'd be doing this, not with Sol. The most straight-up guy ever to walk the Earth. He became dad to my little girl, father of my two sons, the perfect life partner I never thought I'd meet. And now he has become a man with too many entrenched, intense patterns that are too obvious for even me, the woman who loves him, to ignore.

Carefully, I turn away from him, slide my aching body down until it is flat and staring at the ceiling. Before I roll onto my side, away from him as we now always sleep, I use the remote to turn off the television and toss it onto my bedside table.

'I hope it's worth it,' I tell him, quietly.

225

I push my head into the soft folds of the pillow: a part of me wants to smother myself rather than say this. But I have to. I have to give him fair warning because if I've said it and he does it anyway, then I know we've gone too far away from who we were together to rescue it. If I keep silent, I'll always wonder, had I voiced my concerns when I first noticed the change in patterns in my husband, whether I could have stopped it all coming to an end.

'I really hope it's worth it, Sol, cos when I find out what or who it is and how far it's gone, it will be the end of us.'

Thankfully, he doesn't insult me by pretending he doesn't know what I'm talking about. Instead, he focuses his attention on his laptop, on going back to a familiar, legitimate pattern.

MONDAY

Cece

5:30 a.m. Harmony is raging. Absolutely furious.

I've not seen her so enraged, not since she was a toddler and had maybe a handful of truly epic tantrums. In general she is even-tempered, stoic, sensible; it seems that someone has injected her with that mythical teenager serum overnight and she absolutely hates me, positively detests this house, totally resents this family. I heard her stomping down here fifteen minutes ago and taking that bit too long to switch off the alarm, knowing it would wake me.

She has either ignored my questions or replied with little more than a grunt, and is now chewing a wasp instead of cereal. I sit down opposite her, flick off the violent movie she has put on. When she reaches for the remote across the table, a sneer on her beautiful lips, I slide it out of reach.

'Use your words, Harmony,' I say to her.

'Don't have any,' she replies.

'I don't think that's true,' I say calmly. 'I think you have a lot to say to me. Just use your words – tell me everything you want to say.'

'I have nothing to say to you.' She delivers this with the optimum mix of anger, contempt and disdain; the perfect sneer to accompany it. That's how I sounded in my head when I was her age and I was staging my private, mental rebellion. I would never have said that to my parents, but in my head, that's how I sounded.

'All right, I'll say stuff to you. That man was not your biological father. If you wanted to know that, all you had to do was ask. You did not need to twist things when you told your dad.'

227

'He so was my father,' she spits at me. 'If he wasn't you wouldn't have been acting so shifty. Everything about that meeting was well suss.' She uses her hands to emphasise her disgust at me. 'If he wasn't, you wouldn't have acted the way you did.'

'All right, look, he and I did have a relationship, once. We were both a lot younger—'

'What, like sixteen years younger?' she interrupts.

'Yes, it was around that time. But I broke up with him months before I met your father.'

'So why did he turn up here, looking at me like I was his long-lost daughter?'

'Because he, like you, like your dad, thinks he knows better than me when I got pregnant.' I reach my hands across the table. 'Yes, it'd be all neat and tidy and easy if Gareth was your biological father. I wouldn't mind so much. He's a decent enough guy – now. Back then he let me down in a pretty spectacular way. But he's not your father.' Harmony doesn't move her hands towards mine, but she doesn't take them away – that's a huge leap forwards from when I walked in here a few minutes ago. 'I'm sure he'd like to be. I mean, who wouldn't want to be your father? You're amazing, but it's not him.'

'Why don't you talk to me about my father?' she asks. 'Why won't you tell me who he is?'

'You've never asked. Not even when you were little. I just assumed because you didn't ask you weren't interested.'

'I thought you'd tell me that Dad was my father and that I shouldn't do anything to upset him.'

'Me? You seriously thought I'd say that?' I ask.

She shakes her head. Her hair bounces as she moves. 'No, suppose not. I thought he, you know, my father might have really hurt you and you probably didn't want to talk about it.'

'He didn't. Hurt me, I mean. Gareth hurt me, really badly, but your father didn't. I suppose you're old enough to hear this now. We had a short thing, we had a laugh, but when I found out I was pregnant, we both knew it was going nowhere so we went our separate ways.'

'How short?' Harmony asks.

'Pardon?'

'How short was the thing you had?'

I sigh. How much honesty is required now? My pattern is being set, the new less-than-honest pattern is being created, and I do not want it to stick. I do not want it to intensify and concentrate, to turn me into the sort of person I used to spend my days exposing. I do not want to become a liar.

'Very short.'

'As in, like, a one-night stand?'

My daughter's eyes are the exact same colour as mine. I noticed that when she was born. I stared down into her eyes and realised that it was like looking into my own eyes. She stared back at me in what I knew was wonder; she was watching me with hope and our brilliant future together mapped out on every crease on her newborn face. And her eyes, they were curious and open, watching me as though she was relying on me to provide the answer to every question she had. I didn't imagine in those moments that she would eventually be staring at me across our dining table, asking about the most contentious part of my sexual history because it was that particular part of my sexual history that created her.

'Not quite,' I reply.

Her eyes widen. 'You mean, it was only a couple of hours? Or an hour?'

'No, no,' I say quickly. 'We spent a couple of days together. It was fun, our time together, he was a good laugh. When we made you it wasn't planned, but it wasn't awful – at all. He was a nice man. I liked being with him. He wasn't anything like your dad, we weren't great mates or destined to be the next great love story, but, you know, he was all right. More than all right, actually. If we'd met at different points in our lives, maybe we'd have got together properly, but I don't know. What I do know is that he didn't hurt me, he's nothing like your dad, and you are very much your dad's daughter.'

Slowly, painstakingly slowly, Harmony's body begins to unclench; the anger is starting to seep away. She isn't completely relaxed because she still has questions. 'If he was such a good guy, why didn't he want anything to do with me? Or didn't you tell him?'

'I told him. He was such a laugh because he didn't really take much seriously. And if there's anything that needs to be taken seriously, I think, it's having a baby. But he wasn't capable of that. It wasn't you he wanted nothing to do with. He didn't want much to do with anything at that point. I'm not sure he would want much to do with anything right now.'

'Have you looked him up?' she asks.

I haven't. In some way, in that way humans can, I've convinced myself that I do not need to find him. 'No, I haven't. I probably should have, but I haven't. I suppose I didn't think I needed to because you've never really shown any interest in him. I should have, but I didn't. I'm sorry.'

Harmony sighs, then stares down at the tabletop. I know what she's going to ask and I will want to say no. I will want to persuade her to rethink, but I can't do that. It isn't about me, or Sol, or anyone else. Harmony wants to know about her history, she wants to know about her biology. She has that right. She raises her gaze to me.

'Will you help me find him?' she asks.

'Yes, sweetheart, if you want me to, I will,' I reply. Of course, it is the last thing I want to do.

5:50 a.m.

I'll help you if you agree to go away afterwards and leave us all alone.

5:55 a.m.

I can't do that, Cece. She might be my daughter. G x

5:56 a.m.

I'll help you if you agree to go away afterwards and leave us all alone.

5:57 a.m.

I can't. G

5:58 a.m.

I'll help you if you agree to go away afterwards and leave us all alone.

5:59 a.m.

Please, Cece.

6 a.m.

I'll help you if you agree to go away afterwards and leave us all alone.

6:10 a.m.

All right.

6:12 a.m.

I have your word?

6:13 a.m.

Yes. When can I come over?

6:14 a.m.

I don't need you to come over.

6:15 a.m.

You do, you need to know what we know.

6:15 a.m.

I don't.

6:16 a.m.

Just tell me when.

6:18 a.m.

This week is half term. Come over at nine on the Tuesday after.

6:19 a.m.

Fine.

Part 8

MONDAY

Hazel

3 a.m.

> I'm sorry. I'm so sorry about the other week, Anaya. Truly. I'm just cracking up a little here. She was blackmailing you, wasn't she? Please tell me. Let's get together, you, me and Maxie. We can talk about it properly. But please, tell me if she was blackmailing you?!!! Hazel x

May, 2017

Yvonne had asked me to come over a little earlier for our meet-up that night. It was at her house, which meant we would be gourmet cooking. Or rather, gourmet drinking while Yvonne barked orders. I didn't like to say – neither did the others – but Yvonne's nights were the least fun. The drink wasn't a nice accompaniment – it was a necessity to get through the night. I was never sure how Anaya managed it sober.

Yvonne had too many rules, too much emphasis on getting the recipe right, too much need to be perfect. And I felt a terrible, awful friend every time I thought that. Of course I deserved to feel like that because that was what I was: a terrible, awful friend. I arrived at her house ten minutes before the others were due to turn up even though she'd said half an hour. I couldn't face it. She wanted to talk to me about something, but as long as I'd known her, 'talking' with Yvonne meant 'confront you about something'.

Ciaran was in the process of moving here, so I wasn't around as much. From the few moments I'd seen Anaya, dashing to and from the gates, I'd gleaned that she had apparently taken on her biggest job in years and was devoting every waking hour to it. And Maxie, who had always been the most elusive one of us, was working hard and was home-bound because recently Ed was often working away. That had meant many cancelled nights with Yvonne, and had probably caused her paranoia at missing out, about all of us meeting without her, to go through the roof. Yvonne didn't seem to understand that things had changed; she was convinced it was part of a grander plan to blow her off.

'This is not half an hour, Ms Lannon,' she said in lieu of 'hello' when she opened the door. I stepped in and received her kiss on the cheek with a sinking feeling inside.

'I know,' I said. 'Sorry.'

'If I didn't know better, I'd think you were trying to avoid me,' she said. She was smiling in a barely concealed crazed manner. I drew back a little inside.

'I am not avoiding you, Vonny,' I said. 'I am just busy. Busy, busy, busy.'

'Don't "busy, busy" me,' she said. She indicated to the kitchen and I walked ahead of her, rearranging my expression from one of frustration to one of remembered friendship, recalled love. 'I'm busy, too, you know. Running the PC and being Year Two class coordinator is not easy. But I still have time for you. I still have time to look out for you.'

I had been settling my cloth bag of food on the floor so I could shed the ankle-length cardigan I wore as a coat, but those words made me stop. I glanced up at Yvonne, wary of what she was saying. 'What does that mean?' I asked her slowly and carefully.

'I wanted to ease into this conversation, but since you've turned up late, I'm going to have to cut to the chase, aren't I?'

'I suppose so,' I replied, still wary, still almost sick at the thought of what she had done.

'What are you doing, Hazel?' Yvonne asked. 'You got a fantastic divorce settlement. You were able to buy your house outright and now you've remortgaged it for your boyfriend? A man you've known for less than a year?'

'What the hell, Yvonne?'

'Sweetheart—'

'Don't you fucking "sweetheart" me. This isn't charming any more, Yvonne. This isn't one of your annoying-but-cute little quirks, this is bullshit. It's a complete and utter invasion of my privacy.'

'My children stay over at your house; I have a right to know what sort of people they're going to be around.'

'You've been researching Ciaran? Are you fucking kidding me?'

'Of course I've been researching him. I know you – I don't know him. *You* don't know him, for that matter. As evidenced by the fact you've just remortgaged a place you had outright. You had no debts before you met him and now you have a huge one.'

I pushed my hands onto my face to stop myself from throwing them around her neck. 'This is one step too far, Yvonne. I've put up with your total lack of boundaries over the years because I love you. You're kind and generous and so giving, but there is a limit. You can go too far. And you have gone so past too far it's not even in sight. I'm mortified that you've done this to him. To me. You know how happy I am with him. Have you seen me this happy in all the time I've known you? You know what that marriage and the divorce did to me. You were there, you saw it. You saw how it almost broke me and you do *this*? What if he finds out that you've been checking up on him? He'll think I was in on it and he'll be so hurt. He'll probably dump me! Is that what you want? Is it?' My heart was racing, panicking. It wasn't there any more, it wasn't there any more, but what if Yvonne had found his name? What if she'd found out?

'No, of course not, but I don't want you being taken for a ride, either, Hazel. You know nothing about him.'

'I know everything about him. How he makes me feel, how good he is to my children, how he takes the time to listen to me. He's moved his whole life and business from Durham to Brighton because he can't bear to be apart from me. I have never been this happy, never. And you're trying to mess it up for me.'

'I'm not! I only want you to open your eyes. He is not the man you think he is.'

'My eyes are wide open. And I can see now that you need me to be pathetic to give your life meaning, don't you? I need to be available and pathetic and open to everything you tell me to do otherwise your life means nothing. Well, you can do that with Maxie and Anaya, because we are finished.'

'Finished?'

I could tell from the look on her face – the way it was open with shock – that this had never happened to her before. She had never been dumped by anybody. 'I am not going to be your friend any more. This is one step too far.'

'Hazel, I know *everything* about him.'

I had been heading for the door. But I stopped. The fear of her knowing was like a spear through my heart. I wanted no one to know. *I* didn't want to know. I loved Ciaran and knowing his secret, carrying his pain, was too much for me sometimes. For someone like Yvonne, she'd have no problem sharing that burden by telling people.

I turned to look at her. My friend who had helped me through so many phases of my life.

'Are you going to tell people?'

I saw surprise flash across her face. It was brief but it was there. Maybe she didn't actually know. Maybe it was all a bluff. It was too late now, though. I couldn't risk calling her bluff; I couldn't risk anything. She probably knew that.

'No,' Yvonne said sweetly. 'Of course I'm not going to tell anyone.' She came to me and placed her arm around me. 'Hazel, you know I only want what is best for you. I'm not going to tell anyone. So no more talk about finishing with me and stuff like that. This is between you and me.'

'Really?'

'Yes, really. Come on, Hazel. You know that. We *support* each other, don't we? Like, I know if there's anything I need you to do for me, you'll have my back. I mean, if I need your *support* against the other two, or for you to come to events you wouldn't normally bother with, you'd come to *support* me, won't you?'

I swallowed hard. She had me. Yvonne had me. There was no need for it: I always supported her. I always went to her stupid events when I could get a babysitter; I usually stood up for her if the other two had an issue. There was no need for any of this.

'Yes, Yvonne.'

'Come on, let's say no more about it.' She took my bags off me and helped me off with my cardigan.

Anaya and Maxie arrived a little while later. Anaya had obviously driven them over wearing her pink candy-striped apron, while Maxie had two bags in her hand – one had the green neck of a wine bottle poking out the top.

'Are you all right?' Maxie asked me when she saw my face.

'Fine,' I said and forced myself to smile.

'Oh, she's fine!' Yvonne trilled. 'Come, come, lots of cooking to do.'

Both Anaya and Maxie studied me for long seconds but neither of them said anything. What, after all, was there to say?

Anaya

3 a.m.

I'm sorry. I'm so sorry about the other week, Anaya. Truly. I'm just cracking up a little here. She was blackmailing you, wasn't she? Please tell me. Let's get together, you, me and Maxie. We can talk about it properly. But please, tell me if she was blackmailing you?!!!
Hazel x

It's no comfort that Hazel still isn't sleeping either. Because Hazel is bad enough as it is – without sleep she will get even more unstable. Not that I'm much better. I wonder what she and Maxie would say if they knew I've been seeing Cece without them. She's just so uncomplicated and she doesn't know. I think that's the most appealing thing about her. She doesn't know. Which means she can't ask me questions like: *was she blackmailing you?* Of course she was. That's what Yvonne did.

April, 2017
I'd see Yvonne at the gates, at drop-off, and she'd wave at me, give me a cheery good morning and then would go back to talking to one of her Parents' Council friends or another mother from Scarlett's year group, and pretend we were strangers. I started to wonder if she hadn't used my parents' name to search for me after all. If she'd stopped being Yvonne for a while and was back to behaving like the real friend I knew she could be.

Yoga night gave me my answer. I was pushing aside the furniture in the back room and about to lay out the mats when there was the usual, quiet tap on the door. None of them came that early because they had children to put to bed and I had only just managed it. I thought for a minute or two as I hurried to the door that it would be a late delivery. But it was Yvonne. She was dressed up ready for yoga, but I could tell by the look on her face, the way she had set her lips, that she had other things on her mind.

In a way, she'd done me a favour having tea with Sanjay's mother. That night, when I'd spoken to Sanjay on the phone, I had laid it on the line. I had told him that his mother had gone too far entertaining people in our home when I wasn't there, and by telling other people things about me. I'd told him that was the last time that would happen, and he had better tell his mother his schedule in detail so she would know not to come round if he wasn't going to be there. He'd listened and agreed, and I'd known he was just doing the verbal equivalent of a nodding dog to me and not really listening, but that was fine. I had been open, I had been clear; the next stage would shock him, but he couldn't claim surprise because I had warned him.

'You're a bit early,' I said to Yvonne. The first pricklings of fear crept up my neck, rushing towards my face. 'I haven't even finished moving the furniture.'

'Oh, I didn't think you'd mind,' she said. 'Do you want me to go away and come back in an hour?'

'Of course not,' I replied. 'Come in. You can help me push back the furniture and lay out the mats.'

Yvonne followed me down the hall to the back of the house, to the room beside the kitchen that was technically a conservatory but we'd made brick and solid with bi-fold glass doors and a glass roof about three years ago. I went to the armchair and began to slide it across the floor. *Damn you, Sanjay, and your need for heavy furniture*, I thought. I thought that every month when I did this.

Yvonne stood in the doorway, her arms in her jogging top pockets, and her left ankle crossed over the right ankle, obviously not about to help at all. 'I wanted to talk to you, actually,' she said.

A river of ice trickled down my spine as she said this, and I had to pause with pushing the armchair because my body was suddenly rigid. 'What about?' I said and began pushing again. I had snacks to make, I couldn't afford to slow down, no matter what Yvonne was about to say. I'd got there before her, of course. I'd searched for myself on the web and it had taken some doing, but I'd found Anaya Ranatunga eventually. The things I'd had to look at to get there, though . . . I'm not sure anyone sane would put themselves through all that willingly.

'Well, you know that big investors' ball at the Grand Hotel coming up next month? I'd really like to go to it. With Trevor, obviously. Trevor mentioned that it would do his career the world of good if he could speak to some of the investors and corporate reps that will be there.'

'What's that got to do with me?'

'Well, Sanjay's one of the main speakers, isn't he? And you've been doing a lot of the marketing along with that big London firm – I know that's why you've been so crazy busy recently, why you've had no time for me. I told Trevor you'd be able to get us a ticket. And a room to stay for the night so we wouldn't have to worry about rolling in drunk and waking the kids.'

I raised myself up from my bent-over position, abandoned the chair where it stood. I threw my head back to stare up out of the glass roof. The sky was still blue, dulled a little by the lateness of the hour, and with the sun still not having completely set. I stared up, waiting for the sun to finally settle down for the night and the stars to begin their dance through the black sky. This room was almost as good as being at the beach hut. It was warmer, sure, and there were fewer midges blowing at you, and less wind worrying at you, but it was still inside. I liked to be outside. I liked to sit outside.

'And what if I say I can't get you a ticket because the event is sold out and all the rooms are allocated, to the point where Sanjay and I are coming home afterwards, as are all the other people who work for Sanjay?'

'I'd say I'm sure you can find two more seats and one more room for a friend. A best friend at that. One who really needs her husband to get the promotion that will come from him making contact with some big-name potential clients. You're a really good friend, Anaya, I know that you'll do whatever you can to help out me and Trevor.'

I continued to stare at the sky and it slowly began to change, to become something different to what it had been mere minutes ago. Mere minutes ago, I had thought that Yvonne wasn't capable of this, but that had changed. Yvonne was something completely different. I remember thinking that sometimes a friend had to call you out, hold up a mirror to show how you come across to others. Friends are there to tame your worst traits; they are there to support your better self. Or are they? Are they simply there to have good times with . . . and then to use when you have leverage and are desperate for something you can't get on your own? Maybe I had put far too much stock in the concept of friendship and ignored the glaring reality of what it was like to have someone in your life that you call a friend who was toxic. Maybe I'd just ignored the fact that calling someone your friend is not going to inoculate you against their worst traits.

'What if I say no, Yvonne?' I lowered my gaze and levelled it at her. I wanted to see her face as she did this. 'That much as I like you, much as I like Trevor, I'm not going to do this? I'm not going to put Sanjay's business and reputation at risk by doing this?'

'Do I really have to spell it out?' she asked.

'Yes, yes you do.'

'God, Anaya, I can't believe you're making me do this. I didn't want any of this unpleasantness, I only wanted you to help me out. Seeing as I'm your friend and everything. Look, since your mother-in-law didn't know why you had a different name before you were married, I'm sure she and your husband don't know that you were once a porn star. I don't judge you for that, and some of those images were pretty extreme, so I think it's quite nice of me to not judge you, by the way, but I think they might. I think they might want nothing to do with you. And if your children were to see those images . . .'

'You'd really do that to get to go to a ball?' I said to her.

Obviously, like most things, the internet was not all knowing, the internet had not given her the full picture. (Ha-ha.) She'd searched and searched and come across those pictures and thought she knew everything, or, at least, enough to get her what she wanted. It *was* enough, as well. I knew that no matter how I explained it, Sanjay wouldn't understand and his mother would never let it go. This would be all she needed to get me into the life of servitude she believed I ought to be living. She wouldn't want me to leave Sanjay, no, that would look bad to the outside world. Instead, I'd have to quit my job, come to her events, wear an Indian sari instead of a Sri Lankan one, become the dutiful and compliant daughter-in-law she'd hoped she'd get. It must have been awful for her to have three such wilful and – to me, anyway – lovely daughters. They'd gone along with arranged marriages but only to guys they'd actually been dating for a long time before the introductions had been officially made, and they didn't base their lives around their family or their husbands' families. I'm sure she'd thought that Sanjay, her only son, her last to settle down, would bring her someone to rule and control. Finding out about those photos would give her the daughter-in-law she craved.

'Of course not!' Yvonne said, genuinely shocked. 'I only need you to get us into the ball this time. I really don't think that is too big an ask. It's nothing, really, when you think about how big a secret I would be keeping for you.'

'So it wouldn't be just this – there'd be other stuff you'd want "helping out with" as a friend,' I stated.

'Look, Trevor is great and he's got so far with his career, but he's kind of stalled. He's always looking for new ways to get on but he's too polite to actually do what's needed to get ahead. I know Sanjay could really help him out. They like each other, don't they? They've always got on at the various events over the years, haven't they? He simply needs a helping hand, that's all. He needs a hand and, with your help, I can provide that for him.'

'You expect me to believe that this is all about helping Trevor and not even a little bit about you wanting to have me at your beck and call? Like pretty much everyone on the Parents' Council and probably half the women in the playground if the way they look at you is any indicator?'

'That is not nice,' Yvonne replied. 'That is not nice, Anaya, you really should think about being nicer to me. The snarky way you behave towards me sometimes is so uncalled for.'

'You're unhinged, you know that? Is this why you've got no friends? Because you're low-level horrible to them for years and then when it looks like they're about to ditch you, you pull out something to use over them?'

Yvonne flapped her arms up and down in exasperation. 'How is any of that nice? Huh?' She shook her head. 'Well, I'm sure you're just in shock, so we'll say nothing more about this.' She took her hands out of her pockets and came across the room, smiling as she walked. 'This usually goes over here, right?' She carefully nudged me aside, to place her hands on the armchair where mine had been. She started to push; not being as strong as me, it took her much more energy to move the chair. *I could shove her right now,* I thought. *Shove her, make her fall against the fireplace, smack her head open and then plead innocence in all of it.*

How dare you! I would scream at her while standing over her bleeding body. *How dare you think you could do this to me and get away with it!*

I stared at the back of her head, the way her blonde hair fell over the back of her skull and down over her shoulders. In the movies people always hit their heads at that point and were rendered unconscious. I could do that to her and I wouldn't be in this situation any more.

I looked away; I was being ridiculous. Like I could ever be violent to another human being unless it was in self-defence. My eyes travelled back. This would be self-defence, though. Just because her original attack hadn't been physical, didn't mean I didn't need to defend myself.

Maxie arrived and as soon as she walked through the door, I flung my arms around her, clung to her, held on to her trying to draw on her strength, trying to erect a shield around myself against the 'friend' sitting in my glass-roofed room, sipping tea. I did the same to Hazel. And both of them stared long and hard at Yvonne, knowing that she was the reason behind it, but canny enough to know not to ask.

May, 2017

'Anaya, this party is simply divine,' Yvonne said to me.

I pulled one of those smiles across my face that I used to wear when I had worked for my particularly odious boss.

'Thank you so much for inviting us,' Trevor chimed in. 'It was so kind of you. I couldn't believe it when Yvonne said you'd insisted we come along.' He leant in and lowered his voice. 'This is something way beyond my league and the sort of thing I would normally never know was happening until I read about it in the business pages. Thank you.'

I was not at all surprised that this was all Yvonne's doing and nothing at all to do with Trevor. He raised his glass to clink mine. I tipped my glass against his. She'd probably heard me talking about it, had seen the invites, had decided it was something she should be attending.

'Thank you for coming along. I hope you enjoy the food and company and, of course, your room,' I said to Trevor.

'We will,' Yvonne said, with a friendly smile – one that she used to give all those years ago when she had genuinely been my pal. She moved her glass towards mine to clink.

'If you'll excuse me, there are a few other people I must speak to,' I said before walking away, leaving her glass untouched in a toast. I'd pay for that, but right then, I didn't really care.

3:20 a.m. I need to tell someone. I need to tell Sanjay. But I need to tell someone everything before then. The first time I speak to Sanjay about this can't be the first time those words come out of my mouth. Who am I going to speak to, though? *Maxie? Hazel? Nope. Nope.*

So many times I've gone to say something to Cece. Just to see what she'd say. And them I'm reminded of the pact I made. And the way that me telling would be the end of me and Hazel. I feel so trapped. Even more trapped than I was with Yvonne.

Maxie

3 a.m.

Was she blackmailing you? Let's get together, you, me and Anaya. We can talk about it properly. But please, tell me if she was blackmailing you, too?

I'm not sure how much longer I can go on so little sleep. Hazel texting in the middle of the night doesn't help. I've finally managed to pack all of it away into a little box and then one text from her opens it all up again. I'm fooling myself, I know that. It never really goes away, it never really stays wrapped up in that box. How can it when it's been there for ten years? What I did. Everything that I did that led to this situation.

June, 2017
If it wasn't for Anaya and Hazel, I would not have been here. The 'Summer Fling', the ball organised by the PC, was the last place I wanted to attend, especially when it was over with me and Yvonne. I really couldn't look at her since that day in the playground a month earlier, when I'd been reminded of what she could be like. She was not a person I should be friends with. I'd done the hanging-around-with-the-mean-girls thing a long time ago. I had gone to the extreme of the mean-girl thing in my previous life. I wanted nothing to do with that again. Anaya had said there was no way she could get out of going. Hazel had begged, too, saying pretty much the same thing. The implication was clear: Yvonne was pressuring them to go and they wanted to invoke the unstated but very real 'all for one' element of our friendship.

So here I was. Dressed up, sitting at a table with my husband. I'd had to do a double take earlier when he walked into the bedroom dressed in a tuxedo. Then I'd gulped as desire flooded through me. He was rarely there at the moment for me to feel this way about him. He was travelling a lot; when he did work in Brighton he was out early, in late; and we rarely sat in the same room. When I'd mentioned this event to him on the phone, he'd said we should go.

'Really?' I'd replied.

'Yeah, it'll be fun. We don't do enough together.'

I'd clung to that. Maybe he wanted us to have a proper relationship, start doing things together, stop talking like good mates and start being open and real with each other. And when he'd walked in dressed up and ready to go, I'd been bowled over by him.

He had paused in the doorway when he saw me, had run his gaze up and down my red ankle-length dress with its wide diamanté belt that sat low on my waist, and then had ended his look at my eyes. He'd moistened his lips and gone to say something but had stopped himself, adding another invisible brick to the wall of them that had been built between us over the years. 'Ready?' he'd said instead.

'Yeah, ready,' I'd replied.

We'd said goodbye to Frankie, who was being looked after by his former key worker from Preppy, and I'd tried really hard not to worry, not to be terrified that he wouldn't be there when I got back.

Ed and I sat next to each other through dinner and laughed and joked like we usually did. But they were sitting with us, like they always did: the things we did not talk about. Anaya and Sanjay had disappeared, probably out on the dance floor, all over each other like they always were. Hazel was off with Ciaran, probably snogging him, since it was one of the few times they were out with each other. I'd even seen Yvonne's toxic minion Teri smooching with her husband at a nearby table. I reached out for Ed's hand – I wanted to connect to him, to be like the other couples around us – but then changed my mind, reached for my glass instead.

The wine was easier. It wouldn't pull away if I reached for it. It wouldn't let me hold on to it for a certain amount of time and then move on.

I drained my wine, reached for the bottle to fill myself up again. I'd had far too many already, but not enough. I wasn't drunk enough to be rude to Yvonne, which was the bar I'd set myself. The second I decided it would be a good idea to have it out with her would be the second I knew I had to stop drinking. She'd done the whole kissy-kissy-hello thing when we arrived. 'Ed!' she'd said, taking both his hands and leaning back slightly so he got a proper look at her in her skintight gold dress, slit up to her thigh. 'How lovely to see you. I feel honoured that you could make it.' Ed had tried to take his hands away, but Yvonne had hung on to him. She'd wanted me to know that she, mean girl, could have any man she wanted. She didn't realise, obviously, that, like me, Ed knew all about mean girls. He'd lived with it longer than I had. Ed had tugged harder, taken his hands away, and it had been all he could do to stop himself wiping his hands over the front of his trousers to get her touch off him.

I'd watched her all night, circling, chatting to people, all the while watching us. She hadn't got the response she'd wanted from Ed and I was sure she was waiting for another chance.

'Do you want to dance?'

The man standing in front of me was the PE teacher. He was my age, we'd shared a couple of hellos at school sports days and matches, but he made me giggly because – as Anaya, Hazel and I agreed – he was a professional 'good-looker': he was excellent at being good-looking, expert at preening himself and filling his sports gear in the right places. We would all giggle when he went by and sometimes chatted about him when we were making cocktails at my house. Tonight I'd watched him dance with lots of the other mothers and was starting to feel offended that I wasn't on his list of women to dance with. He'd done Hazel, he'd done Anaya, and Yvonne (twice). But not me, until now. I looked at Ed, to see if he minded, but he was inscrutable as always. A tiny spark of rage ignited in my chest. He'd looked at me like he wanted me earlier – not just sexually, but like his wife – and now he was acting as though he couldn't care less.

'Yes,' I said. I put down my drink and slid my hand into his. 'I would like to dance.'

The music changed as we hit the dance floor – no more 'Jump Around', now it was Barry White. Mr Professional Good-Looker immediately stepped up: he came forwards, slipped his arm around my waist, took my other hand, and started a sort of waltz that needed him to keep his hand very low on my back and our bodies very close.

'You're a very good dancer, Frankie's mum,' Mr Professional Good-Looker PE Teacher said.

'I bet you say that to all the mothers,' I replied.

'Yeah, I really do,' he said. 'It saves me time in remembering who I've said what to.'

I laughed, and he laughed. He held me a little tighter and I definitely felt his hand shift lower, to a fraction below my diamanté belt. He was pushing his luck, but I didn't mind. The wine I'd drunk made me especially not mind. I stopped looking over his shoulder and chanced a look at his face. He stared back at me. And then my husband was standing beside us.

'We're going,' Ed said.

Mr Professional Good-Looker immediately took his hands off me and stepped back. The place was packed; it looked like everyone had come with someone and was enjoying themselves, and PGL clearly didn't want to become embroiled in something that could set tongues wagging. That was why he'd danced with so many women: he didn't want to be seen to be favouring one woman. If someone's husband objected, he wasn't going to do anything but disappear. Which is what he did, straight away. He blended into the background, a chameleon that immediately vanished among the bodies on the dance floor. I was left with my husband and one of the world's best singers crooning in baritone in the background.

'We're leaving,' Ed repeated, loud enough, angry enough, for those around us to hear and to look at me.

'Are we?' I replied, I'd drunk enough to be quite keen on having a row. Maybe we'd even say those things we never said to each other.

'We're definitely leaving,' he said.

Outside it was cool. Summer was not far away, but in my dress without a wrap, in my drunken state, I felt every molecule of air as it moved over my exposed skin and warm face. Ed was marching ahead of me. His body was almost rigid with rage; he was clenching and unclenching his fists.

Without warning, he turned on me. I stumbled into him and then swayed to a stop. We were a little way away from the main entrance to the gym, and he grabbed me to steady me, then he tugged me to one side. A bit further on and we were standing by the side return of the building. We were out of view of the main entrance, of where people were starting to dribble out of the gym at the back of the school, like water from a tap with a faulty washer. Soon that dribble would turn to a gush as the place started to close and babysitters grew restless for payment and home.

'The hell did you think you were doing?' Ed hissed at me. He was so close I took a step back, only to find myself literally with my back against a wall. I'd never seen him so angry. No, wait, I had. There was the one time, and I remembered – vividly – how that had panned out. It was because of *that* night that we were together at all.

'Nothing. I was dancing. Just dancing.'

'That was not "dancing".'

'Yes it was. And I don't know if you noticed, but he danced with most of the women in there. Their husbands didn't make a holy show of them.'

'I *did* notice him dancing with most of the women in there. And I also noticed he kept looking at you. All night he's had his eye on you. And I also noticed his hands seemed to go much lower on your body than any other person's he danced with. Oh, and I noticed that you didn't seem to mind.'

'What are you saying? You think I'm cheating on you?'

'Are you going to start behaving like her? Are you? Tell me now so I know where I stand and I can get myself ready for it.'

251

'No one is forcing you to stay with me, you know. I didn't force you into any of this.'

'What the hell was I supposed to do after what happened?'

'Don't you mean what were you supposed to do after what *I did*? I'll tell you what you should have done – you should have gone to the police and spared us the last eight years of purgatory.'

'We both did that—'

'No we didn't,' I cut in. I can't stand his nobility sometimes. I can't bear how he wants to split the blame fifty-fifty when it was me. All of it was me. 'I did it. I'm the one who caused all this. I'm the one who stole the baby.'

The gasp from my left reminded me why I never said things like that out loud. Why we never talked about it. Not ever. Because you never know who might be listening. Who might be lurking around, hoping to catch a snippet of something they could use against you.

Ed and I both turned towards the gasp.

Yvonne. Of course, Yvonne. She'd probably seen the mini scene that had almost unfolded, and had followed us out here. If I hadn't drunk so much, I would have known that. I would have held my tongue until we were far away from here.

She spun on her heels and then walked away quickly, her bum wriggling in her tight dress, her mind probably already turning complicated somersaults as it calculated what she could do with this news.

3:10 a.m.

Was she blackmailing you, Hazel? M xxx

June, 2017

'So how about you start with how you stole a baby?'

Yvonne. I had toyed with chasing after her on Friday night, or calling her over the weekend. But I didn't. I knew Yvonne – I knew she wouldn't tell anyone until she had worked out the best way to hurt me with that information. And she'd have to tell me first, what she was going to do. She would have to gloat and wait for me to beg, and *then* tell everyone.

'We have to go after her,' Ed had said. All anger towards me gone. 'We need to shut her up.'

'No point,' I'd replied. 'She won't say anything tonight. She won't say anything until she's done her research and has told me what she's found out.'

'What if she goes to the police?'

'I don't know, Ed. We'll have to deal with that when it comes up. But I'm telling you, she won't do anything until she's talked to me. That's the sort of person Yvonne is.'

And here she was, true to form. Ready to talk, here to demand answers to her questions or promise retribution and destruction for my refusal to cooperate.

'How about we don't?' I replied, and walked away from the open door to allow her to come in.

This had been the weekend from hell. Or some other place where marriages go to break down and you watch the person you love visibly decide if they want to be with you any more. I'd always known he didn't love me the way a husband was meant to love a wife, not the way that I loved him, but I never thought we'd be here. Where we had to make a decision . . . And poor Frankie had been virtually hugged to pieces. Neither of us could stand to be away from him. Despite my confidence that Yvonne wouldn't do anything, I'd been waiting for the knock on the door, the footsteps in my house, the authoritative voice that told me I was finally being arrested for what I had done.

'I knew Frankie was too pale-skinned to be your real child. I knew something didn't add up despite all that guff you gave me about your father being white. And now I have proof. I knew it.'

'Is that what you know?' I replied. I was trembling, my hands quivering out of time as I filled the kettle and set it back on its cradle. 'OK.'

'You can't "Maxie" your way out of this. I know your secrets now.'

I stopped myself from raising a huge belly laugh at the idea that she knew even half of my secrets. Instead, I concentrated on making tea. Hot, wet, a dash of milk, a hint of sugar. Then I concentrated just as hard on sliding it towards her across my dining table before I grabbed my cup and sat down.

'Sit down if you're staying,' I said to her. 'And don't worry, your tea comes without added poison.'

'I can't believe how calm you are. You really are hard-faced. All this time and you've never let on what you did. I can't believe it.'

'Would you believe me, Yvonne, if I told you I was a different person back then? It was nearly ten years ago and I was a different person who did some things she wasn't proud of then, and isn't proud of now. Would you believe me?'

That stopped her. Would she believe me? She wasn't sure. The cruel, bitchy face she'd worn ever since I ditched her in the playground wavered slightly. Maybe she was wondering if she could say the same. Maybe she was wondering what roads she would be travelling on if someone had given her the chance to explain when she had done the most heinous, but most defining thing of her life.

'Stealing a baby isn't even in the same league as "not being proud of the things you've done". This is huge.'

'What happened to you, Yvonne?' I said in frustration. 'What happened to turn you into the person you are now? We were friends. We all liked you. And then it's as if you've morphed into a different person. What happened to make you like that?'

'What do you care? When have any of you three *ever* cared about me?'

The chair scraped the stone floor as I flung it back to get to my feet. I'd had enough of this. 'How many times, Yvonne? How many fucking times? You are our friend. We like you. That's why I was so shocked in the playground. You were my friend and you were being so horrible about another person, a woman who could have been your friend too if you'd just taken the time to go beyond what she looked like and talked to her. All of us, we loved you. But you act like we're always plotting to have a friendship behind your back.'

'Because you are, aren't you? I know you look down on me for being class coordinator and being on the PC; I know you're all too fucking cool to even think about joining in and supporting your children's school. I know you all laugh at what I do because I don't seem to have anything else in my life.'

'But we don't. We literally have no time to gossip about you. Actually, I'm starting to wonder if the way you carry on is in reality just an act. No one can be like you after all this time. I'm starting to wonder if you're just a manipulative, soulless bitch who wants us to feel guilty all the time so you can control us. Exactly like you said your mother is.'

She slapped me – a stinger across the face to show me I'd gone too far.

I stared at her in shock for a moment, then I slapped her back. Because no one hit me and got away with it. My slap was lighter than hers, had less venom behind it because it was a response to something, not an act of anger, but her hands still flew up to her cheek; her perfectly made-up face tremored with the shock of it. The second my hand made contact with her face, I'd been horrified. I wasn't violent. I wasn't violent by nature, not even when it was in self-defence. She'd hit me first, but it seemed worse when I did it. Maybe because Yvonne was so much more like Bronwyn Sloane than I'd dare admit: she was awful to you but you always felt worse about it if you retaliated.

'I'm sorry,' I said to her. 'I'm sorry, I shouldn't have said that and I shouldn't have hit you.' I pointed to the chair. 'Can we sit down and talk?'

'Talk?' she replied. 'I'm not talking to you any more. And you don't even know the meaning of sorry yet.'

3:20 a.m.

Hazel? Are you going to answer me? M xx

'Yvonne came over today,' I told Ed once he'd done his goodnights with Frankie. He'd walked into the kitchen to grab his evening beer and had been startled to turn on the light and find me sitting on the counter by the sink.

He went to the door and shut it, just in case the sound filtered upstairs into the bedroom and into Frankie's head while he slept. 'By the look on your face, and the way you've been quiet all evening, and the fact you were sitting in the gloom, I'm guessing it didn't go well,' he said.

'No, it didn't go well. In fact, it went pretty badly.'

'Is she going to go to the police?'

'I don't know.'

'We could pack up and be gone in a few hours,' he said. 'We can send for the rest of our stuff. I can work from anywhere, you know that, so can you. We can just pack up and go.'

I shook my head. What would be the point? In this day and age when everything needed ID, everything was electronically connected, we wouldn't get very far at all. I'd thought about it, but it would be too difficult. With a child in tow, and a need for money, we'd have to stop after a while. Besides, Frankie had a life here. It could all be ripped away, but rather that after a few more days or weeks of living a normal life, than going on the run and then having all that ripped away. Better to live on borrowed time than run on borrowed time. We had to see it out.

'Let's see what happens, shall we? She might not say anything.'

'Do you want me to talk to her? Explain?'

I shook my head vigorously. 'Definitely not. Let's leave her.'

'I hate that woman,' he said. 'I actually hate her. I know she's your friend but she's one of those people . . .' He stopped talking but stared directly at me and I knew he meant Bronwyn. We never talked about Bronwyn. Even when we occasionally ran into people who remembered Ed from his former life, who would ask how he was, and would ask about Bronwyn, he'd mumble something about them no longer being in touch; we'd pretend afterwards that the person hadn't asked about her, just like we pretended she didn't exist.

'Yvonne might not go to the police,' I told him.

'Yeah, she might not.' Ed tugged open the fridge and retrieved his beer. Then he took his bottle into the living room to flick through the channels on the television.

More than likely, I knew, Yvonne was going to use the threat of the police against me. She already had Hazel nervous, and Anaya cowed; now she had me where she wanted me. Going straight to the police wouldn't appeal to Yvonne at all. I still had time to keep my family together. I still had a chance for a miracle that would stop Yvonne from ruining my life.

An hour later, my mobile bleeped with Yvonne's text tone.

> I've decided to forgive you for hitting me earlier. I'm sure we can work it out somehow. I'm sure there'll be some way you can make it up to me at some point. Now, honey, let's put all of this behind us. Yvonne xxx

I threw my phone onto the side. I needed a huge miracle, I realised. A giant one.

3:30 a.m.

Hazel??????

Part 9

TUESDAY

Cece

9:05 a.m. Gareth has spent the last few minutes taking in my kitchen. He's looked over the surfaces, the set-up, the mound of papers on the side of the table, the chalkboard with the week's menu I started ages ago but never got round to updating, the sofa with its unplumped cushions, the marks on the tiled floor, the cooker that I have to clean. He has looked at all of those things, but of course he has stared longest at the pictures of Harmony that surround us. He has stared and stared, trying to find the similarities, trying to convince himself that he has a place in her life because he thinks he contributed to her DNA. I don't want him here, staring at pictures of my daughter – my and Sol's daughter – but I can't risk us being seen together. If I am going to do this, I can't risk anyone catching on.

'Have a seat,' I say to him.

There was a time when Gareth and I couldn't be alone in a room without wanting to tear each other's clothes off. I wonder, if things hadn't gone the way they did, if we'd still be like that. Or if, like it has with Sol and me, real life would have got in the way.

He comes out of his stupor, where he is clearly imagining what it would be like to spend dad-and-daughter time with Harmony, and looks at me blankly for a moment. When he remembers who I am, why he's here, he takes a seat at the table and I move towards the kettle. 'You must never tell anyone I have talked to you about this. Only my boss and I know about it – this is top secret.'

'Coffee?' I say. I'm not going to indulge his whole top-secret/secret-undercover-agent thing.

I told him when he turned up, like I told him before half-term, that I didn't need him to brief me. I wanted to do this my way. I wanted to approach it with fresh eyes and my own perspective. I got the impression, though, that Gareth has done a lot of work on this and wants to show his skills off to me. He tells me he'd like a coffee and chatters about confidentiality and suchlike while I make us both a drink in total silence, and then bring both cups to the table.

I sit on the longer side of the table and he sits on the shorter side, where Sol usually sits. What would Sol say if he knew who had been sitting in his seat? He'd probably go mental. To be fair, in his place, I'd go mental too.

'My boss is only letting me talk to you because you're ex-police,' he says. 'Most of the stuff I'll tell you is stuff you could technically find out via other means. So some stuff I'll have to keep back.'

There's an atmosphere, a heavy pall of the past that hangs over us like a thick shawl, embroidered with the threads of what we did together, how we fitted with each other. I can feel the heat starting to rise. I knew it was a risk, letting him come here, but I had no real choice.

'Look, Gareth, I do not need to hear any of this,' I say to him. He is staring at me and when I glance up, our eyes meet. I stop speaking as a memory reverberates through my mind: *Him staring at me, stroking my face while we lie on his narrow bed, naked and close. 'You're incredible. You make me feel incredible when I'm with you.'* I clear my throat, look away. 'I know you will have done a lot of background research into them, but I don't want the things you've found out to cloud my judgement. This is all from you so even if it's just facts, it'll still be the facts as you've seen them. Not stuff that I might notice.'

'I know you don't want me to, but I really have to at least tell you what I can about what we know so far.'

I sip my coffee and mentally prepare myself to listen. I can hear him, fine, but I need to listen, to not let anything cloud what I remember about what he says because I won't be taking notes and I need to see where the patterns are.

'Yvonne Whidmore, forty-two. Has lived in Brighton for nearly twenty-five years. Has been married to Trevor Whidmore for nearly eighteen years. We know some background information on Trevor Whidmore and obviously he would have been our main suspect but he was at home with the children the night of the attack. Neighbours heard one of the children wake up in the night with a nightmare and he went in to resettle them. The child confirms it. The child is also a poor sleeper so did wake up several times in the night. And his mobile phone says he did not leave the house all night, but he did make several calls to the suspects in the early hours of the night when his wife didn't come home.

'They have a normal marriage, no financial worries although a little debt. On the night in question the things we know for sure are that Yvonne Whidmore had drunk the better part of a bottle of wine before leaving her house at around nine p.m. She drove – drunk – to the beach, which is where we found her husband's car that she used the next day. She went to the beach hut owned by one of her friends and there was an altercation. All of the women there – apart from Whidmore herself – confirm that. After that, things are sketchy. She's caught on some CCTV cameras leaving the vicinity of the beach hut, but no one knows how she got from there to the school. For some reason she had keys to the school and the code to the keypad entry system. Her fingerprints were found on the gate keypad and the padlock, as well as the alarm keypad inside the front door to the school. The keys were found in her pocket. The right-hand pocket, before you ask, and she is right-handed. Her fingerprints were all over the keys in the way they would be if someone was using them. She was found by a dog walker walking past the school just before six a.m., who saw her through the gates and at first thought she was just drunk so called the police to have her removed. We know that the alarm was disabled just after ten o'clock, so she was probably bludgeoned between that time and when she was found.

'She was bludgeoned with a large rock that came from a set from the beach hut she visited earlier in the evening. There were no sets of fingerprints on the rock – not even the victim's – suggesting it was wiped clean but none of them could explain what the rock was doing at the school and not at the beach hut. Well, they could explain, but none of them said the same thing so we could only conclude they were lying. We found very little foreign DNA evidence on Yvonne, and what we did find pointed to one or all of the women we think did it. Coupled with the fact all their stories vary a little in some places and then wildly in other places, it's clear they're all lying. Even the bits that they corroborated – like the fact they all left together – sound so rehearsed we're sure they're lying.'

He stops talking and when he starts again, he's lost that robotic, formal tone he told me that information in, and he speaks much softer, more naturally.

'Which brings me to what I know about them.' He places a hand on the table and I look down at it. Wrinkled, the skin a slightly baggy dark pink around his knuckles, his nails neatly clipped. 'If you know the background on these women, you'll see why we think it was one of them.'

'But from what you said, you don't know it was one of them. People lie all the time when they're scared, especially when the police are on their case. You know that.'

'Cece, you need to listen to what I know.'

'I don't, you know. It's going to be hard enough facing them with this agenda, but knowing stuff that I shouldn't about them will make it even more difficult.'

'You used to do it all the time,' he says. 'That was your job for years remember?'

'Those people weren't my friends. I respect my friends' privacy. The people who I used to investigate had signed something saying I – well, the company – was allowed to monitor their activity. I'm not saying it was morally right, but it was legal and above board. This is underhand and sneaky. And I'm only doing it to get rid of you. I don't need to know stuff about them before I find out what happened that night.'

He says nothing for a while, probably because he knows I'm right. Maybe waiting for me to look at him again. I can't, of course. Look at him, that is. It's too difficult. I thought all of that would be long gone, eternally erased. I was disgusted by what he was saying in the street the other day, but it's not gone, of course it's not. We never finished properly; I still hate him for what he did, but I kind of—

'All right, compromise,' he says when I don't look at him. 'I'll give you the short version, a precis of all the things you should absolutely know. Right, well, one of them has a caution on record for assault; one is being investigated for possible fraud and one, I don't know, one of them there's something about her. There are lots of little things that don't add up. We were focusing on her first of all because she admits following the victim to continue their argument, but then says she went back to leave the beach hut with the others.'

Bloody hell. Am I really going to do this, to make him go away? This is stuff I don't want to know. This is stuff that I'd rather be able to say, REALLY? I had no idea, she was capable of that about, than sit there knowing. Because what do I do with this knowledge once it's in my head? How do I behave with them after I have looked into all their secrets? Some friend I am.

I push my chair out hard and stand up. I move towards the sink and lean on the worktop beside it. Deep breaths. Deep breaths. *I can do this. I'm sure I can. I have to, but what sort of person does this make me? Will I really ever be able to call any of them my friend if I do this? If I find out that one of them is a potential murderer what will happen with the other two if they find out what I did to help the police? Who would trust me again? I wouldn't trust me. No way. And what if they all did it?* 'Are you absolutely sure it was one of them?' I ask.

'Yes. As I said, they've all admitted they were with her not long before the attack; theirs is the only DNA found on the victim; we know they're lying to us but we can't seem to break them and—'

I hold my hand up to stop him talking. I don't need to hear any more. I don't need to listen to this at all. This is a different kind of nightmare. The only way to rid my life of the ex who betrayed our friendship is to betray my friends.

I stand very still while Gareth gets up and slowly crosses the kitchen towards me. I hear his footsteps approaching and I focus on the way the bevelled edges of the white tiles above the sink disappear into the grey grouting. I concentrate on the way light from the patio doors falls on the stainless steel tap and drainage rack. I focus on the tiny speckles of black mould I'll need to remove from the clear glue-like sealant between the wall and sink. I should move, I should stop this, but I don't. I stand very still and concentrate on my sink until Gareth is close enough for me to feel the heat that was always between us, until he stands behind me, slightly off-centre so the right half of his body presses ever so slightly against the left half of mine. I should stop this, but instead I concentrate on the sink, on biting my lower lip as he places his hands on my shoulders. I should stop this, but instead I close my eyes and inhale his scent, the essence of him – musk, sandalwood, peat – as he lowers his head and presses his face against my hair.

'Cece,' he eventually sighs. 'Do you ever think about us? About what it would have been like if we'd stayed together?'

I should stop this. Despite the heat, despite the way my body is responding to him: unfurling, unclenching, unwinding because I'm desired in a way Sol seems to have forgotten, I should stop this. Despite remembering how physically and mentally hedonistic it was to fuck Gareth, I should stop this. 'I think you'd better leave,' I say to him. I am stopping this. I *am* stopping this.

'Cece,' he breathes again. 'I think about you all the time. I think about *us* all the time.'

'That was fifteen years ago. We've been apart sixty times longer than we were together.'

'It was sixteen years ago, but that hasn't changed anything. I've slept around, yes, I've had relationships, and I've tried to settle down but—'

'You need to leave now, Gareth,' I interrupt. I do not need to hear any more.

'I want you so much,' he whispers and presses his body closer to me. 'So much.'

My treacherous body responds by pushing back, moulding itself to him. I want him so much I can taste it in my mouth, the scent of him is filling my mind. I want him. I want him to press his lips against my neck and cover it in kisses; I want him to slide his hands under my clothes and caress my skin; I want him to unbutton my jeans and tug them down over my hips; I want him to unbutton his trousers . . .

'Gareth, I'm married. Even if I wasn't married . . . we can't go back in time. We can't go back to before what you did . . . Just go.'

'I meant what I said last time,' he says. 'I loved you . . . I think I still—'

It'd be so easy for me to do it. The way Sol and I are breaking apart right now, the way I know my husband is hiding something from me, most likely doing the dirty on me, the way he makes me feel when I am around him, it would be so good to do it with Gareth. To stick two fingers up at Sol, at my failing marriage, and exact a quiet but powerful revenge. It'd be so easy to do it, too, especially when my body, each neglected part of it, wants me to. But wanting to screw someone and doing it are two very different things. There are a lot of steps you have to take in between those two things and you can stop at any time. I am stopping it right now.

'Sex isn't love,' I tell Gareth, my tone harsh but necessary. 'No matter how good it was, sex isn't love. You *really* need to leave now.'

Finally. He steps away and I can at last breathe. I can at last mentally shake myself and tell myself to stop being so stupid.

'Cece . . .' he says.

'Yep?'

He says nothing, does nothing, until I'm forced to look at him.

'I know you said sex isn't love but did you ever, you know, feel . . . ? Did you ever, even a little?'

We are talking about a past history, but it still feels like a current betrayal of Sol. Of the life we've built.

'You know the answer to that,' I say to him. He may have not been able to read me all the time, but he did back then. I was an open book to him back then.

He grins at me. 'Really?'

I nod.

'Thank you,' he says. 'For your help with all this, I mean.'

'I haven't done anything yet,' I state.

'You will. I know you will.'

I know I will too. And that thought makes me want to retch.

2 p.m. I need to find out what they are hiding so I can work out why they are lying to the police. Because even though I am doing this thing, I don't believe any of them has done it.

The strongest link in the pattern that is 'Anaya, Hazel and Maxie' is actually Hazel. She is the one I will have to do more labour-intensive stuff with because so much of her story is known. She is very open about 95 per cent of her life. The 5 per cent she keeps hidden has been squirrelled away for specific, devastating reasons and it will take something big to get her to reveal it.

From what I know of them, what I know about human nature in general, people like Anaya, Hazel and Maxie do not lie for personal gain, they lie to protect other people. Which is why I am baffled why Hazel is being investigated for fraud. Unless she has debts that are astronomical, but she told me she had managed to secure enough in her settlement to buy her new house outright, so why would she? Fraud, the type that requires a long investigation, is not small stuff. I am assuming the fraud investigation is of Hazel because she works for a building society. Which, again, is odd, because why would she? Why would she risk it all when she has three children to bring up essentially on her own? It must be the link to her boyfriend, Ciaran, that has caused her to be investigated. It must be. He is the one I have to do a deep investigation on.

Maxie and Anaya.

Anaya is the weakest link. She wants to talk. She wants to tell the truth to someone. Not only about that night, but also about what led to her accepting a caution for assault. I know it's her because out of all of them, she has the calmest disposition. It stands to reason that if any of the others were to get into a fight, like me, they would argue the toss, they would see it through to the end. Anaya would accept a caution to have it over with. Anaya. She wants to open up to some-one, so I need to focus on her, first. Find out why she is lying to the police. Who she is trying to protect. Why someone of her temperament would lie about being involved in Yvonne's attempted murder. That's the thing as well. Someone who has taken a caution for assault will most likely do it again if threatened. Was Yvonne threatening her?

Which leaves Maxie. The enigma. It could go any way with her. I like her so much though. Out of the three, she is the friend that is most like me – she speaks her mind, she can be volatile, but she cares.

Maybe I'm fooling myself, but I'm doing this for them as well. They are all, in their own ways, cracking up. I see them at the gates, trying to be normal, pretending they aren't carrying this heavy burden, when it's clear none of them has had a good night's sleep in months. If you do not have psychopathic tendencies, things like this will slowly tear you apart. So, a tiny, tiny part of this is for them. The truth will set them free. I know it will.

I have to tackle them in different ways.

My chest tightens when I pick up my mobile. I have to do yoga breathing – deep breath in, long breath out – several times before I can type. Shame shakes my fingers, and I have to delete the rouge letters that come up. Finally I press send and I almost fling my mobile across the room at the thought of what I've started.

Part 10

MONDAY

Anaya

6:45 p.m.

Hey Anaya. How's it going? Love Cece x

She's not technically been in my life long enough for me to call her a friend. But I'm relieved every time I see her name on my phone. She's been sending me 'How's it going?' texts for the past week, and even if I don't reply, they make me feel better. I don't have that clench I get whenever I see Hazel's or Maxie's name come up. She's simple, uncomplicated. Maybe she's the person to practise on before I set off that bomb in my life.

TUESDAY

Cece

7 p.m. Anaya is at the door. I've been sending her 'How's it going?' texts for the past week, hating myself every time I press send, but today it's paid off.

'Hi?' I say. 'Are you all right? Is there a problem with the children?'

'No, no, they're fine. They're with their dad. Although, what they're up to I don't want to think about, so maybe I was being a bit optimistic when I said they were fine.'

I grin at her, remembering how endearingly crazy she sounded the first time we met.

'I sound crazy, don't I?' she says.

'Only a little.'

'Can we go somewhere for a chat?' she asks. I watch her dry the palms of her hands on her tight black trousers and I know she's ready to talk. She's wanted to for a while but now she's ready.

I glance over my shoulder. 'Give me a minute.' I step back in, take off my apron and hook it in place of a small black fleece, which I shrug on before I put on my teal-green leather jacket, swap my fluffy slippers for ankle boots, wind one of my many scarves around my neck. I go to the bottom of the stairs and shout: 'Just nipping out for a bit. The kids have had their dinner, just homework, reading, teeth and bed to do. Don't worry if you don't get around to the washing-up.'

'What?' I can hear from upstairs. 'Where are you going? When will you be back?'

'You're glad you've got my back? Ah, thanks, love. Don't wait up.'

'No, no, Cece, I'm meant to be going out. I said I'd meet a few—'

'What was that? "Have a nice time, Cece"? Oh, thanks, I will.' I can hear movement upstairs so I go quickly to Anaya. 'See you later, kids. Be good for Daddy.' I then usher Anaya out, slamming the door behind me. I take her hand and drag her down the road at a fast run/walk.

'Oh, no, your husband said he was going out. I don't want to cause any trouble. This chat can wait till another time.'

'No, for you to have come here, I really don't think this chat can wait, can it?' I say. 'If you back out now, you won't ever do it. And I suspect this is something you really need to talk about.'

'You're right, but I feel bad, though. What about your family?' Once we reach the street that leads up to the main road, I slow down and let go of her hand.

'They'll be fine . . . well, the kids will be. Sol will be narked for a bit about it, but he does need last-minute reminding that they're also his children and just because he earns the cash, he doesn't get to opt out of all the drudgery bits of parenting.'

'If you're sure?'

'I am sure.'

'Oh, that's great. Do you mind if we walk and talk? I need a cigarette, and bad.'

Anaya

7:15 p.m. We walk over the road, towards St Ann's Ricks Park. I don't light a cigarette because I don't really want to smoke. I want to talk. I need to talk. The park is quite threatening in the dark, large looming shapes of trees, bushes, hills and children's climbing structures all sit like cut-outs against the inky-blue sky.

'You know how I knew Yvonne Whidmore, the woman who was attacked at the school?' I say to Cece.

'I do.'

'Well, I was with her the night she was attacked.'

She nods.

'And I have to tell you why I was there. And to do that, I have to tell you about a certain time in my life. Look, let me just start at the beginning. Well, as far at the beginning as I can get.

October, 1993

'Kalani! Kalani!' My tatta sat in his office, looking at me like I'd sworn at him, and shouting for my mother. Amma came running, thinking something terrible had happened.

When she arrived and found that neither of us were bleeding, or unconscious, she stopped panicking and glared at my father.

'Tell your mother what you just told me,' Tatta said, still with the look of horror on his face.

It was small in Tatta's office. The walls were lined with not-quite-level shelves, stacked with books and journals and papers. He was an intellectual and liked to collect books and papers and other things to expand his mind. He worked for the government, was quite high up in the civil service, and he got the train from Wimbledon station every morning to Victoria and then came home every night the same way. After dinner he would retreat to his office to read, to continue to pen the philosophical articles he was always submitting to journals.

After what I had asked, the office seemed smaller, claustrophobic and confined. My parents were more laid-back than most of the non-white parents whose children went to my school: they didn't force any of us to be vegetarians; they allowed us to follow any faith we chose as long as we chose one; they let us go out like our white friends. But there were limits, boundaries, and I had just crossed one.

Amma smiled at me as she waited to hear what I had just told my tatta to make him call her like he was on fire.

'A man gave me his card today and said he thought I could be a model. He's looking for models for a magazine shoot and thinks I would be perfect for it.'

Tatta nodded his head, confirming that I had sworn at him, and looked at my mother to see what she would say about it.

I'd known they'd be like this. Always, always, always we had been taught to value our brains, our capacity to learn, the chance to intellectually stretch ourselves above all things. Going for something that valued physical beauty above all else was, I suppose, the equivalent of swearing at my tatta.

It was Amma's turn to look at me as if I had sworn at her. She stared at my father, he stared at her, the pair of them clearly shocked that I had even considered doing it.

Amma adjusted the *pallu* of her sari, straightening and restraightening it on her shoulder – something she only did when she was anxious. Then she spun her large gold bracelet around her dainty wrist. She was very anxious about this. Eventually she said, 'I do not think so, Anaya.' Amma rarely said no. Not outright. She talked to you, explained to you, got you to see that her no was wholly warranted and justified.

'But Amma—'

'Your mother has said no,' Tatta interrupted. 'Respect that, Anaya.' Tatta had no worries about saying no.

'Why can't we even talk about it? Why are you being so unfair?' I could hear my voice rising.

'I don't want you out there, exposed to goodness knows what,' Amma replied. 'That is a world we know nothing about. I do not want you to be out there with all of that.'

'But Amma, I'd be one of the first Asian teenage models,' I said. 'I could be a role model for other girls like me to think they can do it too.'

'I'd rather that came from your achievements in the world of medicine, law, science, literature . . . anything but this, this . . . *This*.' Tatta couldn't even think of the word to describe it.

'But I could do both. I wouldn't be a model for ever. It'd only be for a bit, then I could go to university. I could even earn enough money to pay for university myself.'

'No, Anaya,' Amma said again. She was much firmer, much more sure of her decision this time. 'I do not want you to do this thing. No. Come, come, you must do your homework. And then straight to sleep.'

'Goodnight, Anaya,' Tatta added.

I spent the better part of a week thinking of the right way to change their minds, to explain why they should let me do it. Why it would be good for me, good for all those other girls out there who were constantly being told having brown skin meant they were not beautiful. They would have hope. They would see that someone like them could be beautiful. I wanted Amma and Tatta to know that wanting to be a model was not about vanity, it was about being a trailblazer for the girls who would come next. I thought of many, many arguments and counter-arguments. I invoked every argumentative bone in my body and in the end it was simple. I forged their signatures on the forms and pretended to go to school when I had shoots. It was easy, really.

7:40 p.m. Cece and I wander down the perimeter of the park, the structures seeming to change and grow, moving like arthritic giants waking from sleep in the dark of night. She's listening. Listening and not speaking.

June, 1994

There I was, wearing a short skirt and a baseball jacket, with my head thrown back laughing at something one of my friends had said. And there I was, sitting huddled on the street with my knees pulled up to my chest, a hat pulled down low on my head and a 'help me' look in my eyes. And there, dressed in a bikini, with three of my other friends dressed in matching bikinis, all ready to rush down over the sand onto the beach. And there I was, about to graduate – smiling but worried about what the future held. There, there, there. I was all over the place. All over my parents' large kitchen table, in the various magazines I'd worked for.

My school bag fell off my shoulder and I stood very still in the kitchen doorway while my parents sat on either side of the table, framing my laid-out work like two shocked bookends.

'I can explain,' I said. That's when I realised that explaining would be all about confessing to forgery, truancy, lying and deception. They had it all laid out in front of them, they did not need me to spell it out too. They did not need me to inadvertently confess to stuff they didn't know about. 'Actually, no I can't,' I amended.

'Anaya, *why?*' Amma said. The desperation in her voice, the utter incomprehension, made me gulp. 'We allow you so much freedom. So much more than our parents allowed, than any other parents like us allow, and you do this? *Why?*'

Because I wanted to, I should have replied. *You wouldn't let me, and I couldn't accept that answer so I did what I wanted.* I shrugged. It was easier than admitting that.

'Your father is so hurt. I am so, so hurt. How can we ever trust you again?'

This was so much worse than shouting. Shouting I could rail against, I could meet with my own shouts about injustice. Hurt, sadness . . . how do you fight them? Answer: you don't. You either cave and beg for forgiveness, or you harden your heart to all such manipulations. It was manipulation, even as a fifteen-year-old I knew that, but it was good manipulation. It was positive and necessary to scare me back onto the right side of truth-telling.

'I'm sorry, Amma, Tatta. I'm so sorry. I know I did wrong, I know I was selfish and wrong, but I'm so sorry, so, so sorry.'

I hung my head, started to sob as I realised how much I had hurt my parents. I didn't actually think of them as having feelings. They were adults, they were people who set the rules, and made decisions about my life and the lives of their other children. They went to work, they cooked, they cleaned, they made us help with regular chores. They worshipped, they partied, they socialised with other Sri Lankans who had built up a life in London. They were all of these many-many-faceted things, but I never thought of them as having feelings. Understanding, let alone knowing, what love was all about; what fulfilment, or fear, or insecurity or wanting to be thought of as pretty and successful meant or felt like. How could they understand what it meant to have so many conflicting emotions living at the centre of your being? They were adults and they functioned without the passions and desolations I felt sometimes on an hourly basis.

'I won't do it again. I am so sorry.' Tears ran down my face, dripped off my chin, the sobs moved through my body in huge gulps as I realised that my parents not only had the capacity to feel, they could be hurt very, very badly. And I had done that. Some of the girls at school were practically caged. One girl, Erise, told me her parents wouldn't let her out without one of her older brothers accompanying her – even to and from school. I had all the freedom I could need and I'd abused it. I had behaved terribly and I had made my parents sad. 'I won't do it again, Amma, Tatta. I won't do it again.'

Amma came to me, cupped my face in her hands. 'Stop crying, my beautiful daughter,' she said gently. Her bracelets tinkled against each other as they slipped down her wrist. She used her thumbs to wipe away the tears. 'You don't have to worry. Bring me any form you like from now on and I will sign it. If I am not here, your father will sign it. No more sneaking around, Anaya.' Amma took her hands off me, adjusted her *pallu* and then went to the other side of the kitchen to start dinner.

Tatta smiled sadly at me and got up and left the room without saying another word.

I called Flint, the guy who had 'discovered' me in that shopping centre in Wimbledon. He'd treated me so well in all my modelling assignments, looking after me, showing me the ropes and stopping other photographers and shoot directors from pushing me to do outrageous things. He was disappointed when I told him that I had to stop, and he'd tried to persuade me to change my mind, but I couldn't. What I had done to my parents had devastated me. I was giving up modelling and I was going to do whatever it took to earn my parents' trust back.

'I totally understand, kiddo,' he eventually said. 'Come over any time to pick up your portfolio. There are some really nice pictures in there. It's a shame though, you could have made it big.'

8 p.m. Cece links arms with me. She seems scared – I'm not sure if it's of the dark, winding path we're taking into the heart of the park, or my story.

August, 1995
My mouth felt funny. It felt sticky, gunky. It was the first thing I noticed. My eyes were still closed because I was in complete blackness, and they felt heavy and thick, but my teeth were coated, my tongue felt inflated as well as covered with slime. My limbs were heavy, unwieldy too, and I had to concentrate to raise my hands to cover my eyes. When I managed it, I rested my hands on my eyes and immediately regretted it. I groaned, exhaled and groaned some more. My head hurt. It thumped and pulsed and I couldn't stop myself groaning again.

This is what Candy – my former best friend who had been so jealous of my modelling career she had 'anonymously' grassed me up to my parents – said hangovers felt like. But I hadn't drunk enough to be hungover. I'd gone over to Flint's studio to collect my portfolio. It'd been over a year, he must have discovered and photographed lots of girls in that time, but he'd remembered me on the phone and had said to come over any time I wanted. I'd actually wanted to see him because I'd had a huge crush on him and none of the boys in my class could match up to him.

He'd made it very clear that I was too young for him and that I should go for boys my own age. Which, of course, had made me like him even more. One of the best things about being photographed by him was his studio. It was pristine. One area was a clean expanse of white that housed his backdrops and had cameras set up all around. The other part of the studio had a waiting area set up with sofas and chairs, a sideboard with a coffee machine and a fridge underneath. Through an archway, to the right of the shooting area, was his living space. A large bedroom that led to a kitchen area that led to a sitting and lounge area. And beyond the lounge area was another archway that led you back to the studio. He had the whole floor of an old box-style warehouse in a pretty grotty part of east London. Outside the world was decaying; inside it was clean and new and fresh. He'd offered me a glass of champagne and said he'd missed me. 'You were a dream to work with,' he'd said. 'Most models, especially the newer ones, can out-diva even the supers. I swear, the ones like you are few and far between.'

I'd been flattered, had blushed and gulped down the drink in my hand. 'Hey, careful,' he'd said to me, 'don't drink it too quickly, especially if you're not used to it. Sip it slowly, OK?'

'Who said I'm not used to it?'

'You do, with everything you do and say. You're a nice girl, gentle, virginal, untouched by life. That's why I like you. That's why all the clients liked you. Don't go rushing to get into the grown-up world,' he'd said. 'Once you're there, it's hard to get yourself out again. Believe me.'

I'd lain back and closed my eyes. I loved Flint's voice. He had a cockney accent that grated on your ears first of all, but when you listened to it for a few minutes, you found yourself rising and falling with the lilts and tilts of his voice, the way he shaped words and allowed them to escape into the air like gentle multicoloured balloons.

Finally, I managed to prise open my heavy, thick eyes and I flinched at the light that came streaming into my vision. I clamped my eyes shut as fast as I could and groaned.

'Ah, look who's awake,' Flint said.

'Nrrr,' I replied.

'Yes, well, you may well speak like that for a while, given how much you drank last night.'

'I only had one glass,' I mumbled through my dry, scratchy throat.

'And the rest. Do you remember me telling you to slow down?'

'Vaguely.'

'Well, you didn't listen. In fact, you didn't listen to me all night.'

My eyes flew open and looked around the room. 'All night?' I was in Flint's bed, covered by his expensive cotton sheets. 'Oh God, how did I get in here?'

'I mostly carried you.'

'Oh God.' I pulled the sheet up over my head to hide my embarrassment. I noticed then that I was only wearing my white bra and black knickers. I stared at them for a second then jerked the sheet off my head and found Flint staring at me. A small smile of amusement played around his pink lips and his blue eyes.

'You were sick,' he explained. 'All over yourself and some of the beach scene I've got set up out there. I had to take your clothes off to wash them off, but your underwear I left on and tried to sponge off as much as possible.

'Oh God,' I said again, cringing at the idea of it. I really didn't think I'd drunk that much. 'Did I . . . did I try it on with you?' I had to know. I had to know how complete my embarrassment was.

'Let's just say I like my women sober and knowingly consenting.'

'Oh God.' I covered my eyes again. The sunlight, which was flooding in through the large windows in his bedroom, was burning its way through my brain. 'I am so sorry. You must think I am awful.'

'No, no, it's fine,' he said. 'I've had worse, and at least you didn't throw up actually on me. I've had that happen before.'

I rubbed at my eyes. I didn't know what I was going to tell my parents about being out all night. They didn't generally mind, but after the revelation that I'd been dishonest with them, I'd been trying to rebuild their trust. Urgh, I was useless at this sometimes. I was useless at behaving like a functioning human being. Why did I get so drunk? And throw up and then pass out and then stay out all night?

'I think I'd better go,' I said to Flint.

'Don't worry about it,' he replied. 'Your parents will understand. I think your clothes should be dry – I think I got everything off, apologies if I didn't.'

I cringed some more.

'Seriously, Anaya, don't worry about it. We all do things like that sometimes.'

He left me alone to get dressed and I did so as quickly as I could.

'I'll see you soon, Anaya,' he said at the large metal door to his flat.

'Yeah,' I replied. 'And I am so, so sorry about everything.'

He shook his head and smiled that smile again. 'No worries, mate.'

I turned into my road, walking quickly, eternally grateful that it was early so the walk of shame hadn't been too bad, and as I approached our house, I remembered I hadn't actually taken my portfolio. All in all, a completely pointless exercise.

8.25 p.m. I can hear Cece breathing fast beside me. I think she wants to cry; I know she feels bad for me. She holds me closer and we walk on. Deeper into the park, back into my past.

August, 1995
I pressed the large circular doorbell that sat beside the large metal door to Flint's studio/flat. Someone had been leaving as I arrived, so I'd walked in and up the stairs to his third-floor apartment. I'd got him a box of Quality Street to thank him for not being offended

after last time, and I was going to get my portfolio and go. No sticking around to drink, no vomiting, no trying it on with him, no passing out. I was going to collect and then go.

'Anaya,' he said when he opened the door. 'What are you doing here?'

I thrust the small purple box of Quality Street at him and stepped forwards. He stepped back, then seemed to change his mind and halted, barring me from going any further. From the way his shirt was hanging open, exposing his bare chest, he probably had a woman in there and didn't want me around. I swallowed my pang of jealousy and reminded myself that I was only there for the portfolio, not to indulge my crush. 'I brought you some chocolates to say sorry for being sick on your studio area, and thank you for th . . .' My voice petered away when I saw what was projected onto the wall of his studio area: me.

A giant image of me.

My stomach turned over itself, a domino effect from the way my throat had somersaulted and my heart had stopped beating and fallen forwards.

I was projected onto the wall in front of me, reclining on a bed. I was naked, my eyes – hooded and vacant – were barely open; my lips, which looked almost bruised they were so plump, were parted because they were being held open by a white male's hand that wore a gold sovereign ring. I tore my eyes away from what he was doing, why he was holding my mouth open, and instead looked at my body, flaccid and immobile on the bed, my dark nipples prominent, the curls of my black pubic hair unnaturally shiny and glistening. I looked away, but the image of the three men, standing over my naked body, all of them naked, their faces obscured while mine wasn't, was burned into the back of my eyes.

I looked at the sofa, where I'd sat many a time to wait for Flint to be ready to photograph me, at the two men sitting there, both of whom were holding bottles of beer, both of whom were staring at me. One, who had his beer positioned near his mouth, had a huge sovereign ring on the middle finger of his left hand, the same hand,

I guessed, that was attempting to open my lips. I slapped my hand over my mouth and stepped backwards.

My chest started to go in and out rapidly, trying to take air in, trying to keep it in, trying to expel the stale stuff so fresh stuff could get in. I was going to be sick, I was going to vomit, just like I had two nights ago.

'Don't make a big deal of it,' Flint said to me. He casually wandered over to the projector and flicked it off. 'It's only a few pictures.'

'You . . . you . . .' I couldn't find the words to describe what he had done, what *they* had done. I'd been violated. There were probably more and more pictures, all of them depicting what they'd done to me. I didn't remember it, though, none of it. I didn't remember drinking so much, vomiting, allowing them to take my clothes off, letting them do that to me. *Did they rape me? Did they take it in turns? Why don't I remember?*

I hadn't even tried to remember the other night. I had vague images that floated like clouds in the sky in my dreams, but that was only of Flint taking off my clothes. But he'd told me he did that. He'd told me a lot of stuff that I could dismiss if I remembered things, I realised. And because I was so mortified by the idea that I'd vomited in front of him, had passed out and needed to be carried to bed, I hadn't thought too much about it. 'You . . . you . . .'

'I, what?' he cut in at the same time as the picture of me disappeared from the screen and the men on the sofa began drinking their beers again. 'I took a few photos of you, that's all. I've taken lots of photos of you, haven't I, Anaya?'

'You violated me,' I said. And I sounded pathetic. Like I was using a word and a concept too sophisticated and complicated for a silly little girl like me.

Flint smirked, confirming that this was all too adult for a girl like me. 'I *what*? I didn't touch you. None of us touched you, did we?'

'Not one single finger,' one of them said.

The one with the sovereign ring shook his head.

I looked back at the blank wall, as if it was still there. Proof that one of them had touched me. It was physically gone, currently out of sight, but I could see the image, every line, every shade, every hue was still there for me to see.

'Ah, I admit, Doug there got a bit overexcited by those lips of yours, he wanted a proper go, but we reminded him of the rules: no touching. We only touch the ones who are sober and willingly consenting.' He shrugged. 'Them's the rules.'

'You drugged me, didn't you?' I asked. It was suddenly clear: I didn't drink too much – I didn't have the chance. He'd put something in that first drink, the conveniently open bottle of champagne.

'I might have helped you to unwind, but I don't think you can go as far as saying I drugged you. And what would I drug you for? I didn't touch you. None of us touched you.'

'You took my clothes off.'

'You were sick all over them. Some people have that reaction to the things that help them relax.'

My chest was still moving quickly, my heart was still sprinting in that rapidly moving chest. 'I'm going to the police,' I said. 'I'm going to the police.' The second time I said it, the more confident I was about doing that. I would go to the police and have them all locked up for this.

'OK,' Flint said, calmly. 'I don't know what you're going to tell them, though. We didn't touch you.'

'But you did *that* to me.'

'And what was *that*, exactly? I don't remember you saying no at any time. You willingly came over to my flat, drank alcohol even though you're only sixteen, stayed out all night. You didn't complain in the morning or anything. You didn't tell me you weren't up for what happened. You left here all happy. In fact, you came back, so you can't have been that upset about being here last time.'

'But I didn't know what you'd done.'

'Like I say, you go to the police if you want, Anaya. They're going to have to know that you forged your parents' signatures on those forms, though. I mean, I suspected, but whenever I questioned you, you just lied to me, didn't you? And of course, everyone you tell is going to have to see these photos. These photos where you don't

287

look like you're protesting at anything. I wonder what your parents will say? I wonder what your school friends would think if they accidentally got leaked? And what about the people at your new sixth-form college? But I'm sure you're not worried about any of that, are you?'

He smiled at me after he finished speaking, allowed what he had said to sink in: everyone would see those photos, they would see me like that – exposed, naked, vulnerable. They would see me and they would judge me. They would wonder what I was doing there with three grown men; they'd question whether I led them on; they would make assumptions about my character because I'd lied to my parents and bunked off school and had signed their signatures to get what I wanted. I could go to the police and tell them about this, and I would be the one who everyone remembered and looked down on. No one would remember the man behind the camera.

'I thought you liked me,' I said in desperation. I was so confused. He had been so nice to me all along, respectful, kind, often acting like a big brother. And he'd done this.

'I *do* like you, Anaya. I like you a lot. I told you before that you're really easy to work with—'

The guy with the sovereign ring smirked and I felt a wave of shame crash through me.

'Stop it, stop it,' Flint said to him. 'Like I said, Anaya, I do like you. I'm going to miss seeing you.'

The other one smirked then. Obviously hilarious since he – they – could look at me, see me, whenever they wanted.

'Please delete those photos,' I said. I sounded like I was begging, that I still felt pathetic, but I wanted to fly at him right then. The shame and horror and disgust had left me, replaced completely by anger. But I had to pretend – if I was angry he would use those photos to torment me. If I played pathetic, he might take pity on me and delete them.

He grinned at me, that knowing smile he'd shot me two days ago, that I thought had been benevolent and kind but was in fact a hidden smirk, a laugh at my expense. 'Why would I do that, Anaya?'

'Please? Please? I'm begging you, please. Please.'

'You're embarrassing yourself now, kid,' he said. 'Look, you were all set to go to the police a minute ago.'

'I won't, I promise you I won't.'

'Yeah, but how can I trust you? I can't, can I? So I'll hang on to the photos as evidence that you weren't touched or harmed, and you can go about your life. As long as you don't try to harm me, no one will ever see the photos. Is that a deal?'

I wanted to scratch his eyes out. I want to throw myself on him and knock him off his feet and claw and scratch at him until he felt how I felt, until he was raw and exposed to the outside world through no fault of his own. He was cruel, unfeeling. To have done that to me, to have let those other men do that to me and then to feed me lie after lie after lie the next morning, messing with my head, rewriting the story so when my memory began to kick in, began to throw at me scraps and reminders of what had happened, I wouldn't think badly of him – I would berate myself, doubt myself, think I was going mad. *He was sick.*

'Did you want your portfolio?' he asked. 'I can nip out back and grab it for you if you want?'

I didn't reply. I just stared at the wall where I'd seen a giant photo of myself.

'Cool,' Flint said. 'Let me know if you change your mind about the portfolio.' I heard him close the door a little as I headed for the stairs, unsteady on my feet, my head light. I could barely walk, couldn't think. 'Oh,' he tugged open the door, 'and thanks for the Quality Street. They're my favourites.'

I heard the others laugh at that, share his enjoyment of humiliating and violating me all over again.

Out on the street, the world felt unsafe. It was night, the crumbling, decaying area that he lived in, complete with boarded-up buildings and broken street lamps, reminded me of what I had done to my parents. How I had let them down. How I had put myself here by letting them down. The world was scary. I didn't know who I could trust. He might have been planning that from the start.

289

I staggered to the side of the entrance of the building and leant against it, hoping the building's strength and solidity would keep me upright. I wrapped my arms around myself, the coolness of the night going through me, rubbing over every raised goosebump on my sensitised skin. I had to stay there. I had to stay there until I could breathe enough to walk, to move, to make my way home.

8:45 p.m. 'Oh, Anaya, oh, Anaya,' Cece whispers. I don't think she's even aware she's saying it out loud. She keeps repeating it, her voice hiccupping with a small sob over the 'oh'.

August, 1995
I was standing in the doorway of the living room, watching my mother pray. Every night, after everyone went to bed, she would unroll her prayer mat, which most people called a yoga mat, and she would begin her prayers, her meditation. She would use her whole body, stretching, holding, breathing, meditating. She told me once that she and Tatta used to do it together, way back before he became a full-time intellectual.

My mother's long, slender leg stretched up, stepped forward, then planted itself firmly at the edge of the mat. Her body moved up, seeming to add inches to her frame, and in one movement she stretched her arms out, moved them smoothly upwards until her palms met in the air, then slowly she brought them down to meet in front of her chest.

'Amma,' I said. I wanted her to comfort me, even though I couldn't tell her what had happened, what I had done to cause what had happened. I knew it wasn't my fault, I knew that he had chosen to do that, but I also knew everyone would blame me. I would be the one in the wrong, I would be the one forever tarnished because of this thing.

Amma came out of her reverie and focused on me. When she saw me, she brought both her feet together, briefly nodded her head to signal the end of her prayers and came to me. 'Anaya, my little one, what has happened?' she asked as she brought me to the sofa and made me sit down.

'I did something really stupid,' I said, on the edge of tears, on the brink of telling her everything. If there was anyone who would understand it was my mother. She would know what to do. But then it flashed through my head again: that man's *thing* so close to my mouth, the other men's *things* near my breasts, near my genitals, so close but not touching. I'd never seen a man's *thing* looking like that before. I'd seen glimpses of them when they were all floppy and flaccid; I'd never seen a real one erect. Let alone three of them. Let alone three of them over my naked body. How would I explain that to my mother? She'd known nothing good would come of me being a model. She'd known I would get in to trouble.

'What have you done?' she asked gently. I felt bad all over again. I had been so awful to them, I had lied to them. And I would have to keep lying.

'I can't tell you.'

'You can tell me anything, Anaya. Anything.'

'I know, Amma.'

I looked into her face. I rarely did that. I rarely noticed my parents and how they looked. Sometimes I noted if one of them looked tired, if one of them was a bit under the weather, but I didn't look at my parents like I looked at strangers in the street and noticed their features, their colouring, the expressions that sat in their eyes. My mother looked like my grandmother, and I looked like my mother. I had the same oval face, and slightly hooked nose, the same large mouth, the same slightly slanted eyes. She was lighter than me; I had a darker shade of pale brown skin like my dad, like his dad.

'Will you teach me?' I asked her.

'Teach you what?' she replied.

'To pray, like you do. To meditate and use yoga to pray.' And to find inner peace. If I could find inner peace, could remove myself from the panic and disgust, even for a little while, I would be able to cope. I would stay away from the ideas I'd had on the way back of doing anything – *anything* – to stop the shame and self-disgust that were eating me up. Maybe if my mum taught me to do what she did, I could escape my mind with the help of my body.

'You would really like to learn?' she asked. She'd tried to teach us all when we were young, but none of us had been interested. And it wasn't my mother's way to force her beliefs upon us. She knew we would all eventually find our path, our way of navigating our route through this life until we found ourselves in the next one.

I nodded. 'I want to learn. I want to calm my mind and my body.'

'Come.' She stood up and held out her hand. She led me to her mat, and left me in the middle of it. 'We will start slowly,' she said. 'I am no guru, but I will try to teach you how to breathe, how to focus, how to find your inner strength.'

'Thank you,' I said.

'Close your eyes.'

I had to take a few deep breaths, I had to brace myself, I had to not flinch when the image revealed itself in my mind. I had to because I needed to get to the other side. And to get to the other side, where I would be able to clear my mind, focus my thoughts, stretch my body, I had to go through the areas I did not like. I had to accept the image would be there until I had found a way to meditate it away. The only way I could do anything about all of it was to learn how to control and relax my mind.

9 p.m. Cece's fingers slip through mine, she holds my hand and we carry on down our chosen path, heading back to the beginning.

May, 2002
'All right there, Anaya girl.'

Flint. Flint was standing in front of me. He looked used up, spent, like everything good about him had been siphoned away years ago.

I was twenty-four now. I was a woman now. I had a degree, a master's degree, I had this fantastic job working for a marketing firm. I got to come to events like this and work with people who did amazing things. I did not need to see this vile specimen; I did not need to have him drag me back to the hell he put me through at sixteen.

'Do I know you?' I said. I had hidden my shock and sudden burst of fear behind a quizzical look and a calm, slightly irritated voice.

'Come on, girl, don't be like that,' he said. 'It's me, Flint. I "discovered" you. Got you your fifteen minutes of fame. Although it was more like half an hour.' He laughed, a donkey-like heehaw, at his own pathetic joke. He'd always been like this. And I hadn't seen it because I'd had that crush on him.

'What do you want?' I asked sternly. 'In fact, what are you doing here at all?'

'I came to see you, didn't I? There I was, flicking through the latest issue of a business magazine, and there you were. The newest recruit of some big-shot advertising firm. When I gave them your name at the door, they just let me in. You must be doing really well for yourself if it didn't take much to get in to see you. Your name opens doors.'

I hadn't had a flashback to that image in years. I had literally meditated it all away. But now it was crowding in again, the panic and shame swirling together inside like the parents of a cyclone coming together, spinning in unison, to produce something huge, scary and destructive. 'What do you want, Flint?'

'Like I said, to see you.' His suit was grubby and fraying around the edges – it sat on him like his mother had bought it and had gone for the bigger size hoping he'd grow into it. When he turned slightly I realised his greasy hair had been slicked back into a ponytail that sat in the middle of the back of his head.

'I was thinking you might want your photos back.'

My eyes stopped scanning the room and focused on him.

'You left without your portfolio, I thought you might want it back.'

He was messing with me. He had probably loved seeing me beg, had probably not got that much satisfaction from anyone since that night. I was sure he and his mates had done that loads of times, but the women never found out about it. Not like me.

'No, thank you,' I said. 'I think you should leave now.'

He nodded slowly at me with his head on one side and a streak of admiration running through his features. He'd obviously wanted me to ask about those other photos; he'd have got a thrill from know-ing I had spent years terrified someone I knew would see them. 'Are you sure?'

'I said no thank you,' I replied. 'And I'd like you to leave before I have to call security.'

'You sure you don't want *those* photos back?'

'I'm sure,' I said. Of course I wanted them. I would have done anything to get them, but he wasn't to know that.

'How about dear old Mum and Dad? Do you think they'd want them back? Or how about your brother? He'd be about sixteen now, so probably does need schooling on what happens when men get horny and girls get slutty.'

He would do it. He would show them. Flint didn't make idle threats. That was what had kept me away from the police all these years. As I'd got older I'd realised the wrongness of what he had done, how the police probably would have been able to prosecute him for sexual assault as well as drugging me, but I also knew that he would have no qualms about leaking those photos, putting them up on the Net, making sure everyone saw them if I reported him. He would definitely show my parents, my brothers, those photos without a second thought.

'What do you want?' I asked through a tight mouth.

He took a step closer to me so he could lower his voice. My stom-ach turned over, at his proximity, at the smell of stale fags, old booze and drying sweat. 'Two thousand pounds.'

'What?'

'Two thousand pounds.'

'Where am I supposed to get that sort of money from?'

He looked around, encompassing the overt wealth of the people around us. Like it was anything to do with me, like I had anything nearing their money – some of them had chairs that cost more than I earned in a year. 'You'll work something out,' he said.

'I don't have that kind of money.'

'Like I said, you'll work something out. And if you don't, well . . . let's just say you'd better work something out.'

'All right, if I were to get you that money, I want those photos back. I want you to destroy every single trace of them and I want proof before I hand over even a single penny.'

'For that, the price is going to have to be three grand,' he said.

'No. I can't get that kind of money.'

'Take it or leave it. Two grand or three. Your choice.'

'All right, all right. I'll get it. But it is three grand for all the photographs, all their copies and everything on your computers to be erased.'

'Three grand and you're golden.'

'OK, I'll have to start saving. I should be able to get it to you in a couple of months.'

'Months? No can do, darlin'. I have a bit of a cash flow problem right now, I'll need it inside a week.'

'A week? Where am I supposed to get that sort of money inside of a week?'

'All right, all right. But don't say I don't ever do anything for you. Ten days. Get me the cash within ten days and no one ever has to find out what you used to do.'

'I didn't used to do anything – you did it to me.'

'You say potatoes, I say chips.'

Ten days. I had to get that money within ten days or he was going to ruin my life.

9:20 p.m. I like having Cece's hand around mine, I realise. It's comforting, makes me feel connected to her, to someone who cares about me.

May, 2002

Flint's place hadn't changed at all.

In all those years, after all those photographs and shoots and models, everything was exactly the same – just grubbier, tattier, greyer. 'Come in, come in,' he said as he welcomed me with a smile that I'd have once swooned over. 'Take a seat,' he said. He pointed to the sofa where his friends had sat and laughed at me while watching photos of what they'd taken part in while I was drugged.

'No, thank you,' I said. 'I'd like to get this over with as quickly as possible.' I knew, on many levels, that this was a doomed exercise. Modern life, new-age technology, all so wonderful and helpful in many ways. So damning, too. Unless I tore his place down looking for memory sticks and memory cards and other laptops, I could never be sure that he had truly deleted everything. All I could hope for was that he would stick to his word, and that he would forget about me after this. Trusting someone like Flint was like building your house on sand, I knew that. But there might be some parts of the sand that were less unstable than others; there might be parts that were solid, almost rock-like.

'Don't be unfriendly, Anaya. We always had something special, me and you, I have good memories of the times we spent together. Don't ruin it.' He smiled softly and I was startled, truly shaken, to realise that he thought I still harboured some feelings for him. After everything he'd done to me, he thought I hadn't merely come to pay him off, with £1,500 of my parents' money, my next month's rent and my tiny amount of savings, but because I wanted to see him too. I cast my mind back, way, way back to how I'd felt about him before I properly saw him, how I would smile shyly at him, and I tried to make my smile like that, to placate him with a similar expression and by sitting meekly on his hateful sofa. He grinned once his delusion was back in place, his role as my crush secure.

'That's better. Now, I'll get the laptop, you get the, you know, out.' He wanted to retraumatise me, of course. He deleted every photo, all right, but he called up every single one – nearly a thousand of them – and made me look at every single one of them before he hit delete. I had to see myself as I had been then, I had to see what they'd done, how they'd posed me, how they'd violated me, how I had been awake but unaware for almost all of it. I dug my toenails into the soles of my shoes, breathed through my nose and pretended I didn't care. He had his money, and I was getting what I wanted.

After it was over, after he went through the files on his computer to show me there was nothing else there, I got up to leave.

'Thank you,' I forced myself to say. 'Thank you for doing that.'

'That's it?' he said, confused.

'What do you mean?' I asked lightly, while moving very slowly towards the door. The atmosphere was electrified. Dangerous. All the fine hairs on my arms, on the back of my neck, stood up, telling me to run.

'That's it? You just come over, get me to delete a load of photos and you leave? Just like that? No reward when I did something pretty huge for you?'

'I paid you three thousand pounds,' I said and placed one foot behind me, rocked back onto it, then placed the other foot behind that, without ever taking my eyes off him. 'That was a fair deal, don't you think?' I took another step backwards, tried to keep it casual. I only had six more steps, seven at most before I was at the door, out of there, out of reach. Five steps. Four steps.

'You always were a stuck-up bitch,' he said in a low, vicious voice. I was expecting it, but when he did it, when he pounced at me and smacked me across the face, I was still shocked and stumbled back against the door, my hands on my face where he'd hit me.

After a second of reeling at the shock of being hit, I peeled myself away from the door as he came towards me, fists clenched, ready to do it again. I went towards him too, grabbed his shoulders and brought my knee up between his legs. Sharply, cleanly, no hesitation. Amma had taught me that. Over and over, until she was confident I would do it without a second thought if I was in danger. He yelped, as surprised by the way my knee knew the exact place to aim for as by the fact I wasn't cowering or trying to escape. I punched him, clean across the jaw, while he was bent forwards. Amma had taught me that, too. 'If you can run away, always do,' she'd repeated, 'but if you can't run, fight back as much as you can. There's no shame in freezing, either. If you freeze, do what you must to survive, but if you aren't frozen, then fight, *mihiri dæriya*, fight.'

While he was down, I turned towards the door and ran for it. I ran down the three flights of stairs and burst out onto the street like a mechanical rabbit at a dog track. I didn't stop when I hit the pavement, I carried on running, dodging people and dogs and cars. The area, unlike Flint's flat, had come a long way in the past few years. Everyone wanted to live around there now; there were no boarded-up buildings, no homeless people lurking in doorways, it was all glass and steel and craving to be on home renovation shows. I ran and ran, ignoring what I must look like – sprinting in an area that was almost too cool to exist – and ran and ran until I was at the Tube station. I pushed my travelcard into the machine, and then sprinted down the escalator, onto the platform, before I threw myself between the doors of a train heading west. I flopped into a seat at the quieter end of the carriage and tried to calm myself.

While the train dashed through darkened tunnels, taking me further and further away from Flint, I pretended I didn't notice people looking at me, at my wild hair and reddened face and heaving, out-of-breath chest. I pretended, too, that Flint wasn't going to now do his level best to screw me over.

9:45 p.m. Cece swaps hands and puts her arm around me too.

May, 2002
'Miss Ranatunga,' the policeman began. They had come to my workplace and arrested me. There was no way that the owners of Oysle & Wade would allow me to carry on working there after this. There were clients in the building, who had most likely seen the police arrive and march up to my desk. My only hope would be that they would give me a glowing reference so I could go off and be someone else's public relations nightmare.

'Yes?' I replied, eager to be helpful. It would go in my favour if I was fully cooperative. At least that's what the good cops, the ones who were in it to make a difference, always said on telly.

'Did you assault Mr Bruce Flint two nights ago?' he asked.

'Not in the way that you mean. Which is to say I hit him, but only because he hit me first and I thought he was going to do something far worse to me, so I kneed him in the . . . you know, and I punched him once, then I ran for it.'

'So you're saying you didn't fracture his jaw and wrist, cause extensive bruising to his stomach and chest area with repeated punches and kicks, and give him a black eye?'

'*What?* NO! I couldn't do that, even if I wanted to. I thought he was going to . . . I don't know what I thought he was going to do, but I thought he was going to do something and he'd already hit me and he moved in to do it again so I defended myself and ran.'

'He says you were having a dispute about some photographs he'd taken for your portfolio a few years back, and you got angrier and angrier about him refusing to give them to you until you couldn't contain yourself any longer, which led to this sustained and unprovoked attack.' As he spoke, he laid out photos of a bruised, battered Flint. My eyes widened in alarm at what I was seeing.

'That's not true! And I didn't do this,' I said, sitting back. 'I didn't do this to him.'

'Look, Miss Ranatunga, I'm not stupid. You and Mr Flint might think we are or that we've got nothing better to do than settle scores between two people, but there's obviously more to this than either of you are telling. The first person to tell the truth is obviously more likely to be believed. So, here's your chance, Miss Ranatunga: tell me the truth.' As he was talking, his voice had taken on a tired, heard-it-all-before, cynical slant; he'd obviously said something like this many, many times before and had yet, I guess, to have someone tell him the complete truth. I wasn't sure when I became such a people-pleaser but I had a very strong urge to make him believe in people again. To tell him the whole truth so he wouldn't feel so jaded about the world we lived in.

'When I was younger, about fifteen, I used to do a bit of modelling for Flint. Then I stopped modelling and a year later I went over to get my portfolio.' My leg started twitching, anxiety at what I was about to say. I wanted to stand up right then and put myself into mountain pose, slip my mind and memory into the safe, serene, wide-open spaces that yoga and praying created in me. 'He . . . he drugged me with something he put in a glass of champagne and then him and his friends . . . they . . . I was barely conscious and they took off my clothes.'

'Did they rape you?' the other police officer asked gently.

I shook my head, wiped at the tears that were cascading down my face. 'They didn't touch me. He made sure of that. They took photos of me. They posed me. In some of the photos they're all naked as well and the photos show that they all . . . you know, on me.'

The policemen were confused for a few moments then one said: 'Ejaculated?'

I nodded. I'd been having sex for years, I could swear with the best of them, but I still couldn't say words like that without a big run-up and almost whispering it. 'I didn't know about any of it until two days later when I turned up at his flat unexpectedly and I saw them looking at the photos through a projector.'

'Did you go to the police at the time?' the first officer asked.

'No. I was too scared, too ashamed. I didn't want my family to find out and he said he'd leak the photos if I told.'

'So what's all this about now? This was obviously years ago – why did you go to his flat two days ago?'

'He wanted money to delete the photos. When I told him no, he said he'd send them to my parents and to my brothers. So I went there to pay him and to watch him delete the photos.'

The officers were silent when I finished my story. I blinked and lowered my head as I tried to dry my tears and still neither of them reacted or even spoke. There was something off about their silence. I knew they believed me, but that was a problem. My story, the truth, was a problem somehow. I looked up at them and saw the looks they were exchanging: regret, frustration, sympathy. This was not going to turn out OK. I'd told the truth, but it was not going to be OK.

'It sounds like you've been through a terrible time,' the first officer said. 'But from everything you've said, no one would blame you for attacking him. In fact, some people would say you were kind to leave him with the use of his legs.'

'But I didn't do it,' I said.

'I believe you, but the evidence says otherwise. Mr Flint says otherwise. Human nature says otherwise.'

'I thought he was going to hurt me again.'

'I don't doubt it, but think about how all of this looks to us, Miss Ranatunga. Would you believe you if you were sitting where we are?'

'But I didn't do it.'

'I believe you. We believe you. But you have no evidence to back up your claims. You should have come to us when he started to blackmail you – extortion is a criminal offence. Hell, you should have come to us ten years ago when he first took those photos, we would have helped you then.'

I covered my eyes with my hands, then slowly ran them through my hair. 'What's going to happen next?' I asked. My voice sounded weary and small and absolutely terrified. Everything Flint had wanted all along.

'Well, I think you should get some legal advice, but one option would be for you to accept a caution.'

'What does that mean?'

'It means you admit you did it. It goes on your record and if you ever need a CRB check done it will show up as a caution.'

'But I didn't do it.'

'I believe you.'

'So why would I say I did?'

'Because the alternative could mean court. Where you would get the chance to stand up and tell everyone that you didn't do it. And he would be able to stand up and show everyone those photos and say you were a willing participant but are now making up stories to save your reputation.'

'How is this fair?'

'It's not,' he said kindly. 'We've done some checking into Mr Flint. He's involved with some very nasty people; he probably got a beating from one of the people he owes money to and decided to use that to get back at you. But we can't prove any of that. All we can prove is that you hit him because you've admitted to that.'

'OK,' I said resignedly. 'I'll speak to a solicitor and then we'll have to see about going to court. Because I'm not saying I did something when I didn't do it.'

'Good. I'm glad you made a decision,' the policeman stated. 'We'll be back with details of the duty solicitor for you and the other relevant forms.'

By the time I'd finished talking to my solicitor, I had, of course, decided to accept the caution. I was always going to, I knew that. But I didn't want the police to think I was simply going to willingly accept being branded as a violent person. I was always going to accept the caution because I couldn't risk another human being seeing those photos.

When I was finally allowed to leave, the stench of having to sign papers saying I was something I was not clung to me, made me feel filthy. It was now on record that I was violent, that I had beaten someone up. I knew what I had to do, though. I'd had the thought while I was signing those forms, while I was listening to the words of what I supposedly did being read out to me: I was going to change my name. This was what I had to do to move on from Anaya Ranatunga and the mistake she once made.

10:05 p.m. It's odd talking about all of this because I have not told anyone the whole story. The police heard bits but no one heard my voice, my intonation, my words shape this whole tale. And I feel sick about it, a see-saw sensation filling and draining at the centre of my being. Cece stops walking. I stop as well and almost give in to the nausea, only just prevent myself from bending over and emptying my stomach into the nearby flowerbeds.

Cece slips her arms around me and begins to cradle me, hug me, hold me like I have been recently hurt. 'Oh, you poor, poor girl,' she says in a soft crooning voice. I imagine she uses this voice with the boys, with her daughter. 'You poor, poor girl.'

I want to cry, but I'm dry-eyed, strangely detached. It's as if I'm standing back in Flint's studio, watching myself on the big screen, knowing that it is me, but not really registering. I want to cry, but I refuse to collapse, to simply melt in her arms and let myself cry.

I was using her, really. Testing out how it sounded out loud before I tell Sanj. 'It's OK, I'm all right,' I tell Cece, and make an attempt to step back from her. It's a weak attempt and she continues to hold me.

'I had no idea,' she says. Her hands stroke my back. 'You must have been so confused about so many things.'

I've never really known how to describe what happened because it wasn't as if I remembered it properly – only tiny flashes came back to me of that night; it wasn't as if there was any trauma to point to how I had been violated – there was nothing but the images. It was a very hands-off crime that altered my life. The blackmail, that was a crime; the assault, that was a crime; but they came after the original 'event'. I have been confused all these years. Scared, hurt, but mainly *confused*.

'Confused,' I repeat. That is the word that describes the world I've lived in since that time.

'What an absolute bastard he is.' She steps back but holds on to my forearms, keeps us connected. '*Absolute* bastard.'

She looks at me in the dark, peers at me with inquisitive eyes. 'Why are you telling me this?' she asks. 'I mean, I'm honoured, but I get the impression this is the first time you've talked about all of that. And how does it relate to Yvonne—'

I flinch inside when Cece says *her* name, when she reminds me why I have to do this.

'What did Yvonne do?' Cece asks, telling me that I've physically shuddered, too.

'What do you mean?' I ask. Why I am trying to obscure the truth after all I have laid bare, I don't know.

'Come on, Anaya, you nearly jumped out of your skin when I said her name then. You said you wanted to tell me what happened the night she was attacked. What's she got to do with all of this?'

'She tried to blackmail me, too,' I say. 'I changed my name to Harshani. She found out my original name; she found the photos that Flint had posted online and threatened to tell Sanjay and his mother about them.'

'*Excuse me – what?*'

I repeat what I have just said. I feel better already. I knew what Yvonne was threatening was a certain kind of evil, but Cece's reaction proves it is not normal behaviour.

'Wow. *Wow!* Bloody hell. I'm not sure what to say to that. Flint I can maybe understand because he's a sleaze, but Yvonne? I thought she was your friend? And nice?'

'She *was* my friend. And she was nice. Most of the time. At first all the time, if a little intense. Oh, I don't know, it all came apart at the seams and towards the en— I mean, before what happened, it was pretty miserable.'

'What did she want? Money?'

I shake my head. 'Money? No. Power, control. Which, when I say that out loud, makes me sound like the crazy one, but that was what it was. She wanted to be in on the world Sanjay is involved in; she liked being in control of me. Maybe because being my friend took too much effort in the end and she couldn't sustain it or be sure I wouldn't walk. I always found her hard work in the beginning and felt guilty about that. When she showed her hand, guilt gave way to anger and fear, I suppose.'

'Did she do that to others? You know, the blackmail?'

'I don't know.' Lie. Absolute lie. That night on the beach, the raised voices, the distorted faces. The pushing and shoving . . . 'We never really talked about it, but, you know, friends fall out all the time. There's no such thing as the perfect friend, is there?'

'Suppose not,' Cece says quietly. She's looking at me strangely – maybe my lie was not good enough. Maybe she's guessed that they were victims of Yvonne, like me. Yvonne, who was almost famous for looking perfect, behaving altruistically, and having your back way before you knew there was a threat looming on the horizon, changed. Probably slowly, certainly when I wasn't looking, but over the years, she stopped being all those things that made her likeable and fun to be around, and instead she became that threat you had to keep around for fear of what they would do once they were out of sight. I was impressed when Maxie binned her; I didn't have that option by that point, not when she had found those photos. I wasn't surprised when Maxie turned up at the beach that night when we were meeting to discuss what to do about Yvonne. When Yvonne arrived and started throwing around threats, things unravelled quite quickly. We were all less than our best selves. We were all horribly guilty of what happened next.

'What happened that night she was attacked?' Cece asks. 'You say you saw her? You say your story relates to her?'

'I . . . I lied to the police. She was saying stuff, there was shouting. I pushed her. She shoved me first, I pushed her back, there was so much going on, all of us fighting and then she was on the floor. And she'd banged her head on one of the rocks we keep in the beach hut.'

'So all of you were on the beach with her that night?'

This isn't my story to tell any more. This now involves the other two. They would go mad if they knew I was talking like this. Especially Hazel, who has only just calmed down with the paranoia. 'I . . . I can't say any more. I'm sorry, I've used you as a bit of a sounding board. I just needed to hear it out loud before I talk to Sanjay about it.'

'Are you going to tell your husband everything?' I know she means about the night on the beach.

'I don't know. I want to. Like I want to tell you, but it's not just about me.'

'Anaya, do you think one of the others did that to Yvonne?' she asks.

'Thing is, Cece, I wanted to do that to Yvonne. That's why I have to talk to Sanjay. This secret has poisoned me, slowly, slowly. I was so sick when Yvonne found the pictures; she didn't even ask how they came about, she just saw them and knew they'd be leverage, which they were. And I hated her for that. More than once I wanted to do her harm. Not to stop her telling, more to protect other people from her. And I wanted to follow her that night. I wanted to follow her and to smash her head in. And then someone did. And I feel awful about it. Because I can understand that feeling. I had that feeling.'

'But you didn't, that's the important thing.'

I stare at Cece and decide that I need to be honest again. 'Didn't I?'

She glances to the ground. Stumped. This is it. This is why I can't go to the police. I learnt last time that it's always your word against someone else's. Whether I did or didn't, if Hazel or Maxie say I did, if I say that Maxie did, or Hazel did, it would be my word against someone else's. And that hasn't gone well for me in the past.

'I'm sorry, Cece. I've burdened you with all of this. I'm sorry.'

'That's completely fine. I understand.' She smiles. I want her to hug me again. To offer me the comfort and care she did before I told her I could have tried to kill Yvonne. I want to relax into her hold, allow myself to let go again. She reads my mind and steps forward, envelops me with her arms, and hugs me. I do it then – I let go, allow her to comfort me, to let me be weak for one moment in my life.

11 p.m. It's only when I'm pulling into the driveway, see Suhani's car there, that I realise I didn't ask Cece not to say anything to anyone. But she won't. She wouldn't . . . I have a feeling I can trust her. Maybe that's naïve and silly, but I do. Anyway, once Sanjay knows, once his mother knows, it won't matter any more. My marriage will most likely be over but at least I won't have this awful secret hanging over my head any longer. I'll be free to tell everyone everything and I won't feel locked into this world of secrecy with Hazel and Maxie any more.

Cece

11:30 p.m. 'Are you all right?' Sol asks.

I'm sitting cross-legged on the bed with my thumbs pressed into the centre of my forehead, trying to push away my headache. I open my eyes and stare at my husband, momentarily confused by who he is. 'No, I don't think I am,' I say to him.

He enters the room and shuts the door behind him. When I came back from talking to Anaya, the children were in bed, he was in his office and I came up here and sat on the bed, shaking. I eventually calmed down enough to stop shaking and to sit myself cross-legged and try to get rid of my headache, but I've not been able to do anything else.

This was what I was scared of. Anaya had good reason to want to shut up Yvonne. They probably all did. How am I going to tell Gareth that it was her, if it was? How am I going to say, this woman was using something truly horrible that happened to a friend to get into a world that she wasn't a part of? If I was Anaya, wouldn't I want to shut up Yvonne? I wouldn't do it, but I'd want to. She admitted as much. She admitted she wanted to, she could have been admitting that she did from the way she said, 'Didn't I?' Because, in the heat of the moment, when you can see everything you love slipping away, wouldn't you do something out of character to protect yourself? Look what I've agreed to in order to get rid of Gareth. I can imagine Anaya's desperation.

'Anything I can do to help?' Sol asks.

'I'm not sure anyone can help,' I say. I sound bleak. I feel bleak. They are all going to have good reasons to have wanted to harm

Yvonne Whidmore, I suspected that. But then, I am doing what she did. I am going to find out information as their friend and then use it against them. How does that make me any better than Yvonne Whidmore? I didn't think this through when I made this deal with Gareth. That isn't like me. I think things through, I look at different angles and I try to work out the best solution. There is no best solution in this scenario.

'I love you, you know, Cee?' Sol says.

I turn to him in the gloom. 'I know,' I reply automatically.

'And I'm so sorry for being so epically crap these past few weeks.'

I say nothing because I do not want a row. I do not want anything else to deal with right now, not when I am battling with what I will do with this information about Anaya. I feel dreadful. Hollow inside, deceitful in those newly hollowed out spaces. I manipulated that story out of her by asking her every day how it was going. I do not want to row with Sol on top of being a terrible person.

'Whatever it is that's bothering you, you can tell me about it, you know, he tells me.'

'Thanks,' I say. I can't, of course.

'And if you can't tell me about it, remember that I love you. And I know you'll always do the right thing.'

I crawl over the bed to him and he opens his arms. We come together in a wonderfully familiar hug. His smell, the salty, fresh, acrid scent of the man I've chosen to share my life with, moves through me, and it feels like coming home, like we're finally together again. It doesn't take long for us to start kissing and slowly undressing each other. It doesn't take long for us to find our rhythm, to slip back into being with each other.

He's said what I needed to hear, I realise before I let go. *I have to do the right thing. And I know what the right thing is, whether I like it or not.*

Part 11

WEDNESDAY

Maxie

1 a.m. Ed is kissing my neck. I was sitting on the counter, thinking. Thinking about my secret and how I want to tell someone, how I want it all to be out there so everyone can judge me accordingly, when he came in from the living room. I didn't think he knew I was here, but he came towards me and pulled me off the counter. The second my bare feet touched the ground he started doing this. Kissing my neck, running his fingers through my hair. His lips never stray towards my mouth, though – they simply cover my neck, my chest, my breasts in kisses until he is moving us across the room, to the table, then he is laying me down, opening a condom and rolling it on and entering me. All without pause, all driven by him, all so unlike the him I've come to know in recent years. Afterwards, he stares into my eyes, breathing like he has just run a race, blushing like he has shown himself up.

'I'm sorry,' he says between breaths. 'I'm sorry, I shouldn't have done that. Shouldn't have done that.' And then he's gone. Leaving me alone in the kitchen – my body quivering with not understanding what happened, my mind reverberating with echoes from our past.

Hazel

2 a.m. My phone bleeps.

It's been silent for a while. Anaya has virtually stopped responding to messages since I ran away from her in the street; Maxie responds but doesn't give anything away. I've tried to go back to normal texts: *Do you fancy meeting up to knit? Do you want to make cocktails? Tea down at the play centre?* And nothing. Always an excuse from Maxie and usually silence from Anaya.

This isolation, this purgatory, is driving me insane.

I move off the close-lidded toilet into the bath and pull my legs up to my chest, wrap my dressing gown around me. It's pink and silk, something Ciaran bought me in the early days; there's no warmth in it, but it will have to do. I have to sit in here because if I don't, Ciaran comes to find me and makes me go back to bed. Then he holds me. I'm sure he thinks it's comforting or reassuring or something, but really, it's claustrophobic. He rests his full weight on me, it feels like. His arm is heavy on my chest and if I move it to my waist, he returns it to my chest minutes later, even in his sleep. He doesn't seem to realise that when he makes me sleep like he wants to, I can't breathe. It literally feels like he is crushing me. The nights that the children aren't here are worse. He will find me, then bring me back to bed with promises of cuddles until I fall asleep. Cuddles that involve sex, of course. No, not sex, not love-making – baby-making.

I hate myself for thinking like that. It's like, since Yvonne's attack, I am trying to destroy everything good in my life by turning on them. First Anaya and Maxie, now Ciaran.

I hunch up a little more. I sit in here because there is a lock on the door. I would fill the bath, get in and allow the water to ease my worries, but the sound would wake the children.

My phone bleeps again, a reminder that someone is trying to reach me. I lean out of the bath, my fingers graze the smooth screen and I press the home button, type in the code.

I think we should all go to the police together. Tell them the truth. We haven't done anything so we shouldn't be suffering like this. Let me know what you think. A xxx

We haven't done anything. Ha. Ha-ha-ha! Speak for yourself, Anaya. Speak for your bloody self.

'Hazel,' Ciaran whispers through the door. 'Hazel, come back to bed.'

'I'll be there soon,' I whisper back.

He turns the doorknob, checking that I haven't forgotten to keep him firmly on the other side. 'Come on now, Hazel.'

'I said, I'll be there soon.' *Now leave me alone!* I don't say that out loud, but I still clamp my hands over my mouth. I need to stop this. Maybe Anaya is right. Maybe we should go to the police and confess. Then this torture, where I am starting to hate everyone and every thing, can finally end.

THURSDAY

Cece

11:45 a.m. I knock on the navy-green door of 83 Turram Lane. I hope, hope, *hope* that the person who opens the door won't be—

'Cece, isn't it?' Ciaran says. 'How nice to see you.'

I find a smile for him, and I watch a moment of suspicion slither behind his eyes before representing itself as a welcoming smile on his lips. He is incredibly good-looking. I can see why Hazel fell for him. I can see why the woman I met yesterday fell for him, too. You do not see someone like him – polished, poised, perfect – and think he is a violent psychopath.

'Yes, it's Cece. Is Hazel in?' I reply.

He raises a hand, scratches his ear. 'Erm, no, sorry. She's out right now. Would you like to leave a message?'

'Erm . . .' I begin, thrown. She is always at home on Thursdays.

'Who is it?' Hazel calls from inside the house.

'Oh,' he says with a little laugh, his face creasing into a beautiful smile, 'look at that. She is in after all. Must have snuck back in while I was upstairs.'

I widen my smile. 'Yeah. Must have. My husband does that to me all the time.'

Without breaking eye contact, he leans back slightly to call into the house: 'It's your friend Cece.' He has a particular inflection on the word 'friend'. I wonder if I would pay as much attention to that 'tell' if I didn't know what sort of a person he really is. What he has planned for Hazel.

'Cece?' Hazel's voice comes closer. 'Hi.' She steps into the doorway where he stands, ushering him aside. He's still watching me, biting

314

his lower lip and trying to keep a genial look on his face. 'What are you doing here?' she asks.

'Look, I know it's cheating,' I say, and reach into the large cream cloth bag I have slung over my shoulder, 'but I was wondering if you could teach me that purl thing, because I found out you need to be able to do that to make something like this.' I pull one of Harmony's favourite jumpers from the bag. It's a raspberry red-pink and she would lose the plot if she knew I had taken it from her room to use it in this. I needed a reason to see Hazel and this was the only way. 'I saw this type of stitching on Harmony's jumper and I found out it was basically purl. I can't do purl. So, could you teach me purl? I know you sussed me out the first time that I couldn't knit to save my life, but you have to admit that I have come on loads since then. But there's only so much you can learn from internet videos before you have to learn from the expert.' Since the meeting up seems to have dried up, this is the only way to get Hazel to talk to me. 'Please?' I say. 'This is my daughter's favourite jumper. If I could knit like it, I do not think I would be able to get cooler in her eyes.'

Hazel is clearly flattered, but guarded. I wonder if something has happened with Anaya and Maxie? Now I know for definite they were all together and that they *did* all lie to the police – an inference from what Anaya said – I wonder if this will work? There is no way she will come to me like Anaya did. I need another 'in'.

'Go on then,' she says. 'But we'll have to be quick, it's school pick-up in three hours.'

'Don't worry,' I tell her as I step forwards. 'Three hours is going to be more than enough to learn everything I need to.'

Yesterday, I drove to Essex to meet a woman called Lynne Smythe. I'd spoken to her on the phone, I told her who I was, I said it was nothing to do with the police or the papers and I just wanted to talk to her. She'd hesitated on the phone, then said, almost resignedly, 'All right, then,' and gave me her address.

We sat at her kitchen table and Lynne Smythe cried. She asked me if it was me really, and not a friend as I'd told her on the phone. When I confirmed it was a friend and not me, she cried again. She was incredibly thin, and her brown hair was greasy and unwashed. She wore a cardigan far too big for her and she constantly, nervously, picked at her nails. She stared out of the patio doors at her two children – a girl aged about fifteen and a boy aged about three – and told me her story. The story of how she had got involved with a man called Kier Hamill, also known as Ciaran Hamilton, Hazel's partner.

She told me: *I met Kier after my husband left me. My ex-husband was a lazy, abusive bastard who couldn't keep it in his pants. You know, most of the time I could just about put up with it, ignore it, but when I found out he was putting it about, trying it on with my friends and the like, I finally had the courage to end the relationship. It wasn't easy, of course, and my ex-husband dragged it out for months. Just when he'd got me convinced that we could work it out, that he was going to change, help out around the house, take some real responsibility for our daughter instead of just being Disney Dad with his grand gestures and days out, he left me for another woman.*

I'm only telling you this because it'll give you some idea of where I was when I met Kier. My self-esteem was bad enough after all those years in a crap marriage, but at that point it was on the floor. I met him on a girls' weekend away. My mum was looking after Monica, my oldest, so I could get all dressed up and let my hair down. Kier was completely different to my ex-husband. We spent so much time chatting that night, and he was attentive, caring – he made me feel so incredibly desirable.

When I came home again, we kept in touch and he'd come down to visit, stay in a luxury hotel nearby so he wouldn't infringe on my time with Monica, and so he wouldn't be putting any pressure on me. I'd go and stay at his hotel and he'd treat me like a princess. Nothing was ever too much for him, and he loved treating me. With him, I totally rediscovered my sex drive. I rediscovered what it felt like to have a man want you, and to want a man. I'd forgotten what it was like to have an orgasm, or to not have someone shagging you like a battering ram. After about six months, he got a temporary contract in the area and it seemed silly for him to rent a house at extortionate rates when I had all this space here. So he met my daughter and he moved in temporarily.

It was only looking back, afterwards, that I realised he was good at convincing me to do things that went against my better instincts. When Monica met him, she thought he was great. We'd go out, the three of us, and we'd have a brilliant time. Being with him was heavenly. He used to bring me flowers, buy me little presents, and if he ever needed to borrow a little cash to tide him over, he always paid me back straight away.

And Kier totally helped my confidence in dealing with my ex. I managed to get him to pay child support, to actually see his daughter; I suddenly had the ability to stand up for myself. That was all thanks to Kier. It was a bit rocky at first, when he moved in, but that's what happens when you start living with someone, I thought. I mean, most of my friends loved him, my mum loved him for what he'd done for my confidence. I loved him.

About three months after he moved in, he wanted us to try for a baby. I was too long in the tooth for that, I told him. And besides, I'd already got my little girl, she's all I ever wanted. But, like with everything else, he convinced me that it would be a wonderful thing, it'd be this unbreakable bond between us. Oh God, oh God . . .

I got pregnant so quickly. We were so happy. And then when I was six months pregnant, he confessed to me that his contract had actually ended a lot sooner than he expected and he was having a few financial problems. He hadn't wanted to worry me because of being pregnant and I'd been so happy, but he said he was going to have to sell the little house he'd grown up in, even though he'd promised his mother when she was dying that he'd never sell because him and his two brothers had been born there.

It was all so sad, but what could he do? I loved this man, truly loved him, so I said I'd cover his shortfall for him. He'd always paid me back before and it wasn't like he was going to do a moonlight flit or anything, not when I was pregnant with his child. In all that time he'd been so good with Monica. He'd actually told her before it was certain that we were going to have a baby. But he was always so careful to make sure she wasn't feeling left out with the baby. He wanted to reassure her that she would always be as important as the baby.

And then, just before the baby was born, he told me that the job he'd been doing had come to an end and he wasn't going to look for another job because he wanted to be at home with the baby, too. He didn't think it was fair that I would get to see the baby all day every day while he was working hard to pay off our debts.

That's what he called them, "our debts". I'd had to dip into my savings I'd had since before I was married to pay off his huge debts and suddenly he was making out that I had helped to run them up. The baby was due in three weeks and he wouldn't work, wouldn't do anything around the house, and all but stopped talking to Monica unless it was to shout at her for something. I was in such a state by this point. I suddenly found out about all this debt that I knew nothing about, some of it in my name, lots of it on my credit cards that I had no clue he knew the pin numbers to. I had no choice but to pay them off with some of an inheritance I'd got from my gran that I'd put aside for Monica's college. I just didn't want bailiffs turning up at the house when I was trying to take care of a newborn.

When I went into labour, he insisted on coming to the hospital so my mum had to take care of Monica. And then he completely disappeared. He didn't turn up until well after baby Kier was born. Of course, he insisted the baby was named after him, but he wasn't actually there to see his son born and I never really found out where he was. He just kept telling me that it was in the past and we needed to focus on the present and the future.

Everything got worse from then on in. Even though he wasn't looking for a job because he wanted to spend time with the baby, he hardly even looked at him, didn't change a nappy, didn't offer to sterilise bottles, didn't get up in the night, never even held him. And his going out, which he'd always done, was just constant now. It was like, now that he had me totally vulnerable and it'd be virtually impossible to leave him now we were living on my savings, the mask came off and he didn't even bother to be nice.

The calls from other women who'd found my number on his phone started, as well as the threatening letters demanding money for his debts. When I was broken, completely and utterly broken with pretty much no money to my name, he told me he was leaving. For a few minutes I was actually horrified, I couldn't think how I would live without him because it'd be me on my own with a ten-month-old baby and a young teenager. I thought I couldn't cope and I was still so in love with him. Then I realised that it was what needed to happen and I was so relieved. But he told me he'd only be able to afford to go if I gave him money. I told him I didn't have any. And he reminded me that I had an investment account with money in that I could cash in. He knew everything about me. I realised then how much I'd been taken in. He knew exactly how much money I had and had worked over two years to take every single penny of it from me.

I told him no. He wasn't having that. If I gave that to him, I'd be destitute, I'd have absolutely no money left and no time to get a job. And he morphed into this monster, right before my very eyes. He hit me so hard he knocked me off my feet, and started screaming so loudly at me that he wanted 'his' money that the baby started crying. Thankfully Monica was at school, but he said he'd ask again, every day, until he got 'his' money.

He truly believed that it was his, he was entitled to it, and I was keeping it from him. All the while he was talking, he was looking at the picture of Monica that used to sit on the telly. I've had to take it down now; every time I saw it there afterwards it reminded me of the cold way he stared at the picture, telling me I had to give him 'his' money. It took a bit of time to close the account and convince the manager that I didn't mind the financial hit, and every single one of those days he would act all nice and calm until Monica was at school then he would . . . I can't even think about it.

I haven't seen him since and it's been about a year. And thank God. With the help of my parents I've managed to struggle on a bit, I've had to sell this house – I've this morning accepted an offer that is well below the asking price but it should at least clear the mortgage and give me a couple of thousand to pay back my parents, who he also borrowed money from. My car is being repossessed because I couldn't keep up the payments on it. He convinced me we should get it as we'd need a bigger car for our family when I'd been happy in my little runaround. We're going to have to move in with my parents for a bit. I have nothing, literally nothing. The bastard took everything, he even took the jewellery that one of my nans and a great-aunt left me.

I didn't go to the police because I was too embarrassed. And scared. He told me more than once that when people cross him he makes sure they're never in any fit state to do that again. After that time he hit me and after the way he looked at Monica's picture, I knew I couldn't risk it. So when the police came about the next woman he'd moved on to, who wasn't stupid enough to get pregnant and who had called them the very first time she found out he'd taken out debt in her name, I lied.

It wasn't easy. I was terrified of lying to the police, I'd never done anything like that in my life, but I was more terrified of the press finding out what a gullible idiot I'd been and it being all over the papers, and I was absolutely petrified of him coming after me. So yeah, I lied to them, I sat where you're sitting now and told them that we'd been having problems for a while, then had a falling out and he moved on. They didn't really believe me. They kept telling me they'd keep me safe, that I had nothing to be ashamed of, that if they got enough people together he'd go to prison for a very long time. But I was adamant, really definite with them that he'd done nothing like that to me.

I'm still scared, you know, of him turning up one day and demanding access to his son. Everyone would say it's his right, that he just wants to spend time with his son, and I'd be a complete bitch who is keeping him away from his child, but I know he'd only be after money. After I get back on my feet, I'm going to disappear, I think. My ex has lost interest in Monica anyway now that he doesn't get the chance to use her to abuse me, so the first chance I get, I'm going to move to another place away from here so Kier can't come back and get at me.

When Lynne stopped talking, I hugged her as much as I could, because I couldn't offer anything else. As I was leaving, she said to me: 'I hope it works out for your friend. She won't thank you for it, though. A couple of people tried to tell me when I was first with him that his stories didn't add up, that he was dodgy with money and that I should watch my back. But I didn't believe them. In fact, I cut them off because he told me they'd tried it on with him. All lies, obviously – he could tell who saw through him and had to get them out of my life. I have no friends left, thanks to him. So your friend, when you tell her, be prepared for her to react really badly. *Really badly.*'

'Thank you. Thank you so much for your time . . . and the warning,' I said.

She nodded and stepped back, tugged her cardigan around her almost skeletal form and waited on the drive until I had pulled away. There was more. I could tell there was more that she didn't tell me, something so much worse than all of the other stuff. I was hoping I could talk to Hazel before she found out what it was.

1:15 p.m. Ciaran stuck it out for over an hour. He made coffee, he brought biscuits, he sat on the other side of the room reading a paper, then flicking through channels and giving up on several shows and movies, then more coffee, more biscuits. Truth is, I understood how to knit purls within ten minutes, I understood how to do the raspberry formation of the purls, how they intricately bound together, within twenty minutes. I had more endurance than him, though, so after seventy minutes of him having to listen to me mess it up and Hazel very patiently point out what I was doing wrong, he said he was going for a quick jog.

He has reappeared wearing some very expensive-looking running gear, the type that Sol has never been able to afford until he got this new job and became Mr Moneybags. Even then, I know he agonised about how much he was spending on clothes he was essentially going to be sweating into three times a week. Ciaran has an Apple watch on his wrist and Bose headphones snaking a white line from his watch to his ears. 'Just going out for a *quick* run,' he says again. His emphasis on 'quick' is telling me that I need to be gone by the time he comes back.

'I can't see this being quick, but I'm getting there,' I say to him, waving the knitting needles – Hazel has replaced mine because they were unsuitable ('crap') – and the wool intertwined between them. 'I am getting there, aren't I, Haze?' I implore, turning sad eyes on her.

'Yes, I think so,' she says, then pulls a 'she's so bad at this' face at him when she thinks I'm not looking that makes him laugh, which he quickly turns into a cough.

'See you,' he calls at the front door.

'Yeah,' I respond. My face is a frown of concentration as I move the needles together, push a needle through, wind wool around it, then pull.

'Love you, bye,' Hazel says.

When the door shuts behind him, I leave it a few minutes, carry on attempting to knit while Hazel watches me, just so he has time to stop standing on the other side of the door, which I'm 100 per cent sure he's doing.

Another ten minutes pass and I am as sure as I can be that he is gone. I stop mid-purl, sit back and then toss the knitting onto the kitchen table. It takes her seconds to put down her tangle of needles and cable needle and to sit back in her seat, too. 'I can't believe I fell for that. What do you really want?'

'Are you trying for a baby?' I ask her.

'That's none of your business,' she replies.

'No, it's not. But . . . are you?'

'I don't believe this, you're as bad as Yvonne. It's absolutely none of your business.'

'Are you?'

She inhales, accepts that I'm going to keep asking until she answers. 'No. Well, Ciaran thinks we should and he wants us to try, but I'm not sure. Not that it's any of your business.'

'I'm sorry to get all heavy there,' I say to placate her. 'One of the boys mentioned Camille said she was going to be getting a baby brother or sister, and I had to ask.'

'Camille? How would she know?'

'Maybe she overheard you talking?'

Hazel stares through me, shakes her head. I'm pretty sure, like with Lynne Smythe's daughter, Ciaran will have told her.

'No matter. I was a bit surprised, since you've only just moved in with him, from what you've told me. I mean, what do you know about him, really?'

'Are you going to tell me you've been checking up on him like Yvonne did?'

'Look, Hazel, when I first met Sol, I was a single mother, like you, so I was super paranoid. He doesn't know this, but I would do all sorts of searches on him, on every available search engine, every possible permutation of his name – and with a name like Solomon Solarin, you can imagine how many versions of his name there were out there. And this was all in the days of dial-up. But I did hours of picture searches, I looked for info about the city where he claimed to have lived, the jobs he'd allegedly had, the people he supposedly knew. Nothing he told me was a fact until I had verified it for myself. Yes, I showed a fundamental lack of trust in him right at the start of our relationship, but I had my daughter to think of and I wasn't going to let just anyone into our lives without knowing as much as possible about him as I could. It could still have gone wrong, of course, but I would have done all I could to find out as much as I could about him before I exposed him to my child. Which is my point. How much do you know about Ciaran, Hazel?'

That is an unfair question. I only found Lynne because I searched for so many, many variations on his name as well as doing an image search that linked him back to a very old photo of Lynne's that she must have completely forgotten to remove from her Facebook page.

'What is it with you people who can't take others at face value? This is exactly what Yvonne did, and it destroyed our friendship. Why can't you just leave us alone?'

'Hazel, I'm only trying to find out what you know about him. And you're right, it's none of my business, but I am worried about you.'

'Why? I barely know you. Why would you be worried about me?'

'Because you look really stressed. In general. You've mentioned Yvonne several times. Did something happen with you and her about Ciaran?'

'What happened was she did exactly what you're doing. She couldn't leave him alone. She was constantly prying into his background, trying to find out stuff. She said it was for me, because she was worried about me, but it was because Yvonne liked to have stuff on people. She liked to use it to get people to do what she wanted you to.'

'But that's only possible if you've got something to hide,' I say calmly. 'How can you have something to hide if you don't know anything about his past?'

'I KNOW WHAT I NEED TO!' she screams at me. 'I know everything I need to about him, all right? And don't look at me like that. We all make mistakes.'

'Mistakes? You call *that* a mistake?'

'I knew people would react like this. He is only on the sex offenders' register because he wanted to spare that girl the pain and trauma of court. He didn't do it. She lied about her age – he didn't know she was thirteen, but still he wanted to protect her. I think that's a pretty decent thing. She almost ruined his life and he still thought of what was best for her.'

What? *What? WHAT?!*

'*Excuse me?*' I say.

Her eyes become like saucers with little spots of brown at their centre when she realises what she has done, what she has told me in a fit of outrage. The colour, which had risen like a crimson tidal wave up her pale neck, finding its whirlpool home in her cheeks, now recedes, drains clean away. 'That wasn't what you were talking about?' she says.

I can barely move as I shake my head. 'No.'

Her hands, lined and parched from spending so much time cleaning up and washing up, fly up to her face then press on her closed eyelids. Then she sits very, very still. Slowly she removes her hands, looks with concern out towards the hallway and the front door. 'OK, look, you can't tell anyone that.'

My response is to stare at her like the crazy woman she is.

'Promise me. Promise me you won't tell anyone.'

'I'm not promising you that. No way. Even if I did promise it'd be a complete and utter lie – I'll tell whoever I think needs to know.'

Hands back over closed eyes, anxious leg jiggling.

'I mean seriously, Hazel, what the hell do you think you're doing?'

Hands away from eyes, clasped together in prayer. 'He didn't do it. If you knew him like I know him, you'd know there is no way on Earth he did it. I mean, it wasn't like it went to court – he accepted a caution. They wouldn't have left it at a caution if he actually did it, would they?'

'What do you want me to say? "Yeah, you're right, he seems like a decent bloke, crack on, Haze, crack on"? Like anyone in their right minds would say that.'

She reaches out, covers my hands with hers. 'I promise you, promise you, if I thought for one second he was guilty I would not let him near me or my children. It was a misunderstanding. He's really not like that.'

Her hands are light on mine; they feel fragile and she is trembling like a little bird, unsure of itself before it takes flight for the first time. I think about Lynne, about the thing she couldn't tell me. About the shame that oozed out of her like an invisible but pungent slime. What did I just say to Hazel? *What the hell do you think you're doing?* And what did she say to me? *Promise me. Promise me you won't tell anyone.* The secret she cannot share. The shame she cannot risk anyone knowing. What kind of a mother allows her daughter to be in the same house as a sex offender? The kind of mother who would do anything, *even lie to the police*, to stop people finding out that she knowingly let a sex offender *live* under the same roof as her children. The kind who, once she saw his true side, would believe he would harm her child.

'Have you actually seen sight of this conviction?' I ask her.

'No, but he didn't do it. I promise you.'

'Have you seen his name on the sex offenders' register?' I ask, even though I know it's not technically called that. But only law people and the police use its proper title. 'Because it will say what he's on there for.'

'No, it didn't go to court so it was only on there for two years and now it's been removed. Again, if he did it, he'd still be on there, wouldn't he?'

'What about a probation officer or anyone like that? Did you have a home visit from the police to check he is living here because there are children in the house? Did he have to register this address with the police when he moved in?'

'No, I told you, he's off the register now so nothing like that would be necessary.'

'When did he accept this caution?' I ask her.

'A while ago, I'm not exactly sure. I can't exactly bring it up and start asking him questions. It's obviously a very painful time in his life so I don't talk about it. And you mustn't either. It took a lot for him to share that with me and I'd hate to think a moment of stupidity has put all that at risk. He's rebuilt his life since then, and he's still very vulnerable about it all, so please, you must promise me that you won't tell anyone.'

Hazel is a good-looking woman. When she smiles the apples of her cheeks bloom, her hair, even when she has obviously taken some time to make sure it is neat and presentable, is almost always endearingly messy. She is intelligent, compassionate, trusting. She's not naïve, she is not stupid, nor gullible or pathetic. She is simply a woman who likes to see the best in people. Despite what the world has shown her of what people can be like, she is constantly overwhelmed with a need to trust the goodness at the heart of the person in front of her.

'I'm not going to tell anyone,' I say eventually. I'm not going to tell anyone because it is a colossal lie. He is not on the sex offenders' register. For one, Gareth would have told me. For two, with the amount of time I spent researching him and the possible variations on his name, there is no way I wouldn't have found something.

He needs Hazel to *think* he is on the register, like he needed Lynne before her to think he was, because it is the ultimate con. It is a huge gamble, but it is perfect. It casts him as fundamentally honest because he has shared something so huge and personal; it paints him as vulnerable because it is so painful to be so wrongly accused; it presents him as a flawed hero who will sacrifice himself if it saves a troubled girl from the trauma of court. Also, it cages the woman he tells, prevents her from ever telling anyone about it because she will be shunned for allowing him near her children or other people's children. And, ultimately, it is the sudden threat of what he might do to her child that will get him what he wants before he goes away. That is what Lynne couldn't tell me. He threatened – possibly even overtly – to seriously harm her daughter if she did not give him what he wanted. And everyone would have blamed her for not ditching him the second she knew he was a sex offender. It is the ultimate gamble for Ciaran and it has clearly paid off many times because he is still doing it.

Hazel believes he is a fundamentally good person who did a good thing for someone else at his own expense. She will not listen to Lynne's story. She will not listen to me and believe me.

'Did Yvonne find out about him?' I ask.

'You keep asking about Yvonne,' she says.

'I don't. You keep comparing me to Yvonne, so I was wondering—'

'If I accidentally told her and then smacked her over the head to keep her quiet?'

'I was wondering if her checking up on you and Ciaran led to you two falling out and that's what's eating you up? Do you feel guilty that you weren't friends any more when she was attacked? Because I hardly know you, Hazel, but something is eating you up. The only time you look remotely happy or relaxed is when you're knitting. Even at Maxie's when we were mixing cocktails you looked bereft.' I pick up my knitting again. The way purls are made is simple; what they result in is something that is deceptively complex. The way a friend is made is surprisingly simple; what that friendship results in is deceptively complex. 'I'm just worried about you, Hazel.'

'I look bereft?' she asks.

I nod. 'And I'm not going to tell anyone what you told me. But please, do yourself a favour: check up on yourself.'

'What do you mean?'

'You work for a building society. Don't you think it's wise to regularly do a check to see if there is stuff in your name that you know nothing about?'

'You're telling me that there's debt in my name I know absolutely nothing about?'

'No. I'm telling you that whenever I've been away anywhere, or Sol has, or we've been to a new petrol station or bar or a new area, I check that no one has cloned my cards, etc. When was the last time you did that?'

She stares at me, baffled, as though I am speaking a completely different language.

'OK, let me put it like this. Does your ex-husband know information about you that could allow him to take out credit in your name?'

'Yes, I suppose he does.'

'Right, given the way you told me he treated you, would you put it past him to have a long-term strategy to screw you over by, say, running up debt in your name?'

She sits very still, obviously remembering something about her marriage. I don't think for a second her ex would bother, but if there is a way to make her open her eyes, to check what is going on and stop being so trusting, to maybe explore the possibility that something is being done in her name without her knowledge, then I will throw Walter under that particular bus.

'I'm not saying there is anything to know, but it wouldn't hurt to check.' I gather up my belongings, return my knitting to my bag and put my mobile away. 'I'd better get going. I need to do a few things before the school run.'

At the door, Hazel throws her arms around me. She buries her face in my neck and she holds me so close I can smell the lemongrass and water lilies scent she uses as a fabric softener, mingled with the notes of something that reminds me of the perfume my mother used to wear.

'I said some awful things to her,' she says. 'Yvonne. I screamed at her and she attacked me and I fought back for once. I was so angry with her. I screamed at her and she attacked me, and Maxie and Anaya stepped in to stop her. It was awful. And even after that, when it all calmed down, I was still so angry. I didn't come straight home. That's what I told Maxie and Anaya. I—'

Ciaran's key in the lock stops her words. She pulls herself upright and we both step back while he finishes opening the door. He stops short. 'Oh. You're still here,' he says to me.

'Not for much longer – we were saying goodbye.'

I grin at him and then look at Hazel. I don't know how she got away with lying to the police because a game face she does not have: she is openly anxious, twisting her hands, her eyes wide and fretful.

'Hazel, it's not that bad,' I say with a laugh. 'I will practise when I get home and I promise you that the next time we see each other I will have mastered purl *and* cable.'

I step forwards, cover her hands with my hand. She needs to calm down. 'I'm sorry I made you anxious about the knitting,' I say to her. 'Maybe you need to sit down and do a few rows now?' *Remember, like I said, it's the only time you look calm and happy.* 'I won't force you to give me private lessons again.'

She clearly remembers what I said, and she relaxes. Smiles. 'You're right. I need to do some of my own knitting to remind me that it's simple and easy. Not complicated, like you were making it.'

'Exactly. I'll see you in an hour or so,' I tell her.

'Yes.'

'Actually, sorry, you won't, the boys have after-school clubs today. So I'll see you soon.' I focus my attention on Ciaran. 'See you.'

'Yes,' he replies. 'See you.' His expression tells me that he's not at all convinced by the act we have put on. Not convinced at all.

He stands at the open door and watches me walk down the garden path, and continues to watch me until I am out of sight.

FRIDAY

Anaya

1 a.m. Usually when Sanj is working late in his office, I end up distracting him. It's not fair, really, considering how ballistic I would go at him if he did the same, but unlike me, he likes it. He enjoys any bit of non-essential contact we have. Especially when I come in and sit on his lap and talk to him. I want to do that now. To wander into his office, tip myself onto him, link my arms around his neck and kiss him. Then talk to him, right up close, so I can see every perfect millimetre of his gorgeous face. Even now, after all these years I still find him thrilling to look at, exciting to be around. Except when his mother is mentioned, of course. Then I look at him and remember what I said to him all those years ago when I had to hide in his wardrobe: 'You're a giant mummy's boy'. I hope no one ever says that about Arjun. Or Priya for that matter. I hope no one thinks of them as infantilised and weak in the face of their parent. I hope that when my children are grown they will be able to put in place and enforce, if necessary, firm boundaries. I hope that if I ever turn into an evil mother-in-law that I will have brought my children up well enough for them to put me firmly in my place. Which is outside of their relationship.

I have two difficult conversations to have with my husband; they are interlinked and if one doesn't go well, neither will the other. It's been a few days since I spilled everything to Cece. I've ignored texts from Maxie and Hazel, I've arrived at the school gates at the very last minute to drop off, and have made the kids stay for homework club so I don't have to see them then, either.

I can't go on like this, obviously. I have to talk to Sanj and get things on the move.

330

'Babe,' I say. I have entered the room quietly, but away from the angle of the computer so Sanjay doesn't see me approach – he nearly leaps out of his skin.

'What are you doing, Ansi? Trying to give me a heart attack?'

'No, no, sorry. I just wanted to talk to you.'

He pats his lap while pushing his chair away from the desk.

'I think I'd better sit over there,' I tell him.

As I arrange myself in his leather armchair, he physically braces himself, preparing himself for the onslaught that is to come. We only ever fall out about one thing and one thing only. Obviously it'd probably be two things if he knew what else I am going to add to the end of this conversation. But for now, I am happy for him to steel himself to talk about his parents.

'I'm going to change the locks,' I say. I surprise myself. I have planned this, have talked over and over in my head about how to broach the subject in a kind, considerate manner so that I won't upset him unduly before I tell him the rest. But this came out. Now it's 'out there', it's as good a place to start as any. 'And the alarm code.'

Sanjay moves his head up and down in what most people would think is a nodding motion but is actually him taking in the information and deciding how to deal with it. 'Erm, why?' he eventually asks.

'Sorry, I should have said: I'm going to change the locks and the alarm code and if you give your parents any kind of access to either of those things, I will leave you. And by access I also mean telling them before it's done that we're doing it so they have a chance to have any sort of say about it.'

I can tell by his slightly amused stance – his head is almost forty-five degrees to the side and his frown is deep, his lips comically pursed – that he's not taking me seriously. He's also working out how much placating he'll need to do to stop this conversation even happening, let alone the rest of what I've said happening. That's why he's a good businessman, and excellent at what he does – he can suss things out, work out what someone needs and then ally that with his wants and needs. 'That's a bit of an extreme thing to say, Ansi,' he eventually replies. 'Why? I mean, with all of it, why?'

'I've finally worked out that in all of this – all the stresses and subtle battles I've had with your mother over the years – *you're* the problem.' I raise my hand before he can interrupt, protest, try to convince me otherwise. 'And I'm the problem. We're the problem. There, I've said it: it's not her fault, it's yours and mine and ours.'

His stance is less comical now; he's a bit pissed off. Sanjay doesn't like to be a problem, he wants – needs – to be liked by everyone. He has a pathological need to be all things to everyone. Which is great in his line of work, but a nightmare if you're married to him and he has a mother who has no boundaries and no filter and control issues.

'Come on now, Sanj, I'm not saying anything that isn't true. It's not natural for adults to live like this. You did it for years and that was fine, but I can't feel like a visitor in my own home any more.' Another move to protest and my hand is up again, stopping him before he can speak. 'We moved from London and your parents came with us. Never mind their daughters who got married and had children way before you, the first thing your parents did when we told them we were moving was to put their house on the market and start looking at houses down here. I mean, what the hell? I thought, I actually thought, because we'd be buying a house together that things would be different, but they're not. If anything, they're worse because I don't feel like I'm living in our house to which your mother has a key; it feels like I am living in your parents' house and while I am there I have to live by their rules. Even though I pay the mortgage and the bills.'

'It's not that bad, Ansi,' Sanjay manages.

'No, it's not that bad – it's worse. I can't relax in my own home. I can't walk around naked, I can't feed my children fish fingers, I can't even leave the beds unmade without worrying about what she'll say and how she'll judge me and if it'll spark a whole month's worth of barbed comments and attempts to get you on your own so she can remind you what a bad wife choice you made. I'm done with it, Sanj.

That's why I say it's you and me. Me because I should have said something years ago. And it's you because you can't see that there's a problem. Actually, you *can* see there's a problem, but you want to ignore it because you don't want to stand up to your parents.'

'That's not entirely true,' he says.

'Which part isn't?'

He licks his lips. I know what he's thinking: *How can I get out of this conversation? How can I avoid having to talk about this in anything but a 'you know what my mother's like, she's harmless really' way?* 'The part about me not standing up to my mother. It's not like she does anything totally heinous that needs standing up to.'

'You know what? It's the little things that sound innocuous on their own that she's expert at. And it lets you get away with dismissing my feelings and making out she's not that bad. Sanjay, she *is* that bad. Like I say, it's my own fault for putting up with it for so long.'

He seizes on that. Something he can use to deflect the interest away from him and his mother onto me. He can make it all about me and my failings so he doesn't have to deal with the real issue. I know my husband well. I love him for being predictable. For following the script that I have mostly written in my head that will lead me to this part of the conversation. (Although I did have to say it was my fault a few times before he snapped up the bait.) 'I think you're right there, Ansi. Tell me, why did you put up with it for so long if it's that bad?'

It's my turn to lick my lips, to moisten my mouth to allow the words to slide out. 'Because when I was sixteen, a man I knew drugged me and took pornographic pictures of me. A few years later he said he would delete them if I gave him a lot of money, which I did. But he didn't delete them. He got me arrested by pretending I'd beaten him up and then he put them on the internet anyway. So, I've been terrified all these years that your mother will find out about it and tell you and you'd leave me.'

My husband's face is fixed on me, his body is very still, but his eyes are roaming around the room as if waiting for someone to jump out and scream, *'ONLY KIDDING!'* When no such thing happens, he returns his focus to me and very slowly says: 'What?' I don't think he realises how slowly he says this, how his mouth moves to form every curve and line of the word.

'I've wanted to tell you for years. Right after we met, before we got serious, before we got married, before we moved here, before we had children. I wanted you to know but then I wanted no one to know. I know you just accepted my surname being different to my parents' as part of me, but your mum has never quite accepted it. She's always digging around, trying to find out what my secret is. She thinks I was married before, which I wasn't. But I didn't want her to be the one to tell you I had this huge secret and to get you on-side with hunting out what it was. And then it didn't seem import-ant – there was no way she'd go searching in the places you have to look to find those photos – and I realised, if she could control me in real life, she seemed to stop looking in other places for more infor-mation. That's why I put up with it.'

'What?' Sanjay repeats. 'I mean, *what*?'

'And I didn't tell you because I am a coward and I did not want to see that look you have on your face right now.'

'Look on my face?' he says. 'Look on my face?' His voice is loud and he is suddenly on his feet. 'You were scared of the look on my face?'

'Kind of, I suppose,' I reply. 'I didn't want to see the disappoint-ment and disgust.' I feel dreadful. Physically heavy, internally awful. I shouldn't have kept this from him. I told him off for being fake, and all along I had kept this secret. First, I guess, because I didn't think it would last, then because I saw that look in his mother's eye. She was determined to get rid of me: I was of Indian heritage, but not good enough for him. She wanted someone else, someone pliable and easy, someone who would either bow down to her or be easily cowed by her – I was neither and she wanted rid. I shouldn't have kept this a secret, I should have let him make the decision whether to marry me or not, knowing all the facts about me.

'What?' he says again. 'You think this is disgust and disappoint-ment?' He points to his face. 'Really? After all these years, you think that I'd be disgusted and disappointed by you being sexually assaulted and the bastard taking photos?' He comes to me and gets down on his knees, almost as though he is about to beg for forgiveness. 'Ansi, I'm *horrified*. I'm horrified that it happened to you, and I am absolutely distraught that you couldn't tell me because of what my mother might say.'

'Really?' I ask him hesitantly.

'Of course really. What did you think I would say, even if my mother had told me?'

'I don't know . . . She might have made out I was a porn star or something.'

'And if she did, and you told me otherwise, I would have believed you. And if you were a porn star, I would have accepted it. You're the mother of my children; you're the only woman I've ever wanted to marry. Yes, you drive me insane sometimes and you frustrate the hell out of me, but that's normal. You being so scared of my mother that you keep things like this to yourself is not normal.'

'I'm not scared of your mother,' I say indignantly. I really am not scared of her. 'I was scared of how much sway she has on you and your feelings.'

'You know what I mean,' he replies. He gathers me up in a hug, holds me close to him. Thinking about it now, what *was* I so scared of? Would I want to be with a man who wouldn't believe me when I told him about what happened? Would I want to be with a man who wouldn't believe their son or daughter?

'I didn't want anyone to know, as well,' I explain into the folds of his sweatshirt. 'I was so ashamed about all of it. I wanted to act as though it was something other to me.'

'I'm so sorry. So sorry. I hate that it happened to you, and I really hate that you've been living with it all this time and not able to tell me. Well, that's all going to change. From now. Tomorrow we change the locks, the alarm code and I will not tell my parents until they try to get in here.' I feel him wince at the thought of it, what it will unleash. 'I'll take a few days off work to make sure I'm here to deal with the fallout,' he then says. 'And don't worry, they won't be getting another key.'

'Are you sure about this? I don't want you to cave. If you have to, we can blame me and I'll take the flak.'

'No, no. It won't be easy but I've got to do it. I'm old enough to do this.' He holds me closer. 'Anything for you.'

'Thank you.'

'What made you decide to tell me now?' he asks.

I almost don't tell him. I've come this far, said this much, I don't want him to know the rest of it, what I had to do to try to keep the status quo. *But no more lies, eh, Anaya? No more secrets and lies.* So I tell him. All of it. Every little thing about Yvonne and what happened.

'Oh, fuck,' he says at the end of it. It is *that* serious, if Sanjay is swearing. Even after I had a go at him all those years ago, he still very rarely swears. It's just not his thing. Yup, it is that serious. I don't know how I have managed to convince myself it wasn't.

Part 12

MONDAY

Cece

11 a.m. It's taken Sol six days to revert to git mode. Six whole days. I suppose I should be grateful I had that time where he was him again and we were us again. And I could pretend I'm not spying on my friends and getting them to reveal secrets about themselves so I can tell the police which one of them was lying about her whereabouts when a woman was almost bludgeoned to death.

With a little bad grace, I collect a trolley from the entrance to the supermarket I've driven out to in Hollingbury. I've come here for two reasons. One, to make sure I don't feel guilty about the row I had with Sol earlier and, two, to make sure I see as few people I know from the gates as possible. Two has already gone down in flames – from pulling into the car park and entering the supermarket, I have seen six different people whose children go to Plummer Prep. Some have smiled vaguely at me, others have registered my face but have stared straight through me.

The main reason for me being here – the row – I am still so angry about I'm sure rage is shimmering around me. Sol rang to ask me to pick up his dry cleaning and would I mind finding his passport and starting on his packing because he'd run out of time to do it before he had to leave for his business trip. When I pointed out that I had no clue he was going away, and that, more importantly, he was meant to be picking up Harmony like he'd promised her he would and driving her to a hockey match because she'd finally been chosen for the team, he treated me to a long silence that revealed he had forgotten. Someone had obviously asked him to go away last-minute and he had said yes, without even bothering to tell me as a courtesy.

If he had mentioned it, I would have reminded him about Harmony's first hockey game he had made a big deal of going to with her because he used to play hockey at school. After the silence, he suggested she get the school bus with everyone else, as she had been going to do until *he'd* insisted on driving her there and back to make the game special. When I pointed out the crushing disappointment she would feel, he asked me to kindly stop trying to make him feel guilty and would I pack his navy blue suit which was at the dry cleaners. 'Go love yourself, Sol,' I told him and hung up.

What I hadn't wanted to do in the aftermath of the row was feel so guilty that, in the interests of peacekeeping, I would look for his passport and start his packing, so I got in my car and drove over here.

I'm going to have to take the boys with me tonight to watch her play. They'll be thrilled that after a day at school, they'll be standing on the sidelines of a cold hockey pitch watching their sister play. Not. Oscar hates the cold and Ore's asthma flares up. If I was in London, I could call my mum. Before I saw Gareth, I would have asked Hazel, Anaya or Maxie, but now he's planted the seed of their potential dangerousness in my mind, I can't really risk the boys being with any of them without me.

I push my trolley towards the dried goods aisle and as I turn in, I spot that woman – Teri Haligan – who took over Yvonne Whidmore's role as class coordinator. She stands at the end of the aisle, a vision in pink Lycra and white trainers and a pink-and-white zip-up top. She is talking to Trevor Whidmore. Teri holds her shopping basket – with its 'all natural' cereal bar and bottle of fizzy water – like a picnic hamper, while Trevor Whidmore has a sandwich, crisps, juice and a bar of chocolate in his basket. Teri is simpering at him, her eyes fluttering, her head tipped at an angle that is sympathetic and 'kiss me' at the same time. He has a certain amount of affection on his face, but when she places a hand on his chest, he steps backwards. There's a pattern being formed there. Or has it already been formed? Is there something about them both being out here at the same time, a way of hiding in plain sight? Whatever, I need to move away to contemplate this because any second, one of them is going to feel the weight of my gaze and then they will look up and I will become embroiled in a fake, nicey-nice conversation I can do without. I step backwards, pulling my trolley with me, and turn to go back the way I have come and—

'Oh, hello, Mrs Solarin. Fancy seeing you here,' Mrs Carpenter says.

'Hello,' I manage to squeak. I'm immediately tense; scared that she's going to tell me off because no matter how old I get, I still always think headteachers are going to tell me off.

There is a posh party going on in her trolley: several bottles of prosecco; platters of olives, cubed cheese, circles of cured meats; and big packets of organic crisps. Party shopping in the middle of the school day? I'm not sure I approve. Shouldn't she be at school, over-seeing the general day-to-day running of the place?

'I'm so glad I ran into you,' she says. While she speaks, she positions herself in front of the trolley to obscure it from me. She doesn't want me telling people about her party shopping on school time. 'I've been meaning to contact you to sound you out about you maybe joining the Parents' Council. I know it can be daunting coming to a new school as well as moving to a new area, so I thought you might like to join the PC to meet people?'

'Me?' I shake my head. 'No. Thank you, but no. It's not my kind of thing at all.'

She flicks her red-brown hair and tips her head to one side as she looks at me. She's not that much older than me, but she has the lined skin of someone who likes foreign holidays, and the body of someone who likes to indulge in the things in her trolley. 'Mrs Solarin, I'll be honest with you: we could use someone like you on the Parents' Council. Fresh blood, different outlook. People can become jaded and it's always important for us to freshen things up.'

Really? I think. *The head of the PC is lying in a coma and you think it's appropriate to be trying to freshen things up?*

'Let me be even more honest with you. Mr Whidmore confided in me that you helped him out recently. You went over one night to watch his children while he went to work? Even though you hardly knew him? He was so overcome with the generosity of this gesture.

As were the other members of the school leadership team when I told them. We all agreed that you showed the true spirit of Plummer Prep and we would like to have you as part of our team.'

Inside I raise another eyebrow. *Did she say that to him? That my helping him out was my audition to become part of his comatose wife's group? Really?*

'I told him not to tell anyone about that,' I say. 'Everyone will be wanting me to take care of their kids if word leaks out.'

She looks stricken. 'Oh, I'm sorry, I didn't realise. We were meeting about—'

'I'm joking, I'm joking,' I tell her. I didn't realise she has no sense of humour. The first time I met her she was quite jolly, relaxed. So this must be another overshadowing from what happened on her school premises.

'Oh, I see.' She offers me a smile. 'I'm sorry, everything that has happened has been so difficult for all of us, as I'm sure you can imagine. That is why we're trying to expand our family, draw people in and hold them close. If you understand what I mean?'

I nod. I don't fully understand what she means – how can I when I've never been in that situation? But I do understand that need to cling on to things at certain points in your life, to embrace the new and try to make it familiar and part of your world as a panacea for all the other crap you can't do anything about. 'I'll think about it,' I say gently.

'Oh, thank you, Mrs Solarin. I can't wait to tell the other members of the Parents' Council and the Senior Management Team that you'll be on board. It will be such a boost for the school's morale to see that the new parents are keen to become part of the school, because you know this was a one-off incident. Thank you, Mrs Solarin. You have made my day that bit brighter.'

Hang on, I didn't actually say that, I go to tell her, but she is off down the aisle, virtually whistling with happiness before I can utter another word. I've so been played.

WEDNESDAY

Cece

4:15 p.m. I really should not be here.

Places like this, events like this, are created and held for parents with better temperaments than I. I stand on the sidelines between the two pitches behind the school, wearing the mums' uniform of padded black knee-length coat, hood up against the drizzle, hands in pockets against the cold, boots up to your knees fighting the mud while I watch my boys play football. When the other school Oscar and Ore are playing climbed out of their minibuses and walked down the path to the fields on the far side of the school, I gulped. They are huge. Overgrown beings masquerading as children, bred to win at all costs. Most of them seem a full head taller than most of the boys in Ore and Oscar's classes, and certainly a width bigger than my two boys.

They played matches in their London school, of course, but they seemed fewer and further between. And, most importantly, I wasn't there for them. I wasn't able to get away from work so I rarely – if ever – saw the other side striding out, looking like they didn't know the meaning of the word 'friendly'.

This by-product of working – not seeing my offspring go up against bigger children – is something I will be eternally grateful for. It's got me this far, relatively emotionally unscathed. These things, these 'matches' – friendly or otherwise – are for mothers who know how to restrain themselves; who can watch their youngest child perform a slide tackle and not flinch; who can see their middle child stand in goal, ready to face a penalty, and not scream when the ball misses his face by millimetres. (It was bad enough on Monday watching

Harmony and she looked the same size as most of the children on the hockey pitch.)

I should not be here, it is not good for me. I doubt it's good for the boys, either. They do not need to see every facet of my neurosis about my children being hurt played out on this muddy field. They need to be able to throw themselves – quite literally sometimes – into the games without worrying about me storming in there and snatching them away to somewhere safe.

'First time?' Maxie says.

'How do you mean?' I reply. I can't look at her, I can't take my eyes off the boys. I'm standing facing the whitewashed cricket pavilion while most parents are facing one field or the other. I have to face the pavilion so I can keep an eye on both matches on both fields at the same time.

'You should see the trauma on your face,' she jokes. 'You look how I feel about Frankie playing. I've mostly got used to it now.'

'How?'

'I don't come to the matches very often. His dad does, if he's around. He can watch without worry. Me, not so much. He's away tonight so I've forced myself to come. It's not so bad but don't get me started on rugby.'

My eyes widen and whip round to look at her. 'Rugby?' I whisper, triggered into my idea of neurotic parent hell with that word. I'd actually ignored that whole section of the uniform list.

'GOAL!' the shout goes up, the ref's whistle pierces the air and I turn to see Ore with his hands in the air, running around as fast as his mud-caked legs will carry him, while his teammates try to hug him. I clap and shout, with the R-word ringing in my ears.

'Sorry,' Maxie says. 'Didn't mean to make you miss the goal.'

'No, don't worry, probably for the best I didn't see. I'm sure he'll be replaying and repeating it for me many times in the coming weeks.'

'I'm sure.'

We stumble into silence. Uncomfortable and awkward, when it's never been like that between us. She's struggling with something, I think. She wants to say something but won't. She's not like Anaya, who has to plan to do it; she's not like Hazel, who will accidentally do it. She is on the verge, but won't. 'Haven't seen you around much, Maxie,' I say to break the tension. 'Are you all right?'

'Yeah, course. Just busy. Busy, busy.'

Abandoning the pavilion, I rotate slowly in the sideline mud to stare at her. 'Really?'

She nods. 'No.'

I move towards the cricket pavilion. It's especially muddy there, Mrs Carpenter explained, because the cricket pitch is unusable except in the driest months. I walk towards there because there are no parents along this area, no one is wearing the type of boots that will withstand those pigsty-like conditions. Maxie follows me. Even then, away from people who don't want to stand right by a mudslide, I lower my voice: 'What's going on?'

'I stole a baby,' she says to me. Just like that. She doesn't even particularly lower her voice, but I know it's masked by shouts from the matches, dissolved in the light drizzle, whisked away on the wind.

'What?' I say with a half laugh. I wait, for her to cuff my shoulder, grin, or double up in laughter at my face.

'You heard me.'

I stare at her. I thought she'd wait a bit longer to reveal her secret, that she'd think about it and then talk about it. I didn't expect this blurted-out confession.

Her eyes are penetrating my face, probing my mind to see what my reaction is, what I'm thinking, what I'll say. Over her shoulder I watch Frankie, Ore and Oscar's best friend, shout to Oscar and the other defenders to get into the goal, while he goes in for a tackle. My older brother used to talk (obsessively) about Pelé, the legendary football player. My brother spent years trying to recreate Pelé's over-head kick, attempting to throw himself just right so he could connect with the ball and slam it into the goal. He managed it once – after years of practice. I watch Frankie Smith throw himself up and backwards, bring his right leg up in a perfect arc to connect his foot with the ball as it comes his way and then kick the ball so hard it whizzes straight past the other team's giant of a goalkeeper.

'GOAL!' roars everyone on the sidelines for Oscar's match. 'GOAL, GOAL, GOAL!' The shouts get louder; the referee's whistle strikes the air.

Maxie continues to watch me.

'Frankie?' I eventually say.

She nods.

This is what Gareth meant: to him, an expert people-reader, she would have been a mass of contradictions. Plain speaker, gregarious, presents as openly honest, but beneath the surface something else lurks, something you can't put your finger on to suss out. Who would guess that this would be it?

'Are you really shocked?' she asks.

I offer her a dry laugh in return, watch Oscar throw his arms around his muddy friend while Frankie rubs his knuckles along Oscar's forehead, leaving a streak of wet earth. 'Yeah, I'm shocked.' I nod. 'I'm properly shocked. I don't think anything has ever shocked me this much. Who else knows?'

'You. Me. Ed.' She inhales. Then exhales: 'Yvonne.'

Knowing Yvonne . . . I look over Maxie again: she's slightly younger than me, but she is beautiful. Really quite striking. I noticed that at the beach hut when Oscar first pointed out Frankie; she is someone who stands out in a crowd. She said that to me once, that I was so beautiful I stood out in a crowd. I was incredibly flattered. Apart from my husband, no one I know who is beautiful has called me beautiful before. Knowing Yvonne . . .

She nods at me. Yes. Nod, nod. 'Yes,' she says. 'In case you're wondering, yes, I did try to kill Yvonne that night.'

Maxie

8:25 p.m. Cece picked the pub right around the corner from her house. She insisted that I bring Frankie over for tea, for a bath, and to sleep over because Ed is away. 'Are you sure, sure, sure you'll be all right?' she asked her older daughter, Harmony, before we left for the pub.

Harmony, who is a shade or two darker than me, so I'm guessing, like me but unlike her brothers, has a white father, rolled her eyes at her mother. 'Oh, please, Mum. If I had no homework, I would be making a fortune out of babysitting. I'll be fine.'

'We're not babies!' Oscar called from the living room.

'No, we're not!' Ore added. 'We're nearly ten.'

'In two years!' Harmony called back.

Frankie was silent. He had been ever since he'd clapped eyes on Harmony. He kept blushing every time she looked at him and stuttered when he spoke to her. Us leaving him with her was a dream come true. There was a time, in Reception, when he had decided that he was going to marry Priya. Yvonne had been offended because he hadn't wanted Madison. 'He told me that Camille's going to marry her,' I'd said to Yvonne to make her feel better. Which it hadn't. 'There's no pleasing you, is there?' I'd told her.

Cece and I walk over to the pub in silence. She orders drinks and we sit at the back. It is quite busy, the place full of people watching a Wednesday-night qualifier for something. I watch Cece take three sips of wine – the first to cleanse the palate, the second to get the tartness out of the way, the third to start to enjoy it. That's what Bronwyn used to say to me.

'Do you want to know about Frankie or Yvonne first?' I ask. Cece is one of those wait-it-out people. I think that's why I told her. Because I knew she'd take her time, she'd think, she wouldn't rush to judge, she wouldn't ask millions of questions.

Another sip. She stares at the table, at the circular beer mats. Ed used to pile them up sometimes twenty high on the edge of the table and then flip them and catch them in one go. His party trick.

'Frankie,' she says.

I'm glad she's asked about that. That will maybe make her understand a bit better about Yvonne.

'I ended up living and working with this high-flying couple. She was like this superstar journalist, writer, television-programme maker, and she was with Ed, who I'm married to now. He'd been with Bronwyn for years before he met me. That's her name. Bronwyn Sloane. I'm not sure if you've heard of her?'

November, 2006

'You're like the daughter I never had,' Bronwyn said to me. We sat on the big, comfy sofa together, as we often did with soft music playing and the lights on low.

'I'm not sure I like that,' I told her.

The cottage was divine. Every single cliché a cottage in the middle of the Cumbrian countryside should be, with its stone floors and uneven walls, the mismatched furniture and draughts we could never quite seal out. The bedrooms were cold but surprisingly cosy and it often felt like we were living on another planet because it could be days before we saw another person.

I lifted my head from her shoulder and sat back and away from her. 'I know I'm not as old as you, but I thought we were equals or at least friends on an equal footing. If I'm like the daughter you never had, then you think on some level you're above me.'

'Not at all,' she said. She took my chin between her forefinger and thumb, to turn my head to look at her. 'Not at all,' she repeated gently. 'I just meant that . . . I have this longing, this yearning to be a mother. It's so boring and primeval that I'm regularly annoyed with my body for making me feel this way, but it's there nonetheless. I have a need to produce a smaller version of myself, someone I have this unwavering love for. Every other type of love I've experienced so far – and believe me, I've experienced them all – they've all been conditional. I know, without a shadow of a doubt, that there's something every single person in my life could do that would make me stop loving them. Except you. That's what I mean, sugar,' she said. 'I can't think of a single thing you could do that would make me dump you. That's what I imagine being a mother is like.'

What she had said to me was huge. As time had worn on, and her fame as an intellectual, journalist, lecturer and TV series creator had grown, I'd got to know the real her. She could be difficult, ruthless, unyielding. She fell out with people, regularly. Someone she was practically in love with one day was someone she hated the next. She could be volatile, her temper brittle and fragile like freshly formed ice on a fast-moving lake – anything, even the slightest ripple, could cause it to snap. She'd never gone for me, but I knew she could.

'Ed comes a close second. There's not much he could do that would cause me to cut him out, but there is something. Not with you, though, sweetness. There's nothing you can do.'

She leant forwards and pressed her lips against mine. The first time she'd done that, it had felt like my heart had stopped beating, like my blood had forgotten how to flow. I'd been frozen, transfixed by the way she'd broken this physical boundary, had done something intimate, sexual. I'd been so confused, bewildered, but she hadn't gone any further. Instead, she'd sat back and carried on with what she was doing as though she'd done nothing out of the ordinary. She did it all the time: a quick peck on the lips to finish what she was saying; a longer kiss after she told me she loved me – constant punctuations of her feelings. All of those kisses, those boundary redefiners, had been platonic, had gone no further. Now, she was saying she felt maternal towards me, but she'd kissed me in a way that was anything but. This kiss was different from the others. This one . . . My heart stopped again, my blood forgot to flow. This one . . .

'Are you going to have children?' I asked her, ignoring the feelings that were bubbling inside me. She was thirty-something (she always fudged that) and she liked sex, had a lot of money now from the success of her journalism and books and the TV series she'd written that had recently been recommissioned – having a baby seemed to be one of those things that someone like her could do any time they wanted.

'I'd love to have kids,' she said dreamily. 'I can't even describe how much I want to be a mother.' Her dreamy smile, her wistful look, disappeared suddenly, replaced by defeat, despair and deep, deep sorrow. 'It's probably not going to happen, though.'

'Why?' I asked. 'Is it Ed?'

She shook her head. She'd pulled her hair up on top of her head, twisted it around to sit in a messy bun. She'd moved her green plastic-framed glasses to the top of her head and they looked like a tiara. 'Ah, no, Ed and I are on the same page – we both want children. We'd fill our house with them if we could. It's me. My body won't cooperate. I've had so many miscarriages. I don't write about those in my books because it's all far too painful. Everything else is fair game, but this . . . I know I shouldn't keep things back when I can talk about everything in my books, but I can't. We've tried IVF, the works. We've got some embryos in storage, but I don't know if either of us are strong enough to go through it again. I know, I know, I'm a complete hypocrite. I should be able to take this in my stride and talk about it, but I can't. I just can't.' She briefly closed her eyes, sighed. 'I know I should just get over myself, I should just accept that this is how it is. But I can't. I simply spend my life hoping for a miracle.'

'What about adoption?' I asked, then could have slapped myself. I shouldn't offer any suggestions. I should let her speak and listen. What did I know? I was twenty-eight. I hadn't even thought about settling down. I was still free-forming it, living a bohemian life working out in the middle of the Cumbrian countryside with a couple I was slowly but surely falling in love with. What did I know about anything? The only thing I could offer in such moments was a caring, listening ear.

'I'm getting there, sweetie,' she replied. 'I'm getting there.'

I nodded, bit my lip to stop myself offering any more 'helpful' suggestions.

'I need to make sure I know that I've exhausted all avenues of having a biologically connected child first. At one point, Ed and I talked about finding a surrogate.'

'Right,' I said cautiously. I remembered the looks. Those looks from the nursery, from the night she'd asked me to come to Cumbria, from many, many times we'd been here. I recalled those looks and my body grew still.

'Obviously nothing came from that conversation,' she said. 'Can you imagine? Asking someone to carry our child and then hand said child over after nine months? I don't know a single person who would do that. Like I'd ever do that if I could. Like I could ever be that selfless.' She laughed suddenly. It smashed up the atmosphere that had been settling like quick-drying cement over us. We were free again, released to be ourselves.

But my mind had been set thinking: *Is this why she asked me to come here? To somewhere remote, where no one would ever know if I were pregnant and then gave the baby to her? No, surely not. She wouldn't do that. It'd be a bust, anyway. She and Ed are white, I'm mixed race, she couldn't pretend any child I had was theirs. Unless they simply want me to carry an embryo? That way, no one would know. I would simply be the incubator for their child.*

But then I was being silly. I was going through my mind and making the pieces of the time since I'd met them fit with this conversation. Because she'd have to know, much as I loved her, much as I loved Ed, there was no way on Earth I'd do it. No way on Earth.

8:40 p.m. I can tell by the way Cece is shifting the beer mat around the table that she's raced ahead in her mind and knows what is coming next. At the time, gullible as I was, I didn't know. I honestly didn't.

*

351

'It's just you and me today, Max,' Ed said.

I had been the first down to gather wood, start a fire and get every-thing ready for breakfast – I'd mixed up the eggs to scramble them when the others appeared, chopped up fruit, cut up bread. I always got the good china out, even though there wasn't a full set (it was a mishmash of lots of different sets), I'd set out the linen napkins and the hand-woven placemats. I always made the biggest effort for breakfast because it was the meal we ate together most often. Ed was meant to be heading to London today for a few nights and Bronwyn was going to go over the notes I'd made for her lecture series.

'How do you mean?' I asked.

'Bronwyn's taking a personal day,' he said. 'She's . . . She didn't want to tell you until we had good news, but a couple of months ago we had an embryo implantation. It was successful but she started bleeding last night. She . . .' He shook his head.

'Do you want me to call a doctor?' I asked.

He shook his head again. 'No, it's nothing new. When it happens, she doesn't want to be around people for a while. I'll cancel my trip to London but we're best off giving her some space.'

'Shall I take her a cup of tea and a slice of toast? She needs to keep her strength up.'

'Yeah, that'd be nice, actually.' He pulled a tired smile across his face. 'Thanks, Maxie, it's really good that you're here.'

March, 2008

No one ever asked, I don't remember even offering, but we were doing this thing. We went to the clinic, I had the assessments, the screenings, counselling, we talked and talked about it. We talked and talked until it was happening and I was being implanted with one of their embryos. I don't remember how I got there, but there I was. On this road. Doing this thing. Helping out two people I loved.

*

In the light from the full moon flooding the kitchen, I sat and stared at the table. The kitchen seemed full of smooth curved lines in the moonlight. I couldn't sleep, not since it'd failed for the second time. I'd felt so hollow since it'd happened and I wanted that hollowness to stop.

'Max,' he whispered. His voice floated over to me on the moonbeams, the sound soft and lulling. I didn't tense or even jump when his hands slid over my shoulders, resting lightly there. 'Maxie.' His hand slid lower, inside the top of my knee-length nightshirt, moving lower until his fingers brushed over my nipple and stopped, resting there. 'We don't have to wait for the next transfer.' Slowly his fingers moved over my nipple, working to make it stand up. When he had what he wanted, when my nipple stood hard and firm against his fingertips, he gently pulled me to my feet.

My breathing was short, hard, fast, and I tried not to react. I kept my gaze cast aside as he slowly opened the buttons of my nightshirt. Then he slowly lowered his head and covered my nipple, painful and erect as it was, with his mouth, gently sucking on it, until it was unbearable and I gasped out loud. He carefully pushed aside the other side of my top, exposed that breast before he covered that nipple with his mouth, teasing it until I couldn't help but cry out again.

'The next appointment could fail as well, there'd be more waiting,' he whispered. He was being careful, gauging how I would react. He knew I practically worshipped Bronwyn – that was why I had agreed to do it in the first place. She was like no one I had ever met before. Doing this with him would be a complete betrayal. He kept his voice low, skimming on the edges of the moonbeams: 'She wouldn't mind. You know she wouldn't mind. As long as she gets to be a mother.'

She had suggested it originally, but I'd been horrified. She hadn't. It would be a means to an end, she'd said. They would pay me more, but I hadn't wanted to be genetically connected to the baby, I hadn't wanted the money but they'd insisted. In all of this, I had wanted to be able to tell myself that I was simply growing their child. But this was taking so long. And after we had thought we had reached success, it'd been snatched away again. Each time, I'd grown closer to . . . *him*. I'd felt my loyalty, my devotion, moving slowly towards him. I was fickle. I needed to only spend time with someone who fascinated me, who wowed me with their intellect, and I could feel my eyes opening up, my heart uncurling, my body reaching towards them like a plant towards the sun. Bronwyn had once been my sun, but she'd been replaced by him.

While I thought about what he was saying, what he was suggesting, he reached for my knickers, slowly moved them aside and slid his fingers into me.

This was so far away from my world. The last three years had been so different, so surreal. I had grown up with the simplicity of people saying what they meant and meaning what they said. I had liked the predictability of living in a small community where people went to school, went away to college, but came back, got a job, got married, had babies. I had loved all that; I had expected all that. And then I'd had my head turned, I'd encountered the brilliance and ideas and reasonings of a woman who had done remarkable things. I had been seduced by the idea of intellectuality; I had begun to follow her, wanting to learn and then needing to learn and then needing to be with her. And then I was working for her, basking in her brilliance, growing in the rays of her sun-like presence. She'd taught me so much, helped me to think, to grow, to dream beyond the bounds of who I thought I could be, would be. And now I was here. With her man, her partner, the man she wanted to be the father of the children she couldn't carry. I was on the edge of doing something the old me would never have done.

You don't go with your friend's man. It was a code me and my friends had always lived by. We'd had severe, Siberia-like punishments for the girls who forgot that.

Ed took his fingers away, and lifted me to sit me on the edge of the table, pushed open my legs to stand between them. 'She wouldn't mind,' he said.

She would mind. No matter how intellectual, and open-minded, she would care. She would be hurt. But she would have her baby; she would be a mother.

Ed rolled down my knickers, took them off then dropped them beside me on the table. I still couldn't look at him, couldn't face him and what I was about to do. Because of course I was going to do it. Of course I was going to betray her. Ever since she'd announced she was going away for a couple of weeks to visit old friends and get her head straight I had known it was going to happen. The surprise had been how long it'd taken – four nights before he approached me.

I saw him unbuckling himself, unzipping, undoing, releasing. *It's what she would want,* I said to myself. I said it again, in my head, louder, then louder still, hoping that at some point, I would believe it. *IT'S WHAT SHE WOULD WANT.*

Slowly, I began to lie back, to ready myself, to do this terrible thing to someone I loved with someone I loved. Because I did love him. More than her. I closed my eyes. It would be quick; it would be a functional act, so we would hopefully get the result we wanted. The baby. A baby. Her baby. *Their* baby. He would enter me, he would move, he would ejaculate. Over in minutes.

'Tell me,' he whispered. 'Tell me you want this.'

I inhaled, steadied myself. 'I want this,' I said. 'I want this.'

I felt him smile, knew he'd get it over with . . . and then I gasped again as his mouth grazed between my legs, his tongue beginning to tease me. Not over in minutes, then, not a functional thing for a sole purpose. I gritted my teeth, my fingernails trying to dig into the table. Then my fingers were caught up in the soft, brown curls of his hair, pulling him closer, urging him on, making this a far bigger act of betrayal than I thought it could ever be.

I want this, I want this, I want this.

9:30 p.m. Cece is watching me now. Her face is a mask – I can't read her, I can't tell what she is thinking, but she stares directly at me. So directly I have to look away, ashamed, thoroughly ashamed.

*

355

'Are you certain you want to sign this?' I was sure someone would ask me that.

Or at least I hoped someone would ask me that. No one did, though. We sat in the solicitor's office and I had the papers and forms in front of me to give it all up. To fulfil the purpose I'd had all those months ago. It was nearly four years since I had first gone to live in a farmhouse in Cumbria, with the space to read and talk to a woman I found fascinating. It was six weeks to the day since I last saw the pale, squawking bundle that I'd handed over in the hospital to his parents. We had never spoken of it. She had been full of gushes, full of kisses and full of hugs – while never quite meeting my eye. And he had stared at her like he adored her, like she had carried the child for nine months, like she had been in labour all this time, like she had given birth and was now handing him his son and heir. It had been surreal. Like that night in the farmhouse when I'd first slept with him, it was all surreal.

After two weeks back in the farmhouse, expressing milk and resting up, I'd gone to stay at a flat I'd rented towards the end of the pregnancy. I'd been concentrating on the bit afterwards so I didn't have to think about the baby growing inside me. I'd been organising my future reality so the present would quickly flit away.

The last four years of being involved with Bronwyn and Ed had been a step off into another world and now I had to get back to reality. I enrolled in a copywriting course, to learn all the secrets of great copy, and then I planned, after this week was over, to start the course, move on with my life, forget that I'd done this thing. After this week was over, I would have so much money in my account, a buffer for my year on the course, a feathered nest that would be comfortable and soft for many, many years to come. After this week was over, I would be free. I would pretend this last four years hadn't happened, and I would look to the future.

The room was silent, so silent I longed for even the ticking of a clock that would mark out the seconds, the moments between now and then, between my pressing the nib of the black ink pen in my hand onto the paper and when I finished making the swirling loops of my name.

They hadn't brought the baby. I had no idea where he was. I had no clue what he looked like now, if he was still pale, if he was still squirmy and squawky, if he cried because the woman who birthed him, who had provided the milk for the bottles for a fortnight, hadn't been able to hold him. I wondered. I wondered. I wondered.

The silence rolled on; you couldn't even hear breathing in the room because everyone seemed to be holding their breath. Even the stern-faced solicitor who had clearly disapproved of all of it, who would have to report us to the police if he knew I'd been paid to have their child, held his breath. All I had to do was start the loops. I pushed the nib deeper into the paper.

I wondered if Ed ever thought about it. About how he hadn't just had sex with me that time she was away. He had seduced me and I had let him. Every time we'd made love he had said my name as though his heart was so full of me, he couldn't stop himself whispering, gasping and sometimes shouting my name as he orgasmed. I wondered if he fantasised about us, if he thought of me as he entered her, wishing we could turn back time and do it all over again.

I began the first slope, the upwards trajectory towards finishing what had been started all that time ago. I wondered if she ever asked him about it. About why we never went back to the clinic. I wondered what she'd thought when I had shown her the stick with X marking the spot. I wondered if she thought we'd done it in the dark, eyes closed, bodies clenched, as few thrusts as necessary to get it done. I wondered if she knew we'd made love so many times, in so many ways, and I'd longed for him every single day for the rest of the pregnancy but he hadn't so much as looked in my direction.

I wondered if I was going to be able to do this thing. To walk away without a backward glance, with all that money at my disposal, my future financially set, and not constantly think about the pale bundle that I'd never been able to hold. *I wonder, I wonder, I wonder.*

I signed my name, scrawled it out clear and easy to read. No shame. No hiding from what I was doing. No pretending that I was a good person who had done a good thing for good friends. Own it. If you're going to do something, own it. Isn't that what Mum had always told me? Wasn't that part of the code of trying to be a good person? Even if you behave badly, own it.

I made the line under my name, a sweeping mark on the page, and the room unclenched. The exhalation of everyone else in the room – including the solicitor – was an almost deafening crescendo of relief as I pushed the papers across the table.

'Thank you, Miss Smith. Now that you have completed the transfer of parental rights, I'd like to remind you that you have agreed not to see or contact my clients again. Are you clear on that?'

I pretended to myself that he sounded sympathetic, had a modicum of admiration for what I had done for his clients, but I had to be clear-eyed about this. He didn't care. He probably looked down on me. Having a child for someone else, for the allowable £15,000 worth of clearly itemised expenses, and then signing all rights to that child away just six weeks later was not something he would think of highly.

I nodded at him, and avoided looking at the two across the table by keeping my gaze lowered. We had spent so much time talking, laughing, being friends and companions and confidants.

Now I was their dirty little secret, and they were mine. They left first. And I walked away from Tapping, Cleat & Anderson Associates, Solicitors at Law, knowing I would never see them again.

9:45 p.m. Cece reaches across the table, takes my hand in hers and curls her fingers around mine. It's only when she touches me that I notice how cold my hands are.

January, 2010
The sound of my fingers rapping against the front door seemed to echo for miles.

I'd been sitting in the car I'd hired down the lane since early afternoon, and now it was dark and I'd finally managed to get the courage to do this. To knock, to hear my knuckles against wood reverberate across the hills, reminding me how alone and isolated it was up here.

After the knock, the anxiety and fear bloomed in full. I didn't know what I expected by coming here, but I couldn't go on how I had been. I was so close to the edge, so close to falling into an endless pit, I couldn't do anything but come back here. Beg for a second chance, for the chance to be in their orbit again, to have the suns of their affection back on me. To have the chance to hold the little bundle.

I'd managed seven months. I had managed to get through seven months of what felt like not living. I wanted to see them, I wanted to be with the baby. Not all the time – I knew he was legally theirs – but I wanted a little time with him. Just to be allowed to see him sometimes, to know what it was like to hold him as he got bigger, got cannier about the world, to see him develop and grow, become a little boy. Not every day, not all the time, but just a little bit. If I could have just a little bit of him, of them, then I would feel better. I knew I would. And I'd be able to move on. I would feel able to get dressed in the mornings; I wouldn't stay in bed, staring at the walls, wondering if there was a point in anything.

Ed's eyes closed in agony when he opened the door and saw it was me. 'You shouldn't have come here,' he said. His words were stern, but not his voice. He sounded almost resigned, as though he had been expecting me to turn up at some point but had been hoping I wouldn't.

'I only want to talk to you. Then I'll go. I'll go. I just want to talk to you. Please?'

He shook his head, but stepped aside anyway. I stepped over the threshold and went straight for the living room. There was a fire crackling in the hearth, the lights were low, there were two glasses of wine on the coffee table and an open bottle of red in between them. They had music on, and Bronwyn was reclining on the sofa. The place did not look like it had when I had been there those two weeks after the birth. Then it had been filled with baby things; now there was no sign that they even had a baby. No cot in the corner, no muslins and bottles and toys and clothes, no changing mats and nappies. My eyes darted around the room, looking for a sign that the baby was still there. The only clues were the car seat and the pram that I'd seen in the corridor. Other than that, their lives didn't seem to have been changed at all by the baby.

'What the hell are you doing here?' Bronwyn demanded. She lowered her legs and stood up, angrily jerking down the folds of her dress over her thighs. 'Why did you let her in?'

'I just want to talk to you,' I begged. 'Please.'

'We have nothing to talk about. I paid you a *lot* of money to go away, and stay away.'

'Why are you being so cold to me?' I asked her in desperation.

'You slept with my husband. Is that not enough?' she replied.

'But I only did that to get pregnant with the baby you so desperately wanted.'

'You keep telling yourself that. I'm sure one day we'll all believe you, won't we, Ed?' I looked at Ed, who was lurking in the doorway, looking pained. He flinched at her words, as if they had genuinely, physically wounded him. 'She hated every single second of it, didn't she, Ed? Begged you to be quick, didn't she?'

I looked at Bronwyn again, and she was transformed. I saw her for the person she was, the person so many others had claimed she was. She was cold. At the very core of her, she had a tundra instead of a heart. At the very core of her was a woman who could not see beyond herself. She had told me this, many, many times. She had told me she only liked me because I reminded her of herself. She had called herself a narcissist and I hadn't believed her. I had thought, because she was showering me with warmth, attention and affection, that she couldn't be cold, she couldn't be what she had named herself. And she had named me as just like her. And I was. I had taken money to have a baby. I had handed that baby over. I was worse than she was, because I doubt she would have ever done what I did. I was cold. At my heart, I was cold.

She carried on, the vitriol spewing from between her perfect lips, the lips she'd kissed me with so many times. 'How long did it take to get her knickers off, eh, Ed? Five minutes? Five seconds? Five nanosec—'

'All right, stop, enough now!' Ed suddenly said. He raised his voice, but not too much, obviously aware the baby was asleep somewhere around here. 'It wasn't anything like that, and you know it, Bronwyn. It was what you wanted. You told me that you didn't want to wait for the clinic anymore, for the uncertainty, you wanted it done as soon as possible.'

'Ha!' she spat, and rounded on him. 'Ha! Ha! Ha! I told you to impregnate her, not to seduce her. Not to fall in love with her.'

'I didn't fall in love with her,' he scoffed.

'HA!' she spat again. 'Even before you did it you had. All those long meaningful gazes you threw her way. You think I didn't notice? You think that wasn't the reason why I didn't want to wait for the clinic? I wanted her out of my house and out of our life as soon as possible. I thought you would actually use a turkey baster – there's about a million of them in the kitchen. Didn't you get the hint? How many turkeys have we actually basted, ever? *Ever?* But no, I tell you I can't wait for the clinic so you screw her the first chance you get.'

'You told me. You told me to do it,' he said in despair. 'I said no for over a year. I said no but you wouldn't stop going on at me. You told me to get her knocked up. "Fuck her every day until she's pregnant," you said. For over a year, you said that to me. Over a year.'

I gasped. I was so naïve. Utterly stupid and naïve. They had never cared about me. It was only about them having a baby. All they ever wanted was a baby, and they had simply played the long game with me to get it.

Ed's head snapped to look at me after I gasped, and his face suddenly changed from a look of anger and frustration to one of horror at the realisation of what he had done. Or maybe it was the shame that I had found out how they'd used me.

'And there you have it!' Bronwyn snarled. 'Proof positive that you're more worried about her and her feelings, and couldn't care less how it felt for me to know you'd screwed the little bitch, probably in my bed.'

He looked as though he was about to shout, then remembered the baby. 'Upstairs,' he said to her. Before she had a chance to respond, he left the room and took the rickety stairs two at a time from the sound of his footsteps.

She ignored me as she went up after him, running to get up there as soon as possible.

'Do you have any idea what we did?' I heard him say as soon as she arrived in their bedroom. The words were muted, softened out by flooring, but I was standing right below them, so I could still hear them. 'We broke the law. We paid for a baby. And we put that girl through hell.'

'Really, is that what we did? We gave her a lot of money for something she should have been willing to do for free; we gave her a job, a home, somewhere she felt like she belonged.'

'Do you really not see how wrong we were?' he replied. 'Really? I mean, what was it about her that made you choose her? Was it that she wasn't like the others? That she didn't fall for it completely? That she didn't "seduce" you like the others had despite how much temptation you dangled in front of her?'

'What are you talking about?' she scoffed.

'Oh, you think I didn't know that you've screwed every single one of your acolytes, all those gorgeous little versions of yourself that you have help you do your "research"? That it's a sport to you? Get them out here, tell them how special they are, kiss them, wait for them to take the bait and make them believe it's all their idea to seduce you and become your lover. And then when you're bored of them, you pay them off to disappear. You're the original dirty old woman. You seriously thought I didn't know?'

'You don't know what you're talking about. And if any of that was true, why have you stuck around for so long?'

'*Because I love you!* I know it seems an impossible thing to you, but I love you. And I convinced myself that – deep down – you loved me. That it'd be OK and that once we had a baby, things would settle down. How fucking stupid that was, eh? You're a complete narcissist, as you keep joking. Actually, I think you're a sociopath.'

'You're just trying to cover up for what you did.'

'Yeah, maybe I am—'

From the room off the living room, I heard a gurgle. A small little baby cough. I stopped listening to the two people upstairs and went towards the sound. The nursery was downstairs. The room, which had been a small study for me to work in before, was now full with everything a nursery needed: plush cream carpet, the walls painted a soft, buttery yellow, a beautifully carved cot in the corner, an open unit stuffed with toys, and the same style of rocking chair that had been in that room where I met Bronwyn.

The baby was asleep on his back, the blanket pulled up to his chest. His eyes were shut but his mouth was open while he gurgled and snuffled in his sleep. I was melting all of a sudden. I'd never *felt* anything before, I realised looking at the little boy in the cot. I had never had a true, real feeling ever in my entire life until that moment when I saw my son properly for the first time. I hadn't seen him alone before. There had always been someone – usually Bronwyn – standing on the periphery, lurking, hovering, making sure I never had a proper look, a complete look-see at the person I had made. He was something I could not describe. A word beyond human language. I, who loved to talk, could not verbalise how incredible he was. He was a human being, *my* human being. I had made him and then I had let him go. I didn't want to wake him, certainly didn't want to break him, but I had to touch him, I had to feel what he was like to hold.

Gingerly, I slid my hands under his body, then carefully lifted him out of his cot, taking his blanket with him. He was soft, plump, as I settled him in the crook of my arm and held him close. His eyes fluttered briefly, but he didn't really stir, seemed to almost sigh and relax a little more against me.

It was because he knew me, I decided. He knew it was me, that was why he hadn't stirred, hadn't been disrupted at all. He knew who it was and he was pleased I was back. In the quiet of the house, I could still hear them. Rowing upstairs. Saying all the things they'd probably bottled up for years, deconstructing their extremely messed-up relationship while their child slept downstairs, and the person they'd dragged into this mess waited patiently to learn what the outcome would be.

I'd allowed myself to be flattered into doing this thing for them. I'd thought I was doing something noble, something good for two people I adored. They had shown me a different type of life, and I was repaying them by fulfilling their greatest wish. My arrogance had led me here, to a place where I was sneaking into a room to have a cuddle with the child I had given away. Given away? Sold. I was a terrible person. I'd had a child and I'd been given money for it. Didn't matter that I hadn't asked for or wanted the money. Didn't matter that they had insisted and then had paid it once I'd transferred my parental rights to them. Didn't matter that I hadn't spent a penny of it, that it sat there in the bank account I'd opened especially for it, a festering reminder of the awful thing I had done, I was still a terrible person. I'd thought I was doing something good, but that was my arrogance and naïvety.

The longer I held the baby, and the longer no one came to snatch him away, the clearer everything became. I could sort out this mess; I could start to make things right. I had already decided to give them their money back; being here, listening to how they plotted to use me, had made me realise the last thing I needed to do was to get back to that state of supposed nirvana I'd existed in when I was with them. I needed to start again. Find out who I was after nearly five years of letting Bronwyn and Ed define me. I had been young and stupid, it was time for me to grow up. To be an adult. To be a mother.

I glanced around the nursery, looking for the stuffed toy that I'd bought him before he was born. I'd wanted him to have something to remember me by. I couldn't see it. They'd probably binned it, just like they thought they'd binned me. That was the final push I needed.

When I stuck my head out of the little room, the living room was still empty. I could hear them, upstairs: screaming at each other, throwing swear words and insults, accusations and short, nasty laughs through the air. I moved quietly, quickly to the front door, where I gently laid the baby down in his car seat. I had to take off his blanket to strap him in, but he didn't seem to mind, didn't move at all. Maybe he knew what was happening and had decided it was for the best. Maybe he couldn't face kicking up a fuss when what was happening was going to happen anyway. Or maybe he was an extremely chilled baby who would sleep through pretty much anything.

The screaming stopped for a moment and I stopped, scared that they were going to come downstairs. I could hear my heart in my ears, pounding out in triple time the wrongness of what I was doing, my ragged breathing telling me I was going to get caught. The silence from upstairs continued to roll through the house.

'I have done so much for you. And you say all this to me!' Bronwyn screamed at Ed and I reached for the door handle, slowly eased it open. I knew the door was loud to shut, so once I had stepped out onto the gravel outside, I pulled the door as far to as I could before I crept over the stones. Each step was suddenly magnified, but I couldn't stop, couldn't wait any longer. They were going to stop shouting at each other soon, and then they would come downstairs and see what I had done.

The thrumming in my ears grew louder, the hammering in my chest like a drill. The air around us was cold and I wished for a moment that I'd thought to grab a hat for him, nappies, clothes, formula. But I hadn't. I'd just done this thing like I'd done the other things that had got him here in the first place – without thinking it through properly.

Go back! I was screaming in my head. Even as I was speeding up, the car seat's handle hooked over one arm, the other hand steadying the main base so that it didn't swing too much. *Go back. Stop this. This will end in so much trouble. Go back, go back, go back.* I could see my breath, escaping from my panting mouth in thick white plumes. My chest ached, truly ached from the pain of running in this cold and in these circumstances. My legs weren't strong enough, they kept wanting to give way, to drop the load in my arms, to stop doing this stupid, terrible thing. But I pushed on, forced myself to keep going, to get to the little turning along the road where I had parked the car.

I couldn't find my car keys. I fumbled one-handed in each pocket, terrified that I had left them in the house. I didn't want to put him down, not on the ground, not on the bonnet of the car. I shifted the weight of the car seat into my other hand, searched through my pockets again: left front pocket, right front pocket, left back pocket, right back pocket. Right jacket pocket, left jacket pocket. They weren't there. They weren't there.

Think, Maxie, think. Where did you leave the car keys? What did you do with the car keys? Think. Think.

I clasped the car seat handle with both hands.

GO BACK. THIS IS A SIGN. GO BACK, part of me was screaming. *Think, think.*

Deep breath. Deep breath. Now think. Don't think about them coming down the stairs, seeing the door open, guessing what you've done. Think about the car keys. Think about what you did when you got here. You sat in the car, you thought and thought. You kept turning the engine on to warm yourself up. Eventually, you got out of the car, you took the keys out of the ignit—

I stopped suddenly. I hadn't done that. I hadn't taken the keys out of the ignition, I hadn't reached over to the passenger seat and picked up my bag. I'd just wanted to get it over with. I hadn't been thinking at all.

I bent over and peered into the darkened car: there was my bag, splayed open with my mobile phone and purse on show. And there in the ignition were the keys. I tried the handle and it opened with no resistance. I'd learnt how to strap in car seats from my time as a nanny and au pair, and it took me very little time to make sure the car seat and baby were secure in the back seat.

Don't do this! I was screaming at myself as I started the car, turned it around and headed back the way I had come. I wanted to speed away, to race off into the night, but I had a baby in the back and I didn't want to risk his safety on dark, lampless roads that I didn't know very well. But they had a far faster, far better car than I did. They would easily catch up with me if I didn't at least get on with it. But maybe they wouldn't drive. They'd had the best part of a bottle of wine – maybe they would know that it would be dangerous to drive.

From the passenger seat, my mobile lit up the interior of the car, right before the ringing started. Loud and insistent. It was Bronwyn's ringtone, of course. I pushed my foot harder onto the accelerator.

The baby started to grizzle in the back, unhappy at the loud noise in the enclosed space. I didn't dare take my hands off the steering wheel for even a second, though, not on these unfamiliar roads in this dark, with the most precious passenger in the back. The phone kept ringing, seeming to get louder with each ring.

I'd done so many stupid, terrible things. This was the first step to putting all those things right.

10 p.m. Cece still has her hands on mine. She's still holding on to me, but I can't look in her face to see what she's thinking. I can't look at anything but our hands.

January, 2010

> Come back, Maxie. Please, come back. Come back and we won't go to the police. We'll say no more about it.
>
> Please, Maxie, please. We can arrange times when you can see him. Please Maxie. Just tell us where you are and we'll come to you.
>
> Maxie. Please. He's my life. I can't live without him. Please. Just let me know he's OK.
>
> Oh God please, Maxie. Please. Ed wants to call the police but I've said no. I know you were trying to make a point. You've made it. Please come back to us. Just bring him home.
>
> Ed says he's going to give it three more hours and then he's going to call the police. Please, Maxie, don't do this. It's not fair on any of us. He's my baby. I love him so much. Please.
>
> We're going to have to call the police. I didn't want this. I didn't want any of this.
>
> Please, Maxie. Please.

*

What did you do, Maxie? What did you do?

I did another bad thing, that's what I did. I sat in one of the longer-stay areas of the motorway services, in the back seat. The baby had started crying during the second hour of driving and I'd been forced to pull over at the nearest service station. He was wet through and probably hungry. I was shaking. I couldn't stop shaking. I had stolen a baby.

'I'm sorry, Baby,' I said to him as he sat on my lap, cradled in his blanket. I'd bought nappies, wipes and cotton wool pads. I'd managed to get some ready-mixed infant formula and bottles that I sterilised with a bottle of mineral water and a bag system. It was not ideal, none of it was ideal, but he'd guzzled down the milk as though he hadn't been fed in a while and wasn't sure where his next meal was coming from, and had been surprisingly cooperative when I'd changed his nappy on my lap. Now I rested my feet on the back of the driver's seat to create a slight slope with my legs and I stared at him. He sleepily stared back at me, gurgling and trying very hard to eat his fingers.

He was pale, like he could have been Bronwyn and Ed's child, but he had my nose, my lips, and he was as familiar as looking at myself in the mirror.

'I should never have brought you into all this,' I said to him. 'Don't get me wrong, I'm glad you're here, I wouldn't change that for the world, but I did some things I'm not proud of and now you're probably going to suffer because of it.' I gave him my finger and he took it, held on to it like he knew we were in for the whole of this stupidity ride I'd put us on. He had no choice but to cling to me, to see this through with me.

I wasn't sure what to do next. I hadn't thought any of it through. I'd literally grabbed the baby and run for it. I couldn't be sure they weren't closing in any second now, knowing that since I hadn't taken anything with me I'd have to stop at some point for supplies. Or maybe they thought I'd planned it, had come ready prepared and had somewhere to stay. The one thing I'd done that would buy me some time to think had been to head north, instead of south like they might suspect. It had been a last-minute decision that I was hoping would be the right one.

I'd just made myself a mother. Did I want to be a mother? No. Not really. Not in that deep, yearning way that Bronwyn had done. Not so much I'd ever entertain letting my husband sleep with someone else. She was mad to have said that even once, but to have repeated it? To have been able to have me living in her house for all those months afterwards, knowing that I had done that, she must have so wanted a baby.

Was that why I had done this? To hurt her like she had hurt me? I hadn't gone there to get him back. I had only wanted to see him. To hold him. To spend time with him. While being a part of their lives. I hadn't wanted him back consciously, desperately, but I must have needed him because from the moment I'd picked him up, I couldn't put him down and let him be someone else's. From that first moment of real connection, he had to be mine again.

'What we going to do now, eh, Baby?' I asked him.

He responded by trying to push my finger into his mouth.

'Yes, you're right, I need to eat. We both need to sleep.' I grinned at him, and gently kept my finger away from his plump little lips. 'So far, I think you're doing very well as a hostage to a fugitive. We need to get you somewhere warm and out of your car seat.' I closed my eyes, then opened them again, blinking hard against the tiredness that made them thick and scratchy.

'I have to stay awake until we can find a hotel or B & B or something,' I told him. He closed his eyes, wriggled then stopped as he pushed out a large sound, followed by a pungent, milky smell. 'Thanks for that, little fella,' I said. I wrinkled up my face against the rancid aroma that was fast filling the car. 'If there's anything that's going to keep me awake, it is that.'

10:15 p.m. 'Do you want to stop?' Cece asks me.

I shake my head. I need to get it all out there. I need to tell. I've started so I'll finish.

*

I was sure he was missing her.

The smell of her, the shape of her, the simple *herness* of her. He'd had me for two weeks, her for seven months. He knew her, he didn't know me. And he cried about it. After he'd been fed, after he'd been changed, after he'd been settled for the night, he would sob. I'd got to know his cries the last couple of days, and this was a sort of desolate cry, him whimpering for his mum. I would hold him, hush him, remind myself that I was a terrible person for inflicting this upon him. I should take him back. I should return him to his rightful mum and dad. But I couldn't. I needed him.

It was all about me, yes. Parents are meant to put their children first, meant to look beyond their hurt and do what they think is right. Everyone would hate me for the fact this was all about me. They would know that I wasn't doing the right thing for him, but because I was alone without him.

I'd waited, these last two days, for the knock on the door, for the appeal on the TV and in the papers, to hear that Bronwyn Sloane had had her child snatched from her by an unbalanced individual and the police were leaving no stone unturned until they found her. I had found a place to stay near where we'd stopped that first night. Partly because I didn't know where else to go, and partly because if they were going to find me, I'd rather it was here. I'd rather be nearby so he wouldn't have a very long journey home. I scoured the papers every day to see if she was mentioned, to see if there was anything out there that would tell me what my fate would be if I brought him back or if I kept him. Nothing. The only hint that something was wrong was his little cry, which would drill through my heart, make me rethink what I was doing to him, what I was doing to her.

I rocked the baby on my shoulder, listened to his little desolate cries as they grew softer and quieter, as he edged himself towards another sleep. Maybe I should go back to Sheffield. Just face the music. Take responsibility for what I'd done these past couple of years. Sleeping with someone's husband, essentially selling a baby, stealing that baby. Maybe I should stop making such terrible, impulsive decisions and face up to what I had done. If Bronwyn and Ed had got my address from Mum and Dad and were waiting for me, then so be it. I lay the baby back in his car seat and began packing up the stuff we'd accumulated in the past few days. I had to go home. I had to give him some semblance of normality. Living in a hotel room, even as nice a one as this, was not good for him. If they were there when I got back, they were there. It would be a sign that I was not meant to be with him, and I needed to be punished for what I'd done.

The baby whimpered one last time before he fell properly asleep. 'It's OK, Baby,' I whispered to him. 'We're going now. And hopefully you'll be with your mother again soon.'

January, 2010

'I just want to see if he's all right,' Ed said. He came towards me with his arms out, his hands up, showing me he was no threat. I'd rented this flat at a great price, using the money I'd got from being Bronwyn's researcher, and hadn't noticed his car when I'd pulled into my road and unloaded my bag and the baby from the car.

The closer he got, the worse he looked: a full beard, unkempt hair, his clothes creased and grubby. He kept his hands raised in peace and surrender, and he approached us slowly. He wasn't looking at me, though: his attention was entirely focused on the car seat.

'Have you come to take him back?' I asked. My heart was thumping as loudly as a jackhammer.

Ed stared at me, almost surprised that I was there. His eyes were a network of red veins, his skin was the dull grey of a winter morning. He squinted slightly. He looked how I had felt all these months away from the baby – shocked, scared, unable to properly function. He shook his head. 'I don't think I have, no,' he said. He refocused on his son. 'I don't know what I've come for. Bronwyn and I have split up. I wanted to go to the police, she didn't. I got your address from your parents. I can't even think. I just . . . I just want to make sure he's OK.' He inhaled deeply. 'Once I know he's OK, I'll be able to sleep.'

'He's fine,' I said.

Ed stopped staring at the baby and looked up at me, a penetrating, withering stare that caused me to shrink a little. 'I'm supposed to take your word for that, am I?'

'Look, come up to my flat and see him properly if you don't believe me. I've been looking after him. I really have.' Another impulsive, terrible decision. Ed could do anything to me up there. He could beat me up and take the baby away again. He could call the police and have me arrested. I was queen of stupid decisions. *Well*, I thought as I unlocked the outer door, *at least I'm consistent*.

In my living room, as small and boxy as it was, Ed got down on his knees to take the baby out of his car seat. I'd driven through the night, but had had to keep stopping to make sure he didn't spend too much time in the car seat, so morning was starting to peek over the horizon by the time we'd pulled up outside the flats.

'Are you going to call the police?' I asked Ed. Carefully, but expertly, he lifted the baby out of his seat, then he got to his feet, stepped backwards and sat down on the sofa.

Ed ignored me. Instead, he gazed at his son, his tired face softening and brightening. 'Are you OK, Frankie mate? I missed you.' He bent down and brushed his lips against the baby's forehead. 'I really missed you.'

'It's fine if you are going to call the police,' I told him. 'I don't care if you are.'

He stopped staring at the baby, and glared at me. 'I'm not going to call the police. I wouldn't put Frankie through that.'

'Why do you keep calling him Frankie? Isn't Frankie his third middle name?' I'd been calling him 'Baby' these past few days because it felt wrong to call him Damien, his given name. I hadn't liked it, I hadn't had any choice in it, and when I called him Damien it reminded me that he wasn't mine. Not legally. Not morally.

'Frankie was meant to be his name but Bronwyn changed her mind at the last minute. On the way to the register office that morning, actually, she said I could have it as his third middle name or not

372

at all. It was another way to punish me for . . . for sleeping with you. She always had the final say in everything to do with him because I could never make up for what I'd done to her. She couldn't stop me calling him Frankie, though, despite how hard she tried.'

'Oh.'

I sat next to him on the sofa. He didn't turn away from me in revulsion; instead he stared at me with a small frown wrinkling the space between his eyebrows. 'Why did you split up with her?' I asked.

He returned to looking at, marvelling and delighting in, his son. 'Because I wanted Frankie back and I didn't care what it would mean. She only wanted him back if no one knew what she'd done. That turned out to be my line in the sand.' He smiled down at the baby's sleeping face again. Suddenly the smile disappeared and the frown was aimed back at me. 'You shouldn't have taken him, Max. I would have persuaded her to let you see him. You shouldn't have done that.'

'Yes I should,' I replied. I'd opened my mouth to agree with him, to say I'd done a terrible thing and I was sorry, but instead the truth had come tumbling out. The truth of it was, I should have taken him. 'Because I should never have given him away in the first place. Sold him. I shouldn't have done it.'

'Yeah,' he said. 'Yeah.' He suddenly held the baby out to me, offering him back, saying he understood that I shouldn't have cleaved myself away from the little boy.

'No, no, I didn't mean you weren't to hold him, I just—'

'I think I'm going to pass out, Max,' he interrupted. 'I have literally not slept since I last saw you. Take him, please.'

'Oh, oh, OK.' I gathered Frankie in my arms and stood up.

'I'm going to lie here for a bit,' he said. 'Don't run away with him again. Please. *Please.* I just need to sleep. OK? Don't run away. I'm not going to hurt you, I'm not going to call the police. Don't run away with him and we can sort everything else out afterwards. Right now, I just need to sleep.'

'Cool. Yeah. I need to change him and stuff anyway. You sleep. And I won't run away. I most definitely will not run away again.'

*

'I've been thinking,' Ed whispered in the dark of my bedroom. Frankie was asleep on the bed between us. Since Ed had arrived, even though he'd been asleep when Ed had held him, Frankie (as I was now calling him) hadn't sobbed. Hadn't cried for his mummy. We'd spent the day playing quietly in the bedroom while Ed slept on the sofa. Ed had eventually woken at five, bleary-eyed and subdued. I'd said he could take a shower and afterwards, he'd emerged with his damp hair slicked back off his face, dressed in only a pair of my grey jogging bottoms. None of my T-shirts would fit him and he couldn't wear his own clothes because I'd put them in the wash the second he took them off.

I'd had to avert my eyes to stop myself from staring, remembering his naked body against mine. Frankie kicked his legs up in the air, while trying to stuff both hands into his mouth at the same time.

'What have you been thinking?' I asked Ed.

'We should get married.'

'What?'

'We're his parents—'

'Actually, legally, I'm not any more. I've technically kidnapped him.'

'*We're his parents*. Let's get married. We could move somewhere, anywhere, live together. I don't want to live without him, you've proved you don't want to live without him. Let's get married and bring him up together.'

'I think that's the perfect plan,' I said. 'Except you're already married, we're not in love, you only just broke up with your wife and I have kidnapped a child. Oh, and it's a stupid plan.'

'I'm not married.'

'But you and Bronwyn . . .'

'We never got married. Yes, she called me her husband, I called her my wife, and for all intents and purposes we were a married couple, but not legally. It's a bit of paper that we just never got around to signing.'

'OK, that's not a stumbling block. But the rest of it is. You just broke up with her. We are nowhere near a relationship. I've committed a heinous crime. I stand by what I said – it's a stupid plan.'

'We do have a relationship – we're his parents.'

'But we're not in love with each other.'

'Look, let me be honest here, Max. I . . . I want to be with my son. I've always enjoyed your company, sex with you wasn't exactly terrible, but we don't have to have sex if you'd rather not. If you look at it overall, though, I think we could have a good life together, the three of us. We could move somewhere like Cornwall? Or Brighton – I've always fancied living near the sea. There's coast up here, of course, but I reckon down south, away from here and all of this would be good for us. I think it could work. I really do.'

'So it'd be a marriage of convenience?' I said. When I said it out loud, when I named it for what it was, it sounded cold. Clinical. When I named all the other things I had done they sounded cold as well. *I* sounded cold.

'If you want to call it that. I suppose it could be. But so many people who are married don't even have that after a few years.'

'I think you're on the rebound from Bronwyn and you're scared that I won't let you see your son. I will, you know. You can see him any time you like.' Apparently, at some point, I had decided I was keeping Frankie. I was talking about him, making future plans for us. That future could also involve Ed in a very real way, if I were stupid enough to do what he was asking. It'd be stupid because of how I felt about him. I couldn't go into it cold, view it as an arrangement that meant we would both get what we want – to see our son – and be happy with that. I would want more from him. I had feelings for him. I had more than 'feelings' for him: I was in love with him. I could not be detached and business-like with him. The most stupid, damaging thing in the world I could do would be to marry him. Which obviously meant stupid me was probably going to do it.

'I'm not on the rebound.'

'Well, I think you are. But you could always prove to me that you're not.'

'How?'

'Let's try it for a year. We could move, like you said, live together – separate rooms – so we get to see Frankie every day and then, if

375

you're sure you're over Bronwyn, and you still want to get married after a year, we do it then.'

'I'm not on the rebound,' he repeated. 'But fine. If it means I get to see him, then fine.'

'What about Bronwyn?'

'What about her?'

'I stole her baby. She's going to track me down and probably try to kill me to get him back.'

He shook his head. 'She won't. She won't come after you. That's the whole point. Why we had to split up. She won't do anything that will jeopardise her public image. Her plan was to wait until he was one, then to throw a huge party, tell everyone she'd used donor eggs and welcome him to her world. If we went to the police, or came to get him back from you and you went public, it would destroy her reputation – rich white woman pays poor brown woman to have a baby. No, she couldn't stand the idea of that being found out. That's why we had to split – I wanted to do anything to find him; she had her limits.'

'You're just saying that to make me feel better about what I did. She may not be a nice person, but she doesn't deserve to have her baby taken away.'

'Sadly, I'm not being kind to you. That's why I know I'm not on the rebound. She actually smashed my phone when I started calling the police and said she would do everything she could to destroy you and your parents if I did. Anything to stop me letting the world know what we'd done.'

'How can you want to marry me – even if it is a convenience thing – when you were calling the police on me?'

'Because, Maxie, if I had been in your position, I would have done exactly the same thing.'

10:45 p.m. 'We didn't wait a year to get married. We moved to Brighton and got married on Frankie's first birthday. It was stupid, of course. Because I still loved Ed. In almost every way, we have a good relationship, we get on really well on so many levels, but he doesn't love me. And, of course, I did this thing. I did this terrible thing and it's always there.'

Cece releases her hold on me and, with a shaking hand, picks up her wine and gulps it down. I want to know what she's thinking, what she's going to do. I chance a look at her and she is staring at me.

'I don't know what to say,' she eventually confesses. 'That doesn't happen very often, believe me. But I . . . Ah, look, come here.' She gets up from her side of the table and comes to mine, gathers me up in her arms and holds me close. I cling to her and she holds me closer, kisses the top of my head and holds me.

She won't be doing this when I tell her about Yvonne.

'Don't tell me about Yvonne,' she says. 'Not tonight. I don't think I can handle any more. Look, let's go back. The kids should be asleep; we could both probably use an early-ish night. All right?'

All right, I replied in my head. 'All right.'

THURSDAY

Maxie

11:20 p.m. Frankie was overjoyed that he got a midweek sleepover at Oscar and Ore's, that Harmony stood over him while he did his homework, and that he got to have something other than porridge for breakfast. His little face beamed with being a boy who was winning at life. He couldn't contain himself, shouting out his good fortune to Mrs Carpenter, who was standing on the gate this morning as always. 'That's lovely, Frankie,' she said and smiled at me. 'Good morning, Mrs Smith.'

I mumbled a good morning, and Mrs Carpenter turned her grin up when she looked at Cece who was beside me. Immediately Cece whipped her gaze away.

'Good morning, Mrs Solarin. Have you thought any more about what I asked?' Mrs Carpenter called. Everyone around us looked at her, wondering what was going on. I noticed Teri openly earwigging – she kept switching her gaze between Mrs Carpenter and Cece, suspicious about what that was about, wondering if she should know about it.

'Erm, still thinking, Mrs Carpenter,' Cece replied, obviously mortified. 'Still thinking.' Teri kept her gaze fixed on Cece, her eyes narrowed slightly. Teri really was trying to take Yvonne's place by acting like she had whenever Mrs Carpenter showed any interest in anyone outside of Yvonne.

I raised an eyebrow at Cece and she whispered as we walked away, 'Mrs Carpenter wants me to join the Parents' Council. I'm the right sort, apparently.'

We got to the end of the road and stood there awkwardly. We

hadn't talked any more about it when we'd got back to her house last night. She'd made me a cup of tea and then showed me the spare room where Frankie was sleeping and said goodnight. I'd slept through, for the first time in months. They do say the truth shall set you free; who knew it would also put you to sleep? Cece, on the other hand, looked like she hadn't slept at all.

'I'm going to go back to bed,' she said. 'I didn't sleep much. Shall we talk in a couple of days?'

'Yeah, yeah.' I didn't know what I wanted her to say – maybe to say it was all right, what I did? That it wasn't that bad?

'We'll talk again soon, OK?'

She gave me a hug and then left.

I've been in my office this evening and left Ed to get Frankie ready for bed. Frankie has talked non-stop about last night's adventure, and where Ed would have been cautious and unsure before, he grinned at his son, genuinely happy for him. Once I hear Ed going to bed, because I'm in the office, I go in.

He sits on the edge of the bed, taking off his socks. He pauses when I come in, gives me a smile and then starts to move to leave. Neither of us has brought up what happened in the kitchen the other night. I doubt he's forgotten it, because I haven't.

'We can't do this any more, Ed,' I tell him.

He stops midway getting off the bed and sits heavily back where he was. I cross the room and climb onto the other end of the bed. He waits for me to finish what I was about to say. When I don't speak because I'm scared suddenly of making such a big pronouncement, his whole body sags and he looks up to the ceiling. 'Do what?' he asks.

'This. Us. How we are. Together and apart. We just can't do this any more.'

His body sags a little more and he lets out a sigh, which sounds like a small sob. 'OK. If you want a divorce, I'll accept that.' Another sigh. 'I'll accept that.'

'You want a divorce?' I ask him.

'No!' He twists at the waist so he can look at me. My husband is weather-beaten, life-beaten. His skin shows his many travels, his heartaches, his many joys. 'You're the one who said it was over.'

'I didn't,' I reply. 'I didn't say that at all. I was trying to say that we can't carry on with this marriage as it is. We have to talk about what I did. We have to accept that maybe getting married to me wasn't the best idea for you, and work out the best way forwards. We can't keep going in this state that we are in.'

'Why do you say it wasn't the best thing for me? What about you?'

I sigh. I've told Cece one of my biggest secrets – why shouldn't I tell my husband my other? 'Because I love you. I married you because I love you. It's painful in all sorts of ways that you don't love me, but there it is. I don't want to get divorced, I know there's no way to make you love me or forgive me for what I did, how I wrecked your life, but there it is.'

Ed lies back on the bed and he allows his arms to flop out on either side of him as he stares at the ceiling. Through the gap of his unbuttoned white shirt, I watch his muscular chest rise and fall. When he is away staying in hotels, he runs for miles, he works out in gyms, he works on his body so he can remove the pain from his mind.

He closes his eyes, takes a few breaths in, lets them out. His face almost melts; he's about to cry. 'You married me because you love me,' he says. He's scoffing at me. I shouldn't have told him – it is ludicrous if you think about it. How could he love me when I changed the course of his life? He would be bringing up Frankie with Bronwyn; he would be living in his cottage in the countryside; he'd still have his original circle of friends. With me he has sex when he can bring himself to, and someone to talk to about everything apart from his past.

'How can you love me when I took advantage of you? I let Bronwyn use you. *I* used you. I changed the course of your life and I've made you live with me and stopped your chance of a proper relationship, hell, a proper marriage with someone else. I see how men look at you – that teacher at that stupid party. I saw him watching you most of the night . . . He's not the only one . . . How can you possibly love me?'

'When you put it like that . . .' I say to him and he tips his head back against the bed to look at me, frowning, trying to work out if I'm messing about with him or not. 'You must have known how I felt about you, Ed? Surely. I wasn't too subtle about it. Why do you think I was so willing to have sex with you all those years ago? Like Bronwyn said, we could have used a turkey baster.'

'She didn't want me to use a turkey baster,' he says. 'She wanted me to have sex with you as punishment for falling in love with you. Did you never realise that? You had to be punished for not doing what the other young women who worked for her did by "seducing" her, and I had to be punished for having feelings for you. If I did as I'd been ordered to, if I got you pregnant, then I'd never have anything to do with you again because of the agreement. And she'd always have that over me.'

'Was she really that calculating?' I ask him.

'Yes. Yes, she was. She's like Yvonne. Bronwyn was an amazing woman, I loved being with her, but she has this side to her. I was weak. And I have hated myself every single day for being a part of what we did to you. I hate myself more than I hate her because I shouldn't have indulged myself in making love to you those two weeks.'

'Did you fall out of love with me because I stole Frankie?'

Ed frowns, then rolls over onto his front, before he sits back on his knees. 'Why do you think I've fallen out of love with you?'

'Erm . . . our marriage? The way I can barely get you to be in the same room as me if Frankie's not there? The way I have to practically beg you to have sex with me? The way you've never kissed me? Take your pick.'

'I've never fallen out of love with you,' he says. 'I just keep remembering what I did to you. I relive it over and over. Every time I touch you, I tell myself it has to be the last time because I don't deserve to have pleasure with you. I don't deserve to have anything good because of what I did. I hate myself for everything I did to you. I thought you must hate me for it, too.'

'Never. I've never hated you. Why would I? You did some questionable stuff but look at me. I am queen of questionable stuff. I've never had a stupid idea I haven't followed through to its stupid conclusion. Except for Frankie. Except for you.'

I go towards him, place my hand on his face. I love the feel of his skin under my hand; I stroke my thumb across the crest of his cheekbone. I stare into his eyes, and find myself lost in the labyrinth of emotions they hold, just like I used to be all those years ago. When we were younger and stupid enough not to be honest with each other.

'I've loved you since the day I met you,' he says. 'In that nursery in London. I remember seeing you and thinking, wow. I do that all the time: I look at you and I think, "wow".'

I kiss him. Without hesitation, he kisses me back.

Part 13

MONDAY

Cece

6:45 a.m.

Can you come over for coffee after drop-off this morning? About 9? I really need to talk to you. Thanks. Cece x

9 a.m. Maxie arrives first. She looks refreshed, relaxed, happy. Not what I was expecting after her confession the other day. Especially not with the other part of her story untold. Or maybe I should expect nothing less, since she is at last unburdened and it is now my problem. I cannot work out how I feel about it. What to think about it. Instead, I replay those other words she uttered: *'Yes, I did try to kill Yvonne.'*

'Come in, come in,' I say. I greet her with a hug, give her my cheek to kiss and gratefully relieve her of the packet of chocolate digestives she's brought with her. *Do the right thing*, Sol told me.

9:03 a.m. Hazel is next. She is chaos, her coat open, her bag only half on her shoulder, her hair wild. She has also brought her knitting bag, as well as the heavy grey bags that seem to have moved in under her eyes. She seems wary of me, and I wonder if it's because she has started looking herself up and has discovered things she'd rather not know. 'What's up?' she asks as she wanders down my corridor into the kitchen. When she sees Maxie sitting at the table, she whips round to look at me. 'What's going on?' she asks. The doorbell sounds so I raise a 'hold that thought' finger at her and dash back to the front door.

*

9:05 a.m. Anaya arrives. She is calm and serene. She is in her gym gear and she seems to have had a lot of her worries lifted. She has sent me one text since we spoke and it said: *'All locked out.'* I assumed it meant her mother-in-law no longer had a key to her house. 'We're in the kitchen,' I say to her.

'We?' she replies and looks down the corridor as though the monster that lives under her bed has crawled here and is waiting patiently to devour her.

I take her hand and pull her along until she is in the kitchen. Maxie is standing by the back door, her arms folded defensively across her chest, Hazel is half sitting on a chair, ready to make a run for it, and I drag Anaya into the main area.

'What's all this about?' Maxie asks, clearly wounded that I haven't just sent the text to her, but to the others, too.

'For one reason or another,' I begin, 'I know a lot of stuff about all of you. And those things all relate in some way to Yvonne Whidmore and what happened to her. I want . . . no, I *need* you to tell me what happened that night at the beach hut.'

'Why should we?' Hazel says. Hazel, the strongest link. The one who will not break first.

Maxie adds, 'Yeah, why should we? What's it to you?'

Anaya, the weakest link, moves to the table, sits down and pulls out a chair in silence.

'When I met you, it was all still fresh what happened to Yvonne, but you were all still friends. From what you've all said, you were really good friends and Yvonne tried to control that? Look what's happened. She isn't even around and she's not only managed to control your friendships, she's ended them. She's basically won without trying. Do any of you want that? Truly? I think you need to talk about what happened that night and then work out what you're going to do next.'

'What do we need you for?' Hazel says.

'You don't. But you're all here, I have coffee and tea, and I want you all to get your friendship back. I thought I'd found three women who I could be friends with and look at you . . . Please don't make me go out there and make new friends. I haven't got the strength, especially when I have three perfectly good mates here in this room.'

Hazel

18 August, 2017

'What did he do?'

When the phone rang, I knew I shouldn't have picked it up. I just shouldn't. No one called my landline except him, and that awful PPI lot. But I'm still a bit Pavlov's dogs about phones: it rings, I answer it. More fool me. I heard Walter's voice on the other end and my heart sank. It always did. I was tied to him for another fourteen years, at least, because I knew, as a person does, it would never be easy to make the children go to see him. And when they were old enough to start making their own choices about it, and having something more interesting on during contact times, it would be me running interference because I could not stand by and let him eviscerate them like he would.

'What did he do?' he repeated.

'I'm busy, Walter,' I said. 'If you've got something to say, say it. If not, put it in an email. In fact, aren't we only on email contact right now? Didn't you say you don't want to talk to me because I am impossible and stupid and you want my mad rantings in writing so the world can see how crazy and thick I truly am?'

He paused, because while he'd never actually said any of that, that was clearly what he was thinking and he was worried that he'd shown his hand by ranting that at me. I'd been fine with email contact – it meant I didn't have to get that stomach-churning pain that accompanied every conversation. And he was far too clever to put his bonkers requests and vicious lies into writing, so I didn't have to put up as much with his himness. Honestly, my life had been a different proposition once he'd left, but it had taken meeting Ciaran to finally discover what good men were all about.

'Hazel, I'm calling about the welfare of my children. I've come across some very disturbing information about that man you have moved into my house—'

'It's *my* house, Walter,' I reminded him. 'My house bought with my money. Nothing to do with you. You've never even stepped over the threshold – not for the want of trying.'

'Stop trying to distract me from the fact that you've moved a criminal into my children's home.'

The world seemed to slow down for a moment, and I couldn't speak. What did he know? *How* could he know?

'I haven't,' I said with a sigh. 'You're the one with the conviction for drunk driving; you're the criminal.'

'More deflection, Hazel. Your friend Yvonne told me her suspicions about that criminal. It's only a matter of time before we unearth his crime.'

'I don't know what you're talking about,' I replied. I couldn't breathe; my heart was racing at a hundred miles an hour in my chest. Yvonne. Fucking Yvonne. She *had* been bluffing me. 'And I don't want to know what you're talking about. Yvonne is clearly wrong.'

'I thought she was the best thing since sliced bread, Hazel dear? This is why I know she was right about this criminal. I know you have very questionable judgement when it comes to people.'

'Walter! I didn't realise you knew how terrible you were for me.'

He was briefly taken aback. Then: 'Hazel, Hazel, Hazel . . . If you only knew what your friends were really about. Do you remember that party that your friend Yvonne forced us to go to?' he said. His voice was soft, silky, like warm honey. He was always dangerous when he lowered his voice like this.

I didn't reply to his question so he continued: 'And remember how I got lost in the school, looking for the toilets? Well, I wasn't exactly lost. I was in the headmistress's office, showing Yvonne my etchings.'

Lie. Absolute lie. Yvonne wouldn't. She was a lot of things, but she wouldn't. She just wouldn't. Not at that time. We were proper friends then. She cared about me back then. 'You are such a liar, Walter. Like Yvonne would ever sleep with you. She found you repulsive from day one.'

'Ahhh, poor deluded Hazel. She didn't sleep with me. She was very adept at fellatio, though. Don't you remember the freshly applied lipstick when she came back? Don't you remember how I needed a shower when we came in? Don't you remember how angry she was when she found out I had left you for another woman? Didn't that all smack of "woman scorned" and not simply "supportive friend"?'

'You're a liar,' I repeated. And I knew he wasn't. Of course she did it. I doubt it was more than once, but she did. Probably because she could. Because at the end of the day, that was why Yvonne did a lot of things – because she could. 'Is this because Ciaran is younger than you and infinitely better in bed? Are you that jealous you're going to make up ludicrous lies?'

'You know I'm telling the truth,' he said, but there was an uncertainty to his voice.

'Yes, of course you are. What is it, don't like the idea that I have sex five or six times a week now I've got someone I actually want to do it with?' I replied. 'Or the fact that when the kids go to you I'm not sat around on my own, but I can spend all day in bed with a fitter, younger man? It must hurt you so much to know that I'm not frigid or asexual after all, it's just you're terrible in bed. In other words, it's not me, it's actually y—'

The dialing tone was a brief reward for finally giving Walter a taste of his own medicine. Very brief. Seconds later my mobile lit up:

When I find out what your criminal has done, I will go for full custody of the children and win.

Yvonne. She'd so done that all those years ago, and it made sense now, why Walter knew stuff he shouldn't. She'd been talking to him all along. She'd been feeding him information. I'd thought it was the children, I'd thought they told him stuff about my life, and because I never wanted them to lie to either of us, I'd let it slide. But of course it was Yvonne. I pushed my mobile away across the kitchen worktop, waiting for it to go black again so it would blank out Walter's message. Thank God I hadn't told her everything when she bluffed me about Ciaran. Walter would fight me for the children. In some ways, I wouldn't blame him, but I couldn't be without my children. Yvonne had obviously still been digging for information and had come up with nothing; it wouldn't surprise me if she'd told Walter so he would think about hiring a private detective to dig up dirt on my other half.

It must hurt you so much to know that I'm not frigid or asexual after all, it's just you're terrible in bed. I shouldn't have said that to him. If it hadn't occurred to him before to find out all about Ciaran, and if Yvonne hadn't already put the idea into his head, then he would now. He'd do anything to wipe that smug tone out of my voice.

At that moment in time, I hated Yvonne. She was a back-stabbing, two-faced bitch. I was glad I was meeting the others later. I would tell them what she'd done, how she'd betrayed me, and that would encourage them to tell me what she'd done to them, too. Between us we could then come up with a strategy to deal with her.

I had liked her so much; I'd thought she was the perfect friend. She had obviously liked the life I used to have and wanted that. When that life had come to an end, had she resented me for letting it all go, or for allowing it to go to someone else who wasn't her? Had she thought she would get Walter another way? But I couldn't believe she wanted Walter. I couldn't believe some of that friendship stuff we'd done together wasn't genuine. She'd seemed so hurt when we met up without her, like she wanted to be one of us. She became one of us. Had she been plotting against us all along because we met a couple of times without her, or was it feeling like the fourth wheel on a trike that had sent her over the edge?

Whatever it was, Yvonne had stopped being my friend. She was now The Enemy. I listened to the kids and my partner going about their lives at the top of the house, and I picked up my phone, put it down again, and instead poured myself a glass of water from the tap. I stood still and tried to do that yoga breathing that was meant to calm me down. I downed the water, I did some more breathing. But my rage wasn't subsiding – it was growing and growing with every passing second.

It was a good thing I wasn't going to see Yvonne that night. Because I knew I would not be able to stop myself doing her some serious harm if I saw her lying, deceitful face ever again.

Anaya

'Ah, if it isn't my three favourite friends.' I knew instantly that Yvonne was pissed as well as pissed off.

Several times, especially over the last few weeks, I had been reminded of that conversation about turning into our mothers and how Yvonne had described hers. She'd said she was a vindictive alcoholic. Maybe it'd been a cry for help, a desperate plea from a desperate woman who wanted one of us, the only people she seemed to have stuck with consistently over the years, to help her. To stop her turning into a vindictive alcoholic. Maybe if we'd realised she needed help, we wouldn't have met up at Maxie's beach hut to discuss the situation that night, and instead, one of us would right then be sitting in her house, counselling her on how to be a better person.

'What's this? A mothers' meeting without one of your friends? Surely you wouldn't do that? Not to me.'

We hadn't got the table out; we hadn't brought yoga mats or cocktails or even knitting. We'd just brought our blankets and our flasks. We certainly hadn't got a chair out for Yvonne.

'Oh, just piss off, Yvonne,' Hazel said.

All three of us looked at Hazel. She was the one who had championed Yvonne all along and she was the most placid person I'd met. Not laid-back like my amma – she simply didn't seem to respond in the same way that most people I knew would. The crap she put up with from her ex-husband was unreal. Every time she'd put her foot down it was the result of Yvonne or, latterly,

Ciaran having coached her to do it. But the worm had finally turned, it seemed.

'What did you say to me?' Yvonne asked quietly.

'I said piss off. I've had enough of your passive-aggressive bullshit. All right?' Yes, this was Hazel. 'You want to know why we're meeting tonight without you? Because we're sick of you. You're bitchy, you're arrogant and you're downright nasty. I know you've been talking to Walter behind my back. Probably fucking him as well, aren't you? I know you told him that Ciaran has a criminal record when you know no such thing. Well, you know what? Piss off. I don't care any more. Tell Walter what you want. At least I know he means me harm, unlike you, who's been pretending to be my friend all these years.'

'I *am* your friend,' Yvonne replied. She appeared genuinely shocked by what Hazel had said.

'Newsflash, as Camille would say,' Hazel said. She used her thumbs to point at me and at Maxie. 'I have friends; they are nothing like you. You wouldn't know how to be a friend without wanting something in return if it bit you.'

'How can you say that to me?'

'How? How? Because you're a *fucking bitch*.' Hazel was out of control, I realised that then. Something had broken in her, and neither I nor Maxie had seen it. She'd been a bit crazed these last few weeks, but something had tipped her over the edge. The fact she had agreed to come and meet me and Maxie to talk about Yvonne should have been enough to tell me she was on the edge of the cliff face of sanity. She was now so far off the edge she was swimming out to sea. 'Sorry, I didn't mean that,' she added. 'I mean, you're an inadequate, desperate, needy, nasty, *friendless* fucking bitch.'

Yvonne leapt at Hazel, claws out, ready, I think, to scratch her eyes out. Really. I think she'd forgotten that no one actually does that, no one actually tries to claw the face off another person. Maxie was on her feet and positioned between the two of them before Yvonne got very far, I was a millisecond behind her, and we made a barrier between them. Yvonne bounced off Maxie, then she shoved me and

I shoved her back, but that didn't stop her. She simply came at us, harder than before. From the corner of my eye I saw Hazel was on her feet, and she must have caught a whiff of whatever crazy Yvonne was sniffing because her fingers were outstretched too and she was suddenly going for Yvonne in the slight gap between my and Maxie's bodies.

'What the—' Maxie began as Hazel bodily pushed her aside and went for Yvonne.

'I know what you did with Walter at that Preppy Christmas do!' she screamed. 'I knew there was something suspicious about the way you two disappeared. He told me you went down on him. He told me! He told me!'

Maxie grabbed at Hazel, held her back; I tried to fend off Yvonne, but it was pointless, stupid. There was a full moon that night, which I think must have added to the craziness. I remember, at one point, almost leaving my body and watching us: four women, four friends, who were standing outside a beach hut, in one of the most beautiful places on Earth, grappling with each other – grappling, fighting, swearing, clawing. A mess of mothers; a foolishness of friends.

I don't know who or how, but one minute Yvonne was trying to fight Hazel, and then she was on the ground, half in and half out of the beach hut, her head having connected noisily with one of the large rocks that held open the beach hut door. We all stopped then, wide-eyed with horror at our behaviour.

Yvonne was also wide-mouthed, screaming as she clutched at where she had banged her head. 'Owwwwww!' she wailed. 'Owwwwwww!' I wasn't sure if she was really hurt or if she was acting up because her moans of pain didn't seem real. But that was Yvonne – sometimes she didn't seem real; her reactions were overblown and out of kilter.

'Oh God, Yvonne, are you hurt?' I said, and went to help her.

'Get away from me,' she screamed in response and started to kick out at me.

I drew back, mortified and angry. *How dare you?* I thought. *Who the hell do you think you are?* But the worst thing I thought was: *Hazel was right – you are friendless.* And the worst thing I said was: 'I think it's best you leave now.'

'Anaya's right,' Maxie said. 'I think it's time you left.'

'Oh, it speaks,' Yvonne said. 'How's your "son", Maxie? Managed to make him look any more like you yet?'

Frowning, I looked at Maxie, and found her glaring at Yvonne with a dangerous expression on her face. She didn't look angry or anything that obvious, it was more a calm, cold detachment. 'Get off my property, Yvonne,' Maxie said, her voice the physical embodiment of the look on her face. Hazel must have heard the menace threaded into her tone, too, because she turned to look at Maxie as well.

Still clutching her head, Yvonne began to laugh. 'You're all so funny!' she screeched. 'You all act like you're best mates, but really? You're all so fucking pathetic with your stupid secrets and lies. I bet none of you know what I know about all of you.' She dissolved into a nasty laugh again, a kind of witch's cackle that, I admit, made me want to go for her. I actually felt my fingers curl into my hands and I wanted to take a step forwards, another step forwards and then . . .

'LEAVE! NOW!' Maxie suddenly roared.

It scared Yvonne enough to have her scrambling to her feet. When she was upright, she had the rock in her hand. 'You don't mind if I take this, do you?' she said to Maxie. 'Memento of our friendship and all?'

I was about to snatch it off her, to remind her that I had found those rocks, I had painted and polished and inscribed them. I had made them for my three friends and she was certainly not one any more. But then I caught hold of myself. Not only was it petty, did I really want to be fighting with her again? Hadn't the first time shocked me enough? Had I forgotten what had happened the last time I fought someone? If I was arrested, my caution would all come out and I'd be in a lot more trouble than either of these two. It would become a pattern of violent behaviour. Instead of fighting her, I turned my back on her. Hazel did the same. Maxie stood facing Yvonne, staring at her until I heard her clicking away on her impossible shoes.

We were all silent for a long time, stood in our places, trying to find our equilibrium, the balance to know what to do next.

'I can't leave it like this,' Maxie said. 'I'm going after her.'

'NO!' Hazel and I both shrieked and stood in her way.

'Just leave her,' Hazel said.

'Please, no good will come of it. Just let her go,' I said.

She shook her head. 'No. No. I'm not letting her get away with saying things like that. Before you know it, she'll say something in front of her kids and it'll get back to Frankie. No, I'm going after her and I'm going to make sure she doesn't say that sort of thing again.'

'Please don't, Maxie. What happened here was bad enough. Don't make it worse.'

'Worse is letting her get away with it.'

And then she was gone. She'd lost her blanket in the shoving thing anyway, and her flask had been kicked over. She took off, in the same direction as Yvonne. And I didn't see her again that night.

Hazel and I packed up, locked up, in total silence. I wanted to ask Hazel all sorts of things, but in the end we left Maxie's stuff inside, locked up and then went our separate ways without even saying goodbye to each other.

Maxie

18 August, 2017
Yes, I went after her.

I left the other two to lock up the beach hut or to leave it open and let it be robbed and looted because I really didn't care at that moment. I just wanted to grab Yvonne by the arm, swing her round to face me and tell her if she ever said anything like that again and it got within fifty feet of my son, I would kill her.

My son finding out what I had done to get him was not something I wanted to leave to the whims of a fucking bitch like her. Yes, I'm out of order considering what happened to her, and yes, it's not like she created the situation – I did that all by myself. But seriously, right then, after she'd made that not-so-cryptic comment in front of two women I trusted more than anything and who would never gossip about me, I knew that Yvonne would stop at nothing to get me back for calling her out that day in the playground. Actually, you know what? She probably had stored up somewhere a whole list of slights, a whole catalogue of times when I hadn't included her, when I hadn't called her first, when I hadn't bowed down to her and her fucking greatness as queen of fucking everything Plummer Prep, and this was her way of exacting a fitting revenge.

I couldn't have that. No way could I have that. She could hurt me all she liked, but if she did it through my son – intentionally or not – I would not be able to restrain myself. So yes, I left Hazel and Anaya at the beach hut and I went after her.

Looking back, I don't know what I thought would happen. It's not like she would throw her hands up in the air and declare that she wouldn't spread rumours and gossip that would eventually get back to my son. I wasn't thinking rationally, though. I just wanted to say my piece to her, threaten her, make it clear she couldn't keep getting away with the way she behaved. When I got to her, she was leaning against a parking meter and she was clutching the stone as though it was her anchor, the only thing that kept her upright.

'I want a word with you,' I said to her.

She looked at me through bleary eyes. I think the bash to the back of her head had been harder than any of us had thought. I should have probably backed off, and I might have if she hadn't gone, 'Oh, piss off and steal another baby, why don't you?'

I got right up close and I said to her: 'If my son ever hears someone say that, I will end you.'

She smirked, swayed, tried to stand up and away from the parking meter, but couldn't. 'Oh please! One little call to the police and you'll be nothing. You *are* nothing, actually. You. Are. Nothing.'

'And what are you? Something?'

'Of course,' she said with another smirk.

I smirked back at her. And through her bleariness and sneeriness she saw my face and she stopped for a second. 'Oh yeah, that's you, something all right. That's why the playground gossip has been all about your husband having someone on the side.' Not true. I didn't listen to playground gossip, but this would get to her so I used it. I made the whole thing up. 'Must be so hard, Yvonne, knowing that your husband can't keep it in his pants and the whole world knows it, too.' I felt bad because I liked Trevor and I knew he wouldn't cheat, but it was the only way to get at her.

Her face almost melted into a picture of horror. This was Yvonne's nightmare. She wanted to be everyone's go-to friend, she wanted to run the Parents' Council and she wanted to be universally respected and liked. She would sacrifice all of that not to be gossiped about. School-gate gossip was never corrected, never totally disproved, only ever got more distorted and outlandish. The thought that people were saying anything negative about her was horrifying to her. Her true Achilles heel.

'Who said that?' she demanded.

'That's for me to know and for you to find out, don't you think?' I said.

'Tell me!' she insisted. 'Tell me now!'

I shook my head. 'I don't think I will, actually. I'm going to let you live with the sick feeling of not knowing who to trust and who to relax with and who is stabbing you in the back . . .'

'Tell me, Maxie,' she said sincerely. 'Please. I need to know, please.'

'And I need you to keep your mouth shut about the lies you keep slinging at me, but neither of those things is going to happen, is it?'

She became Yvonne again, poised, cool and calm, straight-backed and the epitome of charm. 'I wouldn't do that, Maxie,' she said. 'I may make a few comments to you when I'm a bit upset, but I wouldn't seriously tell anyone that. I mean, I know it's not true, for starters.'

If I didn't know her, I might have fallen for it. She's very believable when she has all her Yvonne abilities working together to deceive. 'I'm glad you know it's not true,' I replied. 'Just like I know those rumours about you and your husband and his lover aren't true.'

'Tell me,' she screeched suddenly and launched herself at me, rock held high as if to try to brain me. I deflected her blows, which wasn't hard considering how ashen and shaken she looked, and she fell back against the parking meter again.

'No. Yvonne, I don't think I will, actually. I'm just going to leave you to work it out all by yourself.'

That was it. I walked away and left her there. Not my finest hour, not my finest decision, but I did that. I left her to her own devices, even though she was hurt and shaken and injured. I hate myself for it now, of course. If I'd managed to put aside my feelings and driven her to hospital, none of this would have happened.

As it is, that was the last I saw of Yvonne in the flesh.

By the time I got back to the beach hut the other two were gone. I don't know where, but they'd locked up so I went home feeling dreadful. And now, I know that, like I said, if I'd taken her to hospital things would have gone completely differently.

Cece

10 a.m. I have listened to them. To what they say, how they say it. I have listened to them and now I know what Gareth needed me for. They are all telling a part of the story, they are all behaving as if they did it together. Gareth wanted me to find out what motive they might have and which one of them would be most likely to break and tell him they'd done it together if he brought them in for questioning.

Maxie is sitting on the kitchen counter; Hazel has been knitting non-stop; Anaya has drunk six cups of coffee, one after the other. I rub my fingers over my eyes and rest my elbows on the table. I am still filtering what they have told me, still running it through what I know of them.

I sit back in my chair and look at them in turn: Maxie, the mysterious one, Hazel the strongest one, Anaya the calm one. 'All right, now do you want to tell me what you're lying about?'

They all – *all* – freeze. It's almost as if they've been practising for this moment when they're found out.

'You're all lying. Aren't you?' Again, coordinated looking down in shame and guilt. 'Tell me what you're lying about. Tell me what happened afterwards.'

They say nothing, the three of them; they sit in my kitchen, the three silent liars.

'Hazel?' She shakes her head, stares down at her knitting and moves her fingers faster, the needles clicking hard together, the wool moving from one needle to another at lightning speed.

'Anaya?' She lowers her head even further, as though she will find a spot when her head is so low she will disappear.

'Maxie?' She turns her head towards the patio doors, stares out into the garden.

'Isn't all of this driving you crazy?' I ask them. 'Has any of you slept the whole night through since it happened? Have you stopped thinking about it? Tell me what happened.'

'I . . .' Hazel begins. 'I went looking for her,' she admits. 'I know Maxie did, but when Anaya got in her car, I waited until she was gone and then I went looking for Yvonne. I went back in the direction where she'd gone, but I couldn't find her or Maxie. I'd been so angry, still. I don't know what I would have done if I had found her. I mean, I was murderous. I know I told Maxie to leave it, but every time I thought about what she'd been doing, how she was working with Walter, how she'd used our friendship over the years to find out information and was feeding it back to him . . . I didn't understand why she would do that. I got so angry.' She speaks through gritted teeth, grips the needles in her hands so tight she could crush them into splinters. 'She was trying to get my children taken away. And the only reason I could think of was that she wanted revenge for us not including her in everything. I mean, why else would she do that? I hated her so much that night.' Hazel drops her knitting into her lap and slowly wipes her eyes. 'I just wanted her to stop. I wanted all of that rage, all of that anger to be out of me and into her, where it belonged. I didn't find her. She was gone. But I found her car. And I used my keys to scratch "bitch" onto the bonnet.'

'Hazel!' Anaya exclaims.

'Oh, what? She was lucky that was all I did. I only feel bad because it was Trevor's car and he obviously had to have it repainted.' (This was probably one of the things Gareth wouldn't tell me.)

'I went looking for her too,' Anaya admits. 'Don't look at me like that. I was going to go home. I drove off, but it was like Hazel said. The further away I got from the beach hut, the angrier I got. It was bubbling away inside. I mean, we'd gone out and there she was. After all she'd done, she turned up and was acting like the injured party. She was actively trying to destroy my marriage or control me and I got so angry. I drove back. I drove all along the seafront, looking for her. I couldn't see her, so I started driving down the individual roads, hoping she was there somewhere.' Anaya stops talking, covers her head with her arms as though she is about to have multiple blows rain down on her.

'I saw her. I saw her with someone. The person was helping her, and I told myself that was good. She'd met someone who was helping her and it was good. But I knew it was all wrong.' Anaya starts to rock back and forth, trying to soothe herself, protect herself from what she did. 'I couldn't see the person's face: they had their hood up, they were very careful to turn their face away from the passing cars. I left her to it. I told myself that she'd be fine and left her. I didn't drive very far away, but it was far enough for them to be gone by the time I stopped lying to myself and came back. I wished her harm, I suppose I'm saying. I was so mad at her, I didn't stop my car and get out and offer to take her home. If I had, she wouldn't be in a coma. I left her to get killed because I was angry at her. It looks like it was pretty much luck that she didn't die. That makes me a terrible human being. She's in a coma because I couldn't put aside my anger.'

'I actually tried to kill her,' Maxie says. Her words hurtle out of her mouth like racehorses out of their stalls, a mixture of needing to get it out and needing to make Anaya see hers wasn't the only heinous act that night. 'I didn't just talk to her. When she attacked me, I fought back, I shoved her against the parking meter, and . . . and . . . I had my hands around her throat. Her scarf was in the way so I didn't actually touch her skin, but I suddenly had my hands around her throat and I was squeezing. I was actually squeezing. She thought I was messing about first of all, then she realised and I realised – almost at the same time – I was serious. I was going to do it. I was going to kill her. I stopped, of course. But for those seconds, I was going to do it.' Maxie tips her head back, tears rolling down her cheeks as she stares at the ceiling. 'That's when I knew, I knew that I was broken. It didn't stop the row, it didn't stop me telling her lies about her husband, but I was scared after that. I was terrified of what I was capable of to protect my son. I can't tell the police that.

They'll think I followed her to the school and hit her. They'll know I was capable of that. *I* now know I'm capable of that.'

'Isn't that the point?' Anaya says. 'We were all capable of it that night. We were all angry enough and scared enough of what she was threatening to do to our families to do it.'

'I wanted to do it,' says Hazel.

'So did I,' says Anaya.

'I tried to do it,' adds Maxie.

I know why they were lying now. Because to outsiders, to Gareth and his colleagues, it wouldn't look like three women who were angry at a friend and wished for the smallest instant for her to leave them alone. To them, they would see three women who conspired to get Yvonne Whidmore alone and to try to kill her to keep their secrets.

It sounds like they did, but they didn't. I truly believe they didn't. There is a barrier, and I do not think any of them breached it, not for Yvonne.

'Are you sure you didn't notice anything about the person you saw with Yvonne?' I ask Anaya. 'Anything at all? Any marks on the top you could tell the police about? Anything about the way they walked?'

She shakes her head without even thinking about it. Lie. She thinks it was one of the other two.

'Are you sure?'

She closes her eyes and stills herself. 'There was something familiar about them,' she admits, 'but I don't know if I think that because I feel so guilty about letting her go off with someone dangerous.' She sighs. 'We have to go to the police, don't we?' she says to the others.

'It'll be better if we go together,' Maxie agrees.

'The kids are going to Walter's on Thursday this week,' Hazel says. 'I'm off work. Let's do it then. All for one and all that.'

'Well, that's that settled then,' Maxie says. She slides off my kitchen counter and stretches deeply when she lands on the ground.

'Don't go,' I say her. 'Please? Can you all stay and I'll put some music on, we can have a talk, maybe a laugh? Hazel can knit, I can pretend to knit and Anaya can show us some yoga moves. I do have spirits for you to mix cocktails, but probably not the best idea at this time of the morning. Maybe you could use juice and fruit to make some smoothie cocktails or something.'

'I really should be going,' Anaya says.

'Thing of it is, I don't want you to go,' I say before the others agree. 'You're my friends. My only three friends down here. My marriage is falling apart. I thought we had a strong relationship, but he's changed since he moved here. I don't know if it's cos he was here for three months on his own or if he is just sick of me now I don't go out to earn money, but things are not good. He's started to let the children down as well as me. I have no one here but you three. So please, can we just have a bit of time together. Seeing as we're all here?'

'Wow, Cece, I had no idea,' Anaya says. 'I'm sorry to hear that.'

'Yeah, me too. I didn't realise,' Hazel commiserates.

'Yeah, you're just as pathetic as the rest of us,' Maxie says. The others burst out laughing.

They spend most of the day at my house, then we do the school run together, bring the children to my place and we have an impromptu party, with pizza and movies and no homework. It's a perfect way for them to be together for what could be the last time.

WEDNESDAY

Cece

3 a.m. I'm missing something. There is something there, something that will solve this mystery, but I am missing it. I can't tell Gareth it wasn't Anaya, Hazel or Maxie until I can tell him who it is.

In the darkness, Sol snores beside me. I have added this to his current behaviour pattern. He only snores when he is anxious. When he had exams, when he was applying for jobs, when he got a promotion and wasn't sure he could do the job, he would be anxious, he would snore. He has been snoring for two weeks now.

The pattern with Sol is clear, entirely predictable. The Whidmore pattern is alluding me. There are links there, connections, that I should be making, but I can't. I close my eyes. The pattern is like a honeycomb. There are parallel connections, there are diagonal connections. A network of interconnectedness that is linear and oblique. Along each thread is Yvonne Whidmore. She is the glue in every connection, she is the person at the centre of the honeycomb. In each hexagonal-shaped bubble that surrounds Yvonne are the people in her life. Hazel, Anaya, Maxie. Trevor. Scarlett. Madison. And more, everyone at Plummer Prep. Everyone she met through her husband and through friends. There are so many. Too many. Too many.

But then, I don't believe that. There was something personal, close, *intimate* about what was done to Yvonne Whidmore. Not that many people were close enough to Yvonne to hurt her like that. It does keep coming back to Anaya, Hazel and Maxie. Trevor? Children can be wrong, neighbours can mishear – maybe he did leave the house. Hazel, Maxie and Anaya.

I hope I'm wrong. I hope I'm wrong.

Part 14

THURSDAY

Cece

11 a.m. Sol's office is glass and chrome and ever so modern. I have driven out to the office complex on the other side of Brighton to see my husband at work. Maybe, outside of our home, we will be able to converse without out resentments taking over.

Those days where he returned to normal were bliss. They seem, though, to have been followed by a descent to another level of hell. We offer each other wan smiles in the bedroom nowadays; we talk like business associates swapping information about our children; we actively move apart when we could come together.

'It's so lovely to finally meet you, Mrs Solarin,' Sol's assistant, Miranda, says when she meets me at the lift. 'I've said to your husband more than once that I think you're actually just a disembodied voice, so it's a pleasure to finally meet the whole of you.'

'Nice to meet you too,' I reply.

She leads the way down the corridor that runs alongside the open-plan areas of the floor where he works. As we walk, I scan the room for familiar faces, anyone I recognise from the autumn event. No one. Everyone is a stranger.

Miranda knocks politely on his wooden door that proudly displays his full name. I double-take: his original job title when he came here was vice president. Now it reads:

Solomon Solarin

Senior Executive Vice President

He has been promoted and didn't tell me. Hurt crawls through my chest like a maggot chewing its way through an apple. It has reached the stage where he doesn't even share his smallest victories with me.

'Come,' Sol calls out from the other side of the door. The vertical blinds which give him a view of the people in the open-plan office are closed, protecting his privacy, shutting out prying eyes, giving rumours room to take root and flourish.

Miranda opens the door and steps in. I step in behind her. I notice the smell instantly. It is delicate, fragile; ripe and *uncontrolled*.

'Mr Solarin, your wife is here.'

Sol sits behind his desk with his feet up on it, his profile to the large corner window. On the sofa on the other side of the room sits a woman in a green skirt suit, with her stockinged feet up on the coffee table while her shoes with their high, toothpick-thin heels wait patiently beside the table to have her feet returned to them.

I smile at Sol first, then I smile at the woman, then I return to looking at Sol so she can sit herself upright, tug down her skirt, which is quite high up her thighs, and can discreetly try to reinsert her feet into her shoes. The scent, the atmosphere, is familiar, obvious. *Obviously*, she is 'T. B.H.'

'Oh, hey,' Sol says. Awkwardly, he gets to his feet, unable to work out how he's supposed to act – not in front of me and 'T. B.H.' at the same time. We're only supposed to meet under carefully managed circumstances, not like this. He comes to me. 'What are you doing here? Has something happened to the kids?'

'No, everything's fine. I was in the area and thought I'd drop by.'

'What were you doing in the area?' he asks. Now he's here with me he's too embarrassed to kiss me, obviously he can't shake my hand, so he sticks his hands into his trousers pockets and rocks on his heels.

'Seeing you. I thought we might go for lunch or something.'

'Oh. I see. Well, it's great that you're here.' He extends his hand to the woman from the sofa, who now has her shoes on, her skirt back at her knees, and is standing, looking like a jewel in her green suit, her mass of thick red hair flowing over one shoulder. 'This is Pia. She's another vice president. Pia, this is my wife.'

Her smile flickers with nerves and surprise. I extend my hand to her and shake it warmly. She's at least ten years younger than me and fifteen years younger than Sol. 'Cece, my name is Cece,' I say. 'I think Sol sometimes forgets that.' Sol and Pia laugh – more nerves. Nothing physical has happened yet. I can tell. Not yet. But if she offers herself to him, if she makes a pass, he *will* turn her down. No doubt about it. That's the sort of person he is. It won't end there, though. He's already down this path; what will happen is that he will turn her down and then begin to question everything about his life and he will decide he doesn't want to be married any more.

'Good to meet you, Pia,' I say. And it *is* good to meet her. It is good to meet the person who will bring about the end of my marriage. She has a face now: I know who to imagine when I argue with Sol. I know who he is thinking of when he doesn't respond to any of my touches, and when 'T. B.H.' and other tells slip from his lips.

'You too, Mrs Solarin,' she says.

We shake hands and hers is confident and assured. She can relax now she's met me. I am older, I am curvier, I am wearing a leather jacket that is nearly as old as her, and baggy jeans. I am not the nightmare rival she expected.

'Pia, we can pick this up later,' Sol tells her and she nods, smiles, leaves without saying another word.

Once the door clicks shut behind us, Sol moves away from me. He returns to his desk, a decent barrier between us.

'Nice office,' I say to him.

'Thanks,' he replies.

His large corner window gives a view right over the Downs, the green hills seeming to go on and on. He has thick carpet, leather furniture, a glass desk. At the edge of his desk there is a chrome-framed picture of our children: Harmony in the middle, Ore on the right, Oscar on the left. They grin out of the frame at their dad, and I know he'll look at that photo several times a day, thinking about them. Telling himself he's working so hard to provide for them. There's no picture of me. Not anywhere. In his last office the place was plastered with them.

Why wait? Why wait until she makes a pass at him to end this? Why don't I just do it now and be done with it? I'd be putting us both out of our misery.

This is familiar. Even though we have never been here before, it is familiar. I take a deep breath in and the smell – the natural pheromones of attraction that have mingled with the synthetic ones in Pia's musky, heady perfume – drifts slowly to me. I close my eyes and I am overwhelmed by it: the smell, the atmosphere of deceit, the future together we're not going to have. I inhale again. Under the smell of sex, and the scent of Pia, there is the smell of calla lilies. Delicate, light, fresh. Synthetic, so probably an air freshener. Calla lilies. Musk. Jasmine. There is a pattern. It's forming in my head. It's a pattern, a memory. It connects. I can see how now.

'What are you doing?' Sol asks contemptuously.

I open my eyes. 'I was working my way up to asking you for a divorce,' I say.

'What?' He sits forward in his seat. His face corrugates quite dramatically for a man who is further down the road to the end of our marriage than me.

'But I'm not now.'

'What are you talking about? Cece, you can't come in here and start throwing around words like divorce and expect me to understand.'

'I'll explain later,' I tell him. 'But right now, I have to go. I have to . . . I'll tell you later.'

'Cece—'

I open the door and across the room, Pia ducks her head, goes back to pretending to discuss something with a colleague so she can keep an eye on Sol's office. I smile and wave at her, but she looks down. I only want to thank her. She's helped me make that final connection. I think I understand it now. I think I can see that link that breaks across the lines of the hexagons, that connects the different parts of the Yvonne Whidmore honeycomb in a way I hadn't properly registered.

If I'm right, then I think I know who did it. I think I've worked out who tried to kill Yvonne.

Hazel

12:30 p.m. They've separated us. We arrived together and said we wanted to tell them everything we knew together, and they still separated us. They're questioning us at the same time, and I think, from the way another police officer will come in and ask other questions, that they are using one person to check our stories.

I am so tired.

I've answered a million questions and I've been honest. Even about Ciaran. I am so tired. I just want this to be over.

The door opens and the policeman who keeps going and coming and asking other questions he can only have formed from talking to the other two enters the room. He's good-looking. I'm probably not meant to think that, and it didn't really register the first time I met him, but he is. 'I think you're going to need to get a solicitor, Mrs Lannon,' he says when he sits down. 'I think you all are.'

Cece

1 p.m. I called him at work but they said he was working at home today so I've come here – I need to see his face when I ask him.

He opens the door after the first ring of the doorbell and does a double-take when he sees me. 'Cece? Hi.'

'Can I come in?' I say.

'Sure, sure.'

I'm probably crazy coming here all alone without anyone knowing where I am, and without calling Gareth, but I need to see if I'm right first. There's no point in putting everyone on high alert if I'm wrong. Although I know I'm not.

'Do you fancy a coffee?' he asks. 'I'm working from home today.'

I shake my head. 'No, I'm fine. I just – well, I need to talk to you about something.'

He frowns and leads the way to the kitchen. 'Sounds ominous.'

When I don't say anything, he stops reaching into the cupboard above the dishwasher for a cup (even though I've refused his coffee), and turns to face me. 'It *is* ominous?' he asks. 'What's going on, Cece?'

Thing is, I like Trevor Whidmore. Not as much as I like the other three, but me and him could have been friends because the boys and his girls are friends and Oscar is quite set on marrying Madison, but this is down to him. Not Yvonne, him.

'Who are you sleeping with Trevor?' I ask so he doesn't have time to brace himself, prepare his face, shore up his body. His response will be real and revealing.

His whole body freezes for a second, his face flashes shock, then settles on anger. Immediately he goes to anger to mask the guilt that runs like a powerful river through a barren valley. 'What?' he says.

'Who are you sleeping with?'

'I can't believe you're asking me this. My wife is in a coma, and you're asking me . . . Get out.' He steps forwards, right up to me, intimidating me with his size. 'I mean it, get out.'

'Trevor, just admit it. I know you've been sleeping with someone else. Who is it? I'm not going to go running to put it on PPY3 or anything like that. I just need to know.'

He leans down, gets right in my face. He is suddenly threatening, and I'm aware of his height, his strength, the fact that no one knows where I am. I don't step back, don't let him know that he *is* really quite scary. I did at one point think it was him, that he'd decided to end his marriage rather than end his affair. 'Get out of my house, you horrible, horrible woman.'

But it's not him. Someone who bludgeons a woman almost to death will not settle for 'horrible woman' as an insult. He didn't do it, but he knows who did. Even if he doesn't realise that yet. 'The night I came and sat for you, you came back smelling of a woman's perfume; your shirt wasn't buttoned up properly. I know you went out to be with her and I don't care about that. I just need to know who it was.'

He stands back, clearly shocked that I've known all this time and have not let on.

'Who is it? Maxie? Hazel? Anaya?'

No, no, no. Not a flicker. None of them, his face tells me so. Someone else. Damn it. He won't tell me.

'Whoever it was, they're responsible for what happened to Yvonne.'

He becomes still. He is finally connecting the dots, seeing how his actions have consequences and the main one of him sleeping around is that his children have been without their mother for nearly four months. 'What? What are you talking about?'

'Whoever you're sleeping with did this thing to Yvonne. So tell me who it is.'

418

'No, but that's —' He frowns, his eyes clearly running through the tangents, the things that are only now starting to make sense.

'Who is it?' I ask.

'Get out of my house. Right now!'

'I wish you would talk to me, Trevor. I can help you work out how to—'

'GET OUT!' he screams at me. 'RIGHT NOW!'

1:15 p.m. I sit in my car, waiting to see if he'll do what I expect him to do, or if I really have got it all wrong and he'll sit there getting angrier and angrier at me and my accusation. I have my seatbelt on, the car parked halfway down the road with the engine running. If he does what I think he will, the first thing he'll do is go to the woman and tell her what I've said.

My heart is racing, my breath is thick in my chest. It feels like my stomach is filled with the stormy and choppy sea at high tide, threatening to explode out of my throat at any second. I remember, at work, whenever we had to confront someone with the extent of their fraud, I'd feel a watered-down version of this. My heart would thump, my stomach would swim and I would be almost deaf with the sound of my own breathing. I never wanted the people I caught to be guilty, I always wanted them to have a proper explanation, for it to work out so they could keep their jobs. I was still waiting for that to happen when I left.

I want to be wrong about Trevor. I want—

The green door flies open and slams shut loudly after Trevor as he races down the steps leading from his house and then virtually leaps over the bonnet of the family car to get to the driver's side. He's in and moving – no seatbelt or mirror checks – before I get the chance to take off the handbrake. He roars off in his seven-seater like it is a sports car and heads to the end of their road. I'm catching up with him when he swings onto Sacksaway Road, the main street that leads up to the motorway, narrowly missing scraping the back of a white van that has stopped partially covering the yellow hatchings at the end of the road. Trevor doesn't stop at the amber light that is flicking onto red, instead he goes right through, turning right at the crossroads and racing on. The camera at the top of the traffic light flashes its displeasure at him, but he's gone. Out of reach.

No, no, no, no! My eyes flick to the rear-view mirror. There are two cars behind me so I can't reverse to get the correct angle to get around this stupid white van. And even if I could, the light is red. I won't be able to catch up with him, not at the speed he is moving – by the time the light has gone green again, he'll be who knows where.

Why did I think I could play detective? I should have called Gareth the moment I realised there was someone else in the mix. Now I've just tipped Trevor off and he's going to tip off his lover – whoever they are.

Maxie

4:30 p.m. When I told Ed last night that I was going to go to the police and tell them everything, he asked me if I was sure and I said yes. He said he would come with me but I said no, Frankie needed him and he was Frankie's legal parent so to let me go and confess to everything. Which is what I have done.

The good-looking detective returns to the room and sits down again, looking weary.

'The thing is, Mrs Smith,' he says, 'no one really knows where to begin with you. My best advice is that you get a solicitor and we take advice from the CPS about how to proceed.'

'OK,' I reply.

'How are my friends?' I ask before he leaves the room.

'I really think you should worry about yourself,' he says.

Cece

5:40 p.m. I have called Gareth and he hasn't answered his phone. I was cautious about leaving a message.

Trevor isn't here at pick-up, making me believe that I was right. He went to see his lover. His girls aren't with the other children who are standing in a huddle at the gates waiting for their parents to pick them up from their after-school activities and homework club.

The boys aren't there either. They never are. Oscar, who has maths club with Madison, is almost always the last one out because he goes back in for pretty much everything. Ore, who is in graphic design club with Scarlett, usually takes an age to do everything but is always the one who comes home with everything, and first time. Ore often ends up waiting for Oscar, or carrying stuff for Oscar even though they have the same amount of stuff. It's a quandary I've never managed to solve.

They're never this long, though. The playground is almost empty of children, and even the just-made-it parents have been to fetch their offspring.

I stare at the doorway to the school but the boys do not appear. I walk up to the gates, to the teachers who are discharging the last of the children. I am not going to panic. There is nothing to panic about.

'Do you know when Oscar and Ore will be down?' I ask them. The teachers look at each other.

'They've left already,' says Mrs Thackery, Ore's teacher.

'Yes,' Mrs Applebaum, Oscar's teacher, adds. 'They left with Madison and her sister. We were told that you'd asked Mr Whidmore to pick them up.'

I will not panic. Panicking will make this all worse.

'I didn't ask anyone to pick up the boys. Are you absolutely sure about this?'

I have told the boys not to go with anyone except when I have told them specifically that someone else is picking them up. I've said, if I am unexpectedly delayed, the school secretary will tell them I called to say that, but she must have the password. Trevor Whidmore does not have the password. Well, he shouldn't. Unless Anaya, Hazel or Maxie told him.

'We're sure,' Mrs Thackery says. 'The message came via the school office. They didn't go to after-school club or their activities. The password was used.' She looks at Mrs Applebaum, who nods in agreement.

'I didn't make any calls to the school today. I did not tell anyone else to pick up my children. Where are my children?' I ask them.

The pair of them look at each other, stricken. But not completely. They think I've lost the plot a little, that I must have arranged this and forgotten. Mrs Carpenter appears at the entrance to the school, obviously wondering why there are two teachers still in the playground and the front door is propped open when it is probably usually shut by now. She pulls up the collar of her navy-blue coat and comes over to us. I need to start panicking. I need to call the police, I need to panic, and I need to call my husband and I need to find Trevor Whidmore. He has my children. Trevor Whidmore has my children. I am suddenly seeing he is not as innocuous as I pegged him earlier. Trevor Whidmore has my children.

'Is everything OK?' Mrs Carpenter asks when she arrives with us.

'Mr Whidmore collected my children earlier without my permission. He lied to their teachers and has taken them.'

'Pardon?' she says, shocked. She turns to the teachers, her eyes searching their faces. 'What is this about? How has this been allowed to happen?'

'Mrs Artum came in and said that Mrs Solarin had asked Mr Whidmore to pick the children up early. She said he had the password. We didn't think anything of it.'

'Have you called Mr Whidmore?' Mrs Carpenter asks. An obvious question. The obvious thing to do at a time like this. 'I'm sure it's all a misunderstanding. He's probably got the days mixed up.'

My hands are trembling as I bring up his number and press 'call'. My hands are trembling and my mind is starting to race ahead. To see the pattern, and where it generally leads.

'This is Trevor Whidmore. Leave me a message.'

I click the hang-up button and lower my phone. 'Straight to voice-mail,' I say. I look first at Mrs Applebaum, then at Mrs Thackery. 'Are . . . Are you sure it was Mr Whidmore that picked them up? I've never asked him to pick them up before. Are you sure it was him? It wasn't Priya's mum, or Frankie's mum, or Camille's mum? It wasn't one of them and you're mistaken?'

'No, it was definitely Mr Whidmore. Unusually, all of those children were picked up by their fathers today, but no, it was definitely Mr Whidmore who picked up your children with his.'

I hit the redial button, and again it goes straight to voicemail.

'This is so odd,' Mrs Carpenter says. 'I've never had this happen before. Never.'

There is not enough panicking going on around here, I realise. There is altogether far too much standing around and not enough panicking, action, desperation to find my children.

'I need to call the police,' I say. 'I need to call the police,' I say again, louder. I know what I need to do, but I am frozen. It doesn't seem to be a real thing I need to do. It doesn't seem a real thing that has happened. I clear Trevor Whidmore's number from my phone screen and call up the keypad.

'Come into the school,' Mrs Carpenter says. Her arm is on my shoulder, reassuring and calming. 'You can call from my office. Then you can call your husband. Keep your mobile free in case Mr Whidmore calls you.' She gently guides me in through the gates, ushering me towards the building. She is talking calmly, but she is walking quickly, almost at a run. She's panicking too. We head up the main stairs of the school, the treads inlaid with marble, and along the corridor of the upper level, the dark wood panels foreboding but familiar.

My heart is beating in double time, I can hear my breath in my ears again. I'm shaking, my body cold and hot at the same time. Whenever they've been picked up by someone else in the past, they've had to ring me to let me know they're safe. Ore will be worried now, because he will want to make that call. Oscar will start to worry because Ore is worried. Are they able to be worried? Are they conscious?

Mrs Carpenter opens the door to her office and we both rush in. My chest is heaving now, not from the dash to get here, nor the stair climb, but from fear. I have never been this scared in my life.

Just inside the doorway to Mrs Carpenter's office, I make myself stop. Physically stop. Then mentally stop. I need to calm down. I need to calm down and then I need to think. I stand still, my feet rooted in Mountain Pose, like I learnt in yoga. I need to breathe deeply. I need to be still. I need to stand here and be still. I just need to be still for a few seconds, to breathe, to think. I close my eyes and concentrate on my breathing. Slowly, I open my eyes and find Mrs Carpenter watching me, obviously wondering if I'm about to completely break down.

'The phone is on my desk,' she says warily. 'I think this is fast becoming a nine-nine-nine situation.'

I nod, quite slowly considering the magnitude of what is happening. 'Yes, I think you're right,' I say. My voice is calm and slow, too. 'That's a nice perfume you're wearing, Mrs Carpenter,' I continue. 'Jasmine, isn't it?'

'Oh, thank you. It was a present. And yes, I think there are notes of jasmine in it,' she says.

I keep my gaze fixed on her as I say, 'What have you done with my children, Mrs Carpenter?'

Anaya

5:45 p.m. 'I've told you this loads of times before,' I say to the police officer who keeps coming into the room with more and more and more questions. 'I didn't see the person's face. Yes, there was something familiar about them, the walk maybe, but I didn't get a proper look at them. And I don't really know anything else.'

'All right. Mrs Kohli, do you go into your children's school to read with the pupils?' he asks.

'Yes, why?'

'Did you submit yourself for a DBS check?'

'Yes, why?'

'Did you list all your previous names?'

'Oh.'

'Mrs Kohli, even if you didn't know that your previous caution would stop you passing the DBS check and signed the declaration forms in good faith, you would not have passed the check if you had declared all previous names.'

'But I didn't do it on purpose. Harshani is my middle name, it's there on my birth certificate. I didn't think.'

'I suspected as much.'

'Am I in a lot of trouble?'

'Yes, you are.'

Cece

5:50 p.m. Mrs Carpenter smiles at me with the grin of a snake that has been caught about to strike.

'Mrs Solarin, I really wish you hadn't said that.'

What I would like to do is grab her and squeeze the information about where she has taken my children out of her. I would like to shake her until their whereabouts rattles out between her chattering teeth. What I have to do is wait. Because if I do anything to her, she will in turn do something to them. I know it. I can feel it. Someone who is able to attack and almost kill a woman and then sleep with her husband weeks later is cold-blooded. Deadly.

'If you hadn't just said that, I would know that you had no clue who Trevor's lover was, so I would have let your children go in a couple of hours. We'd have all laughed about the misunderstanding. As it is, you know too much.'

'I don't know as much as you think I do,' I say. I am keeping my body loose, fluid, unthreatening. I want her to think she can easily intimidate me.

'Have a seat, Mrs Solarin. We have another fifteen minutes or so until the school completely empties and we can talk properly.'

'Where are my children?' I ask her instead of following her outstretched arm as it indicates the two comfortable green leather bucket chairs opposite her desk. I remember sitting in the left one when I first came to look at the school.

'Take a seat,' she repeats, irritated now.

'I will, when you tell me where my children are.'

Her face, which was quite pleasant minutes ago, even seconds ago, tightens in displeasure. I'm playing a dangerous game, but I am testing her. I am trying to see if I can negotiate with her. If not, then I need to think of something else to do. It's a small, simple test, one that will tell me how to go forward from here. Because the panic, which is lighting up my body like a domino chain of firecrackers lining my veins, will not help me right now. It will at some point, I'm sure, but right now I need to suss her out as quickly as I can.

'Sit,' she orders, like a dog trainer with a particularly difficult puppy.

'When you tell me where my children are.'

She screws up her lips and flares her nostrils as she exhales loudly. I notice the broken veins of a drinker showing through the otherwise flawlessly applied make-up, I see the spidery threads of lipstick that have broken free of her lip line and are radiating outwards from her mouth. She always looks so well put together, so chic and poised, even up close. Ultra close, the little faults show. The tip of her tongue darts out from between her lips and runs over her lips in what might be a nervous gesture.

'They are not far away. Not near enough for you to find them if you choose to do something as crass as run out of here, but not too far away that I can't get to them whenever I want.' She gestures again, much more firmly this time. 'Sit.'

I move to the seat and lower myself into it slowly, holding my bag on my lap.

'Please hand me your mobile phone,' she says.

I hesitate.

'Please, Mrs Solarin, I do hope I will not have to keep repeating myself. Remember, what happens to your boys is mostly down to how cooperative you are. Please hand me your mobile phone.'

I do as I'm asked and she faffs about, looking for the off button. Once it is off, she drops it onto the ground and without pausing or hesitating, she puts her heel through the screen. I hear the crack. Was she this cavalier when she went for Yvonne Whidmore? Did she hit her without ceremony or hesitation?

'Isn't that better?' she says to me. She sits back in her leather seat, which is ostentatiously larger than the chair in which I sit.

'Not really, no,' I reply.

I am trying not to think of my children's fear-twisted faces, their terror-tensed bodies. If I think of them as 'my children', not Oscar and Ore, I will be all right. I will be able to function and get through this and get to them. If I start to worry about what they're feeling, if they're in pain or shock, I will begin to crack up. The thought of any of my children hurting terrifies me. I know pain is a natural consequence of being alive, but the idea that I cannot do all I can to spare them from any form of agony is probably the thing I fear most.

'None of this was meant to happen,' she says. 'You don't think I enjoy doing this, do you? But you backed me into a corner.'

'No I didn't,' I reply.

'Of course you did!' she almost screeches, but collects herself. Gathers together that poise she is famous for, and stops talking while she observes me with a cool, dangerous haughtiness.

Knock-knock at the door startles us both. Her face relaxes back into its usual pose and she sits back, giving the impression of someone relaxed and assured.

'Come in,' she says, smiling at me.

The door opens and I do not turn around. If I do, I might give the game away, I might scream at whoever it is to call the police while I leap across the table at Mrs Carpenter to stop her dashing off to hurt my children.

'I was wondering if you wanted me to hang on for the police?' Mrs Thackery asks.

'Oh, no, sorry, Zaina, it was all a misunderstanding,' Mrs Carpenter lies smoothly. 'It seems Mr Whidmore got the day wrong for picking up the children, like I thought. Hardly surprising with all the additional pressure he's under. The children are quite safe and are on their way home as we speak. I was just reassuring Mrs Solarin that mistakes like this don't often happen, wasn't I?'

I inhale, catch a nostrilful of her perfume and almost gag, before

I put on a smile and turn to the woman in the doorway. She is still anxious, worried that she has done something wrong. 'Yes, it's all been a bit of a misunderstanding,' I parrot.

'Oh, thank goodness,' Mrs Thackery says with a relieved smile and a clap of her hand over her heart. 'I was so worried. I'll make sure I triple-check from now on so this doesn't happen again.'

'Thank you,' I say.

'Yes, thank you, Zaina. I'll see you tomorrow.'

5:55 p.m. 'How do you intend to get away with this?' I ask her. 'I mean, if anything happens to me now, at least two people saw us together. Coupled with what happened to Yvonne Whidmore, they're going to know you were involved. You have no way out of this. Why don't you just tell me where my children are and we can leave it at that? I won't tell anyone; we'll just pretend it didn't happen. We'll even leave the school. If I can't convince Sol to move back to London, I'll take the children and go back with them myself. If you think about it, there's no way for this to end well, so if you just take me to my children, we can find a way to move on.'

Mrs Carpenter's face tells me she is indulging me, allowing me the luxury of trying to talk my way out of this situation. 'Do you want to know why Mrs Whidmore is currently in a coma, Mrs Solarin?'

Because you are a psychopath, I decide. 'Tell me,' I mumble.

Mrs Carpenter smiles. 'Shouldn't you be a bit more enthusiastic about all of this?' she asks. 'I mean, you did work it out, didn't you? You worked it out and couldn't possibly contain yourself before you went rushing off to tell Trevor. I'd have thought you'd be gagging to know, if I may use such a crude term.'

The thing is, only a little bit of me wants to know. I'm curious, sure, but seriously, I'd much rather have my children back. I'd much rather not be here with her and not be panicking about what they're going through. Ore always leaves going to the loo till the last minute. He very often doesn't go during the day at school and has to rush to the toilet when he gets home. He'll be desperate by now. Oscar will be worrying, panicking that he's done something wrong, fearful about not having anything to eat.

To get them back, I have to allow this crazy woman her moment. This is where she reveals her genius, shows off how superior she believes herself to be. It must have been awful for her all this time not being able to talk about it, not being able to show off how she got away with it. And now she's got a captive audience, she wants me to beg her to tell all, to give her attention like I would a misbehaving toddler.

'Yes, I want to know,' I say to her. 'Please tell me. Please.'

Attention is like a warm spotlight being shone on her and she lights up and relaxes at the same time.

'The story starts thirty-six years ago,' she begins. 'I bet you didn't know that, did you? It began when I was seven years old and I was in the second year at Plummer Prep and I had a best friend called Trevor Whidmore.'

18 August, 2017

Winnie Carpenter stood a little way away and watched four parents from her school fighting. It was odd. They were like little girls from this distance, shouting and shoving, trying to scratch each other's eyes out. But obviously, being bigger, they were deadlier. She'd been watching them for a while, following them to the beach when they were there knitting and drinking; sitting outside various houses when they went to someone's home. She had to keep an eye on Yvonne. To find out all she could about the woman who'd stolen her life.

Yes, yes, it was all a long time ago, but she had been in love with Trevor. He was meant to be hers. That sounded so simplistic, but she didn't know how else to explain it. He had been her best friend since they were seven. Seven! He'd become her boyfriend at fourteen. They'd lost their virginity to each other at fifteen. They'd signed up for teacher training together and they were going to build a future together. They'd have two children – daughters – and they were going to live in a big house in Brighton.

He wasn't supposed to go away to university, but his parents had insisted he saw a bit more of the world. Winnie and Trevor already had their plan: they were going to study, gain their qualifications, *then* they would go off and see the world together. Teaching would mean they could pick up their careers when they got back from travelling. Winnie had been sure that Trevor's parents had been trying to break them up, that they thought she wasn't good enough for him or them. But it hadn't worked. They'd stayed together all through the first year at college, and every time they were together they had simply picked up where they'd left off.

It had changed in the October of his second year. He'd changed his course and only told her about it afterwards. He had gone back to first year, and of course, it had been because of Yvonne. He had met her and wanted to be with her.

Winnie was a pragmatic person, even back then, even when it came to love. She'd understood that Trevor needed to spread his wings. He would have an adventure, maybe sleep around a little, but he would come back to her. They were meant to be together and it would happen if she played the long game. Besides, she could have other lovers and liaisons, too. This had probably been for the best. But then, he had done the unthinkable – he had stayed with that woman he'd changed the course for. They had stayed together all through college, and then he'd had the adventure *they* were meant to have – with her! She couldn't believe it. She'd been all set to go and see the world with him and he was off doing it with someone else.

Her pragmatism had kicked in and she'd got on with her life, but with a little ache for Trevor and the life she was meant to have. She had a short-lived but passionate marriage, and carried on with normal life.

Then he had walked back into her life. She had recognised him straight away when he'd come to look around the school on an open day. He'd shown up with the blonde on his arm and she had hated him for looking so happy, so content. She hadn't found anyone to have children with. Sure, she'd had liaisons, sure, she'd had that brief, intense marriage, and her current relationship with Crispin was full and rich, but it still wasn't the life she had planned with Trevor.

She knew Trevor's face lit up when he saw her, and she could see that Yvonne didn't like it. But Winnie had decided she was going to get herself back into his life, and that involved befriending Yvonne.

Winnie followed Yvonne that night as she walked away from the other women on the seafront. This is what happened with female friendships, she'd found over the years. She had seen this intense closeness develop between groups of girls. They always had one who was The Friend, the alpha female who the others flocked around. Slowly, though, surely, though, the others would stop being happy with their role as betas, they would start to talk behind the back of the alpha, they would start to meet up without her and once the alpha found out – usually because one of the betas developed a conscience and told the alpha – they would have a confrontation that would become physical. That was why Winnie avoided groups of women. She had seen all of this play out with her students, and it'd happened to her once in college, where she had been the alpha and she had been the one who was wronged.

That night, Winnie followed Yvonne and she watched the confrontation between Yvonne and Mrs Smith – Maxie – who she suspected was in line to be the new alpha. After Mrs Smith had gone away, she went to Yvonne, said hello. Asked her what she was doing there, asked her if she was OK, told her she was bleeding. Yvonne, usually so poised, especially in front of Winnie, was disorientated and blurred. Winnie told her that she would take her somewhere, administer first aid and drive her home. Yvonne was grateful to her; she went willingly to the car, clutching the rock inscribed with her initials.

Winnie had decided she wanted Trevor back. He was her destiny and he had come back into her life. She had worked hard over the years: she'd moved up from being a deputy head to being head of the school they had both attended as children. This was her time and she had to be clever about it. Know thy enemy. Which is exactly what she had done. She had begun to watch Yvonne, to be where she was. To find out who she was away from her role on the Parents' Council. Once she was sure of Yvonne's movements, how long she was away from Trevor on her nights out, Winnie had begun the next phase of her plan. She would follow Yvonne to wherever it was she would go, and she would put forty-five minutes on her phone. She would go to Trevor's and she would be with him for forty minutes. No more, no less. She would bring cigarettes, she would bring good whisky, and they would sit in the garden chatting. She would only ever let him smoke one cigarette and she would help him to disguise the smell, would only allow him a small shot of whisky sipped over half an hour. It was a slow plan, but Winnie was a patient person, she was planning for her future and she was as diligent with it as she had been with everything else in her life.

434

Winnie would appear at Trevor's house and would never say it, but she would imply it wouldn't do her well if anyone at school found out about them drinking together. As a result, he never told Yvonne, which is what she wanted. She needed him to have secrets, things he kept from his wife. It created an exclusion zone around them; it made them intimate and made it easy for him to take those next steps. To allow her to kiss him. To kiss her back. To allow himself to stroke her breasts. To allow her to perform oral sex on him. That had been risky. She'd purposely left it to the last minute so it had been rushed and she hadn't had time to finish it. So when she had asked him to meet her at the school the next night, obviously he had turned up. That had been the end of meeting at their house. That had been the start of their regular liaisons at the school. That had been the start of the next phase of her plan: to rid their lives of Yvonne.

Winnie drove Yvonne to the school. She wasn't sure what she would do; she hadn't planned this far ahead. It wasn't meant to be like this. She would have liked more time to plan for every eventuality, but she knew this was the moment. The possibility, the anticipation of it, tingled on her tongue, at the back of her throat; it fluttered in her stomach. Her mind was racing ahead: she had to get Yvonne to the school, where there was no CCTV. She parked her car a few streets away; she was already hiding her face by wearing Crispin's jogging top that he kept in the back of the car to change into after longer runs.

She had to support Yvonne, even though she herself was walking on legs as shaky as a newborn creature's. She was trembling and wasn't sure why. Was it because she was scared of what she was about to do, or was it that she was excited? Or was it a swirl of both, each feeling sliding into the other like different-coloured paints bleeding into each other to create a new emotion? Winnie wasn't someone given to extremes of emotions. Her affair with Trevor, while exciting and reconfirming in her mind that they were meant to be together, was controlled, tidy and, beyond the centre of the orgasm, did not disturb her core. Nothing really ruffled Winnie, except this. The idea of doing this. The idea of putting an end to someone.

*

When Winnie had decided to rid her life of Yvonne, she had planned on it being through divorce and forcing Yvonne to move away, ideally with the children. Winnie had seen it time and time again with the parents at her school: they allowed their emotions to overcome them, they couldn't keep themselves in check, their marriages fell apart, they made huge, rash decisions, and she was, more often than not, served with notice of a pupil being withdrawn or, even more excruciating, having a meeting where the parent begged to be released early from the contract they'd signed so they could retreat and lick their wounds. Winnie, as head teacher, never relented: this was the consequence of divorce and separation, after all. Yes, they nurtured the children, but it was a business. She would be doing a disservice to the other owners and shareholders if she allowed these people their money back. She and her business partners could not be out of pocket because of other people's inability to keep their lives on an even track.

To be honest, she'd thought that was what would have happened with Yvonne. Divorce, move, the way clear for her to 'go public' with Trevor in a year or two. But then a passing comment from an alumnus revealed what Yvonne had been up to. Winnie had befriended her rival, had given her as much support as she could to take over the Parents' Council. She had given Yvonne keys so she could be one of the emergency contacts. All of this was done so that Yvonne would trust her and would let her guard down and allow Winnie to find out something that would hasten the end of Yvonne's marriage. She hadn't realised that Yvonne was doing the same. The alumnus mentioned that Yvonne had been looking into raising funds, had been talking to the other owners so she could oust Winnie. Yvonne wanted to be an owner, she wanted Winnie to be nothing more than a figurehead, to not be able to make policy, to not be involved in steering the school. This was why Yvonne had insinuated herself into the role of head of the Parents' Council – she wanted to demonstrate to the owners that she knew the parents; she was more in touch with the fee payers than the head teacher. That was when Winnie calmly – because that was how she did most things – had decided to kill Yvonne.

*

'Do you have your keys with you?' Winnie asked a swaying Yvonne. 'I obviously don't.'

If Yvonne didn't have her keys, she'd have to magically find her own keys, something she didn't want to have to do. She needed to leave as little forensic evidence as possible. No one would question why her fingerprints were on various things at the school, but it would be so much better if Yvonne's were the last set on there.

Yvonne was still unsteady on her feet, and needed Winnie to help her. She opened the gate, and then she opened the front door to the school. Winnie allowed Yvonne in first, allowed her to turn off the alarm, which she did almost on autopilot, Winnie realised. She'd obviously been in there before out of hours.

'Come on then, Yvonne . . . it always feels very odd to call you that,' Winnie said to her prey. And she *was* her prey. The thought of what Yvonne had tried to do had angered her. The realisation that she had been in Winnie's school on her own was the push she needed. This was the right thing to do. She was sure of it now.

'My head,' Yvonne said, rubbing her eyes.

'I know. Let's get you to my office. You looked like you really banged your head when they pushed you.'

'They're a pack of bitches,' Yvonne mumbled. 'But I'll show them. They're going to regret taking me on.'

Winnie stepped forwards, pulled her sleeve over her hand to push open the inner door. 'For what it's worth, I think they all treated you appallingly.'

For some reason that seemed to shock Yvonne out of her stupor. She didn't move forwards, following Winnie into the dark school – she stopped. When Winnie turned to find out why she wasn't being followed, Yvonne was blinking at her. The light from the surrounding street lights allowed Winnie to see Yvonne's face, and with every rapid movement of her eyelids up and down, Yvonne was becoming more sober, more lucid, more aware.

'How do you know what happened with my so-called friends?' Yvonne said, and took a step backwards. 'How did you know they pushed me?'

'Is it important?' Winnie replied. 'You're injured. You need first aid.'

Yvonne looked Winnie over again, noting the raised hood on a man's sweatshirt, the way she had covered her hand before reaching for the door, the darkness they were about to head into, the semi-darkness around them.

Yvonne took another step away from Winnie. She didn't think much of the head teacher. She was an oddball. Someone who didn't have children, who didn't seem to like children, really. She was pleasant enough to them, but she never really seemed to connect with them. That was why Yvonne had wanted her removed as anything other than a figurehead head teacher. She wanted someone warm, who 'got' children, to run the school. Someone you could go to and feel that they not only knew your children's name and academic record, but took the time to speak to them, to get to know how they ticked, found out if they liked sports or art or music or reading. Someone who gave the impression of actually giving a shit. Winnie was not that woman.

It baffled Yvonne every time she spoke to Winnie, spent time with her, learnt more about her background, how Trevor could have been with her for so long. It seemed inconceivable that someone like Trevor would be saddled with someone as cold as Winnie. *Trevor.* Yvonne's heart seemed to turn over in her chest. *Trevor.*

Maxie, in full-on bitch mode, had said that thing. And she had known it was true. For a while now there'd been something furtive and detached about him. Something not quite right. And as he'd detached, she'd looked for connections elsewhere. She'd turned to her friends and they in turn had turned their backs on her. The more they'd distanced themselves, the more she'd had to show them that they couldn't just leave her out, reject her. The only person who could make him so unengaged was . . .

'How do you know what my friends did?' Yvonne repeated and took another step away.

'I saw. I was on the beach and I saw you all fighting.'

'How did you see? Why were you on the beach? You don't have a dog. You don't live near here. Why did you drive down there?'

'It's a free country. I'm free to go wherever I wish.' Winnie went towards Yvonne and she stepped even further back into the playground, jittery and visibly scared.

'You've been following me, haven't you? Stalking me because you're sleeping with Trevor.'

Winnie shook her head, opened her arms to show Yvonne she had nothing to fear. 'Yvonne—'

'Get away from me!' she screamed. 'GET AWAY!'

Winnie ran at her then. She had to shut her up. On this side of the school there were houses a short distance away, near enough to hear screams, to not dismiss them as people messing about because that generally didn't happen in this area. She barrelled into the slender blonde woman, her college rugby training coming to the fore. She heard Yvonne's head crack on the soft AstroTurf of the front playground, and it was so loud, a brutal snap in the still night air that she expected Yvonne to lie still, felled by the weight of a slightly broader woman. But no, she was a squirming, fighting mass, and in seconds she had pushed Winnie off and was crawling away. She was whimpering, sobbing, her voice catching in her throat like screams strangled before they could hit the air.

Yvonne moved like she was hurt, but Winnie, who had also been jarred by the fall, went after her. Winnie found herself panicking, something she never normally did. She couldn't detach, step back, watch herself from a safe distance. Panic gambolled through her as she scrabbled after the woman who had stolen her life. It wasn't as easy and simple as she'd thought it would be. What had she planned to do when she got Yvonne into the school? A shove down the central staircase, to make it look like an accident? Probably. Murder removed. She could hear Yvonne's laboured breath, the strangled cries, the sobs of shock. Slowly she realised some of it was from her: *she* was breathing loudly, *she* was sobbing as *she* was as shocked as Yvonne Whidmore, but she couldn't stop now.

Yvonne would tell.

Yvonne would tell everyone that Winnie had tried to kill her.

'Stop, stop. Yvonne, stop,' Winnie sobbed. 'Please, stop.'

She was on top of her now, but again Yvonne did not capitulate. She fought, and struggled, a many-limbed creature that would not be contained or restrained. Winnie grabbed the rock, she felt its weight in her hand. She pushed at Yvonne, trying to keep her still with only the weight of her body. Winnie wanted her to stop, to be still for a moment so she could hold her down. But Yvonne was wild; a desperate creature, trying as hard as it could to escape. Winnie had no choice: she brought the rock down on the back of Yvonne's head to calm her down, to steady her. Yvonne was still for a moment, shocked by the sudden blow to the back of her head, almost on the original blow. Then she was fighting again, harder this time, it seemed. Terror made her stronger, more determined to get away.

'Stop,' Winnie whispered through her sobs. 'Stop. Stop. Stop. Stop.' She just needed Yvonne to stop. Each time she spoke she brought the rock down, she tried to show Yvonne what she wanted. *Stop, stop, stop, stop, stop.*

She finally did as she was told. She finally stopped. She was finally, *finally* still.

'I just wanted you to stop,' Winnie told Yvonne's still form. 'It's not how you think. It's not like that at all.'

Now she needed Yvonne to move. To acknowledge what she was saying, even in the smallest of ways. Winnie knew Yvonne wasn't going to reply. She knew this but she continued to speak to her. She told her that it was destiny with Trevor. That he did love Yvonne, yes, but what he had with Winnie was bigger than that. Yvonne did not move, she did not respond. Winnie looked down at the mass of blonde hair, matted with a dark liquid that wasn't truly visible as red in the darkness.

She pushed herself off the dead body in front of her and couldn't look as her stomach lurched at the realisation at what she had done. She threw down the rock, slick with the same oozing, dark liquid on the back of the woman's head in front of her. Winnie struggled to her knees and stared wide-eyed. With a shaking hand she reached out and tried to turn the woman over. It wasn't easy. She had to use both hands and her stomach lurched again when the body thumped over and just lay there. Her eyes were closed, thank goodness, her face was squashed; the same sticky liquid had poured out of her nose and smeared itself over her lips. There was a cut on her right cheek that looked like it would swell if she was alive. She looked so . . . messy. Winnie knew that Yvonne would hate that. No matter what, she would want to show her best face to the world.

Power streaked through Winnie. She was in complete control of how Yvonne would look. She had finally won over Yvonne. Yes, she was sleeping with Trevor, but Yvonne had been plotting behind her back. Now she had won. Another surge of power, ultimate power, thundered through her. She had won. The sick feeling that had washed through her swept away again, like the tide receding, but this time never to return. She had only done what was necessary, what would stop this woman from taking away her future again. Winnie shoved her hands into the pockets of Crispin's top and found a neatly folded-up tissue in the right one. Of course. That was the sort of man Crispin was: organised, neat. He would want to have a tissue to hand, always. She used the tissue to pick up the rock, then used the edge of Yvonne's white top to wipe it down. She was meticulous, careful, exacting. If she was not careful, not diligent, a stray print could give her away. She cleaned each crevice, each crease and bump, making sure it was free of evidence.

She was going to drag the body out of the open, but then she didn't want to transfer any more DNA, hair, skin cells or whatever onto her. It was bad enough that they had fought, it was not ideal that in this darkness she could not see if she'd left any hairs on the body, but the longer she stayed here, the longer someone might see her. As it was, the CCTV from further down the road would probably show that Yvonne had been with someone; she did not need an eyewitness who could give more details.

'I hope there are no hard feelings,' Winnie said to Yvonne before she left her. 'All's fair in love and war, and all that.'

Winnie walked a long way, in the opposite direction to her car, to give the wrong impression to the CCTV cameras. She walked and walked, with her head down, the hood hiding her face and hiding her hair, hopefully giving the impression she was a man. The air was cold on her skin, biting and cruel, in a way that didn't seem to bother the other people she met on the way. She felt, though, like she was on fire, an inferno walking and walking, with every step replaying what had happened. On one level it surprised Winnie how unemotional she felt about it all. She wondered if she was in shock, if it would hit her at some point that she had committed the ultimate crime, but in reality Winnie knew that no such guilt or remorse would come.

She simply wasn't built that way. She ducked into the tavern at the end of Hove Park, packed with late-summer drinkers enjoying their pints and drinks and the company of friends. In the toilets she removed Crispin's top. She folded it as small as she could then went to order a drink. She sat and sipped the drink, all the while what she had done running through her head. She watched the people around her carefully; no one noticed her, not even that she was a woman on her own. She waited and watched until a group of seven or eight people got up to leave together and she went with them, slipped into their group and followed them slowly until she could break away and go back for her car.

It seemed so simple. Uncomplicated. It amazed her that people who planned this stuff would come undone so easily. She retrieved her car, put the top into a carrier bag she found in the boot and then drove out towards Brighton marina, pulled into the supermarket car park and disposed of it in one of their large bins. Then home. Home to Crispin, who'd fallen asleep in front of the television, as he usually did. He'd been practically asleep when she had left earlier, nodding off and then waking up. He'd probably woken up a couple of times, had thought she was off having a bath or reading in the study as she often did, then nodded off back to sleep. This was the usual map of their evenings when she wasn't out having sex with Trevor in her office.

Winnie showered, removed the stench of what had gone before, washed away the persona she'd had to adopt to do what she did, then she returned to the living room. She sat on the sofa she always sat on, reclined like she always did later in the evening. She put her head down and forced herself to go to sleep. Yvonne's face kept coming to her, sure, but she pushed it aside. She had to sleep. She had to establish an alibi. She had to make sure that she got away with this because if there was one thing she knew, it was that Yvonne was not worth losing her freedom over.

Sleep, she told herself. *Sleep, sleep, sleep.*

Cece

7:15 p.m. 'Imagine my shock when they explained that she had survived,' Mrs Carpenter tells me.

She has been very calm about it all. She has told me how she did it, and why she did it, and I can see that she is talking to me like this because she doesn't believe I'll be telling anyone.

'I actually expected to feel some relief and gratitude that I hadn't killed someone, instead I was disappointed in myself for not doing the job properly. If any of my staff had done such an incomplete job I would have disciplined them, severely.' Mrs Carpenter runs her hands through her hair and settles them under her chin as she leans forward on her desk and stares at me. 'What am I going to do with you, Mrs Solarin?'

'Realistically, there's nothing you can do, Mrs Carpenter,' I reply. 'It won't be as easy to get rid of me as it was Yvonne Whidmore. And the fact you've brought two children into this whole mess will make it worse for you. For example, how are you going to explain it when Trevor Whidmore says he didn't call the school and he didn't take my children? And the school secretary will say the message came from you.'

Mrs Carpenter smiles at me. 'No, Mrs Artum will say she found a telephone message on her desk, just like I did, written on message pad paper from the staff room.'

This situation is rapidly deteriorating by the second. She has planned a lot in a short amount of time, like the night she tried to kill Yvonne Whidmore, but this improvisation, this behaving as though there is a possibility she will get away with it, means she is losing touch with reality. She can't see that there is no way out of this. Even if she manages to do away with me and the boys, there is too much that she can't explain or undo. She has just told a staff member that the children are safe. They will remember that. Trevor has probably already gone to the police. Yet she still thinks she will get away with this. She is not going to give me back my children. And she is going to try to kill me.

I watch the clock on the wall above Mrs Carpenter's head tick, the second hand jerking from mark to mark, counting out the length of time my children have been holed up wherever they're being held. Seconds have turned into minutes have turned into hours. It is past seven o'clock. Harmony will have been texting, asking where we are, what's for tea, do I want her to start cooking? Sol will have called, asking where I am, and what did I think I was doing acting all crazy by coming to work like that, and where are the boys? Gareth has probably returned my calls, and is now wondering where I am and why I've suddenly gone silent on him.

'Why did you take my children?' I ask Mrs Carpenter.

'Because I wanted you to listen. The only way you would listen to me is if I had something so precious to you that you wouldn't be distracted. When Trevor came and accused me, said that you had made up these lies about me, I wanted to speak to you. I wanted you to listen.'

'But it wasn't a lie and it has nothing to do with my children.'

'OF COURSE IT HAS!' she screams. Her voice returns to a normal level, but her eyes are wide and her nostrils flared. 'It's *always* about the children. That was why Yvonne was trying to take my school away from me. She didn't think I was good enough to be in charge of her children's education because I hadn't given birth. It's always about the children, don't you see?

'Don't you think Yvonne, in fact all of these parents, would treat me differently if I had managed to have children? Don't you think they would understand whatever I did if I could use my get-out-of-jail-free card of being a mother? I would be able to not work. I could swan around all day not bothering to earn any money, expecting the world to praise me for simply not being smart enough to use contraception. Everything is about the children, and the women who pushed them out earn sainthoods for the privilege.'

'Why did you become a teacher, a job where you have to deal with mothers and parents, if you have such contempt for them?'

'Because that was the plan! Are you really so dim? Do you not understand? Are you not listening? That was what Trevor and I had planned. I was meant to have him, I was meant to be one of you – a mother – *with him*. He changed the plan but I didn't. How could I, when I had a plan that was perfect?'

She has spent more than thirty years living out a plan she formulated when she was tiny.

'Where do you think Trevor is now?' I ask her.

'At home with his children or at the hospital visiting *her*.'

'Really?' I say to her. 'You really believe that after finding out that his affair possibly led to his wife almost being killed that he'll just go about his business like nothing has happened? Do you *really, honestly* believe that?'

For the first time since we have entered this room, sat at her desk with the light fast dimming from the large picture window to my left, she looks genuinely uncertain, worried.

'If you were him, wouldn't you be wondering if you should go to the police and confess all about the affair, and see what the police will say about these accusations?'

The streaks of worry broaden on her face, start to tense up her shoulders.

I am talking, but I am also thinking. I am ransacking my mind, searching, desperately trying to work out where she would take the children. It will be in the school. This place is her life so they are here somewhere. Away from where the teachers and staff normally go so they are not discovered. I am trying to remember. I walked these halls. When she showed me around I walked these halls with her, I saw her school, I mapped out the place with my feet and my eyes, and I know I can remember if I try.

This is what my mind does: it makes patterns. I can remember

445

the pattern of the tour. I know I can. In through the front door, approach the large sweeping staircase, up to her office. Then down the staircase, to the ground floor, to the lower year groups' class-rooms. Along the glass walkway towards the huge library. Turn left, towards the art department, a generous space with a glass wall and patio doors that open out onto a paved area so the students can paint and draw outside, overlooking the playing fields. On towards the science block, with its two labs.

Continue on to a storage room, to arrive back at the staircase, or back the way we came. Start again at the staircase, this time, right. Down towards the middle years' classrooms, all decent-sized and light-filled, moving you round to arrive back at the staircase. Then back, up the stairs this time. Left to the upper years' classrooms. Then back, and right, to the head teacher's office, to the school office, to the staff rooms.

No, none of those places. They are all too public, too frequently accessed.

'Trevor Whidmore has as much to lose as me in all of this,' Mrs Carpenter says.

'Really?' I say to her.

They must be in the outbuildings. We went to the wet-weather gym space, situated beside the netball/basketball courts, where they hold exams as well as indoor sports. We went to the left side of the building, to more playing fields.

'You really believe he has as much to lose as you?'

We didn't complete that pattern. It'd rained the night before and that playing field, for some reason, was unusable if there was rain. They had a mini cricket pavilion but she had explained that it became waterlogged in autumn, rock-hard in winter. They'd spent thousands trying to sort it out but no joy. For some reason, that part of their land was unstable. They hadn't given up, though. 'The head of the Parents' Council is trying to raise funds to allow us to come out here even in the later months,' she had said. 'Watch this space.'

They are at the cricket pavilion. I remember the football match where I had to stand facing the pavilion because I had a child on each pitch. They are there, I am sure of it. No one would go out there at this time. But if they are there, they will be cold as well as scared and hungry. I have to get to them. I have to take the gamble that they are in the cricket pavilion.

'I think your best bet, Mrs Carpenter, is to run while you can. You can either stay here and plead self-defence while praying that Yvonne Whidmore doesn't wake up, or you can dash home, pack a bag and your passport and go before they come to talk to you. You could probably get on a flight somewhere since we're so close to Gatwick.'

'Don't be ridiculous. I am not leaving my school.' She points outside, to the fields and buildings she can see from her office. She can see the cricket pavilion from her office – that is the perfect place to keep an eye on them and the comings and goings from that area. 'It would fall apart without me.'

I glance at my bag in my lap. I can't run with my bag. Any sudden move I make will mean leaving my bag and running for my life. For my children's lives. This is a gamble. The weight of it bears down on my shoulders. If I'm wrong and they're somewhere else, or if I can't get there first . . . She knows the fastest way. The fastest way, of course, would be out of the window. But obviously not an option. I walk the pattern in my head again. If I could get down the side of the school, that would be the quickest way, but it will be locked up. Padlocked. I need to go down the stairs, to the left, through the art room. I don't have a key, so I will need to smash through the doors, both sets. Or fire exit. I will use the fire exits that sits at the bottom of the stairs to get to the back of the building – through those fire exits, across the small courtyard.

I do not have anything to smash through the fire exits if they are against me. My eyes scan her desk. She has a small, clear paperweight sitting beside the nameplate. When I run, I have to grab that.

'Fine,' I tell her. 'You stay here.'

I throw my bag at her as I leap to my feet, grab the paperweight and run for the door. I meant to throw the chair behind me to block the way but there is no time. Mrs Carpenter cries out in surprise.

She wasn't expecting me to do this, but what else was I going to do, when the only thing that could happen next was her trying to do away with me and the boys?

I race down the corridor to the staircase, take the steps two at a time, and I can hear her behind me, her sensible head-teacher shoes clattering as they come for me. I leap down the last four steps, land awkwardly, my left ankle wobbling, acting as if it will give way. But I ignore it. I turn at the stairs and find the fire exits are propped open. I don't know why, when the school is empty, and it's as illegal to do that as it is to deadlock them, but they are. I run for the first exit, aware I can hear her behind me. I kick aside the brick holding the door open and tug at it, the door's stiff, slow-closing hinge almost fighting me as I try to slam it shut. She is halfway down the stairs when the door finally relents and works with me. It slams shut just as she nears the bottom of the staircase. I run again, aiming for the next open doorway, waiting for me like an extended hand, urging me to reach it, to touch safety. This is the door that will make the difference. Even as her hand reaches for the opening bar of the first clear-glass fire door, I am pulling this one shut, tugging and tugging until it comes to. I see her face contort into a scream as she realises what she'll have to do to get through it. Maybe let herself into one of the classrooms and come round that way. Or set off the fire alarm to release the door, but that would bring the fire brigade.

I run through the next door, slam that shut, and chance a look behind me. She's gone. The small courtyard I have just run across is empty and I don't have time to stand and search for her. I race through the final fire door, out onto the small paved area that runs around the outside of the school. I hesitate, brace myself to run out into the silky darkness that hugs the school.

I can see the pavilion, an old white, weatherboard building with a red-tiled roof and a large clock sitting proudly above the large patio-style doors. There is a terrace that you need to step up onto from the ground, where I imagine they put out tables for the match tea, and windows almost all the way around the building. There are two wall lights that are lit along the side of the building and they cast a weak, yellow-orange glow around the pavilion, its patio and a good few metres of grass around the area.

I begin to run again, my chest contracting painfully at the sudden cold. As I pass the gym building, the motion-activated outside lights snap on, blinding me. I stop, blink away the flashing and get moving again. As soon as I hit the first pitch, my feet skid. It has poured with rain for the last two nights. I've lain awake both nights listening to the rain, trying to work out patterns, listening to Sol snoring away the remainder of our marriage.

I push on, the ground more mud than grass, and the soles of my shoes disappear into the brown mush. I stop for a moment to pull my feet up, steady myself. In the stillness, the lights go out. When I move again, they snap on, and I see them: footprints. Clearer at some points than others, two small sets of footprints flank one large adult set of footprints. The wavy patterns on the smaller footprints are the inverse of ones I've had to clean from the corridor tiles many times. I look up at the pavilion.

Forgetting the mud, its slippery surface and the danger it poses to me falling over, I break into a run again. Slipping, sliding, but moving as fast as I can, until I reach the pavilion. I skid sideways, and have to put my arms out to stop myself completely going over.

I reach the raised terrace and jump on, grabbing for the door handle. I rattle it, but it's locked of course. I still have the paperweight, and raise it to break the glass.

I have a sudden sensation of movement behind me and I turn to see Mrs Carpenter, her face a murderous red, coming at me with a hockey stick raised aloft. I don't have time to move, I can only raise my arm to protect myself as she brings the stick down. I feel the crack at the exact same time as I hear it, before the pokers of pain shoot through every part of my arm and stinging stars of agony explode in my head.

Mrs Carpenter raises the stick again, this time aiming for my head, and I step backwards, slip on the mud from my shoes and land painfully sitting down, my arm automatically coming down to help brace me. I scream as the pain shoots through me again, the agony erupting a sickness in my stomach. I'm about to heave, more and more stars fire behind my eyes, a never-ending cacophony of fireworks.

She raises the stick, steps forward with her face contorted, this time knowing she has a clear shot at my head, and I manage to move and she instead dents the white weatherboard. Again she swings, and I manage to move and she leaves a deep impression in the wall behind me. I catch my broken arm again and the pain explodes again; I'm dizzy and I can't keep myself upright. She swings again, this time coming from above, and before she can bring it down I kick out, aiming for her front knee, the one bearing all her weight.

My foot connects, muddying up the front of her skirt and knocking her off balance. She stumbles backwards, her face lit up with surprise, and catches the edge of the terrace, which causes her to lose her footing. She lands flat on her back in the mud. I struggle to my feet, and go for the hockey stick. I snatch it up and step back so she can't kick at me.

'DON'T MOVE!' I scream at her. 'JUST DON'T MOVE!'

She ignores me, instead moaning, sobbing, while rocking side-to-side in the mud and cupping her knee with her hands.

'Cece,' Gareth's voice says.

I know I must be hallucinating, that the throbbing pain from my arm, the jarring agony in my spine, is making me hear things.

'Cece.' I hear him again. 'Cece, look at me.'

It's him. It's really him. He has his hands up – scared of the hockey stick and what I might do with it, I suppose.

'Cece, it's me. It's the police.'

The police? The police. I look up and the playing field, waterlogged and muddy, has several people on it. Most of them uniformed police officers. They are rushing towards us; a couple of them go straight to Mrs Carpenter.

He points to the stick in my hand. 'Can I take that?' he asks, still signalling surrender and peace.

'Yes, yes,' I reply and hand it over to him.

'Trevor Whidmore came and told us everything. We were trying to get hold of you but your phone was off, you weren't at home and neither were your twins. We thought we'd come to talk to Mrs Carpenter and found the school wide open and then saw you both out here.'

I stare at him and listen to him but he is talking another language. The pain is dulling my senses, stopping me from properly understanding anything. I think I'm about to pass out.

Two officers help Mrs Carpenter to her feet, but when they let go of her, she almost falls over again.

The boys. My boys. I run the short distance to the pavilion's door.

'The boys!' I say to Gareth. 'She's got them in there. They've been in there for hours.' He pulls me back and tries to shoulder the door. It shudders but does not relent. He tries again. Nothing. He stands back, then kicks at the door, aiming for the join of the lock. On the third kick it shatters open, both doors flying backwards and opening up the gloomy interior of the building.

'Oscar? Ore?' I call. 'It's me. It's Mama. Boys. Boys, are you . . . ?'

The silence that inhabits and coats the dark space terrifies me. It's unnatural. When two boys who are as relentlessly noisy as my twins are in a place, it should not be this quiet.

'Boys!' I call again, desperately. I am trying to keep the terror out of my voice. Because if I hear it, then I will accept that they might be— 'Boys! Oscar! Ore! Where are you?'

Gareth comes in behind me, followed by two police officers. I need to hear them to find them. I stand still, close my eyes, listen for them. For their voices, their breathing, a sign that they're still here.

I can hear Gareth breathing loud and fast, I can hear the rustle of the police officers' uniforms, the thrum of the wall lights outside, but I can't hear the boys. The two officers go to the right, I go left, using my one good arm to feel my way.

There is a semicircle of chairs, right at the back of the space. It has the shape and feel of a fort they would have made to protect themselves. They must have been so scared, especially when the light began to fade and Mrs Carpenter didn't come back.

'Oscar! Ore!' I call at the top of my voice as I run towards the arca. 'Ore! Oscar!'

At the centre of the semicircle, on the dusty white-wood floor, they are two crescents, wrapped around each other. They are very still, facing each other. When I was pregnant and I used to imagine them, this is how I saw them, how they found a way to fit together in a small space, facing each other, communicating without words. My heart turns over at how immobile they are. In this dark I can't see if they're still breathing.

I kick aside the chairs and not even that noise stirs them. 'Oscar, Ore,' I call. 'Boys, boys, wake up.'

Before I can throw myself to my knees and touch them, Gareth is there, moving me aside and effectively blocking me from going any further. I know he's trying to protect me, trying to stop me being the one to find out if they're—

He touches Ore first, obviously not knowing that Oscar is the older one. It's Oscar who's meant to be first. Then his fingers go to Oscar's neck, checking his pulse.

'We need another two ambulances,' he tells the police officer beside me. He points to another male officer. 'Come here,' he orders. The officer sidesteps me to do as he's told. 'Pick him up,' Gareth orders, indicating to Oscar. 'Unzip his coat. Now hold him against your body, and put your coat around him, like this,' he says, all the while doing the same with Ore. 'That's it, that's it. You're trying to warm him up using your body heat.' He snatches the navy-blue woollen hat from his head and places it on Ore's head before pulling up his hood again. 'Cece, your hat,' he says. Moving like a robot, I take off my hat and hand it to the man holding Oscar. The officer copies Gareth and returns to cradling my boy.

'The rest of you, wrap your jackets around us,' he orders the other officers in the pavilion. 'We need to warm them up slowly.' We all recoil as the overhead lights buzz then blink on.

'They're OK,' Gareth tells me. 'They're just cold. Probably hypothermia from being out here so long, which is why they went to sleep. Clever boys, though, eh, trying to share heat by curling up together? But they're OK.' He holds his hand out to me. 'Come. Come and wake them up.'

'Oscar,' I whisper to my little boy, pressing my lips on his cold cheek. 'Ore,' I whisper to my little boy, pressing my lips on his cold cheek. 'Wake up, boys. Wake up now.'

I stroke their faces in turn and try to ignore the stillness in their usually lively bodies, the unnatural chill in their normally warm brown skin.

Part 15

THURSDAY

Cece

9 p.m. Sol and Harmony come charging into the boys' room in the A & E department of the children's hospital. I am wearing a temporary bandage, and I have moments when I think I'm going to pass out despite the painkillers, but I've made it clear I am going nowhere away from the boys until Sol and Harmony arrive.

Harmony throws herself at me, bumping my arm and detonating another round of pain explosions. 'Pain, Harmony, pain, pain, pain,' I gasp as I hold her close to me.

'Oh, sorry,' she says and shifts slightly, but doesn't let me go. The fact I can hold her, albeit with one arm, feels like a miracle when not long ago I thought Mrs Carpenter was going to kill me. I bury my face in her hair and kiss the top of her head. 'Are you all right, Mum?' she asks. 'Are you all right? Are you all right?'

'Yes, yes, yes. I'm fine.'

'Oh, Mum. Are you sure you're all right? Are you sure?'

'Yes.'

'What about those two?' She drops me like a hot stone, and turns to her brothers. She leans into Ore's bed and peers right at his face. Then she spins, does the same with Oscar. 'Are they all right? When will they wake up? Is there any permanent damage?' Her questions run one into another, as though this is all so exciting for her she doesn't know how to slow herself down.

'They're fine. Mild hypothermia. They'd practically come round by the time the ambulances arrived. They've had a warm drink and they're both exhausted so they've been allowed to go to sleep. No permanent damage. They'll be discharged first thing in the morning.'

'Mum, this is all too weird. You lot were like almost murdered by like a psycho headmistress. That is too weird. Even for this family.'

'Can you stay here with the boys? I need to talk to your dad.' I struggle to my feet and raise an eyebrow at Sol.

'Oh, I think Dad wants to talk to you all right,' Harmony says softly. 'I think he has lots and lots of words he wants to use with you.'

We're the only ones in the small waiting room in this area and despite the door being shut, Sol still gives it a full three minutes before he speaks – I know because I count them out in my head . He's probably been counting to a hundred and eighty, too, to calm himself down. 'I don't know if I should hug you or scream at you,' he eventually says.

'I think the result – pain – will be the same whichever you do.'

'*Man!* Cece! Have you lost your mind?' he says, his voice raised. 'The whole drive over here, actually, when the policeman turned up and started to tell me what had been going on, I couldn't get my head around the whole thing. I still can't.'

'Shhh,' I reply. 'Keep your voice down.'

'No!' he replies. 'I think everyone here should know how catastrophically you've fucked up.'

I blink at my husband. *All right, enough,* I decide. *Enough now.* 'I want a divorce, Sol.'

He lowers his voice then, the shock apparently robbing him of volume when he replies: 'What are you talking about?'

'I'm talking about you and me not being married any more. I'm done. Finished.'

'Excuse me? You have secret meetings with your ex. You endanger our children's lives. And I'm the bad guy here? How does that work?'

'You're a liar and I don't want to be married to you any more,' I tell him.

He almost leaps across the room to stand in front of me. His fingers poke into his own chest; his face is incredulous. 'I'm a liar?

I'm a liar?' he says. 'Are you having a laugh? I can't believe you're trying to twist this onto me.'

'Patterns, Sol,' I tell him. 'Remember? I see things in patterns. Your pattern of behaviour since you came here to work is that you don't really want to be married to me any more.'

'That's not true,' he says, although he won't make eye contact.

'You're lying again. What is it, Sol?' I ask. 'I see the pattern but I don't see the why. I don't think you've slept with someone else, yet, but it's not long before you do. And you've been trying very hard sometimes to make that my fault. But what is it that's driving this behaviour? Is it debt? Drugs? Gambling? Attempting to time travel? What?'

Sol sighs and stares down at the ladybird rug we're standing on. He prods at a black spot on the back of the ladybird with the toe of his shoe and takes a few deep breaths.

'I, erm, look, I wanted to tell you, all right, but I didn't know how.'

'Well, you might as well tell me now because our marriage is over anyway.'

'Don't say that. All right, look . . . Not long after I got here, a bit before you arrived, I was offered another promotion, in another city.'

'They wanted you to move?'

He nods.

'This was before we moved from London?'

'Yeah.'

'So, when you were all "the Brighton office will shut down and all those people will lose their jobs if I don't come down to save it", it wasn't a fair representation of the situation since they want you to move in less than a year?'

'That's not what I said.'

'Oh please, that's exactly what you said. You . . . We could have stayed in London, you could have properly commuted to Brighton so when they offered you another job, you could have commuted there. Oh, Sol. You are so lucky I love you despite not liking you right now cos . . . grrrr . . . And I never say grrrr . . .'

'It's not that simple,' Sol cuts in. 'They want me to go to Ontario.'

'Canada?'

'Yes. It's a big deal. I'd be running a department twice the size of this one with a view to becoming second in command of the whole company. The CEO even flew over to see if they could change my mind. Every couple of weeks they offer a better package and, I don't know, it makes me—'

'Resentful that I'm holding you back.'

'Not you.'

'Yes, me. Me and a family that won't want to move again. Bloody hell, Sol. Have you been behaving badly in the hopes that I'll dump you so you can go off and follow your shining career without any guilt?'

'No. Well, not really. I'd hate it if you dumped me. I panicked earlier when you mentioned divorce, I was truly terrified, and I thought I was going to throw up when you said it again. I don't want to divorce you. I don't want to live without any of you. And the stuff I was saying before? I'm sorry. I was jealous. I couldn't handle the fact you'd met up with your ex and didn't tell me. And then he helped to save our boys' lives and he may or may not be Harmony's father. How do I compete with that? I was jealous.'

'How do you think I felt when I saw you and that woman in your office? You might as well have been shagging her on your desk, the atmosphere in there. It's all right to fancy other people – I thought we always agreed that. But it's not all right to cross boundary after boundary to the point where you're about to start an affair – which is clearly what I saw in your office.'

'Yeah, that was a bit out of order.' He wobbles his head. 'It was a lot out of order.'

'Yeah, well, I was out of order helping the police behind your back. And I may have come close to crossing the line, too. But believe it or not, I was doing it so that he'd go away. He is not Harmony's father – biological or otherwise – but it was the only way to get him to agree to stay out of our lives.'

'I can believe that you'd do it for those reasons. Do you still have feelings for him?'

I immediately think of Gareth's face earlier. He stared at me as though he wanted to say a lot more than 'Someone else will come and take your statement' before he left. He stared at me as though he was thinking of reneging on our deal and sticking around to see if I had feelings for him, to see if he was Harmony's father.

'It's all right to fancy other people,' I reply to Sol. Saying yes would hurt him too much; saying no would be a lie. But I will have to tell him one day how close to the line I came.

'Right.' Sol looks away, jealousy stamped all over his face. 'Right.'

I could point out that he's crossed so many lines with his crush, that he sees her every day – probably several times a day – but I don't. It'd be point-scoring. Instead, I reach out and take his hand. Tug him towards me. 'Let's talk about the Canada thing,' I say to him.

'Seriously?'

'Yes, seriously. I don't want to move to Canada, and I told Harmony that I'd help her find her biological father—'

'What?'

'She wants me to help her find him. I said I would and I know you won't mind because it's her right to get to know him if she wants. But that aside, let's have a proper discussion about Canada. You know, like two people who are married should do? Even if it means you go on your own for a while and we move back to London so it's easier for me to work and have a support system. Let's at least talk about it.'

'Yes, let's talk.'

My husband steps forwards, and it feels like he's taken that step that will bridge the gap that's been forming between us these last few months. It feels like he has come back to me, finally. Finally. I'm not sure how I've lasted this long without him, how we've managed to function when we've been so fractured, but he's back, we're back. I close my eyes as he leans in to kiss me. Our lips meet and all sorts of memories from our history blossom in my mind, all sorts of desires uncurl in my heart.

I pull back a fraction. 'Sol?'

'Yes?'

'Pain, pain, pain, pain.'

FRIDAY
Cece

10:30 a.m. From the top of the hill where the children's hospital is, I can see the sea. We stand at the top of the winding road that leads down to the main road, the boys each holding one of Harmony's hands. She clings on to them like she is never going to let them go. Sol has his arm around my waist and we pause outside the hospital, looking out across the city.

'This is like the end of a TV drama,' Sol says.

'Is it?' I reply.

'Yeah, you know, one of those ones where everyone gets to live happily ever after.'

'Right. So it couldn't be one of those walks that ends with us not having to walk miles and miles to where you parked the car?'

'Yeah, none of them end like that.'

MONDAY
(TWO WEEKS LATER)

Cece

4:20 p.m. 'Go on then, go be with your "peoples",' Sol tells me.

'Look, is there any point in you doing the school run if you're just going to sit in the car?' I reply. 'You go.'

'Nope. You are not getting out of this, Cee. You've got to face them sometime – this is as good a time as any.'

Today is the first day of the school reopening and the second to last week of term. They offered an abject apology as well as a refund of a term's fees to all the parents who were prepared to stay, but not even that stopped the mass exodus of people from the school. We are still there because the boys begged us to leave them there. They were quite impressed that they'd been a part of a police investigation and that they were witnesses. They'd been gagging to go back to school so they could tell everyone how they'd been kidnapped by the head teacher.

The deputy head teacher and most of the staff resigned with immediate effect, because they were horrified by what had been going on right under their noses.

The school run this morning was odd. I saw Hazel, Anaya and Maxie, but from the safety of the car because Sol did the actual dropping off at the gate. And there were less than half the usual amount of children there. A lot of them, I suspected, were only there because their parents couldn't take time off work so were waiting on places at other schools.

The scariest part of all of it is that there is no evidence to charge Winifred Carpenter with the attempted murder of Yvonne

Whidmore. It is all stuff she told me, with nothing that physically links her to the attack. Until Yvonne Whidmore wakes up, Mrs Carpenter is only being charged with grievous bodily harm (me) and false imprisonment (the boys).

Trevor Whidmore came to see me a few days after we came home from the hospital. He wanted to apologise for calling me a horrible, horrible woman and for what his affair had led to. He seemed small and defeated and he confessed that he'd been horrified when he heard what Yvonne had been doing to her friends. 'I've had to apologise to Anaya, Maxie and Hazel, too,' he said. 'This whole thing is an unholy mess. I don't know what to do about Yvonne. A lot of this is my fault but she is certainly not the person I thought she was. But, then, I love her. I suppose I have to wait for her to wake up and see what happens next.'

I'd listened but didn't know what to say. Sol had hovered in the background, making it plain he wanted Trevor Whidmore to leave so I didn't start to feel sorry for him. But I didn't turf the poor man out. He was in such a state that I couldn't. I listened, hugged him and told him I hoped things would work out. I hadn't heard from Hazel, Anaya and Maxie and I stopped myself from asking Trevor Whidmore how they were.

'You see the thing is, Sol, I'm not actually going to go out there,' I tell my husband.

'You get out of the car and go over there, or I start honking this horn and draw a lot of attention to us. Take your pick, Cee.'

'Git.'

'Beautiful.'

They're the first here, standing on the pavement outside the gates, waiting for their children, and I walk slowly across the road to go to stand on the other side of the gates, away from them.

'I can't believe what you'll do to get out of knitting.' Hazel.

My face grows a smile before I turn to face her. Anaya and Maxie are with her too. I quail with the fear of what they might say to me.

'Really, knitting's not that bad, is it?' Hazel adds.

'No, no it's not,' I say.

'Does it hurt?' Anaya asks.

'Yes. Especially when it comes up to my next lot of painkillers.'

'Oh good,' Maxie says. 'I'd hate to think you got away with all of this unscathed.'

I lower my head. 'I'm sorry,' I say. 'I shouldn't have kept what I was doing from you. I completely understand you all hating me.'

'I don't hate you,' Anaya says. 'I was pissed off when I found out but I don't hate you. It was for the best. I was finally able to speak to my husband and tell him everything about me. And after that, I got to take back my house and my life from my mother-in-law.'

'Same,' Maxie adds. 'I mean, not the mother-in-law bit. I quite like my mother-in-law. I mean the talking-to-my-husband bit. We were finally honest with each other and, you know, we're going to start trying for another baby.'

'Oh my God, that's amazing!' I say.

'Thank you!' she replies with a huge, face-splitting grin. 'But don't think I'm not pissed off with you. Because I am. In between all the love I have for you, I have a serious amount of pissed-offness in there as well.'

'Well, I'm not pissed off with you,' Hazel says.

'Not even a little bit?' I ask. I'm surprised, since she was the prickliest of them when I met them – the one least likely to want to be my friend, as I sometimes thought of her.

'Nope.'

'Hark at Saint Hazel over there,' Maxie says. 'It's natural to be pissed off with someone who has, you know, pissed you off. You can still love them, you know.'

'Why would I be pissed off with Cece when she was the one who found out that Ciaran Hamilton, aka Kier Hamill aka about a trillion other aliases, is a huge con man and psychopath who was using my identity to commit several acts of fraud including credit card theft, money laundering and deception?'

'WHAT?' Anaya and Maxie say at the same time.

'Oh yeah,' she says. She sounds confident and strong, but we can all see the strain around her eyes, the tension around her mouth. 'The police came and arrested him today because the children are at school. They think he was working up to finding out my login details at work to try to defraud them, too. This is the man I had living with my children.' She gulps and the flippant tone and expression slip for a moment. Then she's back to where she was before. 'He's done it loads of times, apparently. Cece spoke to one of his past victims. After she did, the woman told all to the police. They were then able to track down some of his other victims and they still think there's loads out there.'

'I'm sorry,' I say to Hazel. 'I'm so sorry.'

'Me too,' Anaya says.

'We are going to need a truckload of cocktails and yoga to deal with this,' Maxie says. When Hazel cocks an eyebrow at her, she adds: 'And knitting. A shedload of knitting, too.'

I hold my arm up. 'I can't do any of that stuff,' I remind them.

Anaya rolls her eyes. 'Oh, here we go. "I was attacked by a psychopath, feel sorry for me."'

'I knew we'd be getting guilt-tripped at some point. Didn't I say it?' Maxie pipes up.

'Hey. I want no sympathy. I just can't join in with the boring stuff you lot do.'

'Excuse me?' Maxie says, affronted.

'I can play cards,' I add. 'Why don't you come over to my place, bring wine and we can play poker. Actually, pontoon cos I have no clue how to play poker.'

'I have no childcare,' Hazel reminds me.

'Oh well, you can't come then,' Anaya quips. She cracks up laughing when she sees our faces. 'It was a joke! We'll come over to yours, Hazel, won't we?'

'Yeah, course,' Maxie and I reply at the same time.

'Thank you,' she says. Her eyes fill up and she has to lower her head as the tears start to fall. We put our arms around her and she tries to shake us off. 'Don't,' she says. 'Don't.'

'Why not?' Maxie asks.

'Yeah, why not?' Anaya says.

'That's what being a friend is all about,' I remind her.

TUESDAY

Yvonne Whidmore

4:30 p.m. I think it's time I woke up.

I've been asleep long enough. I've been hiding here long enough and it's probably time to pick up the children from school.

I've listened to him talking to me, telling me he loves me and wants me back. I've heard their voices, the different intonations telling me who was who.

I think it's time I woke up.

I have things to do.

I have children to love.

A husband to build up.

A life to live.

Scores to settle.

It's been perfectly lovely here, but now, I think it's time I woke up and picked up where I left off.

THE END

Dorothy Koomson, the knitty-gritty . . .

Dorothy Koomson is the author of twelve novels including *That Girl From Nowhere*, *The Chocolate Run*, *The Woman He Loved Before*, *The Ice Cream Girls* and *My Best Friend's Girl*. While writing *The Friend* she took up, in the name of research, knitting and cocktail mixing – two things that are oddly compatible. Give it a try.

For more information on Dorothy Koomson
and her novels, including *The Friend*, visit
www.dorothykoomson.co.uk